NOCTURNE FOR A
DANGEROUS
MAN

NOCTURNE FOR A
DANGEROUS
MAN

MARC MATZ

A TOM DOHERTY ASSOCIATES BOOK
NEW YORK

NOCTURNE FOR A DANGEROUS MAN

Copyright © 1999 by J. Marc Matz

This book is printed on acid-free paper.

A Tor Book

Published by Tom Doherty Associates, LLC

175 Fifth Avenue

New York, NY 10010

Tor Books on the World Wide Web:

www.tor.com

Tor® is a registered trademark of Tom Doherty Associates, LLC

Designed by Lisa Pifher

Library of Congress Cataloging-in-Publication Data

Matz, Marc.

Nocturne for a dangerous man / Marc Matz.—1st ed.

p.   cm.

"A Tom Doherty Associates book."

ISBN 0-312-86935-5 (hardcover)

I. Title.

PS3563.A8686N63   1999

813'.54—dc21   99-22968

CIP

First Edition: July 1999

Printed in the United States of America

0 9 8 7 6 5 4 3 2 1

for Maritha

for giving freely what really matters:
love, patience, faith.

For *very* professional assistance,
I would like to thank Algis Budrys,
James Minz, and Deborah Miller.

NOCTURNE FOR A
DANGEROUS
MAN

HOOKER WAS IN THE HEART of the South Bay colonia, being invisible in a crowded brahmin bar. Slowly nursing a beer, with his finger-nails sketching lines on the frosted lager glass like a child drawing on a wintry windowpane. He should have been calm, easy. He wasn't. He had thought it would be better to wait in a place where no one would know him, where no one would expect him to be, than to prowl restlessly over rain-lashed streets. A mistake. His temples were throbbing painfully. He ached to be anywhere else. Away from this room, the air thick with useless, monotonic talk. Away from the parasites with their rusted-out souls.

No, it wasn't true that he wanted to be just anywhere else. He knew exactly what he longed for: the porch of Abbie's white-washed cottage, his bare feet up on the rail, listening to the sing-song of the katydids. Watching the late light caramelize his wife's tawny shoulders and cheeks, the shadows slowly gliding down her damp shift, the cotton twisting at her hips as she would turn to him, watching him.

Like a prayer, he quoted to himself words from her favorite poem: "'Sorrow and silence are strong, and patient endurance is godlike.'" It wasn't a comfort.

But it was because of Abbie, and what they, he, had lost, that he was here among these zombies. He and the team. He stood up abruptly and drained his glass.

Hooker was wrapping his scarf around his neck when he heard a man speak with an inflection, a turn of phrase, that shouted his memories back. The voice from the end of the bar called out again, "Melissa, *cher*, come by me!"

Another lost Louisiana boy. A fellow refugee from one of the long arc of drowned parishes: Orleans, Saint Bernard, Plaquemines, Jefferson, Lafourche, Terrbonne, Saint Mary, Vermillion, Cameron, Iberia. A rosary of dead names, villages, people, and the lost, once inexhaustibly sweet land. With a clarity that he hated, he could still see it all. He knew he should let it go, but it had been such a long, long, time since he had heard home.

He worked his way down the length of the bar to where a sallow-skinned blond was embracing a woman. Their shoulder wraps had the same corporate tartan: deep gray and turquoise braided with crimson helixes. From his student days he vaguely recalled the pattern as belonging to one of the lesser biomed combines. On the woman's muscular arms dangled delicately filigreed lifemonitor bracelets, fetishes for the self-obsessed. There was a clear spot next to them. He unobtrusively filled it; leaned against the shiny marble counter with his back to the man, and listened.

". . . So I told Martinez not to take it so hard. Po' Jenkins had it worse when the Serengeti Alliance banned our rectal KV-12s—you didn't hear about that, *cher*? Ahn, Jenkins told me that the yammers claimed they were causing brain damage!"

Hooker sighed, turned around, loosened the left cuff of his jacket, and waited politely for the woman to finish laughing.

Then he knifed the man.

Not literally, of course. He was a sometime believer that punishment should fit the crime. While mindless bigots were a never-ending disease, they weren't the plague carriers. But there were times . . . The s/m was already on its way back into its wrist holster.

For the blond man, his nervous system was shrieking as he felt a cutting pain rip upward from a point just below his back ribs, curving through part of his left lung, and ending as if a cold steel needle were punching into his heart.

Before the man fell to his knees, Hooker was already more than ten feet away, moving with ease through the unknowing crowd. The man's companion just stood there, fright clawing at her face. Finally she screamed.

From the corner of his eyes he saw a waitress running over with the bar's Zoll medpac and fitting it over the stricken man's chest and face. In seconds the device would adjust itself to the victim's size, run puzzled diagnostics, and attempt emergency treatment. From the doorway, with only zombie backs to see him, he nodded approvingly as he slipped out to the street.

"Sorry, Abbie," he whispered to no one, "I've fallen too far for endurance."

The rain was thinning to a drizzle as he strolled casually to his bike. He popped the canopy and slid into the saddle. A press of the starter and BMW-Honda's flywheel purred quietly between his legs. He was happy with his choice; he had driven the motorcycle from Amarillo to L.A. in less than twenty hours and it had performed flawlessly. Always steal the best and leave the poor fools the rest—the one part of the bastards' credo he believed in.

He tugged his right earlobe. "23:31.17," the comlink murmured like a drowsy lover. Then the slight hiss of a clear channel. Good. The target was supposed to be primed and ready by 0100 hours. He had plenty of time to get himself into position.

He took the empty back streets to the beach, feeling the bike gently shudder as it drifted over the sweaty bricks. The tall villas pinched together on their narrow lots glowed like steamy hothouse orchids in the bike's soft beam. He had to swerve carefully around some broken solar shingles that had been blown down during the rainstorm. They were as black and sharp as shattered obsidian. Before dawn the tinkers would scoop up the pieces and recycle them to the high desert communes. An example of what the zombies laughingly liked to call trickle-down ecology.

When he got near the seawall he killed the lights, cut the engine, and coasted until he was about a hundred meters from the Flower club; the Blue Azalea. The party club was housed in a trapezoidal structure partly—defiantly—cantilevered over the levee. Some local half-wit tagger had recently sprayed with reflective paint Dykes Against the Wall along the building's foundation. He pushed back the bike's side windows. The only sounds were of the surf ghosting onto the massive pile of concrete boulders, and the faint thump of the club's ocean generator, its piezoelectric panels flexing with the tide.

The Blue Azalea's sign, a bright cobalt swirl of tubeless neon, illuminated the row of great cars situated across the wide intersection from the club entrance. He smiled. This part of South Bay was a restricted zone with limited access for automobiles—even the richest and most powerful had to keep their limos parked vulnerably out in the open. Prudence and the weather kept the drivers in their vehicles. But they had spaced their cars well apart, motors idling—standard security procedure.

He thumb-keyed his saddlebags. He took out his tools, put them on his lap, and sighed.

He wished he could have been inside the building working the wing position, but the Blue Azalea was for women only. So he compensated for his disappointment by half closing his eyes and imagining the scenario. The cavernous interior would be filled with glittering mist and music. Each distinctly colored plume of smoke, guided by dozens of microfans controlled by origami processors, was a stream of neuroactive agents: euphorics, kinesthetic stimulants, topical aphrodisiacs. An agile dancer moving the long length of the main room could undergo a dozen distinct sensory impacts, matching each to the music's beat and rhythm.

Teresa would be one of those dancers, feeling shamefully awkward in her Cretan style bodice—bare-breasted, waist tightly cinched. Little Havana and its morals still pulsed in her blood. But she was an experienced wing. Wearing nose filters and flesh-colored skin block, her attention would be wholly fixed on the players within the zone: Chloe, the team's center; the target that Chloe was seducing—and most importantly, the target's body-guard, who Teresa knew would be as protected and alert as she was.

Chloe wasn't shielded from the drugsmoke, but after years of playing in Flower clubs she had a high threshold for its effects. And more than that, her will and determination would carry her through. Only the unsuspecting target would be completely help-less. The woman had come to the club looking for quick love; the team had used her profile to transform Chloe into an irresistible force. The piercing looks, the promising words, the melting touch—the physics of desire are remarkably simple if you know all the right formulas. When Teresa was certain that Chloe had snagged the target and had positioned herself to neutralize the bodyguard she would give the signal. Then he and the other mem-bers of the team would handle the rest. . . .

"12:47.2. We're leaving, ETA two minutes hard. Harvest moon." Over the comlink, Teresa's voice had a slight, uncontrollable tinge of excitement. Despite her Ch'an training, she still had trouble keeping herself fully calm. Hooker smiled thinly; courtesy of other people's wars he had his own resources. The comlink began count-ing down the seconds.

He put his helmet on and pressed hard under his left armpit, triggering his implant. *"107 seconds, 106 seconds . . ."* The pro-prandol/amphetamine/cortisol mix filled him like a blessing. In moments a rush of absolute focus came over him. *"89 seconds, 88 seconds . . ."* He started the bike's main engine and took it smoothly up to within a thousand rpms of the redline. *"65 seconds, 64 sec-onds, 63 seconds . . ."* One of the limos, a Mitsubishi Koten, fast-blinked its parking lights twice, redundantly confirming which vehicle in the row was to be his objective: the pewter-colored Rolls, two cars down, its adiabatic armor creating subtle bulges along its long flanks. He checked the action on the 12mm H&K and put it on the magnetic strip he had installed above the instrument panel. *"33 seconds, 32 seconds . . ."* He pulled the firing pin off the ring airfoil grenade. *"11 seconds, 10 seconds . . ."*

The bike almost jumped off the ground as it flew across the intersection. At the beginning of the tee, Hooker spun the bike around. As the tires skidded and squealed harshly on the rain-slicked tarmac he corrected his balance without thinking and finger-snapped the grenade at the Rolls. The RAG, exactly like its ancestral frisbee, soared, dipped, and then swooped under the car's chassis. The explosion caused the Rolls to lift and buck like a crazed horse, flipping over on its side with a sickening crunch. The Koten was already on its way to the club's entrance. He drew his pistol and started to lay down a barrage of flash rounds in front of the limos. On the periphery he saw the brief struggle by the door. The target had collapsed in Chloe's arms. A tough-looking woman, guard or patron he couldn't tell, started to move toward the melee, saw the twin-fingered shine on the barrels of the scatter gun sticking out from the car and reconsidered. A sudden burst of red— Jesus! Teresa must have used a torch on the bodyguard. The burning, howling figure spun wildly back toward the club, scattering those few of the crowd that had remained frozen by panic. At the door the blaze collided with a rushing guard armed with a wide-bore sonic. His scream merged with hers. Then the team and the target were in the car and moving.

Hooker wheeled in a circle. The street was a maelstrom of light and chaos. Nobody was trying to be a hero. He slowed the bike and carefully put a shot into the Blue Azalea's sign. The phosphorus flare blossomed, engulfing brilliant blue with blinding yellow white. He gave a rebel's shout, a Lucifer's yell to the night: "All ain't lost!" As if it heard, the sky shuddered and brought down a sudden curtain of rain. He grinned, twisted the bike's handlebars savagely and took off in the opposite direction from the getaway car.

"12:52.3" said the comlink.

CHAPTER ONE

IT WAS TURNER'S *SHADE AND DARKNESS*, the clouds and canyon sides merging together into a swirling black-brown vortex, a halo of light centered in the east where the rising sun was feebly trying to burn through a thick white veil. The image complete even to a flight of defiant crows wheeling high over the sky. I pressed my nose against one of the leaded panes of the conservatory and cheered the birds and the deluge on. The first storm of the season. And if (crossed fingers), the forecasters have finally, correctly, worked out the new steps in the intricate fandango between the Pacific Niños and the Milankovitch rhythms, the end of seven years of drought and the beginning of seven years of rain. We live in Biblical times.

I sat back down on the stone bench under the silk tree and took Jessie out of her case. I like playing in this room. It has a lovely resonance and the jungle of plants makes for an agreeable, nontemperamental, audience. "Okay, old girl, what shall we greet this dawn with? The Kodaly? Oh, come on, Jessie. Just what I need, another proof of my failings." I caressed her scrolls, trying my best to cajole her, but she wasn't buying. "Yes, I know, humility is good for the soul," I muttered as I tuned her two lower strings down a second and then leaned her gently against me.

Despite the chill and slight damp, she was in her usual form: beautiful beyond words. Still strong-hearted after nearly four centuries. Cellos are meant to sing and this piece gave her full voice. No wonder she was eager to keep at it despite the frustration, my frustration. Jessie has the implacable stubbornness of the old, and the great.

We were about to start the third movement when I opened my eyes and noticed that the phone was glowing orange—the house genie discreetly turns off its voice when it hears us playing. Someone was calling me on my confidential line, a very private one thanks to serious cash and the efforts of the Digital Collective. Supposedly, not even Bell Systems or any of the other major telcos know of its existence. At the moment, only two people have that number: my attorney and my mistress. Since Kit's currently not speaking to me—*"Another brilliant understatement, querido,"* she said in my mind, her voice soft and cutting—I knew it had to be Ethan. But work can wait. I closed my eyes again and returned to the music with as much joy as I could muster.

We finally made it through. The critics weren't cruel. I put the bow on the bench and hugged Jessie.

"Answering visual," I called out. The conservatory's phone rolled forward, unwrapping its Soltan cube. "Okay, counselor, I'm listening."

Ethan's grizzled head floated in the middle of the long room like the ghostly bust of some old, battered Roman emperor. His eyes blinked slowly as he regarded Jessie and me. "Hello, Gav. I hear you are having some foul weather, the rain coming down so hard it's bleeding red."

"I'm alone, Ethan. Still."

"I am sorry . . . a case has rather unexpectedly come up. Available?"

I absently rubbed my thumb across the grooved calluses on my left hand while I thought about how I felt. Despite the stigmata of my fingertips, I'm no musician. Not hardly. Most of the time I work at being a freelance fine-art recovery specialist. Which means I do everything from giving advice on ransom negotiations, dealing with those fences who handle stolen art, to acting as a go-between, to attempting to physically retrieve the artwork if it has been taken for the purposes of acquisition, not ransom—although that's the least advertised of my skills . . . tends to throw curators into a panic. I get as much business as I want; art theft is a perpetual growth industry. And whether it is because I'm considered competent, or equally likely, because of Ethan's prestige, I can pick and choose among an impressive list of clients. The gigs are sometimes challenging, and since I usually charge a 10 percent finder's fee, lucrative as hell. And I like to believe that it's worthwhile. That it helps justify the space I take up in the world.

Still, there are times. Nothing special. The usual things for a man older than he should be. When he can't quite recognize the face in the bathroom mirror at 4:00 A.M. When his work, however rewarding, isn't enough. When wine, a loving woman, and even Jessie, fail to smother an autumn's bleakness.

So, when he has the nerve, he goes hunting. Not for a missing masterpiece or some priceless antique, but for a resolution, for a life. To put it as simply as it rarely is: he tries to recover people who are lost and need, badly, to be found.

The code word for those kinds of cases that Ethan and I use is "available."

Well. I had a fair night's sleep. My last consultation had a pleasant outcome. Jessie's been demanding of late, yet she's easy to forgive. I just bought at an estate auction two cases of Brunello di Montalcino '12—the first bottle told me it deserved its price. But there were no haunting sloe eyes to call laughter into. And being left alone leaves me too much with the past. Excuses.

"Probably."

He waited a moment, measuring my face to my word. "The injured party is the Groupe Touraine. They would like to see you at their Los Angeles offices. As soon as possible."

The music was still with me. It took a second for what Ethan said to register. When it did, I sat up sharply. Jessie's endpin scraped the slate floor in protest. "Ouch! Sorry, sweetheart. A *corporate* situation?"

He nodded gravely. "So I said. I know, Gav, I know. But from what they told me, this one I believe is worth considering." He stopped to rub the back of his neck. "There's something else. They called me and specifically asked for you."

"They called you?" He released his neck and shrugged. While our friendship and business relationship is hardly a state secret, over the years we've managed to keep Ethan's involvement in my personal activities known only to a handful of trusted people. We have a solid rule: The people who have lost someone never know or meet him. In turn, I usually don't know his referrals, and if anyone sees me it's only fleetingly—when I am successful. As the proverb goes: The wise man embraces obscurity. And anonymity is the only security I can offer. Ethan didn't look too worried. A decent man—and perhaps a fool.

I asked softly, "What is it about?"

"I think you should let them tell you."

That completed the breakdown of our system. But while I don't trust easily, I'm also not quick on giving it up. Not with Ethan. I tugged a sleeve of my black wool kimono. "All right, give me a chance to get into something more formal. Tell them— damn—tell them I'll be there in about an hour."

"I'll do that. Can you hold on a minute? Leah would like to speak with you."

Spark of light in the darkness. "Of course."

A blur of images as the receivers changed and Leah's face replaced her father's. "Hi, Jessie, hi, Hawk!"

I gave her an exaggerated shudder. When she was thirteen, as long-legged and wide-eyed frisky as a spring-born colt, she decided that I might be worthy of romantic interest. At about the same time she made the twin discoveries that I'm part Native, and that my given name comes from the Spanish word for sparrowhawk. The crush passed—they always do—but ever since she insists on trying to call me by that absurd nickname. "Hello, Gazelle!" Two can play that game.

She wrinkled her nose at me. "All right—*Gavilan*—I just wanted to remind you—I know, for about the tenth-umpteenth time—that the wedding is still, finally, set for New Year's Eve and if you're not in Fredericton the night before, your shriveled heart, and any other useless parts I can find, are history."

New Brunswick in dead winter—lovely thought. It would have been a sensible May wedding if it weren't for her mother being stuck in a long-range mobile somewhere on the North Atlantic shelf. The date has been moved at least four times in as many months. The oceanographic expedition that Ann's heading is supposed to be a breakthrough one. So far it's only been frustrating, for everyone. "Do you think I'm likely to forget and miss my bloodthirsty—albeit favorite—goddaughter's wedding?"

"Your only goddaughter. No one else would have you." She noticed the suddenness of my frown and without missing a beat changed the direction of the conversation. A well-brought-up lady.

She asked hesitantly, "I know she doesn't like to travel, but would you mind bringing Jessie?"

"Sure. For the reception?"

"Good God, no, I want to see you ta—dancing."

Took a long measured breath. Kit had taught me how to tango. I've never quite understood how, or why, a woman with pure Aegean blue in her veins had fallen in love with the all-but-forgotten soul of Argentina. It doesn't matter; it was a wonderful gift. A few years ago when we spent a weekend with the Hills, we extravagantly rented a skycar and flew Leah down to Buffalo for dinner at a great taverna that belonged to some distant cousins of

Kit's. (Ann and Ethan hadn't been alone together for almost three months; they waved good-bye very happily.) After the restaurant the three of us went to the Piola, a small club in Toronto that was owned by an extraordinary Porteño family.

The air is cool, perfumed with the smell of spilled sherry, old coffee, sweat, anticipation. On a tiny stage a woman sings to the almost empty room in a hoarse, liquory voice, her small rough hands on her hips, her legs spread with intentional arrogant mockery. Her husband and her crippled brother sit on low stools behind her, their heads bowed over their guitar and bandoneon as their fingers move like a smoldering fire with an intensity that is half anger, half love. Kit rises, smoothes her long dress over her hips, and steps out onto the dance floor. In her chair Leah hunches forward, her elbows resting on her knees, her hands tucked under her chin, and watches with eyes that are wrapped up in the music, the moment. As Kit waits, not looking at me, I walk steadily toward her. I put my left hand on the small of her long bare back and my right on her waist. She wraps slim arms around my neck. We close. She kisses my neck, then abruptly turns her head away. Starting with slow dragging steps we glide, spin, break apart, and then find our way back to each other across the blue shadows. We do it again and again. We take all the fierce longing of that legendary woman's tristeza into our bodies. . . .

On our last embrace the song ends. I move my hands from her hips to her hands. She leans into me. I smell roses and mystery. The guitar starts softly playing a milonga. Our eyes meet. We let go and return. Leah doesn't stir, she just raises her head and whispers huskily, "So that's how it's supposed to be." Kit keeps one hand on my shoulder and reaching down, ruffles Leah's hair affectionately with the other. "When you're lucky," she tells her. "When you're ready."

There are evenings that underline a life. I let my breath escape.

My goddaughter had lowered her eyes. The walk hadn't taken long. Even though the phone was only giving a head shot, I knew she had just snagged her right foot around her left ankle. She said quietly, "For before the service. Just for me."

"Jittery?"

"Me? No way. A little anxious perhaps, there's so much that—" She sniffed. "Really, Gav, the jittery bride—thank you very much for that platitude."

"Trust me, it isn't an insult. And if it's any consolation, Richard probably feels the same."

"He better not!"

I managed to hold myself to a smile. She tried a glare but it didn't stick. "Oh, hell. I know I'm being a tensored cliché, but I want so much for it to be perfect, for us to be perfect. And music, you and Jessie, always seems to soothe this savage breast."

"Mine also." I took a mental note: Debussy's *The Girl with Flaxen Hair.* "I'll be sure to bring her."

Perfect; nothing is ever perfect. Leah was old enough to know that, and young enough to still want to try for it anyway. And any way I could, I would help.

She sighed happily. "That would be so nice. Thank you, kind sir."

"You're welcome." Tensored? Grad school slang?

She took a long count; that foot was still snagged. I made the assumption that it was about Kit. It was going to be difficult. I had worried when they first met; the crush had passed, but a strong proprietary interest had remained—and if you've ever spent any serious time around a too-smart teenage girl, you know what that can mean. But it took the two of them maybe fifteen minutes tops to decide that they were sisters from a previous life and to renew the relationship. She finally said, "Uh, was Dad talking to you about a job?"

Bad guess. I tried not to sound as wary as I suddenly felt. I nodded. "He has something I might take on."

It was her turn for a frown. "It isn't one of those stints that you tell me about and make them sound all foolish and silly. I didn't smell anything on his breath but Rita told me she didn't have to make his bed. Don't try to lie to me, you know you can't. He's got something bad for you."

Ethan in a darkened study drinking slivovitz, the only liquor that seems to have any effect on him. That was news. Many years ago when he was a brand-new jurist he drew the short bloody end of the straw and was assigned to juvenile felony court; a great place to learn how to roll with punches to the heart. Brooding is one of my vices, not his. It was he who originally asked me to use my skills this way—the brother of an old client of his firm had vanished. I found the man, not well, not well at all, but alive. That success, and what it did for me, caused him to urge me to continue doing it. But there's a price for everything. For every life there's been a grave. Or worse, just an emptiness. It could be that in the process of trying to help me he may have picked up a touch of my disease. We were going to have to talk. Soon.

Answering Leah was a more immediate problem. Not only did she suspect far more than she should know, but she could sniff out deceit faster than a bloodhound can find a skunk's trail. She looked at me as if she wanted to say something but couldn't. Her eyes darkened to indigo. "You're talking to a judge's daughter." Her projection did an abrupt, scratchy fade.

And I had awakened thinking it was going to be one of my easier days.

I stood up with Jessie cradled in my arms and carried her to safety. The original owner of my house had been a minor movie star way back in the early years of the last century. He must have been quite a character. The house is an odd mixture of styles, even for Los Angeles. The exterior is Spanish mission, complete with two-foot-thick walls—fortunately concrete, not adobe—heavily arched columns and deep bay windows. Inside it's mostly California craftsman; nearly all the surfaces are faced with rare hardwoods, the joinery rounded as sweetly as a woman's hip; the whole of it backbreakingly hand waxed to a rich honey glow. But here and there are odd dollops of art deco; the main hallway's walls are a cascade of polychrome tiles done in gem colors: sapphire, emerald, topaz. The clerestory windows in the living room are Tiffany glass, and the two-story-high conservatory running across the rear of the house is a riot of lacy ironwork that Gaudí could have joyfully designed. There's a story, probably apocryphal, that Wright visited the place shortly after it was built and called it "a wonderful embarrassment."

But the house also has some quirky touches, such as the ceiling peepholes set with magnifying glass in the guest bedrooms, and instead of the traditional steel box hidden behind a panel, the original builder had installed a vault in back of the slate fireplace. To gain entrance to it you have to press twice on a very well-concealed catch up by the chimney flue, and then part of one side of the fireplace neatly pivots aside. The small cavity doesn't show up on the house's original blueprints. The fragile brother and sister that had so reluctantly sold me their home—they couldn't take the winters anymore—despite living in it for almost thirty years and during that time extensively upgrading the house's electronics, never learned that the vault existed. I only found it when I had to replace some warping floorboards and stumbled upon the clever bronze gearing that allows the heavy stonework to be moved. When I opened the coffered vault, all that was in it were some stacked cases of ancient Haitian rum, a set of Turkish hookahs, and a few handwritten journals filled with some very bad verse. A synopsis of a life.

I suppose if someone managed to get into the vault now they might also be bemused by the unusual bits and pieces of equipment I keep there along with a cello case made out of whiskered titanium.

As for the security on the rest of the place, except for the reinforced door and window locks—mostly to keep out the more in-

quisitive members of the raccoon tribe that I share the land with—
and the normal sensor array for the genie, the house is not fortress
wired. Given my trade, I have greater faith in the skills of professionals than in hardware. Instead I mostly rely on the Jing
ideogram discreetly carved on the front and back doors. The Sino-
Hispanic Benevolence that controls the crime sector from the eastern San Fernando Valley down to Mid-City honors it, and the not
many remaining independents are usually smart enough to be
scared away.

After putting Jessie to bed in her case, I went into the bathroom and quickly stropped my straight razor—yes, I know, I'm seriously retrograde. Not to mention vain—there's still no better way
to get a close shave. As I lathered, I allowed myself to think a bit
about what Ethan was sending me to. When it comes to this particular brand of folly, he knows my prejudices, and my weakness.
That I don't do any kind of bounty hunting, or for that matter, do
any work involving major organizations—private or public.

And I don't search for children. There are some things that are
too hard.

What my old friend doesn't know is that the good-works cure
he suggested is for me the equivalent of having a stiff drink to take
the edge off an endless hangover.

Ethan said that it was worth taking. I was wondering what I
would have to give.

The blade on my skin stopped my descending thoughts. Living hazardously as therapy. Some life.

Finished shaving, got dressed, threw on a weatherized cape, and
selected a hickory cane from the rack beside the front door before
I went out. Like a ship's cat on a wet deck, I scrambled over the
flagstone steps to the garage. I hesitated at the Lotus, running my
fingers dreamily over the long hood. It had taken three years, with
the massively comforting assistance of a skilled friend, to restore it

from the battered wreck it had been turned into by a kid with a rock & roll trust fund and too much argent *lody* in his veins. Like me, it's a semirelic, but even if gridpilots had been available during the late Teens I doubted that Colin's heirs would have incorporated one—they knew that people really buy this kind of car not for its state of the art, but for their state of the heart. But that means no automatics, and I wanted to use the travel time to prep. Besides, I hate driving myself in the rain.

So I unplugged the Land Cruiser, woke it up, gave it the address and curled up with my pad. Keeping one eye on the road, I logged onto the *Times* and asked for a brief historical digest on the Groupe Touraine and its widespread affairs, with a subsearch on any problems it might be facing that they wanted to drag me into.

Despite my specifications the *Times* datastream threw me a multiblitz. The contemporary version of a twenty-pound newspaper. Guaranteed to make one know more and understand less. I opened up the galley, flash-heated some water, got out the press, and made a cup of strong, thick coffee, my favorite defense against overload.

Business histories, even the uncensored ones, are generally boring as hell unless you're one of the winners. This one read like it had been massaged by an editor with lazy fantasies. A small but plucky French civil engineering firm based in Anjou picks up a brilliant but nearly ruined Italian design team out of Torino. Finds an entrepreneurial Dutch company with some great ideas on teleoperations, and trying very hard to avoid being swallowed up by NV Philips Gloeilampenfabricken. Lord, no wonder that language is almost extinct. The revamped outfit gets capital from a swashbuckling British merchant bank with connections in the Balkans. They pull off some risky contracts—lots of detoxing, lots of land mines—and even before they knew it, they were numbered among the global big five engineering design/construction firms. And among that exalted group, GT was the one with a nonpareil reputation for both innovation and a willingness rare outside the East

Asian *zaibatsu* to take the very long term view. Or so saith the *Times*.

The factoids that followed the Touraine summary gave a sight-and-sound montage of the range of their high-profile gigs: Completion of a new major Lake Maracaibo port complex in Venezuela. An experimental land reclamation undertaking on the Bengali archipelago—no profit on that one, but good publicity. Outbidding the Nakajima Alliance on the latest New Singapore floating exurb deal; that apparently wasn't unexpected. The Japanese have been losing their grip on the Asian Pacific theater for some years now. They were never respected—memories run very long in that part of the world—and like the seventeenth-century Holland their modern history resembled, their golden age is past them. There was the huge Congo Basin Project—a sort of TVA for central Africa. A co-op agreement with Groupo Centiva, the dominant Mexican construction company, to finally build a decent transportation infrastructure for the Chiapas region. I'll bet their North American competitors like the Bechtel Group and Exxon Heavy Industries must have loved being outbid on that deal.

Their CEO, an Olivia Fouchet, had just arrived in town with her entourage (glossy snap of a slender, ebony-haired woman disembarking from the corporate hypersonic) for the formal presentation of GT's open grant of three hundred million dollars to JPL for research and development on a workable hyper-geomag drive. Well, for whatever it was worth, that had my stamp of approval. Growing up in this century it's easy to become jaded, but to me the geomagnetic drive is still one of the unexpected wonders of our age. A wonder that I'm soft about. Without the drive the Last Frontier would have stayed lost.

Until that technology got discovered, investing in space was like buying a sailboat—you get the same result faster by standing fully clothed in a cold shower and tearing up cashcards. It was the development of the geomag that permitted the cheap—if excruciatingly slow—movement of megatonnage up and down the gravity well that changed the equation. No geomag and it's doubtful that even the moon would have been settled at all. If you consider a couple hundred-odd astronomers, research selenologists, remote-equipment operators, and multitudes and multitudes of arthobot miners much of a settlement.

Understand, I don't care much about pioneers, settlements, the whole bloody lebensraum mystique—given the best part of my heritage it's not hard to see why. But I do care about wilderness, places that are unsoiled, untamed, uncontrolled. Those places are gone from the earth, or soon will be. But the solar system is still full of raw vistas that have only been sensed by our telemetric alter egos. Places that have never been seen first hand, never been touched, awed, by us, by people.

We need that vast, far place and the prospect of it, not for our pockets, not for knowledge, not for breathing room but for what it can give to our imagination, our spirits. So that we don't end up drowning in our reflection.

I'd like to think that I'm not alone in that opinion. And if they can really soup up the drive, maybe develop a solar, no, heliomag-netic drive, then Jupiter, Saturn, and all the rest of the glorious outer system—we might get our chance.

I know. We will bring along our moral wilderness. Our touch will leave irrevocable scars. We'll exploit as recklessly as we always have, mold our new lands to our whims. But it will take centuries. And perhaps there finally will be enough time for us to learn Thoreau's truth. That people are rich in proportion to the things that they can afford to leave alone.

Now, isn't that romantic of you, Robie? Yes, it is. Hopelessly.

Back to the more immediate. What was Touraine's angle? The firm was strictly a terrestrial outfit. They weren't even involved with the LEO platforms. Three hundred million Kennedys was a lot for what seemed to be a nonprofit grant, even for a closely held company like the Groupe. When it comes to philanthropy on that scale, there's usually a good reason and the real reason. With that thought I shook my head; cynicism is too easy a foxhole.

The subsearch gave me nothing, not a whisper of recent trouble. Just to be sure I ran a quick check with Reuters, Fujisankei, Escudo de San Paulo, and some of the more reliable local pools. Zilch. Either GT's problem was so minor that the news combines hadn't noticed, or there was what is politely called a courtesy delay of information—a freeze. Given my current state of mind I didn't know which was the preferred prospect. I turned off the pad and put it back in my coat pocket.

The Cruiser plowed onto the long southern slope of Western Avenue. The street was a fast-moving sheet of tea-colored water; the sewer runoffs were clogged with debris. The truck slowed to a crawl and with a grinding clunk from the transfer case shifted into low-low. I looked up again as we crossed Sunset Boulevard, taking in my adopted hometown.

The rain had stopped with the suddenness of a monsoon. The linear glide track running across the boulevard's meridian glowed with an iridescent, oily sheen. A small crowd of day servants was huddled patiently in doorways, listening for the plaintive cry of the trolley's airhorns. A few of the women wore batiked sarongs, clutching their wraparounds with thin fists. They were mostly Indonesian Chinese, the last wave to get past the gunboats and come hopefully crashing on our shores, only to discover that the Gold Mountain had vanished a couple of generations ago. Whether they ride the trolleys east or west, into Latino or Anglo enclaves, it doesn't make any difference. Most of them will spend their lives working for wages that still drive the home robotics industry to despair.

South of Sunset, Western's lined with discount appliance and furniture outlets, old strip malls converted to open air markets, Pentecostal churches and Buddhist stupas—ecumenically sharing the same skyboards—always-crowded betting parlors, struggling to survive nickel-and-dime vircades; and never-closed cantinas. Lots of cantinas. Where "vive y deja vivir"—live and let live—is a motto enforced by the Benevolences and the police as much by battered flesh as by a smile and a bow. In short, except for a sad scattering of trademark palm trees, Hollywood is indistinguishable from too many other Pacific rim villages. A mosaic cemented with tears.

GT's North American headquarters took up all the frontage on Western between the wide expanse of the Wilshire Xeriscape down to Olympic Boulevard, the heart of the neighborhood that used to be called Koreatown before the fires wiped it out in the aftermath of Crazy Eight. The building was a viridescent mound, a tangent half dome rising up to the local limit, about sixty meters. A double row of massive American chestnuts surrounded the base. That had been a nice political touch; while our forest dieback wasn't as bad as what happened back East, we were still hurt. The thick collar of yellowing leaves and intertwining branches softened the bulk of the structure, gave it a vaguely Parisian reference. It was a subtle reminder that it was the French who won the race to develop a gene therapy that had ultimately saved the most beautiful of our native trees from the fungal blight. The same bioengineers also made them grow four times faster than normal, with a third less water, consume half again their usual amount of CO_2, and have a far more efficient version of ATP, adenosine triphosphate—a tree's energy store. The history of the twenty-first century, you could say. In a nutshell.

I had the truck drop me off at the front and drive itself around to the parking structure. The security station was a low concave bastion of steel-and-ceramic armor set before the entrance. The guards were sharp and crisp. Either they were pumped up with their jefe in town or the trouble their company had was definitely local. Sentries, no matter how well trained, get a sloppy edge in the absence of danger. Those three weren't careless. They took the precise amount of time with my bona fides all the while staring at me with pebble eyes, showing off what they had learned at the sheriff's academy of method acting: cowboy cool. Meanwhile an EEN detector array, its rods spinning like a Gatling gun, shifted around me in a semicircle; sniffing for any anomalies in my body chemistry, scanning for concealed hardware, listening on wide band for any transponders I might have tucked away in an orifice or two. It was going to be disappointed. I live a virtuous life.

Finally one of the guards moved his head a fraction and unlocked the main door. I decided not to salute them as I went in.

CHAPTER TWO

THE FRONT LOBBY WAS LIKE that of a luxury apartment building: a small series of neatly proportioned glowing lapis columns rising high and blending without a seam into the curving ceiling, a few scattered pieces of modern furniture in ivory silk and black-enameled steel. On the roughly polished travertine walls some watercolors and pastels—among the latter a ravenous Nevelson and a languid, thoughtful Frankenthaler—and interestingly, a framed set of large preparatory drawings. The kind of pen-and-ink sketches a few artists still do as schematics before embarking on a major work.

The carpeting was faux moss, green as a myth, soft as down. Quietly chic and apparently deserted, no sign of the corporate equivalent of a concierge. Almost deserted; a few seconds after I entered a swarm of brimstone butterflies the size of handkerchiefs roused themselves from a brushed-copper table, and with synthetic precision fluttered and swooped through the air. Their vivid yellow wings wobbling only when they strayed across a shadow's edge. While I enjoyed the welcoming ballet my palms got cold. I leaned on my cane and wondered how long it would take the welcoming committee to arrive.

Not long. They appeared without warning, neatly triangulating me. The two who loomed up on my sides were both hard, wide, and powerful looking. The one on my right had his waist jacket unbuttoned, the one on the left leaned slightly on his right leg. They stayed just out of arm's reach. The third man stood about twenty feet away at the apex, apparently waiting for me to walk to him. He wore his creased gray linen suit as if it were a uniform. A tall Asian, about six three or so, a couple inches taller than me. Unlike his comrades, if he was armed he wasn't showing.

Their house, their rules. I went forward. From his height I had assumed the man in front was either Manchurian or Japanese. As I approached him I realized that he was more likely from Southeast Asia. He was working hard to keep an expression off his long face; disapproval was the clear guess. That did not surprise me. Speaking to me in French did.

"Monsieur Robie, je suis Paul Thinh, chef de sécurité pour la Groupe Touraine. Je vais vous presenter au president."

I so appreciate having strangers casually display an easy knowledge of me. I reached back a few years, bowed politely, and replied: *"Chào ông."*

He flushed slightly, revealing tiny dimpled scars, one on each cheek. "I am sorry, I do not speak Vietnamese," he replied, this time in English. He cocked his head and seemed to stare a little above and behind my left shoulder. "You are Gavilan Robie?"

It occurred to me that he might be more unsettled by my new voice than by the childish display of one-upsmanship. It has a similar effect on friends who haven't heard me in a while—hell, it sometimes startles me. Not too long ago I got my larynx smashed up pretty badly. I still get a sweat when I take that memory out of the locked recesses, where most of us who have had the misfortune to rub up hard against death park our nightmares. There are a lot of ways to die. Asphyxiation is not my first choice.

The chondroplastic replacement for the destroyed cartilage gives my voice an unusual timbre. Llewellyn Liu, my bodywork partner, when filled with the poetic exaggeration of his Welsh grandfather, is fond of saying it sounds like fine whiskey running over rough gravel. A busted-up baritone with too much vibrato would be more accurate. I could have it fixed—it wasn't the sort of memento I'm prone to keep—but there have been some moments when having an unexpected voice was an advantage. When it gives a clue as to how much a stranger knows about you. I answered Thinh soberly, "Unless my parents were lying."

Somewhere, no doubt deep in the bowels of the building, an identification routine must have run through enough iterations to reconfirm that I was, probably, me.

He nodded. "Gunther will take your cape and cane." The man on my right held out his arms. When I handed him the stick he took it gingerly, too gingerly.

A chin jerk from the security chief and the two associates padded silently away on the deep biocarpet. No footprints as well as footsteps. I would have to remember that. Thinh led me behind the main bank of elevators to a mirrored door. I frowned at my reflection and tried to fingerbrush my hair; once it had been raven black, now it's mostly the color of wood ash, but still as hopelessly unruly—my mother's despair—as when I was a child. The door opened onto a lift not much larger than a teacup. As soon as we squeezed in, carefully not touching each other, it began to rise.

No doubt they were going to add a knowledge of Viet to the list of things they had on me. Good, because I don't speak that tongue—except for some useful phrases such as the "Good morning, sir" that I gave him, and others like "Thank you," "Goodbye," "Please drop that weapon," and "Get a doctor."

Thinh had to be a former member of *les estates flics:* Sûreté, Bureau Deuxième, Armée Superiore, or perhaps from lower down on the pecker order, DST, CRS, PRR—a log jam of police specialties that the French claim is very logical, very precise. They would. In North America inverse manners usually mark the enforcement hierarchy; a part-time deputy from a tumbleweed county will try to give you the most grief, while National Security wetworkers almost always win the geniality award. In France it's not the manners but the quality of the ubiquitous leather coat, or the shoes. I looked down: dark tan boots with a scuffed sheen, an ambiguous clue. From the way he was staring straight ahead I supposed he wasn't in a conversational mood. I watched the old-fashioned diode indicator lap the floors. Odd, the building had an eighth floor listed. A sure bet that not many locals were willing to work on that level. Our superstitions have been hard earned. The elevator stopped at the top. Where else?

From the way the lobby had been laid out, I didn't expect the neotraditional executive suite: spectacular view, half acre of bare desk, walls with mahogany wainscoting and a few overpriced examples of contemporary art. A room that functioned as a mask for the dull and privileged. However, I had expected to see a crisis-management team huddling, with most of its members giving me the same distasteful look that Thinh had let slip in the lobby. Instead there was just one lone woman with her back to us sitting on a couch intently reading something off a minitel. The *Times* photo had lied; her hair was very dark brown, the color of bittersweet chocolate. Without turning, she raised her hand and held her thumb and forefinger a fraction apart. We were to wait.

So I cased the place. I've seen my share of wealthy sanctums; this one you could say was impressive, in an offhand, stunning sort of way. The windows that ran completely around the room would have revealed a great panorama of Los Angeles if they weren't showing instead a view of an informal country garden at the hour just before twilight, when the colors of the earth seem to glow like the freshly dyed threads of some magnificent Persian carpet, a tapestry that only gods and a handful of painters ever manage to weave. But it wasn't an imaginal. That garden existed somewhere.

With all those windows there was hardly any place to hang art, but set on a low pedestal not far from the lift was a piece of sculpture. I glanced at Thinh; he was standing as motionless as a pointer at heel, and shifted over to get a better view of the object. A Pietà. The quarter-scale figures were cast in unpolished bronze with copper highlights. Their pose was the conventional one: Jesus down from the Cross, sprawled on his back across the lap of his mother. The artist had used twisted sheets of sand-blasted lead stained with umber and burned ocher for the clothing. The Christ was sketched in a rather perfunctory way, but the Madonna was fully modeled, the sleeves of her robe pushed back to show veined, sinewy arms as she held the heavy dead weight of her son, the arms of a woman who had toiled all her life. Her face was gaunt, lined, full of abiding sorrow. . . .

Thinh's too-loud voice brought me back to the world. "Madame President, this is Gavilan Robie."

I turned to face the woman. She was rubbing her left temple with her fingertips. She said, "Mr. Robie. I am glad you consented to come. Please, be seated."

I gently parked myself in one of her truly beautiful chairs.

"Paul, for now I wish to talk to this gentleman alone." Thinh didn't even flick an eyelash. He spun on his heels and took the waiting lift down.

She smiled apologetically. "You must pardon his manners. It has been a difficult day for him. I am Olivia Fouchet. Would you care for some coffee, a glass of wine?" With an offhand gesture, she indicated a tray showing various comestibles. Her accent was classic mid-Channel, halfway between Cambridge and the Ecole Normale.

"No, thank you, Madame Fouchet."

She pointed to a bottle. "Are you sure? I know it is early, but this is special."

Took in the label. Romanée-Conti '17. The last good burgundy vintage—perhaps the very last good vintage. I sighed and passed.

"Then you will excuse me if I dine while we talk. My stomach is still in Europe."

I shrugged and took the opportunity while she uncovered the hot dishes—turbot au beurre blanc, slender spears of asparagus, a little baked Brie speckled with black truffles—to get a realtime look at her. She moved and spoke with the kind of graciousness that is more bred in the bone than learned. Age fifty plus, somewhere in the third quarter, but way ahead on points. Her features were angular, almost harsh. With her hair pulled back into a tight bun, her pale skin looked almost painfully taut against her cheekbones. If she had some sculpting done, it was past my ability to spot. She was wearing a black-and-gold drape-collared jacket over a dark lavender one-piece of hand-loomed wool. No jewelry. A faint scent of fresh lilacs. Beside her on the cushions were a pair of buff-colored datablocs and a slim metallic briefcase.

She became aware of my inspection, let it continue for a few seconds more and then straightened up. "Last night one of our executives was kidnapped in South Bay City. Her name is Siv Matthiessen. This was dropped off in front of the building an hour after the crime." She handed over the valise.

In one sense she was typical. I never met someone as far up the spectrum as she was who believed in wasting time. I took the case from her. It was a standard courier case—standard, that is, for people moving certain types of contraband. All the surfaces are coated with a synthetic resin that ruins any biotraces. Not that tracking down the carrier would be of much use. In all likelihood the items within and the payment for its delivery would have been handled with no personal contacts. I put it on my lap and snapped open the latches. Inside was a single sheet of paper and a tiny ampoule.

I took the harddoc out. In the upper right corner was one of those fluorescent Casio stickers. It had been set to count up in stopwatch mode. Lime green numbers ticked off 7:23.45. Meticulous kidnappers.

As they go, the missive was unusually brief: no rhetoric, no strident syntax of self-validation. Just two demands: abandonment of the Congo Basin Project and payment of one hundred million ecus. Upon agreement—a "*Oui*/GT" in the *Times* personals—details on the guarantees, method of deposit, and the exchange would be forthcoming. The deadline was ten days away, less the time on the counter. It was signed "The Erinyes."

I rolled the ampoule about in the case, watching the blood sample inside turn into a bright ruby bead. "There was a positive DNA match?"

"There was. Your sheriff's forensic lab estimated that from the rate of cellular breakdown, the sample must have been drawn almost immediately after she was taken." She spoke with the studied evenness of a glider pilot calling off altimeter markings on a fog-blind descent.

Modern science. Sure beats a photo with the victim holding up a piece of dated newsprint.

"Are you familiar with this *otriad?*" Fouchet asked.

Curious, the very old Russian term for the Partisans; the behind-the-lines guerrilla movement that had gnawed relentlessly at the feet of the Nazis. Instead of answering her right away I reread the letter. I pay only a modest amount of attention to what passes for public news, yet I recalled that international protest about the Congo Project had been unusually muted. The tragedy of Equatorial Africa—a play in which the French and their Belgian cousins had written the first blood-soaked draft—seemed to have made it difficult for all but the most ardently dogmatic to object to a plan that appeared to offer real promise to a place and a people that had suffered too much, too long. Whether the optimism was justified I'm not wise enough to say. But as to the suffering, to that I could give my own small testimony.

But in order to break the chains of misery, there would be a harsh charge. There always is. And there are those for whom the pain, the sacrifice, is too much. . . . The Erinyes. Or the Kindly Ones, as the ancient Greek euphemism went. The inexorable punishers of those who broke the taboos, commonly known as the Furies. A strong name, rich in symbolism, rich in righteousness. Any group that took it would be ardent enough. I didn't know them, but I knew them.

A last glance at the note: one hundred million ecus, three hundred million dollars. The same amount Touraine was giving to JPL. Nice. And utterly impossible.

I put the paper back into the case and rubbed my face. "Not specifically familiar, no. And if I was I would have thought that I would be speaking to someone from the Sheriff's Special Investigation Bureau, not the head of GT."

It was a facetious remark. For a moment she looked at me the same way that her security chief had when he first heard me—are you really who you're supposed to be? Then she realized that I was being deliberately ironic. She responded in kind, "We know that you are not an informer."

I took a deep breath. "Fine—why then did you call? As Ethan Hill must have told you, this isn't the kind of problem that I get involved in. I'm not political." Thought of saying that I was only an amateur, but I didn't particularly want to hear her laugh. "There's a slew of federales and their local cohorts who are maintained at great expense to handle situations like this. And I'm sure you have your own considerable resources. You hardly need someone like me."

"The appropriate government agencies are already involved. And yes, Justice Hill was quite clear about you." The dismissal in her voice bothered me. She leaned back against the settee. "As for our resources . . . some years ago, given our vulnerability, my predecessor decided to commission the implementation of a heuristic, sibylline program to evaluate ASK scenarios and develop nonconventional alternatives. When—"

"I'm behind the jargon. 'Ask'?"

"Assassination, sabotage, and kidnapping."

"I see."

"When this event occurred, we called." Her fingers drummed

a quick tattoo on the settee's arm, "We called WOTAN—yes, we have some access to the European Union's strategeo; now you know one of our secrets. It gave a twenty-eight percent confidence level to conventional approaches. Then your name came up. You were assigned a fifty-seven percent confidence." She stopped for a moment and poured herself some more wine. "Frankly, I was astonished. This is not the kind of operation that lends itself to individual success. And your vita file was the most quilted—no, sorry, *patchwork*—that I have ever seen. However . . . one of the few traceable accounts of your unofficial work was about the Tartini boy. As it happens I'm acquainted with them and I heard, very obliquely, a little of the story. That was what, five years ago?"

"Six."

"Yes, they were so very desperate. . . ." She raised her glass in salute. "Bravo, Mr. Robie. No, there was no mention by the Tartini of who had helped them. You have managed very well to stay hidden."

"I do my best." Although not damn well enough. Searching for Francisco Tartini had been an exception to my rules. Not that his family was rich; I don't discriminate. Nor because they already had a brigade of searchers out. When Ethan puts a case before me all the other channels have been exhausted. If I'm not the only recourse, I am usually the last. The problem was with the family's fame. That creates too many risks that I'd rather not take. But I was also acquainted with the family—not personally, but through their music; I owed them. It took almost four months, and in the end a truckload of luck. Contact with them couldn't be avoided, but only the family's patriarch, Arrigo Tartini, and his son, Giovanni, knew who had found the boy. They had agreed to the set of plausible lies that I constructed about what had happened. That they hadn't kept to it completely was sad, but understandable. Couldn't fault them; their music is great because of their honesty. I touched the memory of that snow-swept morning in Cremona, the expression on their faces as they waited in the little piazza, the way they looked when they saw who I was walking with. No, no regrets.

She had said that they were very desperate. What must she be to even consider bringing me into this? I said, "So, you want me to see if I can find her. And then, if I do, you'll send in a hostage rescue team to take her out?"

She cocked her head at me. "Not quite . . . Your file indicated that you and your associates are capable of performing that task with more success than most police teams—and your government would prefer to take some prisoners. I would prefer to see them completely terminated."

I stood up slowly; the chair at least deserved my respect. "Your program somehow overlooked a small bit of information, Madame. If you want a sicario, the whole sweet hemisphere's full of sewers and talented sixteen-year-old assassins. I don't kill."

She waved a hand. "Please, sit down, Mr. Robie. We do have that part of your past. What I did not know was whether you still kept the ethics of an ARC operative. Although I admit I suspected so." She looked at me musingly. "It must be like being a Jesuit; there are some disciplines that stay with you your entire life."

Patchwork she had called it. They had too many of the scraps that mattered. She had the terrifying audacity to sit there and smile at me.

"And, Mr. Robie, as to you not being political—really? The Action Rescue Committee . . . most people would consider that quite political."

"Some people would. Anyhow, I haven't been part of them for a long time."

Unspoken the words passed between us: I will never know you well enough to know why. No, you won't.

"Then you're definitely not planning on negotiations?"

The smile left her. "In the last ten years there have been one hundred and forty-seven documented cases of political kidnapping in Europe alone. There were but eleven effective negotiations, and all of those involved only demands for a monetary ransom. Of the remainder, nine, only nine, of the hostages were finally released unharmed."

"How many rescue attempts?" I asked.

"Thirty-one. Five succeeded." She looked out toward the windows. To the landscape she must have called up for its comfort. "When I was young I never thought that those statistics were going to be part of my job. What a marvelous world we live in. . . ." She turned back to me. "A footnote, Mr. Robie. Two years ago we experienced a similar situation. Another group took one of our key persons hostage and made the same kinds of demands. That time the issue was a very large potash-mining operation we were setting up in the Atlas Mountains for the Maghreb sultanate. We worked out what we thought was a reasonable compromise, transferred funds as a sign of good faith. Then it fell apart. A few months later we were told where we could find the sun-bleached bones of our employee. . . . Sit down, please. I only want Siv back."

"I'll stand. You don't really expect me to find her."

She leaned back into the settee and stared at me with clouded eyes. "I want to believe you can, I want to believe like dear Arrigo does, that you— No, probably not. But I've never let the possibility of failure stop me. And once I have made a decision I do not let it fail from halfheartedness. I will not lose her for lack of trying. Nor, I believe, will you."

The best trick someone can use when they are trying to con you is to tell the truth. "May I see a photo of her?"

Instead of handing me one of the datablocs, Fouchet slipped two fingers into a pocket and pulled out a slim billfold of meshed silver. Inside was a snapshot of a young woman, barely out of girlhood. She was laughing, leaning against a raked mast, the sail behind her luffing gently in the wind. Very dark auburn hair. Bluish green eyes, more teal than hazel. A face almost too sensuous to be taken seriously. A *belle à se suicider*—a woman to kill for, or die for.

"*Oui.*"

I hadn't realized that I had thought out loud. I could feel my face warm. "Recent?" I asked, stalling for time, finding my center.

"Last summer."

"Tell me about her."

She reached for the blocs. I waved a hand at her. "I'll look at those later. For now, I just want you to talk to me about Matthiessen. Anything."

The drawbridge was raised, the portcullis was dropped, the cauldrons of pitch fired. "Why?"

"Then she won't be an abstract, a stranger."

For the first time something I could feel for moved across her face. She closed her eyes, looking for a place to start.

"She is twenty-three; Norwegian; when she is happy in her work she whistles. . . . Like all the young she hasn't yet learned enough to be sentimental. Unlike so many of them, she has an optimism about her life. . . ." Eyes still shut, she sighed. "Pardon. It is difficult."

I kept silent and waited.

Finally she opened her eyes and took a sip from her glass. When she spoke again it was in French. "*Bien.* Some months after Siv was born, she was diagnosed as being mildly retarded. It had not shown up on her genetic indices. The disability probably occurred during her birth, something to do with a lack of oxygen; hypoxia, I believe it is called." She shrugged. "Medicine is not yet a perfect science. Despite that fact, poor Freya was nagged for years by an irrational guilt."

"You know her mother?"

"Siv's parents were both old friends of mine. They died seven years ago in a skycar crash. When Siv was born Freya and Alvar— Siv's father—asked me to be her guardian in case they should . . ." She took a gap in time, going back. "I told them that I was too old.

They laughed at me and said that I would be around when the sun went off sequence—Alvar's words; he was an amateur astronomer—and they said they saw how well I had raised my sons. . . . They said that I would be able to protect her."

She stared at me over the rim of her glass, challenging me to comment. I didn't have any to make. "When her condition became clear, Freya and Alvar decided to have her undergo the Lorca treatment. Siv received a series of fourteen spinal injections. Do you understand what that means?"

Thanks to Kit I understood more about the Lorca treatment than any nonprofessional could possibly want or care to know. The process fell into Kit's area of interests, and when Kit's interested she generates a tsunami wave of such passionate involvement that lovers and other innocent bystanders had better learn to ride it or drown.

Sometimes it's fun.

Moonlight limning her skin. Cheek and chin resting in one slender, strong hand. Dolphin gray eyes fixed on a half dozen rotating displays. I hand her a round wooden cup with a silver straw. "Mmm, maté, thanks, darling. Why am I still up? I got a call from the hospital. We've got a three-year-old who fell headfirst off a roof. Yeah . . . Lucky for him, Dezhnev's team was on duty. Josh and his gang got most of the damage cleaned up, but the kid's subcorticals are a mess. He'll be a good candidate for an LT if we can pull off the repair job. It's going to be a long run on the table. I want to be sure the mapping is—oh, LT?" Maybe it's professional armor, or maybe it's too-thick calluses—no, it's not that, not for her, not for me—but the melancholy of her work passes through us quickly. She looks up over her bare shoulder at me. During the summer when she works late in the night out on the canyon terrace she likes to wear only an old pair of faded blue denim shorts. I'm torn between wanting to run my lips over the gently rising slope of that shoulder up the magical hollow of her throat, or hearing what she has to say. Decide reluctantly on the lat-

ter. She grins a little, feeling my dilemma. Adding to it. But I had asked her a question, on a subject she cared about.

She says with more than a hint of her soft drawl, "You don't know? Every couple of years or so there's a media blitz on it. The Lorca treatment—it's the most spectacular of the Pb therapies. When it works. For some lucky recipients it can permanently recover or enhance one or more of the seven primary MCA's, the multiple cognitives. Sounds great doesn't it? However, those sometime improvements are very unpredictable in number, type, or degree. Yeah, you guessed it, there also can be some real shitty side effects. We use it principally on the most severely injured or congenitally handicapped individuals. Kids mostly—the Lorca, like many of the Pb's, seems to have the best chance of success with the very young."

That's enough. Thank you, Kit. She was younger then and still a bit naive. (Spend some time with me and watch that go away. The gifts we give.) More than a few brahmin parents, heedless of side effects, have found pediatricians willing to add an extra postnatal upgrade along with the usual mess of vaccines, lymphatic strengtheners, serotonin modulators, and Lord knows what else those precious toddlers are loaded up with. Why not? The race has always been to the swift, and the field is very crowded nowadays. Nonetheless, the usual number of shots is from five to seven. Fourteen . . .

"Yes," I said casually, "I've got some idea. The procedure was successful."

"Most people would think so. She graduated from the University of Strasbourg with a triple: Industrial Design, Environmental Engineering, and Fine Arts. First Honors in all of them. She was seventeen. She also ranks in the top twenty among European amateur ten-meter divers. What can I say; she is already a most extraordinary young woman. And she is still quite young, really. One day—"

"Problems?"

She understood what I was referring to. "Siv has a bipolar latency, and sometimes she is hyperkinetic. Outside of that . . ." Fouchet swirled the dregs of the burgundy in her glass. "She has an exceptionally high libido."

Time, I thought, to move on. "That sculpture—the Pietà—it's hers?"

Fouchet smiled fondly. "It was her thesis piece. Splendid, isn't it? Since she started working for us she hasn't had much time to concentrate on her art. I feel badly about that."

Not that badly. "I imagine between her job and having an affair with the boss she must have been kept pretty busy. How long was it after her parents, your friends, died, that you become lovers?"

How fast can ice freeze? "Mr. Robie, is there a particular reason for your rudeness?"

I used the famous Robie tact: "Just clarifying some of the vectors."

"Clarifying." She pursed her lips and gave me one of those eloquent, unduplicatable Gallic shrugs. "Yes, I doubt there would be any question that was the premier reason they selected Siv. Their intelligence on her was extremely good. Too good. We believe that somehow they managed to gain access to her personnel files."

"Which includes a complete psychological profile and evaluation? The Scherzi matrix?"

"Of course."

She made me feel not quite like a simpleton.

"A mole or a worm?"

"We do not yet know."

I felt a flicker of pity for Thinh. "What is her position in the firm?"

"Siv currently heads a peripheral development section. Yes, our grant to JPL falls within the responsibilities of her unit. That, and only that, was the reason she was in Los Angeles with me." The skin across her cheeks was very tight.

I did right, it was not my fault, she was saying. I said softly, "How many people know why you called me in?"

"The real reason? At the present only myself, Thinh, and a Pierre Lessage over in Geneva, he is our interface with WOTAN." Assuming that was true it's bad, but not necessarily fatal. "The rest of my staff thinks that I am talking to you about another matter entirely. A problem involving some missing watercolors that belong to my family."

"And they believe that?"

"Mr. Robie, besides my duties with the company, I am also the *geraint* of my family's private estate. I take all of my responsibilities seriously. There are some drawings we recently acquired that have been discovered to be forgeries. They must have been switched with the originals shortly after we bought them. How, we don't know. Several of the missing watercolors are by Turner. Ones that he did during his last visit to Italy. Given your public reputation, it is natural that I asked for you."

Elegance. Blended into steel. The hardest alloy.

I thought back to the Furies' missive. "The deadline. Why ten days?"

"My birthday."

I nodded slowly, and said to her, "This is how we'll work it. The only contact I'll have is with Thinh. Any information I need, any word on the progress the authorities and his staff are making, I will get it from him alone. That will be a one-way communication—you will get no feedback from me. I won't talk to you personally again unless absolutely necessary. And from this point on, no one will involve Ethan Hill in any of this. Agreed?"

She shrugged again. "*D'accord,* but Paul may prove difficult. Although he respects the ASK program—it has proved its worth— he has serious doubts as to the veracity of the data that it used to base its predictions on you. He was not happy that I chose to go ahead with its recommendations."

Good for him. "And he wouldn't like an independent running around, perhaps muddying things up."

She shook her head. "No, that is not a calculation in his thinking. Much of the Groupe's success has come from its flexibility. We use a multiple-scenario approach for many projects. We know that the first, strongest solution is not always the best one. Paul fully understands that. But our techniques are always grounded on a solid foundation. As I said, he doesn't believe that you are as good as the program says you are."

"Then he won't be difficult. Either he'll ignore me or try to prove that he's right by outdoing me. Since I doubt that you tolerate idiots, I expect the latter. Which is fine. By any chance are one of these blocs her personnel files?"

"Yes."

"Does it include transcriptions of her private psychiatric sessions?"

"No, of course not. I do not see why you would—"

"Would I tell you the best way to design a bridge?"

She wasn't happy with the demand. Understandable, if for no other reason than the relationship she had with the young woman. I could end up knowing things about Olivia Fouchet that madame would not care for a stranger to know. If I had a vindictive streak I would have been feeling gleeful. Thankfully, that isn't on my list of defects. I didn't have to, but I gave her something: "You bothered to find out if I kept to the committee's disciplines. That implies you have a good idea of what they are, of what they mean. They're interlocking links of chain. They don't break easily. None of them."

Fouchet put her glass down and rubbed one hand over another. Hands that reminded her what her real age was. She nodded abruptly. "It may take a day or so to obtain them."

"I would appreciate it as soon as possible. My expenses will be covered by cash from you, whether I succeed or not—and honestly, my doubts are as great as yours. Your program's inference engine needs a major overhaul. It's too damned rich on the optimism. As to my fee—"

"Yes?"

"That I cease to exist in your corporation's memory. From WOTAN on down, I am deleted, erased, out—except for one final copy sent to me."

"Is that all?"

"Come on." I said roughly. "We are both too old for games, Madame Fouchet. For Paul Thinh and Pierre Lessage, and anyone else that you forgot to mention, I want the fiction that you invented for my being here to be the only fact that's remembered about me. And the only reason I am not including you is that they may need the support of your lies."

Mnemochemistry is a black art—illegal, immoral. She stared at me without blinking. "It will be exactly as you wish."

What you wish for, and what you get . . . "Assuming that I am—*heuristically*—lucky. Are you absolutely sure that you want me to get her without calling in a posse?"

She let long seconds pass before answering. "A man who does what you are supposed to have done without killing, or being killed, is either God's fool or . . . I believe that the less blood that is spilled, the less chance that some of it will be Siv's."

"Does that opinion come from WOTAN?"

"No."

God's fool. If You exist, by taking this on I'm certainly meeting Your prerequisites. "Ten days. Not a hell of a lot of time."

She stared at me bleakly. "Is there ever enough time?"

Neither of us were expecting me to answer. I leaned past her, smelled again the sweet scent of lilacs, took the blocs from the settee, and headed for the lift.

Her parting words seemed to be a complete non sequitur.

"Mr. Robie?"

"Yes?"

"Did the Tartini really give you their Guarneri cello?"

"I consider it a loan."

"A loan. I see. It is truly a Bartolomeo Guarneri, a del Gesù?"

"Yep."

"None are supposed to exist."

I touched a finger to my lips. "None do."

CHAPTER THREE

DECIDED ON THE WAY DOWN there wasn't any point in talking to Paul Thinh, not this morning. I expected that most of what I needed to know at the moment would be in the data blocs. Eventually, probably, I'd want to hear about what progress was being made by the main teams, but it would be far easier on both of us if we talked later. After retrieving my cane and cape—cautious Gunther again—I left the building and walked under the chestnuts, their boughs sighing in the sharp wind. For all the "improvements" added to them, they still were wonderful, majestic trees. I stopped and listened for a few minutes, letting them calm me.

I headed slowly toward the parking structure. They had managed to assemble a meaningful dossier on me without my getting even a hint of a warning. I work hard at my housekeeping. I try to stay away from places that I can't clean. I have friends and debtors with sharp ears. A lot of effort, never enough success.

Behind me in a tree a rare gray squirrel chattered. "Are you vouching for or mocking me, stranger?" I called gently back up to him. He was too busy pouching a nut to answer.

My wristband guided me to the open rooftop. The truck was standing by itself off in a corner. I circled the vehicle and opened the rear hatch, tossing in my cape. I got in the front, took it off the grid, and started out to my first stop.

As I was pulling out, a single-rotor chopper landed with a precise thump on the helipad; a Kaman FleetExecutive with Department of Justice markings. It disgorged a half dozen stripes clutching their wraps against the backwash. Recognized one of them: Arthur Cormac, director of the Investigative Taskforce Office, Counterterrorism section. Well, now, I thought, the heavy cavalry is arriving. I could only hope that he hadn't noticed one of the very irregulars leaving.

Went east a few blocks to Crenshaw and headed south crossing over the Santa Monica Freeway, the demarcation line between Hollywood's yellow/brown and Southside black. The border used to be a lot farther north, but the ghetto's long been shrinking. L.A. may have lost about half its population in the past forty years but the African-American community lost a lot more than that. Politicide, a constant dynamic at work.

I was lucky, Jonah was in his garage (yes, he's got the mouth of a whale painted around the garage bay). I could see the back of his plain caftan leaning over a cluttered workbench. I pulled up alongside a late model hydro Mercedes that was parked next to the bench. Got out and smiled genially at Beni, Jonah's mastiff-rottweiler mix. Beni sniffed the air, showed drooling, unimaginable teeth, and slowly lowered his head. Nice dog. Known him since he was a pup. We maintain a cordial, hands-off relationship. I waited for Jonah to finish swearing at a manual. Apparently it had decided that he spoke German. When he said something long, fluent, and filthy in Arabic, it became positive that he knew Romanian. He looked up at me and we both started laughing. With one final curse, he unhooked the guidebook from the Mercedes D/R panel and lobbed it toward Beni who instantly caught in midair—I'm positive that dog can teleport. There was an unnerving crunch as it disintegrated between massive jaws. Beni trotted over to the cycle bin, pushed the lid aside with his snout and disdainfully dropped the remains inside. Instant disposatech.

Jonah nodded approvingly, turned, and took my hand.

"*Salaam alaikum,* Gavilan. Looking fancy this morning." With his free hand he touched the sleeve of my blazer. "Italian threads—nice."

"*Wa alaikum as-salam,* Jonah. I had to deal with some fancy people."

"Hope they 'preciated it. Smart clothes are the only thing I miss on the straight path. What can I do for you?"

"Nothing much. The truck could use a wash." Which was certainly true. The rain had turned a year or so of dirt into a fine coat of crackled mud.

He kept his anthracite hand in mine. "A wash, huh? Praise Allah that I'm not looking to be rich. D'you want it detailed?"

"Not enough time. I've got a lot of ground to cover today."

He gave me that wide grin of his that never shows his teeth. "Enough said. I'll get to it now."

Jonah took his hand away. Nobody knows exactly where palm-sign came from. The most popular rumor is that it originated with a gang of Guatemalan mutes who were doing forever time on the Pecos Ditch. Wherever it started, you'll find various dialects of it informally taught in most of the hemisphere's prisons. Jonah picked it up in old Folsom when he did a hard dime for being the only survivor of his crew after they had a lethal encounter with some rivals. He had gone in as a fifteen-year-old horror in the making, and came out a Sufi. Sometimes there is redemption. Sometimes.

From our dual conversation he knew that I suspected an infestation problem—a private one, not public, which made him happy—and that I thought the Land Cruiser had been entered. Grown-ups should not stand in puddles.

Jonah retreated into the interior of the garage and returned with a pail of water, a sponge, some additions to his work belt, and a hotcard container—the kind restaurants use for takeaway. He went over to the truck, put a restraining hand on the engine hood, and nodded to me. I told the Cruiser to pop it. He let the hood come up a few inches, and stopped it. He opened the container and started feeding its contents into the engine well; blue-banded finger snakes. Or rather organic carbon/silicon composite mobile sensors. I think.

He dipped the sponge in the water pail and started going over the truck—rearranging the dirt. When he got to the back he stopped washing, put on a headset, took an instrument shaped like a minisoldering iron, plugged its jack into the set, and began waving it around. Magic.

After a couple of minutes he glanced up. I covered my mouth. Jonah gave me the okay sign twice; no overhears anywhere on, or in, the truck. He screwed onto his good eye an oversized jeweler's loupe—what it really was I have no idea—opened all the doors, and gently popped the hood all the way. After he double-checked the engine, he went to work on the truck's interior. Jonah is a great mechanic—he was the man who made the Lotus live again—a good electrical diagnostician, and as my father would have admiringly put it, a bloody dervish as a bug terminator. I watched him with a smile. Seeing somebody do useful work superbly is the best spectator sport there is.

I kept an eye on my watch. It took him exactly seven minutes. "There's three. One's a simple directional, hidden loose—even you'd find it."

"Thanks."

"Welcome. The second's a telcomm monitor—hope you haven't been talking to anyone important—hidden hard, but not too hard. If you know what I mean."

Perhaps they were grown-ups after all. "The third?"

"Not sure; it's a thumbnail-sized patch; a grid tap maybe." He rubbed his beard again. "If you don't mind, I'd like to keep it, give it a quick look under the scope."

"All yours. Just don't hold on to it too long. Will there be any difficulty?"

Jonah shook his head, "I'll take them out live, feed the directional some dirt—you were on manual? Good. They'll never know their babies were off-loaded, until they fail. I'll call my niece Narya and give them to her. She'll bike down to the Shaw depot and slap them on the next trolley going out. Sound safe?"

"Probably. The usual donation to the lodge?"

"The hajj fund. We've got some sickly brothers and sisters that long to make the journey before they get called."

"The hajj fund, got it." GT was going to pay for a planeload. He returned to his work. I went into his office and sat in one of the wicker chairs. Against one wall Jonah has a line from Jalaluddin Rumi painted in a beautiful cursive script: Die in Love, and You Will Always Stay Alive. Maybe not, but there are worse things to strive for. I closed my eyes and went over the Debussy piece I planned for Leah. It's a short beauty, a little over two minutes. I decided to add to my practice the transcription I did of "En Bateau"; that would be another four minutes—if Leah needed them.

Jonah finished the extractions with time to spare. Before I left we shook hands again, this time just because.

"'Morning, Gavilan."

"'Morning, Jonah."

The rain started up again. Told the truck to take the surface streets down to South Bay City; the thought of joining the Saturday morning semi convoys as they merrily hydroplaned across the freeway lanes had all the appeal of an offer to stick my hand into a mill press. Faith in cybernetics only goes so far.

I picked up the data blocs that Fouchet had given me and

looked them over. Sterilized, tamperproof, copyproof—I shook one, feeling the heft—probably bombproof as well.

The first was labeled S. Matthiessen. I put it aside. Even though it would have given me a richly detailed biographical breakdown of her life back to what her Apgar score was minutes after she was born, I wasn't in the right mood to be a vivisectionist. Besides, I thought I had a better way.

The other was what the local cops call an abat, short for abattoir, a slaughterhouse. It contained all the files of an investigation in progress concerning a violent crime. Material a private detective would normally never get to see. I know I wouldn't. No requisite local "friend on the force." Not on this continent. I plugged it into my pad. Almost all of the terabyte on the bloc was filled. There was a lot of background stuff on the scene of the crime and the quote "alleged perpetrators"—now, there's an anachronism for you. Lip service to an all but forgotten ideal of jurisprudence. There was only one unique note, and it had seemed very minor to the file. One of the group—a woman—had made some moves the file deduced were from an obscure martial art called *capoeira*. I noted that, and then fast scanned the information on the Blue Azalea; except for a few unimportant details it was typical of the Flower clubs that operate on the county's Westside and in other brahmin enclaves across the country. They were dutch-legal: as long as there were no sales inside and no exporting of drugs out, the authorities didn't care. Not that the latter condition was of much concern; the chemicals favored by the clubs and their patrons were both non-addictive and too expensive to find much of a public market.

The file on the group that called themselves the Erinyes took hardly any space at all and most of that was mere generic speculating. The group was but one of myriad sects throughout the world that were waging jihad on behalf of their particular Just Cause. This particular team—if it was the same one; it's a not uncommon trick to swap names in order to confuse the enemy—was relatively new, but it had already engaged in a busy handful of direct action missions: blowing up some power lines in northern Ontario; derailing a train carrying construction equipment for a cogeneration/ waste incinerator in Cuba—the investment money coming from a brace of firms whose reputation stank only slightly less than the offal they produced. Thoroughly sabotaging an automated detox operation in New Mexico—that sounded wrong.

I did a quick cross-ref with L.A. Central Library; the cleanup was on an old copper operation bordering on the Apache Nation. The company that had bought the land from the previous owners were planning to reopen the mine using a new thiobacillium process. For reasons sacred and mundane, the Apaches hadn't been happy. Between their lawsuit (one of the loveliest ironies of this century is that the Nations now produce the finest legal cavalry in this hemisphere) and the cost of the Furies sabotage, the would-be germ miners surrendered. I thought about some contacts I had within the Cheis society. Dismissed it. Saw no reason to break my rule about not involving any of the Peoples with what I do, certainly not with this case. I returned to the Furies. A few months later they found and cut the water pipes to an illegal pesticide plant in Honduras.

I continued reading. After Honduras they blew up a whole shipping yard of trucks that belonged to a Guatemalan agro-monopoly. Burned a warehouse that held tons of newly tailored seeds that would allow cultivation of lands held in a National Reserve only because they were otherwise considered useless.

Then the Furies started being more personally violent. They kneecapped a banker in Suriname whose company was bankrolling an exploratory offshore methyl hydrate rig. In the now thinly forested foothills of southwestern Colombia they captured a professor of ethnobotany freelancing for one of the big German pharmaceuticals and forced him to give them access to one of the company's research systems—the gatekeeper didn't have a stress analyzer. Unusual mistake for a German company; about the only way you can usually break into a data vault is by holding a gun to

the head of somebody. Once in, the Furies ripped off some unidentified data, but didn't do much damage—the internal defenses
were up to normal Teutonic specs. Afterward the scientist's three
local assistants, students recruited from the agricultural college in
nearby Cali, were let go. The botanist and his bodyguard were
found a few days later, swinging from a tree.

There was another note. Found under the bodies of the men
was a small flat stone with a rune carved into it. The symbol for
Odin. The evaluation that followed was a series of guesses, but I
liked the one that pointed out that in one of the stories about the
god he had hung himself from the branch of an ash tree in order to
experience death and resurrection. So that he could understand
the true meaning of life.

If that was the intent of the stone, of the gesture, it spoke volumes about the Furies. About who they were and what they
wanted to say.

I looked at the snap of the rune. Turned it slowly around. For
a moment I wished I had the stone itself to handle. Not sure why. I
don't have a psychometrician's talent—objects don't speak to me,
not that way. Perhaps it was the same kind of urge my mother used
to have when she did a historical: she had to wear something—a
piece of clothing, jewelry, a trinket, it didn't matter exactly what it
was—from the time of her character. Somehow it made things easier for her.

Nothing spoke up; the feeling didn't set bells off, so I let it fade.

That was the short list of actions that the compilers assigned a
high probability the Furies had committed. Boldness, speed, good
intelligence and funding, no apparent patterning of targets, increasing violence, ability to freely jump around the Americas. Just
what I didn't want to find out.

No hard information on the group itself. No successful identification on any of them, nor of key supporters in the ocean of sym-
pathizers that such groups had. In a funny way that was good
news—if data in the bloc hadn't been too heavily censored. The

danger for the Erinyes of maintaining that tight a seal is that their intelligence about what unofficial outsiders might be doing could be seriously hampered. Which meant that, if I got any breaks, I might be able to find them before they found me.

Moved on to the meat of the book. The simulation of the crime put together by the reconstruction artist. And an artist he—I touched the screen [Marianne Sumner, Graphic Integration Specialist Level II ID# 3745265b]—she was. Starting with a 3-D blueprint of the club and the streets surrounding it, taking the reports of the investigating detectives, the criminalists, the medical examiner, the forensic psychs.

I ran through it as if it were an unfamiliar piece of music. The first time fast, just to get a sense of the whole. Then slowly, looking for the hard parts, the key changes, the measures that would allow me to get at it from the inside out. The first thing that jumped right out was that the kidnapping was too well planned and too well executed. You need a lot of time to get that kind of precision, and still things can go wrong, horribly wrong.

Off the top I could see three rough spots. How they got to Matthiessen, the fight with the bodyguard, and why didn't the report deal effectively with what happened after they left the scene? Start with the last. The Azalea's security had been swift in calling South Bay PD. The limo wasn't registering on the grid—not a real surprise—so an all-points had been put out and the subsystem monitoring the major intersections was instructed to flash red on the traffic lights and give a yell if any vehicles resembling those of the perps got within camera range. But they spotted nothing. The best the local cops could do now was post a request on the community's data-wells and hope that some night owls saw something. A double switch on the getaways. Reasonable. But that meant that the strike team had more than five or six members. At least seven, maybe nine. I whistled softly. Timing difficulties are exponential; that was a cold, hard fact. But the Furies had had no problems.

Getting at Matthiessen. The two in the club. One was a guest of a regular member [Sally Keller, genetics counselor at LifePerfect]; she had met "Angie" at a flame bar in the Hermosa district a week before. It was the first time they had gone to the club together. When "Angie" started moving onto Matthiessen, Keller had split from the club in a huff. The other, a "Donna Marcella," the one who had dealt with the bodyguard, supposedly had an affiliated membership from a New Miami club. The Flower clubs may be as fiercely private as the old gentlemen's clubs of London but they weren't as exclusive. Money would open their doors.

Too easy, too good.

The bodyguard. [Marguerite Vassey. Narrow face framed by frizzy brown hair. Six years with GT security, assigned to the office of the CEO. Skills: Savate, small arms, etc]. I reran the simulation on the fight. She had gone out slightly ahead of Matthiessen, taking the normal shield position, when a woman came out of the happy crowd around the entrance and slapped her face. That kind of totally unexpected attack must have shut the bodyguard down for a split second—and everybody else. Her assailant followed up with a high side kick to her head. Vassey fell back but came up fast, blocked a kite blow to her neck, knew there wasn't enough time to draw a weapon, didn't bother to counterpunch, but went after the other woman who was grabbing Matthiessen.

I lifted my mug in salute. That presence of mind can't be bought or learned. It's about who you are. That was when she got torched. Third- and fourth-degree burns over 20 percent of her body, left shoulder melted down to the bone. Vassey was in very bad shape.

What was wrong was the weapon. You don't use flamethrowers at close quarters. Especially if you want a live hostage. It certainly did not fit the immaculate workmanship of the operation.

That was all I could get at the moment. Not much. I turned off the pad. Professionals, soldiers of a faith, a class I hadn't dealt with in years. And they were at least as good as I was once supposed to be.

Better.

CHAPTER FOUR

IT WAS A LONG CHEERLESS walk from the city's visitors parking lot to the pier. The ocean and sky were nearly matching shades of charcoal gray, the horizon line roughly smudged by haze. I went out on the deserted pier, the sea grumbling under the pilings. A squad of gulls with rainbow-flecked tips (a new spontaneous mutation—that's what they swear) checked me out, saw that I wasn't carrying any bait and decided to ignore me. Studied them for a second as they turned as smoothly as a drill team and faced into the wind, their multicolored wings ruffling. Joseph's coats, that's what they're calling them. As good a name as any, except that they don't have to worry about their brothers' jealousy. They, and a few thousand tagged and fretted-over terns, are pretty much all that is left on this stretch of the coast. There are rumors of some sandpipers north of Moro Bay; a handful of puffins around the Channel Islands; the tiny colony of cormorants that still manage to breed down south on Point Loma. But that's about it. All the other dancers of the wind and sea are gone from these shores.

They will be reassembled, brought back, that's the promise. Sure.

Leaned over the railing. Last night the surf would have been pounding sullenly against the seawall, the rain falling like grapeshot. But by midmorning all the storm had left behind was the usual complement of lousy waves. Three-footers with little curl—at least it was more than the regular ankle-lapping mush. About a dozen surfers were out, jockeying in a friendly way for position, trying to get the most out of their short rides into the spit of sand in front of the high barrier.

It was easy to spot Daniel Sullivan. Not because he's huge—they've been naturally breeding giants in South Bay for generations—but because he was the only one riding a big gun. A board Ted Brewer would have been proud of. Ten feet of perfection, made for serious waves. A senseless choice for this kind of surf, but none of his fellows kid him about it.

Danny was at Rincon on the last day of Big Dog Winter, when the greatest of the great ones came. The handful that stood watching on the bluffs understood what they saw. Like cats that hide before a quake, the countless days spent on the ocean's pulse had given them a preternatural warning about the dawn, they, the human race, were facing. He was among them as they went down silently to the shore, boards and hearts clenched tight in cold hands, to see if it was possible. To see if they could live one last dream without dying.

If you think that they were just stupid children playing at some macho game like those glide lugers, well . . . enjoy your sleep.

His wave was forty feet, maybe fifty, of sheer unbroken power. Want to imagine what that is? You don't need to fire up the VR board. Take a chance, stretch your mind. Go to a high-rise until you're about a foot away, then look up and count off five stories; that high. Keep staring until it seems that you're falling up—a reverse vertigo. Look down, shake your head, squint, and see that wall in front of you become liquid, moving blur fast, shifting— below, above, all around you, your universe—with a rhythm, a beat that you can't ever follow, not consciously. Throw in the visceral certainty that if you slip, you're gone. And that doesn't tell you a fraction of what it, she, was. How she can make you feel. Nothing imagined or imaginal can.

For two minutes, an eternity, Danny rode her, straight into the center of his life. And those who watched, knew.

He doesn't ever mention that dawn, that ride. But from Santa Barbara down to Baja, the fading members of his tribe understand—and the few tadpoles get quickly taught—that after thirty years he's still waiting for another, still an optimist, still filled with grace. No one laughs.

Thirty years or so, that is how long we've been friends, on and off. Separated by distance, by hard years, by harder choices. And yet joined back again.

The best luck is in the draw of your friends.

He owns the Rush, an old-fashioned surf shop, just boards and suits; he's even got a master shaper working in the back room. The shop barely covers its expenses, but his uncle left him a sixth share of Borlote, the best cantina in the South Bay. That, plus an occasional investigative gig, allows him to live in the town where he was born.

I swung my arms until he spotted me. He pointed to the beach and flapped back a yes. I got down to the sand before Danny did. He couldn't resist waiting for a swell to skim him in. I stood by his gear, the wind biting into my face.

He came out of the water looking like a golden-green Poseidon, holding his board up over one shoulder as if it were a trident. He joined me, jammed the board effortlessly into the sand, took a rag out of his bag, splashed the scrap with some rubbing alcohol and began wiping antisep gel off his face and hands.

"Nice suit. New model?" I asked.

"Yep, under a quarter mil thick, moves like skin, keeps you toasty. Decent."

"Great color too, almost matches your hair."

A quick glance at one of the sleeves. "Screw off, mate, I'm getting paid to do a bit for the manufacturer. The color changes with temp and bac count. And there's a softwire feed on vectors." He snorted. "Like they think we don't already know."

Like cats before a quake . . . I said innocently, "Sorry, thought you were trying to make an anesthetic statement."

He came back quickly, "Feeble, Robie, mucho cochin'. But considering what a pain you can be—"

"That's true; have been from the first."

The lines of his brow creased. "Really need to remind me of that?"

"This was the spot, remember?"

He took in the small remaining stretch of beach front. His face clouded a little, remembering what it once was. Then it cleared. Danny mostly believes that looking backward only leaves you with a sore neck. He grinned. "If I'd known you could fight a hell of a lot better than you surfed, I would've turned away."

It had been a territorial thing, with a touch of race. Some of the locals didn't take kindly to a lanky, dark-skinned boy messing awkwardly about on their waves. I broke Danny's arm. "Didn't know you were going to be on my side."

"You didn't exactly give me a chance."

Four against one. Not an excuse. Not for me. I had too much fear and speed then, and not enough brains to give anyone a chance.

"Didn't stop you from surfing the next day."

"Nothing stops me from that."

I spread my hands. "Well, then?"

He shook his head, laughing, spraying me with drops. "All right, I give up. So what are you doing down here this early? Fixing on taking *Shiloh* out?"

"Nope, got a job."

"Shame, looks like it's going to be a good day for a sail. What got nicked, something valuable?"

"Valuable, I suppose so. . . . It's a girl . . . a young woman."

The humor ebbed from his face. "Sweet Mary Mag, are you still doing those?"

"Now and then. Did you hear about the fracas at the Blue Azalea?"

"Hey, when the waves are up the only thing I listen to is the weather report. But Suzanne's a fount freak so I caught some of the gossip—"

"Suzanne?"

"A new pillow friend. The Azalea . . ." He whistled, splitting a note into thirds. "The way it got reported made it sound like it was a raw show."

"It was, and I find myself caught up in the second act. I need your help on this one, Danny."

He leaned against his board and started stripping off his wetsuit. Trying hard not to be shocked. "I'm flattered. You never invite me to those parties."

"For the same reason I don't ask you to go to the dentist for me."

He stood naked to the world and stared at me. "And that, mate, is what I suppose you'd call an incisive metaphor. Expect I should be grateful."

"You should."

Danny is a proud man, but he heard the tone in my voice; he's one of the very few who can usually tell when it's real, and when not. And he knows that I have never counted him short. In his day he's done a thing or two himself. He said slowly, "Yeah . . . Considering what kind of shape they can leave you in, I guess so. Hand me those pants, will you—thanks—so what's the deal?"

I told him. Almost everything. Well, the salient points. He listened impassively, keeping his gray eyes on the water's edge. He grunted once when I took out my pad with the police bloc and ran through the local cast of characters. When I finished he asked me to repeat the names of some of the witnesses, then grunted again. "Do you have a membership roster for the club?" he asked.

I checked. "Seems not. The Azalea uses the Swiss system: no names, only a number and a retinal ID."

"Sloppy of them," he commented. "Holo eye contacts that'll fool a sys have been available for a while now."

"True, but contrary to popular belief, few bastards are able to get hold of them."

"Bet this gang can. I wouldn't be surprised if they had one or two more in the club for contingency backup."

I hadn't thought of that.

A muscled barrel of a man caught a strong little wave and did a nice hard bottom turn on it. Luke Peterson, a member of Danny's cliqua since they were both ten. Danny gave him the righteous sign and then looked down the tiny strip of sand reflectively, "Y'know . . . out here they'd have a rooting section."

And not only here. But far fewer than what their parents and grandparents would have thought. Denial, anger, depression, acceptance—each stage took a decade or so to go through. For most. Some are still working their way.

"Will it be a problem for you?"

A decisive shake of his head. "No. Grief isn't an excuse for anything. What do you want?"

He was right, it isn't. "Oh, lots of things," I said. "A long weekend on *Shiloh* with the spinnaker run out and an interesting long-legged woman at my side. The loan of a Turner, any Turner, but as long as I'm dreaming one of the late paintings would be very nice. Doing the Dvorak with the Denver Phil. Let's see, a mistress that will talk to me—"

"That great a morning?"

"Mate, it's been a lovely morning and it looks like it's going to be an even lovelier week."

"Then let's get past it. What's my piece?"

I squatted down and drew spirals in the sand. Danny was experienced and nobody's fool, but sometimes it helps to review the clearcut. "To carry off that flawless an operation you've got to set a pretty deep matrix around the target. There are the visible units—the attack team that took her out—and the hidden units, the planners, the logistics, the outriders, and as you pointed out, the redundant backups to the primary team. I'm thinking the best approach may be to find her through that hidden part of the matrix. To figure out the pattern that they make with the attack team. And for that I need to find the connections." I shook my head. "For me to go straight after the visible would be an exercise in futility—besides, the thundering herd are going to be trampling off pretty much exclusively in that direction."

"A rock thrown in the pond."

"Hmm?"

"Freddie saying. Stay with the first ripple and you'll find the rock. Simple, but true."

"Most of the time."

He nodded—the slow dip of chin that comes from knowing about failure—and said, "Yep. They're going to be pressured to work fast forward. They'll concentrate from when the victim was taken. The trail is going to be hot for the first forty-eight hours; it's hard for even the most elusive quarry not to leave tracks. If that fails, then they'll try alternatives."

"And it's Cormac's style."

Danny has one of those wonderfully expressive faces that acts like an accent mark to what he says. Not this time. "Arthur Cormac?"

"Saw him arrive a little while ago."

He spat downwind. "He's still in the business? *Mierda.* Why am I surprised? Great guy." His face took on what was for him a dark look. "His field handle used to be Meat Cleaver. From what I hear, he still tries to live up to it."

I nodded. "And that's puzzling. Touraine must know his reputation. They could have vetoed him."

"Maybe they're interested in setting an example."

A sudden rush of bile at the back of my throat. "You're a great cheer."

"Sorry. Can't you bail out of this crap? So they found out some stuff about you. So what. You're good at rewriting scripts."

"I didn't accept the gig just to get back some peace of mind. The girl is . . . special."

Danny ran his hands over the curved edges of his board and smiled sadly at me. "You poor bastard, you let yourself get snagged."

"Kit calls it an addiction."

"Does she?" he said pensively. "She's sharp. Sharper than the two of us put together. But she hasn't had the—that's why she keeps on leaving?"

"Among other reasons."

"They always have them, don't they?" He was thinking of his Nancy. She was one of the few exceptions to his rule about looking back. We stood there, awkward in the moment. That he hadn't said it bitterly didn't make it any easier.

"Yes . . . Well, for right now I'd like you to ask some questions, make some random moves, shake South Bay up a little and see how it resettles."

"Or in other words, you want me to act like a breathing Boltzmann machine." He scratched his scalp. "Sweet Jesus, now where did that come from? Oh, yeah, hick phizz."

"Very good," I noted admiringly. "I didn't think that jocks woke up for anything except anabolic chem."

"Not at Septic High. Even us great football stars had to go through the Revised New Syllabus—or as we used to call it, 'The Real Nasty Shit.' And unlike somebody I know, I wasn't born a bull artist."

I clucked in mock sympathy. He flashed me the finger. Sometimes, without intending, when we're together we're sixteen again. Giving each other our youth, the better parts.

His shoulders shifted slightly, the child retiring to the man who was smarter than he pretended; smart about grief, and about work. "Okay," he said, "I'll see if I can arrange to use a liability investigation as a basic cover. Since Juarez-Lang passed, that'll be an easy excuse for my asking questions about any local involvement with that fracas. Watase Assurance is the major carrier around here for the clubs. Their town agent is Tom Philips. He's given me work before, and he's a mate. If Watase doesn't carry the paper on the Azalea, I'll find out who does and work with them. Shouldn't be a problem. As for the local blue, I know most of the boys and girls, and they're usually willing to give me slack. And lately the chief's been nervous around anyone that has a fed jacket, even if it's an ex."

I try to never stop paying attention, but there are always things that you miss. "Really?"

"There's trouble with a capital T and that rhymes with P and that stands for guess who?"

Danny's fond of light—very light—opera. Don't hold it against him. "I thought that the South Bay cops were paragons of virtue, the best money could buy."

"Buy is the operative word, which is why the chief's scared. There's a new corruption and racketeering taskforce that's looking at all the coastals. It's a joint fed and state squad. Stone guys. Rumor has it they've got data in plenty."

"The Erinyes seem to have money."

Danny raised his thin eyebrows. "I'll look into it," he said. He rocked his right hand side to side. "It's an iffy. The department's going to be tighter than a mule's sphincter." He scowled heavily. Danny has little tolerance for cops who can't live by their oath, and less so for those who would shield them in the name of brotherhood. Why he's no longer in the business. He used his hands like sandpaper to rub the expression away from his face. A smile appeared. "I'd also like to put in a snitch request on the underground creeks. We've got our share of less-than-public-spirited citizens. How fat an award can I go?"

"Whatever you think will appeal. GT's paying all the freight. It sounds good. But Danny, be careful; there are sharks in the water."

He laughed and gently punched me in the ribs. "So we'll be dolphins, mate. We'll butt their asses if they get too close."

"Yeah, and remember what the one-armed fisherman said, 'Never make a mako mad.' I'm serious; be careful, these people are committed and deadly."

He spoke so softly I could barely hear him. "Hey, Gav, you brought Dano back."

So I did. Daniel Xavier Sullivan y Ortega. Nancy and Danny's only child. Called Dano since his first day in kindergarten. The beach joke was that the boy was a chip off the old board. Not exactly true; he definitely had his mother's eyes, her laugh.

He thought that "The Mission in the Rain" was the greatest song ever written. His paternal grandmother had been a never-say-die tie-dye. Besides seventy-year-old folk music he was crazy as nearly every kid his age was about Nueva Canción. He broke his old man's high school record for most interceptions. Like his mom, he was too shy to break hearts. He could swim before he could walk. What he lacked in smarts he made up for with unflinching persistence. He tried to surf every morning. (For his fifteenth birthday, Danny and I sailed with him on *Shiloh* to Hawaii, the North Shore pipeline, where sometimes, just sometimes, there are still good serious rides. I learned new, exciting ways to get wiped out; the two D's experienced satori).

And when he was twelve he spent a summer with me at my cabin on the North Platte, while his parents tried to sort out the ruins of their marriage. I had my own wounds at the time—both inside and out—to mend. During the days we went fly fishing, and later, when I healed up a bit, I taught him how to ride bareback. Took him camping out on the Great Preserve. At night, under a vast moon, I would tell him ghost stories and the tales that my mother's mother taught me about the Tsistsistas, the people. One evening he saw his first meteor shower, orange sparks streaking all the way across a blackberry sky. He was the first, and only, person I'd ever seen actually jump for joy.

He helped me.

After he finished school he did his national service with the C-Corps. When he got discharged he found a job as a service tech with a company that manufactured rockworms. He had to relocate to Monterrey, a hard wrench for a boy close to the sea and his family, but he wanted to make it on his own and you have to go where the work is.

It was a tough gig. Always on call, being sent on a few hours' notice to rugged, quite literally godforsaken parts of the world, monitoring flows for twenty-four hours at a stretch, troubleshooting hundreds of thousands of dollars of sensitive equipment with potentially enormous investments on the line. But the pay was good and the company had promised him a chance he'd get to be a moonwalker—a childhood dream he had caught sitting with me on a ridge under the stars.

Instead they sent him down to Venezuela, to the steamy Pakaraima Mountains on the border with Guyana and Brazil. A mining survey team was having some command-and-control problems with some of their gear. Apart from it being a site where the sixteenth century had barely arrived, it should have been a relatively safe assignment. The brief border conflict between the three nations—two nations, really, Guyana sensibly took a boxer's dive—was then eight years past. But wars there, or anywhere, rarely end cleanly.

Sat down on the wet sand with an arm curled around my knees remembering what I never told Danny. I was driving down a road that was the devil's idea of a good joke in a Jeep so old it should have had Willys stamped on its side. No windshield, no working instruments, a clutch that screamed every time I touched it. Dano was lying across the front seat, his head in my lap, one hand wrapped in the webbing of my strikesuit. He had taken a chest hit from a 8mm Agni.

The "insurgents" may have had antique vehicles, but their weaponry was on the edge. On vid, lasers are depicted as nice clean shots, instant cauterization of the wound and all that, but they never mention what happens to the inside of a body when it's been stabbed by a beam the temperature of a thermal lance, say four thousand degrees or so. His right lung was gone, collapsed or exploded. The shot or the shrapnel-like debris of his ribs hadn't punctured any major arteries or else he would have been dead. His left pupil was a fraction wider than his right. If it blew—I didn't want to think about that. How bad his other internal injuries were I had no idea. My first aid is better than good, but I'm no medic and anyway I didn't have the equipment. I think—I know—it was a miracle that he was still with me.

I had him stuffed with painkillers, hemoboosters, and anti-shock. He kept passing in and out. I drove like we had a chance. He looked up at me, and said, "Daddy, please, my head hurts." Before I could speak he passed out again.

He lives with his mother in Arizona, near Flagstaff, in one of the new hill settlements. He can walk now and helps out in the aquafarm, but not for too long. He tires easily. He doesn't talk but seems to understand what others say. He's got a new lung and nerve augmentations for his left arm and leg; everything that could be rebuilt or rejuved was done by the best—after I became part of Kit's life she did an exhaustive review for me. She agreed the work had been superlative. But there is only so much that can be done for someone who had a massive embolic stroke hours away from a hospital. We can work wonders, but not true miracles. Not yet.

Yes, I brought him back.

Danny put a massive hand on the back of my neck. It felt like a cold compress. "Let go, Gav."

Shook myself. "Yeah, it's okay." I stood up. "Dano's not ever going to be a marker with me, Danny."

"You *are* a stupid bastard. Had breakfast yet?"

"No."

"Great! I've got a surprise for you."

Astonishment; it was *chistorra,* deeply smoked and loaded with chewy, pungent garlic.

A room with the high country's piercing morning light pouring through the open windows. Filled with short lean men sitting around a scarred wooden table. The chilly air thick with the smell of hot food and sheep. A small boy on tiptoes next to his grandfather being handed a loaf of heavy dark bread, sawing at it with a brand-new Buck knife that for three days running hadn't left his hand, the soft laughter of the men stopped by the sudden whiplash stab of the grandfather's blade as he speared a sausage and put it carefully on the wedge of bread the boy had carved off.

Between mouthfuls: "Danny, you're wonderful."

He worked up a proper belch. "I know."

"Where did you find them?"

"Remember the night when you wandered in here loaded to the gills, finished the job, and then got on the stage and recited line after line after line?"

"Alcohol doesn't obliterate my memory. It was a Thursday. A Santa Ana was scouring the city with hot dust, the featured entertainment was poetry, you were nuzzling a redhead who was—as usual—too wise for you, and 'The Tree of Guernica' is not that long."

"It is when you hear it in Basque."

I looked down and concentrated on a surgical cut across a fat link. "You were all enthralled."

He snorted. "Blindsided was more like it. Anyway, it turned out that the only one who half understood what you were saying was Josie, the cook—"

"She did better than *el diablo.*"

He pointed his fork at me. "Hey, mate, if you're going to interrupt me you gotta speak up."

"Sorry. The story is that the devil wagered with God that he could learn Basque."

"So?"

"After seven years the only two words he managed to learn were 'Go away.' That's why you can't find a Basque in hell."

"Uh-huh, guess that means that you might get lucky. . . . Any-oh-how, after I laid you out on the office couch, Josie brought the spray from the bar. While we were trying to get a squirt up your nose she told me that she had heard your serenade before. The old patron of the restaurant where she learned her trade, in Bakersfield of all places, would get up and sing it—thank Jesus you didn't do that—on special occasions. Or whenever he had a skinful of wine." He kept the tines of his fork pointed meaningfully in my direction. "Well, it seems that on weekends and certain holidays the patron had the kitchen fix all the old Basque dishes—what does *'Zapiak Bat'* mean, Gav?"

It means lost wars. Death squads and car bombs. The bygone dream of a people and a land being an indivisible whole. A boy, a grandfather, who had to run from his home. From his enemies, from his friends. It means sorrow. I said, "It's an old rallying cry, 'The Seven are One.' It refers to the provinces in Spain and France that the Basque considered their homeland. The name of the restaurant?"

"Yep. Had a bet with myself it was something like that. Anyway, so I asked her if she could score some of these here sausages and she came through."

I remembered a round-faced woman with a sweet frown firmly holding my head while Danny put what felt like liquid hydro up my sinuses. There's nothing like Sobert to take the fun out of a painkiller. Ah, well, not their fault; they thought they were doing me a kindness.

"So where's this angel of mercy? If she'd like, she's got my best kiss coming."

"I expect Josie would, she thinks—and trust me, I'm only quoting—that you're a beauty."

"Exact quote?"

He grinned. "Close enough. But she's working the dinner shift." His grin widened, wickedly. "However, I'll be sure to mention your offer to her husbands."

"How many does she have?"

"Only two. She acquired them when she was working down in San Dee . . . they're both ex-marine Raiders."

"So?"

"Feeling full of vinegar are we?"

"No," I breathed on him. "Not vinegar."

It wasn't just the *chistorra*—and the scrambled eggs light as air, dusted with fiery pepper, the mountains of crisp hash browns—it was sitting on the little patio under the bougainvilleas late blooming with liturgical flowers; listening to the genuinely glad customers as they briefly stopped by the table to greet Danny; the notes drifting up from below where the Thomas Trio were working their way through "If Anyone Falls"; watching the light slant across the thick clouds and sparkle the waves. It took a major effort to pull back into focus.

"I'd like to use the office," I said.

"Go ahead, I think's it's empty—mind?" He gestured toward the remaining sausage.

Friendship won over greed. I slapped him on the shoulder and went downstairs to the office. As I passed the bandstand, Fuzzy Thomas took his clarinet mischievously through a quick riff of "Born Under a Bad Sign." He got a grin. Private joke. After closing the door and turning on the baffler, I ran an unauthorized route through a buccaneer's telsat and started making my calls.

The first was a note in Ethan's mailbox telling him that I took the case, that he wasn't to contact me, and that he was to immediately, repeat immediately, shut down his web.

The next call was long distance, to France. The tiny village high in the Auvergne where Sophie lives doesn't have a visual link—some squabble between local politicians—so the Soltan fell into a three-color moiré pattern as the phone rang. I thought about having a drink.

"Allo?"

"Je ne regrette rien."

Delighted laughter. "Robie, c'est toi?"

"Oui, ma vielle."

She spoke slowly in heavily accented English. "I have a friend here, a neighbor's daughter that I am teaching how to tat lace. Wait a moment until I can send her on her way."

I heard her speak to the other woman in the scruffy local dialect. A coincidental thought crossed my mind as I waited: Olivia Fouchet and I both spoke French with the same accent.

Sophie came back on the line. "It is sad, the young, they know so little that is worthwhile."

"Are you teaching her anything else besides how to tat lace?"

"Of course not, Robie!" she answered in a shocked voice. At that moment I was sorry we didn't have visual. Sophie was extraordinarily good with her fingers. She was the one who got me started on sleight, but her real talent was in pocket picking. I once saw her switch a billfold that was tucked inside a man's vest while they were close dancing. Still don't know how.

I apologized and we talked a bit about simple things; the weather, terrible as usual; her garden, so-so; my music—the same; a little innocent gossip about some old friends who are still alive. Sophie did most of the talking. Not the way she used to be. But then, after a large life, it's no surprise that she finds her rustic retirement somewhat boring. I did get in a quiet question whether there had been any recent inquiries about me. She answered a bit crossly that if there had, I would have heard. I apologized. Finally we got around to family, which gave me the entry I was waiting for.

"So, how is Lila?"

Her voice got complicated. "She is fine. She came to stay with me for a little holiday last August. She asked about you. You haven't called her in a while."

Lila is Sophie's niece. About ten years ago I was in Paris returning a stolen Bonnard to a family that cared more about the painting than the vast amount of insurance money they would have gotten. The insurer was quite happy to pass along to me a not quite vast fee. So I had a ridiculous amount of money on hand, some free time, and a lovely girl had just started her first year at the Sorbonne. She didn't know Paris very well—she had been raised in Saint Etienne. I did. We went for long walks along ancient streets with new trees, I took her to my favorite restaurants and galleries, introduced her to some agreeable people, went with her to a couple of parties. And we slept together.

Oh, yes . . . On my part it wasn't intended, but Lila wanted a final confirmation for herself. I didn't mind. She's a woman that is easy to like, and the three nights we spent together were filled with sweet affection if not overwhelming lust. There are times when being used is not bad—come on, Robie, let's try to be more honest. It was springtime in a city whose eternal seductiveness had been ravished, but like a twilight beauty was even more compelling. I was feeling wistful; I thought Lila Perrault was, still is, a very sweet-looking woman. I saw the offer coming. I had no intention of refusing.

The problem afterward was Sophie. Not that her niece and I had a passing affair; she's wise in ways that most people couldn't begin to understand. The trouble was the truth that Lila had resolved: in her heart and her body, she preferred women. For some it takes a while to find out who we are—some never can, or want to. And even when we do, there are still the paradoxes. There is so much that Sophie can accept; she is utterly indifferent to color or creed. But she was born in the last century and came from harshness. There is nothing like the rural poor—especially among the French—for that deeply burned-in brand of prejudice. To make it even more painful for my friend, Lila is the very image of her lost sister, and the niece is smart enough to adore her aunt.

"Is she still running a Desk on the Eurobourse?"

"Yes, she is doing very well. She was just promoted to senior analyst." It wasn't the prestige of the job that made her sound grudgingly proud; any well-designed Desk can do the technical work. It's the critical quality of your intuition that gets you into a chair behind them. Sophie is one of the shrewdest people I've ever worked with. For her to see that trait in her niece . . .

"That's great. And does she still frequent the salons?"

"I believe so. We do not talk much about such things."

I'm sorry, Sophie. "I would like to ask a favor from you, and her."

The line was silent for a while. "Go ahead, Robie," she finally sighed.

"I want Lila to do some sweeping. Some of it she may be able to glean from her work, but I suspect mostly it will come from the salons. I would like for you to be her handler."

Another moment of quiet. "Is it a job for—"

"No, Sophie. It's for me."

This time the response was quicker. "Very well, Robie, *pour toi.*"

"Thank you. Will it be difficult for Lila?"

"May I tell her for whom it is for?"

I weighed risks. A pleasant chore. Sophie wouldn't ask if it wasn't significant. "Yes."

"Then she will not let it be difficult. Besides, she was always fascinated by my stories. After all, it is in her blood."

Carefully edited stories. Lila knows a little more than she should about her aunt, but Sophie is very adept at hiding the dangerous things—and not just those that deal with security. There are nightmares that even if you could, you don't share. Not with people you love. I said, "Make sure you tell her I want only low-hazard information."

"I think I can still remember how it works," she replied dryly.

And I can still remember how to feel chagrined. I gave her the basics of the case and an outline of what I was looking for: friends, lovers—especially recent ones—and enemies of Siv Mattheissen; corporate gossip, who hates who and why in the Groupe Touraine and among their business rivals. Wasn't sure how much Lila might be able to provide me on the latter, but unless I was guessing wrong, Mattheissen was almost certainly a habitué of the salons. For the last quarter century they have been the realtime social centers for the bright and beautiful; it fits the image of the New Enlightenment that the Euro intelligentsia are so fond of writing about. While they are not segregated, each of the salons has its own topics and particulars, and although again it was a guess (not that transparent, in Paris, sexuality isn't that significant a divisor—there's always the anxiety of subversion), I was pretty sure Lila and Mattheissen would gravitate toward the same gatherings.

"Shall we use a crypt key?"

Asking the obvious, a little dig back at me. "Do you still have the Bonhoeffer?"

"It's around here somewhere." Her voice became lazy. "Robie, for this personal job, will you be putting together a strike team?"

I blinked hard. You are too old, I thought. Your hands are still incredibly good, but your strong legs are too slow now—they were shattered once too often. You've gotten too heavy. And you had sex with men you hated to save the lives of strangers. Never flinched at anything, but knew when to be afraid, and when not to be. You kept our disciplines better than I ever could. . . . And you only retired because we finally had to force you to. Among extraordinary people, if you weren't the best you were the finest.

I made my tone as easygoing as hers, not easy. "No, if it comes to it, I plan on closing this one alone. But if I were, you know you would be the first I'd call."

"Still a lovely liar—thank you. Alone, oh, my Robie, *mon coeur*. Always so reckless. Always willing to rush in where even fools are unwilling to tread." She coughed low in her throat, clearing it. "I will call Lila right now. *'Voir.'*"

One down, one to go. This one wouldn't be as difficult.

The Lius' factor answered: "Good morning, sir. Thank you for calling the house of Jiao. Master Llewellyn Liu is presently engaged with a class. Do you wish to leave a message?"

"This is Gavilan Robie. Is it possible for Llewellyn to come to the phone?"

There was an almost imperceptible delay. "Ah, Mr. Robie. I shall inquire immediately. May I ask if you plan to revise your appointment schedule with us?"

"That depends on my conversation with Llewellyn."

"I understand, sir. Please stay on the line." Its image kaleidoscoped away. The phone started playing Walton's Passacaglia for Cello. Custom-tailored Muzak. Haven't had the heart to tell Llewellyn how much I hate the perfect lie of canned music. He came on in the nick of time.

He was wiping a thin sheen of sweat from his face as he sat down behind the simple low table he uses for a secretary. Lew has an oddly chiseled face, the contours more hard straight lines than curves. Except for that Welsh grandfather, his family is supposed to be pure old Hong Kong; countless generations of fishermen. But that face spoke of the steppes, of the rapacity of Tartars—which disproves the notion, if it still can somehow be current in this day and age, that a face shows character.

At the edge of the field I saw that he had his black iron-and-stainless-steel chess set out. Like a lot of the newer Chinese émigrés he's become obsessed about the game. "*Quiubole,* Gavilan!" he said. "You called at an opportune moment. My students are being particularly clumsy this morning." He shook his head sorrowfully. "It has been trying. This break will give them an opportunity to recover from my remarks."

"Having been on the receiving end myself, my sympathies are purely with them."

His eyes almost disappeared. "You at least pay attention."

"Don't have much choice, considering the size of my ears."

In the face of irreducible truth, he laughed. So much for the stern *sensei* image. I growled, "When you're through chortling over a man's deformities, I need to talk business."

He managed to shift into contrite—almost. "Apologies, Gavilan. To what do I owe the honor of this call?"

"I am going to need a major tune-up over the next few days, but my hours are likely to be erratic. So if I can, I'd like to reserve all of your time."

"One moment, please." The phone muted while he conferred with his factor. One of the pleasing things about Liu is how he takes my idiosyncratic requests in stride. He came back swiftly. "I have a master judo class Monday at seven A.M. that I would loath to cancel. They are at a delicate cusp."

"How so?"

"I have been working at shattering their confidence. Now they must be helped in rebuilding an honest foundation. And Wednesday evening I will be in Kyoto. Some friends in the Budoin have invited me to join them as one of the judges at a mixed match."

"Between which arts?"

"Aikido and Kasai jujitsu."

"I'm not familiar with that school."

"They are quite small, but they have a great deal of talent and a very pure, yet original, approach. All the participants are supposed to be top flight. I am quite looking forward to it."

The Kokusai Budoin is one of the oldest interdisciplinary martial art associations in Japan and the one with far and away the most prestige. Deserved. From the first they were broad-minded; talent and attitude were the only criteria they cared about. But that isn't a viewpoint usually shared by people who believe in purity.

I glanced at his dark hazel eyes, the legacy of his grenadier grandfather, and thought: the schools have the right to decline a judge. Besides talent, that little dojo had damned good sense.

He went on, "Barring flight delays, I should be back by three A.M. Outside of those—" He suddenly snapped his fingers. "No, I am sorry. Sulinn's film has its first showing this Thursday. If I do not attend she will of course poison me."

"Only poison?"

"For an American, my wife is a subtle woman. Almost as subtle as you, Gavilan."

It seemed to be my morning for backhanded compliments. "Why, thank you, Lew. I've got another request. Can you arrange a session with a *capoeira* practitioner?"

He cocked his head pensively toward me. "I was not aware that the Brazilian art was among your skills."

"It's not, but I've run into it."

"Indeed?"

"Yes, indeedy."

Lew knows the rules of the road and what a stop sign looks like. "How capable do you want the individual to be?"

"Oh, I'd say just good enough to take me. Also it has to be a woman, preferably around average height and under thirty."

"Those are rather narrow parameters. Are they critical?"

"I don't know. Maybe. Sorry for the vagueness. Can you arrange it?"

He rubbed his bottom lip. "It's certainly a challenge. . . . Yes, I think so, although it may take some time."

"Unfortunately right now time is one of 'necessity's sharp pinches'—within the next three days?"

Llewellyn frowned, leaned back in his chair, and played with a steel rook. He's aware—if not for what, or why—that I sometimes take on more than my ordinary load of trouble. Like all my living friends in some respects he knows a lot about me, and in some, nothing at all.

Late at night, Kit's husky, sleepy voice murmuring, "Such a fractional life, Gav. But what do the numerators add up to?"

I do know what the sum is, my querida. And the cost.

"It is a difficult case?" he asked quietly.

"I think so."

He put the piece back down on the board. "Then if it is possible, it will happen."

"Soon."

"Gavilan, I heard the urgency."

"Thank you."

He shook his head in a way that acknowledged the gratitude and said it was unnecessary. "May I watch the match?" he asked.

"Certainly," I answered. "I'll want your critique."

"Sensitive ears and all? Now, that should be interesting. Well, I should get back to my students."

"I'll be in touch."

He nodded, and with a wave switched off. Interesting. A good term for sex, music, or philosophy. A lousy one for violence.

I went back up to the patio to say adios to Danny. He was engaged in a friendly conversation with a young ponytailed woman who sported loud diamond wristbands on each arm. From the laid-back expression on Danny's face I knew he was already working. So I left the cantina and hailed a jitney. Paid the lot's outrageous nonresident fee and headed up the New Coast Highway. My next call lived in the mountains above the Malibu Wreckage.

CHAPTER FIVE

A CONGESTED CRAB-CRAWL UP, AND over, the highway. The storm had brought with it the usual number of landslides. They had rubbled millions of cubic meters of cliff to build the barrier and the road that ran on top of it, but they hadn't torn down enough. When it comes to public works, graft is as Californian as a tortilla. The slides are why NCH is one of the few routes out of L.A. that isn't on the grid; it's considered a waste of time to constantly have to respray wire. And that makes the road a favorite drag for racers and outlaws. Wondered briefly if the Erinyes had used it. Went past Charmlee Park—a sad smoky smear against the brown hills—pulled off on Decker Canyon and headed up the twisting, lonely road. Holguin's last-century pseudoTudor was at the top. A quick automatic check at the gatehouse and I was let onto the grounds.

Parked in the weed-choked courtyard. A couple of Holguin's prize jaguarcitas were lying about on the front steps. They inspected me with dun yellow eyes. They were one of the things I detested about Vladimir. At that moment they looked like oversized, languid tabbies enjoying the break from the rain. One of reality's not-so-little lies.

They're legal, and expensive. That tells you all you need to know about local politics.

I got out, walked very carefully past them to the door, and smiled for the sensors. Waited a polite period of time; found the rusty bell hidden by the ivy and leaned on it. From somewhere inside came a female cry of "Goddammit, aw'right, aw'right!" The door flew open.

"You're too late," the woman barked at me. She was wearing a black bib overall crusted with a rainbow of paint smears over the front and sides. Early thirties; stocky, with thick eyebrows brought together by her scowl. Faint blue half-moons under clear brown eyes. Her hair was a mass of curly russet that looked as if it had been cut in a salad bowl. She held a thermal brush in her fisted hand as if it were a weapon.

"Story of my life," I replied. "I'm here to see Holguin."

"Mr. Holguin is busy screwing his dreams. He doesn't want to be interrupted."

"Screwing his dreams." Pacific Northwest for going under the wire. Not true for Vladimir, appearances to the contrary . . . "Tell him it's Galahad."

"Who? I told you he doesn't want to be—" I moved gently around her and touched the wall plate. "Vlad, I'm here."

His squeaky voice came through the speaker: "Come up in ten minutes."

She looked at me half irritated, half awed. "You must be someone fuckin' important."

I shook my head. "Only stubborn."

Head to toe examination, softened voice. "Sorry about the greeting, that was rude of me. . . ." She hesitated, wiped her free hand on her bib, and offered it to me. "I'm Jordan."

"Nice to meet you." After letting go of her grip I closed the door behind us. "Are you a friend of Holguin?"

"Friend?" She clearly had doubts about how well I knew Vladimir. Her neck muscles tightened. "I'm working for him."

I nodded. "Of course. You're doing a hot painting."

Those thick brows rose. She seemed to be testing my words for irony. A short lag and then she decided that I was innocent. We walked together into the great room. It smelled of spilled wine, oil resins, *yesca,* and faintly of honeysuckle. The heavy oak furniture had been pushed against the walls and body-sized pillows covered the floor. The entryway to the long gallery where Holguin keeps his precious collection was sealed by a new door; looked like a Chubb, composite tungsten steel, plain, not fancy, and still a long sweaty afternoon to break through. Unidentifiable stains ran down its stippled surface. Must have been a high class hooley. Then the stale, tobaccoey scent of the *yesca* tickled my nose and I sneezed. And started laughing.

"That your *considered* opinion?"

In the backwash of artificial lust I thought she was referring to herself until I saw that she was standing in front of an easel. It was tucked into a corner under the grand staircase, almost hidden behind a rack of fans and speaker panels. On it was a work in progress. Cloudy red chalk drawings and freeze snaps were tacked around the edges of a five-by-eight-foot canvas.

It was a bacchanal—what else?—perfect bodies entering the various doors to ecstasy. But it was set in shadows that ranged from the deep endless black of the Spanish masters to a misty gray. It made a composition that would otherwise be crowded seem spaced, private. It transformed what they were doing into a sensual solemnness. Working in thermal oils with their deep glaze effect gave it a gravity that pulled at you. It was only about a third done, but it was a painting already worth remembering. Told her I liked it.

She answered too flippantly, too quickly, "As in you don't know much about—"

"As in I noticed that you adopted Holguin's favorite point of view, fly on the wall, and that some of the foreshortening is deliberately queasy—not enough to throw off the structure, but a real cute way to flip him, one that he's smart enough to get. That you handle black, the toughest color there is, damned well. That I can see that you're focused on the natural awkwardness of bodies, which turns what they are doing into something both wonderful and terrifying. Something real. As in under the best of circumstances, that's always hard. . . ." A long glance at a detailed sketch of a couple shudderingly coupled. "And as in, unless the viewers suffer from some serious dysphoria they're going to feel the heat. . . ." I sighed and turned to her. "Doña, underestimating people is the second most stupid thing you can do, and being defensive is only justified if you don't have any talent."

Except for her mode of dress, or rather lack thereof, she looked exactly like a schoolgirl catching hell from a principal—now, there's an archaic vision. "Oh, damn, lecture's over," I said. She peeked up through her bangs. I gave her the peace sign. "Honest. Forgive me, I was just blowing off. It's been a rugged morning."

"Must have been. You're in the business?" I shook my head. "A collector?"

"An admirer."

She studied me as carefully as I had her painting. "You're certainly not like Holguin's other visitors."

"Lucky me."

She smiled again, a dynamite smile. I turned around and took in the room. "Knowing Vlad, I'd guess it was his idea to have live models."

"He wouldn't have it any other way. I don't know where he found them." She glanced critically at a series of quick blocking snaps thrown together on a small bench by the easel. "They weren't professionals, not the usual, anyway. They were mostly from one of those floating troupes where everybody seems to have been involved with everybody at some time or another. In the beginning they were shy—not how I thought they'd be. They certainly weren't used to having to set this kinda scene." She chuckled. "And it wasn't the sort of scene I've had a lot of experience describing." She paused, and then drawled deliberately, "But it was an *interesting* experience—artistically, I mean."

There was that word again. "I can imagine so," I said, and bit the inside of my lip.

She was a fine woman. The skin below her neck was slightly flushed, her pupils were wide. She had a lovely back, and worse yet, she was talented. She knew what I was feeling. It would be not easy, but possible, to hurry my business with Holguin and together with her find that nearby bed-and-breakfast—one that I never took Kit to—that has an upstairs turret room with a real working fireplace and a sweeping view of the sea. The owner used to be a wine importer. He has a cellar filled with—honest to God—vintage cases of Montrachet and the Widow's best; the beds are covered with the softest cotton sheets. . . . The tips of my fingers traced the contours of her cheek and jaw. She turned her head toward my hand, and closed her eyes.

Her face was warm, a soft heat. I took my hand away. Slowly.

Knew what was putting the bridle in my mouth. While I've never taken a vow of abstinence—always firmly believed that chaste makes waste—I could still smell that damned honeysuckle. There are some things I still try to keep honest.

Holguin's voice saved me from having to be awkward.

His office was up on the top floor. The interior walls of what had once been the attic and servants' quarters had been torn out to provide space for his workshop. Holguin was at the opposite end of the room, in the cluttered midst of what he likes to call his atelier. He was lying back in a lounger, his elbows on his stomach, fingers steepled under his chin. The target of his fixed attention was a rotating mandala floating above a pooltable-sized projector. The image looked like a pink-blue pointillistic cascade of waterfalls pouring out in all directions into pitch-black space. What it was and what it really looked like, I had no idea.

I loudly cleared my throat; a decent bull moose imitation. It managed to get him out of his rapture. He let out a satisfied moan, turned, and smiled broadly at me. "Gavilan, fortuitous timing. I was thinking about you."

Not too hard, I hoped. "Yeah." I nodded toward the mandala. "Another espionage gig?"

"Competitive intelligence is the correct term," he replied as acerbically as someone whose pitch hovers just below a falsetto can. "You know that sort of dusting is merely a peripheral interest of mine. This, compadre, this comes from the heart. My latest masterpiece. The visual manifestation of a political gestalt; its entire self-organized criticality."

I blew on my fingers as I walked around the projector. Always curious about things I don't understand. "Some kind of multiphasic database?"

If he could dare he would have sneered. "Ah, Gav, it's no more a base than you are a collection of viscera, muscle, and bone. What you see here is more than some mere historical topology. What I have captured is the very soul of an organization." He took his gaze away from the display and propped his shades back up on buttercream locks. He had his eyes redyed since the last time I saw him; the irises were now chipped amethysts. The only exotic parts of a face otherwise molded into a cherubic blandness.

When I first met Holguin I figured him for a dioxin neut. He was the right age, under the university brahmin patina there was the nasal accent, and he appeared to have the tragic physiognomy. One of those poor genetic eunuchs whose fathers had committed the sin of fishing for food over the drowned New Jersey estuaries. Men who, like their fathers before them, had worked in the chemical plants that had spewed out the chromosomal twisting wastes— TCDD, remember that lovely?—and were left with not only the legacy of their own killing cancers but the fetal castration of their sons and daughters. A sad story, and like most from the beginning of this century, buried under the avalanche of others.

If he was a neut it might be an excuse. Maybe. But what was stunted about Vladimir Holguin wasn't his sex but his personality.

He was pointing to a chair. I declined. I'm picky about who I sit with. He shrugged and lit up a matchstick-thin joint. Took a toke, sucked air, and after a minute, blew out a perfect ring. "I would offer you some—to share in my celebration—but alas, my supplier in Cuba is undergoing some labor problems, and the artistic endeavors last night put quite a crimp in my stock."

"That's all right. I've had my fill of chemistry for the day. I take it you got your money's worth?"

He finished off the *yesca* in one inhalation, cupping the ashes carefully in his hand. A fastidious man. "Certainly," he said, coughing a little. "Watching the creative process of others so energizes my own—the ceremony of regeneration. It was just what I needed to polish off this design. It gave me the spark to find the most elegant solution to the $1/f$ noise problem as it relates to quasi-cyclic events—a splendid breakthrough if I may be immodest."

Watch, that's all the courage he has. "Would you care to explain that in layman terms?"

He quoted in the original Greek: "'Give me but one firm spot on which to stand, and I will move the earth.' Such a beautiful truism. My design will tell someone, with the highest degree of confidence, where that firm spot is—in regards to one tiny state."

"Or in other words how to disrupt a country, or an alliance, for fun and profit. I don't suppose you'd tell me which state is going to have some minimum damage applied to it?"

He's too self-absorbed to notice when someone isn't being serious. "Please, Gavilan. Again like you, my projects and my clients are strictly confidential. I wish it were otherwise. Even though the nature of the medium constrains me to be a miniaturist, still profound art can be created on that scale. How I long for acclaim from those who—"

"Sure you do." I had a pressing need to do something with my hands. A few feet away there was a burled walnut campaign table with various knickknacks on it. I picked up an hourglass filled with gold dust, a slim print book covered in morocco leather, and a hefty owl figurine that looked like it came out of a sixth-century B.C. Athenian workshop. I started juggling.

An F-sharp: "Stop that!"

It was tricky with unequal weights, but I managed a double over the shoulder, and put them down. Leaned back against the edge of the table, folded my arms, and grinned.

He stared at me. "Why are you here, Robie?"

"The usual reasons. To take advantage of your brilliance, and your knowledge of dirt—pardon me, that's a redundancy." Red spots appeared on those flawless, poreless cheeks. He could have thrown me out. He could have tried.

Instead he turned off the display with a snap of his fingers. "First, shall we discuss payment?" His voice had turned as monotonous as his face.

"Fine by me. What's the tab today?"

He sank back into the lounger. "I have decided to sell one of the pieces in my collection. A work that I have had for a number of years. Unfortunately, should it become public, certain authorities would take the wrong view of the transaction. It's a shame, isn't it, the lack of respect our government has for private property. I am looking for a discreet channel to an appreciative buyer. Given how successful you are in your line of work, I'm sure you know all the best people."

I could see another layer of regret coming. "Having some labor problems of your own? Which piece?"

"One, given your sensibilities, I haven't shown to you. A central Indian stela with a relief female figure." He described it with the pedantic detail that collectors often use as a disguise, or a substitute, for passion: "Typically iconic, almond eyes, large spherical breasts. Her left hand is raised above her shoulder holding a lotus. Her right cradles a very delicately done water jug against her hip. She is wearing a dhoti and jewels. In the foliage of the tree above her is a monkey. It is about seventy centimeters high. Tenth century, quite exquisite."

"Sounds like a number of pieces from that period. . . . Buff sandstone?"

He shook his head, savoring his reply. "No. Alabaster."

"That's not—oh, I see—the Mhow find." I whistled. "Except for the gold figurine of Rama that was on tour, they're all supposed to be radioactive dust. So not all of the artifacts ended up in the Delhi museum."

He smirked again. "You understand how it is. Impoverished peasants, underpaid bureaucrats, the chance of several lifetimes. Some items that were not clearly devotional were made, shall we say, available."

This I did understand. "It must have been damned difficult to get it into the country. Diplomatic pouch?" He waved his hands about innocently. "And given its provenance," I continued, "even harder for you to sell." At the price you'd want, I added mentally. The market discount on stolen art rises dramatically in proportion to the amount of heat on the item. A simple equation I had used more than once to advantage.

"It has been a dilemma," he said genially.

He hadn't shown me the piece because he knew that when it comes to my profession I have the bad reputation of being ethical about certain things.

Some values no computer can weigh for you. It would have been easier if I knew that the information I wanted from Holguin would be of use. But I was sailing on dead reckoning, drawing the charts as I went, using only questionable instinct for a compass.

"Okay, Vladimir. Recorders off."

He called out, "*Hold infinity*. Done, Robie."

"All of them."

I will give him this, he did try his best to stare me down. Lips twisting, he reached over to an archaic keyboard and clicked a few keys. "Very well, Robie, they are all off."

"I hope so." So I told him who, where, and how; and when I finished, as a professional courtesy I added a warning: "Play nice with these people, Holguin. They are far, far worse than I am."

His purple eyes picked up a muddy yellow tinge; they looked like foul bruises: I scared him once—before I found out how fundamentally a coward he was—very badly. "Galahad" is a bit of wish magic for him. My ethics don't stop me from being a son of a bitch.

Waited patiently for him to regroup. He pulled his shades back down, swallowed tightly, stopped trembling. "Go ahead."

I had decided on the drive up that trying to misdirect him with garbage questions would be a waste of time. So I opted for honesty. "For now, take a dip in the streams and give me a wide reading on the Congo Basin Project and its problems."

"Hunh . . . Now, that is an original request from you. Ah, I see. What interest does your Benevolence have in Africa?"

Despite my denials, Holguin is convinced that I work as a consigliere for one of the syndicates. Luckily for both him and me, he's kept that mistake to himself. The padrinos take dimly to false advertising. "None, as far as I know."

"If you say so." He sat up, lowered his shades, and started whispering into the mike attached to his shades. What he saw beyond its dark amber lenses I could only guess at. Datastream virtuality is something you have to train for starting at a very young age. That's all right, I'm not jealous; the side effects too often include some damned unpleasant pathologies.

I glanced at the campaign table. The Athenian owl was a copy—I hoped; my juggling isn't as good as it used to be. I thought about what the bird symbolized: wisdom. Except that during the renaissance and through the baroque, portrait painters often used it as a witty prop, an inside editorial joke: the owl can also stand for deceit. I remembered explaining that to Kit once, and how she flashed me a thin smile and asked me to tell her again what exactly was my totem animal. Gave her a kiss for an answer. I shifted my attention to the goatskin-bound book that I had also tossed around: *Der Wille zur Macht,* the Musarion edition. Nietzsche; it figured. Looked back at Holguin, he was still except for the slight kicking of his thin legs. When he gazed into a mirror, what did he see? Took my pad out, turned it on, and laid it on the table. It was going to be a long, orotund lecture.

"Intriguing," he said eventually. "The surface is beautifully arranged. The Congo basin has fifteen percent of the world's potential hydroelectric power, essentially untapped. The concept of using that vast capacity to develop an economic growth rate above the five percent necessary to break the poverty cycle has been around since the last century. Only the lack of will and capital has held it back. The lower Congo has always had the possibility of becoming an African Ruhr. The deal worked out with the European Union and the Community of Equatorial Africa has the right amount of pragmatic self-interest tinged with compassion to make it work. The grand trine of money, timing, and need is there. The Africans get a much-needed energy grid, a maintainable transport system, a strong boost to their nascent industrial base. The EU gets serious access to a major resource sector."

He started to go into various projections of raw material shortfalls for the European theater over the next twenty years. Some of it was commonplace knowledge, some of it—especially the numbers on shortfalls—didn't sound public at all.

Every so often he would break down some of the obtuse parts that he correctly assumed I didn't understand into terms I could follow. The only impatience he showed was in a little fidgeting in his arms. The little nightmare I had put him through had its roots in his once trying to short me.

I finally interrupted him. "Environmental?"

He switched tracks smoothly. "The ecocrats have their thumbprints all over the project. There was a five-year depth-impact study, a little fast but still acceptable; they used Gottesman and Harcourt, a very blue-chip assessment firm—I have found their studies to be most reliable. The project has been optimaxed to the hilt. What is left of the rain forest goes into preserve—mandate run. Except for renovating the Inga Dam, the big one south of Kinshasa, all the new constructions will be minis instead of those old monstrosities. Fisheries along the river and new lakes. No plans for an irrigation system; the topsoil wouldn't support more than a few years of plantation agriculture anyway. Some agroforestry: shade-tolerant chickpeas under the usual mix of pharmacopeia trees and select fast-growth hardwoods. Exclusivity zones for any threatened species. EU Class Two standards for pollution control. The whole smorgasbord of monitoring. Given the mediagenic appeal of the project it is about all the plus-ultra cliques could have hoped for."

"Downside?"

"I will get to it," he answered tartly. "That's on the second strata."

"Perdone."

"As I was saying, resource access is apparently the main impetus for the Europeans. Shades of the past, eh? Within the consortium's zonal contracts there are two obvious areas of exploitation: The Kiku natural gas fields in Zaire, and that remarkable lithium find near Brazzaville. With the exponential growth in demand for lightsteel, from those two alone the consortium and its allies should over time reap excellent profits. Which leads us to the next level.

"Remember that grand trine, Robic. Money. Global capital is extremely tight. Yes, I know that is an old tiring refrain but it *is* true. Surpluses, like inflation, are now largely a thing of the past. What free investment capital there is gets fought over hungrily. Now, the financing for the project is supposed to be handled by a balance between short-term loans from the World Bank and a few of the biggest Euro moneycenters, bridge loans from the participating governments, and long-term bonds. Those bonds are being offered at four and three-quarters, a very competitive rate; with the added bonus of being tax exempt in those participating member states of the Union—so far only the French, the Flemish, and Scandinavians have made that exemption available to buyers."

I could see his brows arch over the shades' rims. "However, over the twenty-year development span of the project, the cash flow versus the burn rate is insufficient. The bankers know this, of course. They also know that the EU Treasury is backing the long bonds. What they appear not to know—hm, possibly they don't care—is that the consortium is secretly planning to defer payment for much of the construction costs. The reason appears to be simple; the Equatorial Africans have given them certain additional, unspecified, mineral rights. Which implies that there have been discoveries that have not been published. I see some turbulence among the great mining companies. You know that they are all interlocked, have been for well over a century. Would you mind getting me some water?"

I found a frosted silver decanter and poured him a glass.

He took a sip and went on. "The question is whether the consortium can absorb the costs, or more specifically, can Groupe Touraine handle it? They are the rajahs of the syndicate. I am sorry, Robie, but that is a question I am not sure I can find an answer to. The Groupe is privately held and you know what that means in Europe. Looking over their public contracts I can say that currently they seem to have a powerful cash flow and they are supposed to hold major reserves. But all that I am receiving is supposition, guesswork." He snorted.

The corners of my mouth curled up. Having little intuition of his own, Vlad doesn't trust other people's hunches. And he dreams he's an artist.

He pushed his shades up and rubbed at where they rested on his nose. "Please bear in mind, what I am relating is only a first approximation analysis. Moving along to the last part of the wheel; there is nothing mysterious about the timing. The interstices between population, economics, and politics are well within the most favorable ranges for both regions—and with the tsetse fly now officially eradicated, there aren't any serious in situ health problems left. However, the precise nature of the needs, beyond those that I have already mentioned, is cloudy. I cannot get a fix on the dynamics, but again the presence of Groupe Touraine is provocative."

"How so?" I asked.

"Foreign economic policy is supposed to be managed by the Union Secretariat, but old habits die hard. There is a moderately high order of probability that the French state government is a secret partner of the Groupe. Not an uncommon practice in Europe—or elsewhere. Given the history, the likelihood that Paris is using GT as an instrumentality to further their own interests is a viable hypothesis. What those interests might be, besides the traditional realpolitik that they have always played in that part of the world, is not visible on my horizon scan."

Holguin stopped speaking for a moment. The datastream, metaphorically constructed and deconstructed with each inaudible whisper, may turn him into an instant authority . . . but it is wearing.

"Let's see. You expressed questions about the environment. The Congo is one of the few regions where the Transition has had only a nominal effect. You might even say that the climatic changes have so far been beneficial, or at least benign. Coastal elevations made surge flooding an insignificant problem except at river mouths. A small but steady decline in rainfall and an increase in temperature variation of less than one percent possibly indicate that a demishift is under way from a Koppen class A towards a class C—"

"You can skip that. We've all taken the Introduction to Natural History course."

"All I was going to add was that thanks to war and plague, the population has stayed level at about eighty million, well below carrying capacity."

I saw: *The charnel house that was Lubumbashi, mothers carrying*

their babies across shattered streets, both dying of extinct diseases.
Peacemakers coming in silently at treetop level to drop shredder
bombs on random villages. An old man and his wife silhouetted
against a rust-streaked sky, scratching at the caked soil, trying to feed
their dead children's children. Bodies laid out in long shrouded rows
behind the clinic where the Sisters of Grace were hitting themselves
with bootlegged gelbeis *so they could work a hundred hours at a*
stretch, the numbers defeating them no matter how hard they
tried. . . .

I was younger than I should have been.

Wrong. For some things there's no right age.

Sometimes it helps when someone else tells you a story that
you already know. "Just tell me what you see," I said.

"All things considered, much of the impacted region comes
near to being primeval. The Congo is the last great river left that is
close to its natural state. The project ends that. And despite the assurances of the ecocrats, when all is said and done, the probability
of avoiding irreparable damage and still sustaining that five percent growth rate is a questionable problematic. Years ago that alone
would have sunk the proposal, but nowadays, except for the deep
enviros, most people are willing to accept the risks for the gain."

Group Touraine and the Furies. It struck me that they were
two sets of self-absorbed missionaries, one trying to bring salvation through economics—at a profit—the other trying to redeem
the unredeemable. In their own ways, although they would never
see each other as such, two sets of romantics. Neither of them
African. "Any other opposition?"

"There have been some financially related protests. Not all the
Europols are happy with the Treasury underwriting the guar-
anties. Also a few of the minor para groups, like the Moutons Enragés, have engaged in some direct action. Their violence seems to
be predicated on the assumption that the project will be of benefit
only to the major alliances and the Africans. There is a lot of xeno-
phobia underlying that spectrum."

"How about from companies outside the consortium?"

He paused. "At the moment I do not seem to have access to any definitive information."

One of Vlad's few worthy attributes is that he doesn't waste your time with gossip. I pocketed my pad. "All right. That'll be enough for now. But I want you to keep looking for any serious opponents of the project."

He took off his glasses and rested them on his lap. His irises glowed as if they had soaked in the light from the stream. "Robie, you were fortunate in coming to me this morning. I have a number of clients that want to use my talents. And while I'm sure you consider your payment generous, you must realize that my art entails a large overhead. If you wish for me to keep spending my time on this, I may have to ask for further payment."

I walked over to him and gently rested one of my hands on his knee. The physical contact made him as stiff as a deer caught in the headlights of a car. "Do you really think so?" I asked idly.

A nice, quick reply. "No—of course not. After all it was a generous favor."

"Yes, it was."

CHAPTER SIX

SHE WAS STANDING ON TIPTOES, hard at work laying in some more of that magnificent black. The stretch gave her back a lovely serpentine curve. Fished a blank phonecard out of my wallet and entered a number on it. I was going to leave the card where she'd spot it, and slip away, when she turned to dip her brush in some paint and saw me.

One of those little moments; at least she wasn't blushing.

"Hola."

"Hi." She looked at the card. "Your number?"

Tried to sound as regretful as I could. "No, it's for an old acquaintance of mine, Amos Ryland. He's a dealer. Quite a good—"

"I know who Amos Ryland is."

Raised my hands in apology. "And I had the temerity to give a lecture on the danger of underestimation. Well, then, I think he'd like to see your portfolio—unless you already have representation?"

Her face stopped being so carefully noncommittal. "I've been in a few group shows in Vancouv—that's where Mr. Holguin—but no, right now I'm not with anyone." With nervous fingers she took the card from my hand. "Ryland, he handles some of the—why?"

"Call it part of a balancing act. Don't question it, Jordan. Just use it."

She looked at the numbers I had entered as if they were arcane runes. Read them correctly and the magic door opens. Hey, sometimes they do.

"Will he really see my work?"

I smiled. "I know Amos has a scary reputation—" I caught a look on her face. "'A hysterical piranha,' and that's a description from one of his friends, but it's just wind and words, mostly. That number is for his personal box. When you call, make sure to clip a shot of this painting. Don't worry about how finished it is." A short, good look again at the painting. "You know . . . when I was a boy I thought art was like medicine. If you took it the right way you would become good."

"Good at what?"

"Just good."

She bit her lip. "This is too much."

"Not really. All you're getting is a chance."

The great room was quiet. I could hear a tree branch grazing softly back and forth against one of the high windows, like a drummer brushing a cymbal. Waited. In her eyes hope finally won over disbelief. She grinned impishly. "Sir knight, you do deserve your name—what really is your name?"

Vlad won't tell, but Amos is careless. I debated, and decided. From a deck of fictions I pulled a name. "David Aquila."

"Aquila . . . a good name for you." She put the card carefully in a pocket and gave me a bold stare. "Well, David Aquila . . . do you like fresca melons?"

"Yes."

"Champagne?"

"Very much."

"Good. Now if you'll give me your address I should be done for the day by eight or so tonight. I'll bring them for breakfast."

Every so often I think my life is little more than a series of bad timings. I shook my head sadly. "I wish we could. But I'm tied up in a rather complicated business deal right now, and I—I'm sorry, it won't work. But I will go to your show when you have one."

She wasn't about to let a minor disappointment get in the way of the rush she was feeling. "Oh-kay . . . I understand. If I do have a show bring a friend—if you have one."

I grinned at the old retort. "That has a lot of hair on it."

"So has my father—he's the one who told me the joke about Shaw and Churchill. Dad's a historian."

"Small world. So was mine." I leaned down and kissed her cheek briefly. "Adios, Jordan. Luck."

And with that gesture I left. Sublimation, I know. So I was born a couple of centuries too late. So what; last time I checked, it wasn't a sin to be an anachronism.

One of the jaguarcitas was resting on the roof of the Cruiser. He yawned broadly and flicked his long ringed tail. We spent a quiet minute staring at each other. Then there was a sudden patter of rain. He leaped off in a hurry. Sixty pounds of feline homicide. I don't know what bothers me more, whether it's the fact that they are all that's left of those beautiful wild cats except for those in the museum-zoos, or that they have been perverted by tinkering that scaled down their size and toughed them up—as if they needed it—into viciously effective bodyguards. A mutual acquaintance, not a friend—we don't have any of those in common—once told me that Holguin sells his less-than-perfect specimens to the hell clubs, where they fight in an arena against a pack of pit bulls. The wager being how many of the dogs the "flawed" cat can kill in three minutes. By breeding and training, the dogs are fearless; that only means that they die quicker. The minimum bet is five; what the max is I don't know—and I don't want to.

Saved by a squall. I'll take all the good omens I can get.

I ran the truck breakneck down Decker Canyon, driving as if I were in the Lotus; heel and toeing brake and accelerator, boxing the corners.

Used Kit's spare pass to get into the Neuropsychiatric Institute's staff parking lot at UCLA. The guard was as careful as the ones that watched over GT, but she knew that being brusque had nothing to do with being efficient. She guided me through the three sets of randomly rolling steel barriers. What a wonderful age we live in. I took the stairs up to the fourth floor. The corridor to Kit's office was empty except for a cleaning crew. Unfortunately I had to pass the reception area. Stepped over the robugs and walked casually.

A doctor—you can always tell them around here by the white snap-button shirts and heavy-duty med bracelets (physician, worry thyself)—was talking to the young man behind the Desk. Most hospitals would have the typical imaged factor, but UCLA's psych workers still own a union and having people around that actually breathe is supposed to make it easier on the patients.

The doctor was Sutherland, a colleague of Kit. He looked up as I approached and frowned.

"Good day, Mr. Robie," he said slowly.

"Doctor."

"If you're looking for Katherina, she's not here."

"Really?" I scratched my scalp absently. "Kit's usually here on Saturdays."

He let a few seconds pass, trying to decide if I was going to be a difficulty. "Actually, Katherina's in Helsinki at a conference." No affectionate diminutives for him.

I snapped my fingers. "Damn, that's right, I forgot; she told me she was going to be gone this week."

Behind his light blond beard he looked nonplussed. Kit's not one to confide her personal life with coworkers, but sooner or later, et cetera. I wondered if Sutherland had a yen for her. I slouched a little against the Desk and flashed the secretary an honest smile. "Qué habe, Mario? They got you working on a Saturday?"

Mario rubbed a thumb and forefinger together, showing his cliqua tattoo. "Overtime—got the new amiga."

I nodded understandingly. Last time we spoke, Mario was negotiating for a '24 Brazilian Lancer: a hythanol two-stroker with a juice boost; chopped and buffed; painted go-to-hell red. He was aching for it and very worried about whether he could get his new love to meet CalEco's zero-tolerance regs. Riding's an expensive romance. Then again, cost and love are complements; always have been. "Listen, Kit left some tickets in her office for an opening— Sulinn Liu's film—and I'd like to go even if she isn't in town. Mind if I go in and get them?" I added lazily to Sutherland: "If it's a problem you can come with me."

He regarded me with what he no doubt thought was professional thoroughness. I remembered that Kit, with a rare sneer, once called him a fast-fake intake artist. "No," he said ponderously. "I'm sure it will be all right. You can let him in, Mario."

The secretary glanced at me wryly and touched a panel.

"Nice meeting you, Dr.—Sutherland, isn't it?"

"Yes. Good to see you again, Mr. Robie." He was a worse liar than I am. Definitely had a yen. Along with a considerable chunk of the rest of the staff. They're smart, if not always bright.

I moved down the corridor before I got tempted to push it a little more. The name plate by her door glowed redly: Katherina Seferides, M.D., MSNE, etc.—the doctor was out. Helsinki; hoped it was freezing. I opened the door Mario had unlocked for me.

New wall paint, aquamarine. Administration finally broke down and gave her what she wanted. Not surprising. The place was neat as a pin save for the pile of yellow legal tablets on her little writing desk that she liked to use for first drafts. The only thing old-fashioned about her, except perhaps for her taste in men. I sat down in front of her console. The chair only raised up about an inch—there's nothing like a long-legged mistress. Knew I had to move quickly. While I doubted Sutherland would check up on me, the time I spent in the office would be logged on Mario's board and I didn't want him to get into trouble. I do have some scruples. My eyes drifted to the empty tiny Baccarat vase next to the screen. When I was home I made the habit of seeing her off to work with a fresh cut flower. And a kiss that would almost keep her from going to work . . .

That's enough, Robie.

Was able to access Housekeeping with no more than Kit's password—that part of the jumbleplex is ancient and as long as it works there's no budget for an upgrade. Took less than a minute to bridge the office with her home rig. No flags were set off—it's a hardwire connection. NPI's network won't handshake with any terminals that aren't on that line. No automatic cross-checking with her calendar; like I said, ancient.

Before I left, I took a card out and folded it in half so that it would look like a ticket. As I strolled quickly past the reception area I waved it at Mario and called out over my shoulder, "All set."

"Okay," he answered without looking up. "Have a good one."

"Working on it."

Before leaving, I stepped out onto Le Conte Avenue and walked a bit under the shedding eucalyptus trees. Considered stopping by the gym and doing a tight workout on the bars and rings—Jordan, bless her, was right about the body, if not the beauty.

Looked around the campus. I had met Kit here. Four years ago. I had just turned forty-five, more than mildly stunned that I had somehow managed to make it to the middle of the journey. I saw her crossing one of the numerous little quadrangles that dot UCLA. She was wearing a laurel green turtleneck and black lace pants, her ankle-length scholar's cape thrown back against delicate shoulders, folders cradled in an arm—an elegant, studious sylph. Her short dark hair was bathed in sunlight. I watched her unhurried stride, the way she held her head, and thought of a proud Botticelli princess. She stopped to talk to someone, then for no reason at all she looked over her shoulder. No bells rang, no lightning. Just a moment of aching acuity. Of seeing more than you ever expect to see. She pressed a hand against her stomach. I stood there, clumsy fingers curling into my hands, not moving.

Three days later, Katherina moved into my house.

Went back to my truck and drove home.

There was an hour to fill. After leaving a message with Amos Ryland's assistant to have her curmudgeonly boss call me sometime today, I changed into some old work clothes, fixed myself a weak gin fizz, and labored in the conservatory. Actually I mostly sat, sipped, and studied. I was trying to understand why one of the fall hibiscus had failed to bloom. It wasn't being very cooperative— must have a bias against sex. Which was funny considering that its varietal name was Sweet Ecstasy. As I tried to figure out why it was insisting on being shy, I had the genie read to me some chapters from Conrad.

When it got to a certain passage I did nothing but listen.

"Going up that river was like traveling to the earliest beginnings of the world . . . an empty stream, a great silence, an impenetrable forest."

The choices we have to make.

When the time got near, I washed up and headed down to the flats. The barber shop I wanted is located off Cahuenga and Orange. The building it's in should have been condemned after Crazy Eight—it's amazing that it actually survived—but it got declared a landmark. Money changed hands. One of the obvious explanations for why the real cash economy never went away. Not that any Kennedys were spent on the creaky edifice since. It had been built around the turn of the century during a brief revival of the California moderne style; flexed lines sleek as a ship; now it looks like a rusted old scow. Found an empty space nearby, parked, and went to the door. Cheap red curtains were drawn across the mottled round windows. I knocked twice, then once, and waited. A rustling at the curtains, and a few seconds later an emaciated-looking man opened the door slowly, eyes sweeping me and beyond. He nodded and let me in.

Inside the place is nicer, a pleasant cliché. Black lacquered tiles on the floor, brass-and-leather barber chairs. A row of variously shaped colored bottles against a flattering self-illuminated mirrored wall. In a corner a small data screen silently running the Caliente sports lines. Not an orchid or VR board in sight. Two other blades, one Asian, one Latino, were lounging on a comfortably worn sofa watching the betting screen as they chattered softly in the Spanish-Japanese mash the Benevolence troopers prefer to use. They pretended to ignore me.

Han Yee was sitting in the chair farthest from the door, his head tilted sharply to one side, a linen napkin tucked around his neck, as an old man with a tiny golden spoon worked at scraping clean an ear. Without moving he said, "Afternoon, Robie. What brings you here?"

"Good afternoon, Yee. I hope all is well with you and your family?"

He grunted, "Well enough."

The man was never much for manners. "I am glad to hear that. I have brought you a present."

He pointed a finger. The man who looked like a time traveler from the Hunger years took the red parchment envelope from me, put it with some identical others into a narrow folder that he tucked back into his vest.

Formalities over with, I said to Yee, "I came here today to arrange an interview."

He straightened up and told the barber in bad Mandarin to go count some towels. The man dropped the spoon into a bowl, took the napkin off Yee, and went into the back room.

I spoke with care: "I am looking for some stolen merchandise—not from your territory—but not far away."

"And for that you want to bother our Padrino?" He waved a ringed hand disdainfully.

"The merchandise is valuable, and the owners are anxious."

"Eh, they always are. So what? He doesn't deal with street thieves." He rolled his eyes over his men: watch me jerk this cit around.

I sighed, there are limits. "Of course not. Over the years I have heard him more than once express his distaste for pillagers. I am seeking advice, his wise counsel on the matter."

Unspoken subtext: You know enough about me to know that if necessary, I can find other ways to reach the Padrino.

Yee thought about my words for a while. As my Basque grandfather would say, I had given him a stone to chew on. "You need a haircut," he finally said to me.

"I suppose so."

"A man should look neat. Come back in an hour. Chung will trim you, no charge."

"Thank you, Han Yee. I'll do that."

I spent the hour eating a burrito, and then checking out the local Shiu Tong Herb Mart—they have some excellent hothouse teas besides the usual assortment of wonderbuds. I bought a pound of fresh Green Mist for the Lius. A woman smiling only to herself swiftly wrapped the package in ebony rice paper.

When I got back to the barbershop, Yee and his henchmen were gone. Chung silently motioned me to a chair. I told him I'd pass on the cut and handed him a five. His weary expression didn't change as he simultaneously put the money in one pocket and took out a slip of paper from another. On one side penciled in was the character for fortune, on the other side a street number in the Valley, and a time: 10:00 P.M. I bowed to the old man.

*   *   *

After leaving the shop I went over to my office on Normandie in the neighborhood that the local Community Council, with perennial hopefulness, likes to call Los Feliz Adjacent—as if a name could, like paint slapped over rotted wood, hide the essential seediness of the area. The office is a converted single in what once was a stucco two-story apartment building. The other tenants are a mélange of small-time entrepreneurs and hard-luck opportunists. It's difficult to tell the difference. What I've got is a single room with a bath, and carpeting in the final stages of disintegration. But the landlord takes cash and doesn't care to know my name.

I keep in the office some second-hand furniture I bought on Western, a couple of good suits, an old upright piano that's weak in the low registers, and a vanilla rig—its softpac I carry with me. Loaded the programs and activated some figments: George Estaban, confidential agent, and supposedly professional snitch for the California Special Crimes Taskforce; Jane Goddard, wealthy anarchist—an oxymoron if there ever was one; Carl Kohler, a Swiss freelancer interested in guns, revolutions, and underage girls. They were fresh except for Goddard, who I had used on a case six months ago that involved some students who thought that great art properly belonged to the people and shouldn't be sequestered behind the walls of a brahmin's fortress. (Did that case hurt? Yes.)

Nevertheless, they were all due for termination; I don't keep figments for more than a few odd months—costly and time-consuming, but safer. I checked to see if anyone had recently looked into their gossamer histories, made sure I had enough money in my Andorran accounts, armored them as best as I could, and then sent them forth into the hazards of the Electric Sea.

In between monitoring my figs as they made their calls—wandering through dusty muds, knocking on doors, tracking shadows—cueing responses when they got questions that their pseudopersonalities weren't up to answering, I used up the remainder of the afternoon playing Chopin on the upright.

The hours passed. The figs roamed through a bunch of reefs in the Sea that had potential but didn't spot anything intriguing. En-bright, the man (?) I was most hoping to contact, who has a sur-prising level of access within Interpol, wasn't available. It was getting to be late in the evening. Well, I had thrown some chum onto the waters, I would just have to wait for a strike. I brought them back home and took them off line for the night.

CHAPTER SEVEN

THE ADDRESS THAT HAN YEE had passed along was for a renovated black glass high-rise on Lankershim. A small grove of arrogant Seville palm trees with their billowing golden-yellow fronds clustered around the building's base. With its steepled solar roof, hovering colored floods, and flying buttresses of spidery steel, it looked like last century's fantasy of a postmillennial cathedral set in an oasis, or a mirage. Appropriate; gambling is an act of faith, and the top floors house one of L.A.'s finer dens. The Pleiades is the official name, but everybody knows it as the Seven Diamonds.

Hardly anyone knows that it's owned by the Mid-City Benevolence.

Around the perimeter of the building's plaza a crowd of overdressed working boys and girls were loitering; the Valley's *hoi pornoi*. Circled around and found the service entrance. A small fleet of armored limos was parked around the loading bay like spokes of a half wheel, each vehicle pointing outward. The milky water vapor from their exhausts and the cool night air creating a swirling knee-high mist over the black top. This way into the building had the most favorable *feng shui* aspect; gamblers like to take every edge they can get. I found a parking space among the lesser gentry. Got past the skirmish line of house guards, stepped up to the bay, and handed the piece of paper through a slot in the armored glass of the head sentinel's kiosk. He looked at it briefly and handed it off to a human runner. After about ten minutes he touched his ear, nodded, and said, "Senor, you are welcome. Come in." I was buzzed through.

Inside, there was a bewildering row of doors. Depending on what you wanted, a light would be shining over a particular door. Mine was a little less conspicuous than most. I opened it. A young Latina was waiting for me beside an elevator. She wore a loose leather jacket over a blue tube top and wide jeans. She was almost pure Indio with clear copper-brown skin. I nodded and raised my hands. She put on a pair of heavy quilted gloves and patted me down. The gauntlets were a simpler version of the EEN detectors that Groupe Touraine used in front of their headquarters. My skin prickled through the clothing as she swept me. She stopped when she reached the left side pocket of my blazer. "A good luck charm," I said.

She stepped back from me, crouching slightly. "Take it out with your right hand."

I removed the two brass balls from the pocket and showed them to her. She lifted sweeping raven brows that reminded me—a soft pang—of Kit. With unexpected wit she said, "I'd think you'd have enough of those."

"As I said, a luck charm."

She looked at me with stone eyes. "You can leave your luck with me."

I put them in the small tray next to her. She finished her scan and after taking off the gloves, inserted a key from a neck chain into the elevator lock. I noticed that she had an amateur tattoo under a wrist. A metallic blue L over a black C. The tattoo was stretched, faded. She must have had the design inked in while very young. The elevator opened. Inside was a man with extraordinarily long arms holding an s/m knife next to his thigh. In the other hand he loosely held a coil of fine-linked chain. He didn't relax as I got in with him. There are those who claim that an s/m is no worse than a zap from a taser—as if that weren't horror enough. All I can say—or ever want to—is that if you're ever faced with that beautiful choice, take the damned zapper. I leaned away from him and made sure my hands were where he could see them.

Two men were in the owner's suite. One sat at a glowing glass desk dealing out hands from a pack of cards. The other was playing pool on a table under a vaulted alcove. I went to the desk and greeted the man they call the Spanish Deacon. He's got that handle because of his light skin, sandy hair, and a constant, dolorous expression. A plain steel .22 revolver—still a favorite for close-up work, for executions—was by his right elbow. It looked like he had recently finished cleaning and oiling his tool. I took it as a pleasant sign. If I weren't in good graces, the Deacon would be dressed far more formally. Watched his hands as he kept on dealing and held up two fingers. Without a change on his dour face, he flipped over the top cards; three aces; he was dealing fourths. Not bad.

"Hello, Gavilan," he said. "How you been keeping?"

"'Bout the same."

He went back to dealing his cards. I left him and walked to the pool table. The Padrino was shooting three-ball. He looked over his shoulder. "Care to play, Gavilan?"

"No, thanks. Never got the hang of it."

"I am sorry to hear that. It's more fun to compete, teaches perseverance." He sounded sincerely disappointed. He took a leisurely puff from the thin claro that had been resting on an ashtray on the table's burled walnut rim. "I understand that you are looking for some thieves?"

He is a decade younger than I am, the only Padrino under forty. He's not brilliant, merely wise; he knows all the roads that lead to darkness. I said, "Some people stole a young woman named

Matthiessen. They took her out of South Bay yesterday. I'm going to try to retrieve her. I was hoping that you could be of assistance."

Another puff. "Ah, yes . . ." He leaned on his cue stick and studied the ash on his cigar. "Others have already approached me on that matter. I said no. I am sorry, Gavilan, my answer is still the same."

The request for help sure as hell didn't come from the Federales or their allies. Working with organized crime is anathema to them—they'd see the woman's body show up in the sewers before they would come to a Padrino for help. Paul Thinh? Or were there other sharks out there? I shrugged. There were too many other things of more immediate importance. "Then I'm sorry to have bothered you," I said quietly.

He put the stick down on the pool table, turned to the alcove's window, and said, "Open shades." The glass cleared, showing us the vast irregular checkerboard of lights that carpeted the San Fernando Valley. A large globe glimmered through the clouds, a stalker's moon. He spoke without looking at me. "How long have we known each other?"

"About eight years."

"That long." He smoked quietly for a while. I watched the sparse string of red lights flow along the Ventura Freeway. The Valley's slowly being abandoned. People just get tired of rebuilding.

"You know, we think well of you," he said. "There are few outside the life who come to us without greed or fear." He walked to the edge of the window and rested an impeccably manicured hand against the glass. "You and I, we are honorable men, Gavilan. And as such, as a matter of principle, we should not involve ourselves in politics. We can find no respect there." He drew a deep puff from his cigar and exhaled a stream of fine blue smoke. "Of course a principle cannot always be followed. Politicians have a way of thrusting themselves in private business—and therefore have to be dealt with. Though that is usually for us a small problem, a matter of money. This situation with the woman, it is not a small problem.

It's a large one. I do not want it in my life. And you do not need it in yours." He tapped the glass. "Do you understand me?"

I watched shadows cross the moon and slowed my pulse. Life always shifts. Understand. Underneath the Brando pose—the bennies love those lousy old movies, it's their romance, their myth, their excuse—I understood he was lying. This was not something he would pass on. The possibility of gaining the gratitude of a global corp like Touraine, the profits that could be gained—and more. Mid-City was relatively small-time, but they had their overseas affiliates and allies. A connection with GT, however slender, would boost the status of the organization and its overlord. And that, more than the simple exercise of violence and wealth, was what men like the Padrino lived for. I understood he had more to gain by not helping.

Lovely, I thought. He knows me, and he has some idea of who I am. Damn. I actually had enjoyed living in L.A.

"I think so."

"Then you will leave this alone?"

"I'll consider your suggestion."

He came back to the table and put his cigar down on the ashtray. He finally looked at me. "You are a free man, Robie, but consider it well."

I could hear the Deacon sit up in his chair. "I will."

"Yes, you always were prudent." He picked up his stick and began playing again.

I thought: *To coin a phrase, that's my damned cue.* And left.

When I got out of the elevator the Latina was waiting for me. She had my brass balls in an open hand. "I figured it out," she said with a satisfied tone. "Too heavy. They're weapons. You throw them."

I nodded. "Steel under the plating."

"You go for the head?"

"No. Joints, elbows, knees."

She looked skeptical. "That's too tough."

Nodding again, I said, "It can be. Takes a lot of practice—and luck."

I looked at her tattoo again and heard her accent. Tumblers clicked. Took the balls from her and put one in each of my palms. Then I touched them together holding my hands parallel, fingers up. The balls, clinging, climbed straight up the inside of my hands to the very tip of my fingers and slowly descended back down to my palms. I made two fists and then opened my hands. The balls were gone. She wasn't so hard that the sleight couldn't bring an appreciative twist to her mouth.

"A man from Arequipa taught me that trick. . . . The same man once told me a story about taking a boatload of crying children out of Lima in the middle of a burning night. They left on an old motorsailer with orange-trimmed sails. My friend tried to hush their crying by playing his harmonica. He didn't play very well. He was a small man, balding, with the shoulders and neck of a bull."

She glanced right and left, as if searching for live eavesdroppers in the empty hall. "This man, he is a friend of yours?"

"He was."

"Was?"

"He's in the wind."

She jerked her head hard to one side so I couldn't see her face and groaned, a low hum that came up from her stomach and got choked in her throat.

An L over a C: Los Cupones. Twenty years ago they were a gang of eight- to fourteen-year-old orphans that effectively ran one of the worst barrios in Peru. They practiced thievery, burglary, and on occasion, extortion—but never among their own. They fed and protected their younger siblings and the other helpless ones who lived—if that's the word—on their turf. Until the death squads of the Social Nationalists exterminated them.

Except for a few of the babies that we got out.

And she grew up to be a personal guard to a—*Gentle laugh.* *"Hey, amigo, so not all those we can save are saints. But then, we're not really angels."* True, Enrique. Too bloody true. But you came close.

INTERLOGUE 1

THEY HAD GOTTEN TO THIS holding point by careful stages. Now they were ready to leave the country.

A knock on the door. "Time to go."

"Sí, un momento." Teresa finished zipping up her carry-all and then rinsed her hands in the little washroom sink. She was always washing her hands. She knew what it was supposed to mean, but she didn't believe it, or care. She dried herself quickly. She was just nervous, didn't like to fly. One hand touched the medallion on her throat, the other reached into her pants and rubbed the derringer in the tiny holster she had sewn into the waistband.

Twin barreled, .375 magnum shells. She was to have used the gun on Vassey. A head shot, had to be. But instead of the derringer she pulled out a flamer. Surer, she pointed out to the team. The team had not taken it well; that witch, Chloe, especially. If Anton hadn't spoken up, promised to work with her on her control, she would have been pulled off the mission altogether.

Poor Anton. Too often he had to stand up for her. But he always did. If he were another kind of man she would think that it was because he was the one who had brought her into the team and her mistakes would smear him. But that wasn't the reason. They were both Catholicos, the only ones on the team. They had met during a retreat she attended at one of the Alaintine monasteries. It had been a last act of desperation for her; her faith had stopped easing her pain, couldn't give a direction for her rage.

Anton could have been one of the monks. He told her there was a time when he had seriously considered it, until the pain of the earth forced him back into the world.

Before each battle they would do the same meditation together, legs folded, eyes closed, facing each other with their knees almost touching. Oblivious to the other team members. They fixed their hearts on the cross in the lotus and let their minds become empty, clean.

When Thomas first joined them he had asked Anton, with that tactlessness of his that was once irritating, now almost endearing, how he managed to keep his actions and his faith together. Anton had wryly grinned at him and said, "I like to think that I am trying to redress man's inhumanity to God."

Thomas hadn't asked her. People rarely did.

It was difficult for Teresa to be close to someone. Anton was her friend, but it had been hard for him to accept that she had killed the guard. No one doubted Anton Palovich's dedication—he would do what he had to—but he also was the only one who prayed for the souls of those lives the Erinyes took. She, on the other hand, had no petitions left for a crying God. Only a promise she had adopted from her family's past—*La Terra o Muerte*.

She touched the derringer again and then the grenades attached to her belt. They were made up to appear to be large silver pesos. The belt's buckle had a hidden knife. She wasn't expecting trouble; their movement had gone flawlessly, but they *were* escorting the team and its prize to the hideout. If the team was going to be betrayed—and who could tell with those bastards—then she wanted to be sure the team had an honor guard into hell.

Another knock on the door. "I'm coming!" She put back on her vest and slung the strap of her bag over her shoulder. The wind hit her as she stepped outside. She tasted the sea on her lips. Hooker was already striding down the strip of wet sand to the Zodiac. Teresa hurried to catch up with him. He didn't say a word to her; he rarely said anything to anyone.

The rest of the transport nucleus was waiting for them; Thomas, Knut, and Chloe. The last still with them because of her expertise with the hostage. As for their prisoner, she was sitting quietly in the middle of the raft. She seemed indifferent to the cold wind despite only wearing the plain minicape and jumpsuit they had changed her into. She hadn't been any problem—not since they pumped her with pacifiers. Even lethargically cooperating with Teresa and Chloe when they applied hair and skin dyes to her. Chloe was hoping to use this last leg of their trip to start debriefing the hostage. Knut would translate if the hostage lapsed into her native tongue. That often happened under interrogation. The mind falls into childhood, the last defense. Teresa looked at Chloe's black gladstone with distaste. She believed in a few things: the sacredness of the earth, the inviolability of the soul. The idea of using drugs to make someone open up their hearts and minds made her sick. Another brahmin legacy: wreck the inner life along with the outer.

What has to be done will be done. What she believed in the most.

Teresa got on by the Penta outboard. Chloe sat beside the hostage. The men pushed the raft into the rough surf and climbed in. The seaplane was waiting for them two kilometers offshore. A bumpy ride. Teresa kept one hand on a safety line, the other on the outboard's control tiller. She kept her eyes on the floating seaplane's sleek lines. With its blue-and-gray markings it was hard to see among the swells, and the rising sun was still behind the tall hills at her back. She was grateful that the pilot had deployed a small drogue to help keep his plane from drifting.

The little motor struggled against the waves. It took them almost twenty minutes to get to the seaplane. Hooker, at the bow, smoothly threw a line to the man waiting inside the open hatch. Teresa turned off the engine. They warped alongside the slender fuselage. Then just as Hooker and Knut awkwardly got through the hatch, getting ready to bring in the hostage, the woman jumped into the water.

For a moment Teresa was frozen by the absurdity of it. Then she hit the starter on the outboard and yelled, "Knut, let go. Thomas, push us off. Chloe, track her!"

The outboard started easily. She put the drive into reverse and swung the raft around. "Got her, Chloe?"

"Yes, she's about ten meters to the right side."

Teresa cursed under her breath and thought, Chloe's sitting facing me, okay, port. She brought the bow toward that heading. If they didn't catch the woman quickly it would be all over. Even on a clear day and a flat sea it's easy to lose someone in the water. And under these conditions she could vanish in seconds. Not that she would really escape; hypothermia would get her long before she made it to the shore. "Thomas, watch the starboard side. Chloe, point where you see her."

The other woman raised her arm. Teresa edged forward, keeping one hand on the tiller and sighted along the arm. There she was, swimming with an incredible stroke. Teresa was a powerful swimmer herself—even if she hadn't been a diver, you don't grow up in the flooded Florida nightmare without becoming one—but she doubted she could match that woman's speed. Maybe the bitch could make it to shore before her muscles became too numb with cold. She wasn't going to get to try.

Teresa increased the raft's speed so that they would overtake the woman. "Chloe, when I tell you, take the tiller. Thomas, get out a paddle." Chloe nodded. Thomas quickly unhitched the rubber strap holding the paddles against the inside of the raft. He picked one up and held it handle out so Teresa could grab it in a moment.

The woman saw, sensed that they were upon her, veered sharply, and dived beneath a swell. Damn the brahmin bitch! Teresa revved the motor, guessed the direction, and swung the raft into an intercepting arc. Hooker came in over the comlink: "If you have to, shoot her." Unnecessary reminder. Teresa didn't bother to respond. She thought how the faint light would work for them as well as against. It would be dark under the water, difficult for the woman to see where the raft was. She should have brought along her hand sonar set with its transducer minnows—a stupid thought. A better, if chilling, one: The woman might be heading away from shore to lose them. The question was, could she have established her bearings? Teresa remembered Chloe shaking her head, looking so scared, when she first read the woman's psych matrix. Teresa decided. She twisted the throttle up and pushed the tiller left, turning the raft out to sea.

The other two said nothing. The ocean was Teresa's domain, and among them leadership flowed like water seeking its natural level, finding the right one for the task. One anxious minute, two minutes, three, four, and then the woman's head popped out of the water two meters from them.

"Now!" Teresa screamed. She lunged forward, almost knocking Chloe over as she grabbed the paddle from Thomas. A wave pushed the raft right up against the swimmer. The woman had time to see Teresa raise the paddle and dove back under the water. Too late. Teresa chopped the paddle down and crashed it onto her skull.

She dropped the paddle and tumbled into the water. It felt like falling into a pile of gravel. She forced her eyes open. The woman was floating legs down right next to her. She wrapped her arms around the woman's waist, kicked and kicked again. Then she felt a man's hand on her elbow. She relaxed her grip as Thomas started to pull the body into the raft. She gave one final kick to push the body upward and reached out to grab a line. Thomas and Chloe managed to get the woman on the raft. Teresa pulled herself in after. She held her head in her hands and coughed out sea water. "Is she alive?"

Chloe peeled back both eyelids, ran her hands over the back of the woman's head. "Yes. Nothing worse than a concussion—

maybe." Teresa watched as Chloe opened her bag and took out an air syringe and pressed it against the unconscious woman's neck. She felt an uncomfortable surge of admiration for the hostage. It had been reckless, desperate, yet smart. Capitalizing on the time and place and concealed strength. Teresa would have tried to do the same. Then it came back to her what the woman stood for. *"Estupida puta,"* she hissed.

They were quiet on the trip back to the seaplane. The argument started after they had gotten everybody aboard and strapped in.

"How the hell did she overcome the meds?" Knut roared over the sound of the starting engines.

Chloe yelled back at him. "I told you I could only guess at the dosages! She doesn't have our kind of chemistry. I wanted to put her out completely!"

"You know it would have been too hard to drag dead weight around with us—not to fucking mention the attention it might have brought."

Thomas, as usual, tried to cool them down. "Look, we got her back and she's alive. Everything's okay, right?"

Teresa watched as Knut and Chloe glared at each other. It didn't take a psych degree to understand that a lot of the tension between them was sexual rivalry. It had been obvious since the beginning of the mission. Even in a stupor, the *puta* bitch was magnificent. Knut was a good soldier, but Teresa had only contempt for someone who would let his balls instead of his brains lead him. As for Chloe, well, Chloe was who she was. Knut rasped, "She nearly got away. That is not okay!"

"Yaah!" Hooker's shout silenced them. He held his hands up and blew on his fingers. "This debate is properly for the nex' full team meeting, *non*?" A reluctant nodding of heads. He jerked a thumb toward the cockpit. "Then let's not distract our escorts." He looked at Teresa. *"Bien hecho, compadre.* You did good." She shivered in her wet clothes and nodded back. As if it mattered.

CHAPTER EIGHT

SAT IN THE CONSERVATORY WITH a Pendleton trading blanket spread across my legs in a rocking chair by an open window. Listening to my neighbor across the wide arroyo blow fragments, indigo fireworks, of old Ellington ballads on his cornet. Many, many years ago, Bowen had been a studio musician, a session man, before the technology retired him. None of us who share the canyon mind his occasional playing into the night sky. Some have been known to join in. Sooner or later, we all get there.

Fell asleep in the rocker. About three hours. Not too bad. I usually develop insomnia when I'm working. Luckily, my body's more than decent at purging toxins. But joints creaked and protested when I got up to take a shower.

It was about 5 A.M., plum dark outside. I fixed myself some hot oatmeal with ersatz maple syrup and a quart of coffee. While I ate standing barefoot in the kitchen I scanned the morning edition of the *Times*. For a change I went randomly through the international press summary:

An updated status report on the forty-six current armed conflicts that meet the 2 percent threshold of public interest. I went right past that. . . . The Swedish Institute of Oceanography announces successful conclusion to tertiary tests of the Guigi/lambda4 zooplankton. Assuming clearance from the World Ocean Commission on open sea introduction, foresees doubling of current population (yeah, from a 40 percent baseline to 80. I know, I know, we were a micron away from losing it all) . . . Death toll in Madagascar rises to over twelve thousand in the wake of Typhoon Gordian. Emergency shelters save countless more—one thing we've managed to do well is raise disaster relief to a science. Only twelve thousand dead. There are two million Malagasy scattered over East Africa, the fortunate ones who made it out—if living in generational refugee camps can be considered lucky. They do, when they look back to the millions still left on an island that can be called a flooded desert. I took myself off that road. . . . Literacy rate in Central Asian republics approaches 90 percent. Achievement attributed to widespread introduction of the cheap Lezak portable teaching Desks—cheap enough so that even females could get one. . . . Cease-fire holding in Papua, New Guinea, between ANZAC forces and the Greater Sunda Republic. More Pacific Force Blue Berets due to arrive Tuesday . . .

The altercation at the Blue Azalea had finally made it to the public screen. A one-page factoid with some old footage of the club when it opened: billowing clouds of party smoke, music heavy on drums and hyperviolins, a crowd of blazingly hued women arduously trying to look indifferent. The report read like a word-for-word copy of a standard police briefing; reassuring, relentless platitudes pushed to within an inch of ennui. No suggestion as to what were the kidnapper's motives, no identification of the victim, save that she was a foreign national, or whom she worked for. Ah, the power of the press.

It was too early to bother local people and I didn't feel up to driving down to my office to fire up my figments. I activated my personal rig and chose the I Ching. A bundle of sticks appeared. I threw about half of them aside, and began with the rest.

When I was done what I had were the lines of the Ta Ch'u: "Restraint by the Strong."

> Danger at the outset. *Wait.*
> They are stronger. *Patience.*
> You will have allies. *Careful.*
> Channel the wild forces. *Rein.*
> Dissipate the force. *Master.*
> The obstacles fade away. *Progress.*

The T'uan, the judgment: A wise ruler entrusts you to succeed; success will be yours.

I thought about whether Olivia Fouchet was wise, whether any ruler was. Still, it was a good throw. But that promised nothing. I opened another screen on the computer and placed a hexagram in the center and began shaping around it. Opened with the two natural themes: Groupe Touraine and its Congo project and the Erinyes with their dreams. Entered the data from the blocs that Fouchet had given me and whatever my agents could find in the public libraries. Played back all that Holguin had told me, distilled it, and put it into the mix. For seasoning I called in the lexicographic history of the Erinyes—the names we use for ourselves have power. Added the glyph notes that defined my experience in a tightly knit team, the way the world outside takes on different colors, how—whatever your reasons for joining—the reality of the team becomes the reason for your life. Then, what it's like to be a prisoner, to live each minute at the mercy of others.

As I moved, one by one the symbol-laden translucent forms, fragile as soap bubbles, sounding gently off each other like a carillon of bells, the chords of a cloudy third theme crept in early, the force that moved the Padrino into neutrality. It had no name, no clef, but it was there, moving in rondo to the other lines. . . .

It was eight o'clock when Danny called. He wanted to see me, down at his shop; that meant he had something.

I told him I would be there right away, did a final scan of the picture—seeing it from the outside it looked as hopelessly complex as a Berlioz score, set it on autocatalyst, and sighed.

"I didn't expect you to call me this soon," I said to Danny.

"I may not be as obsessive as you, mate. But I do know how to move fast—and I had a stroke of luck."

"Is that how you got that shiner?"

"Kind of. Spent last night with a volatile group, brahmins and bastards. I thought there might be some possibilities. Unfortunately they were drinking too much and behaving too blah. So I tried to liven things up by venturing the notion that there's no such thing as a private beach. Mate, it was inspiring to see how our local lords and ladies try to reconcile their love of possession with their love of nature. There's nothing like politics to get people to act like they really feel." He gingerly touched the liver-colored bruise on his cheek. "I gotta say I didn't expect some of them to start punching each other out; must've been passing pills I didn't see. I got this even before I knew there was a fracas going down. I wish I could say you should see the other guy, but he came barely up to my elbows. . . ." He shrugged. Two-hundred and sixty pounds, only about 3 percent of it body fat, and Danny's got the gentle manners that decent big men have. They know how much they can hurt somebody, and so they don't. "I hope I didn't take you from anything important."

"Just some creative inaction. Besides waving that ol' black flag and getting into a fight,"—stupid, Danny, real stupid—"what else did you get?"

"A character that thinks he's a radical and likes to hang with rough trade. Name's Jason Nancarrow. He was the host of the party. One of his *friends* is staying with him and helped settle the dispute—a tough SOB. Afterward we settled down, shared some chemistry, and talked too much. It seems that some of his other friends were in town Friday night, 'doing the daring.' Gav, I may start asking for wages. Anyway, the SOB, calls himself Jammer, derailed that trolley before it got out of the yard. Given Nancarrow's politics I got a strong feeling what he considers daring is worth another talk."

I asked, "You want me to deal with his friend?"

"I figured you could deal with both of them, if you got the time. I've got something else. And there's a problem with Nancarrow. He lives on the Pen."

South Bay is a wealthy colonia, and the very richest live on the heights of the Palos Verdes Peninsula. Danny's life is the South Bay. I could see the problem. "All right. What's the something else?"

"A waitress who saw something she wasn't supposed to. A guy last Friday had a heart attack where she was working. At least, that's what everybody thinks. But the waitress spotted a tool, recognized the signs—the guy got hit with an s/m. That's not a toy played with in this neighborhood."

"What's the relationship?"

"She went outside when the bravo left. Saw him ride off on a bike that matches the make that the police have. And from the way he handled himself in the bar—I think he's got the style."

I muttered, "Not exactly a trout in milk."

"What did you say?"

I repeated, "A trout in milk—overwhelming circumstantial evidence."

"Holmes?"

"Nope, another detective. Okay, Danny, it's a popular bike and there are a lot of people who are stylish at hurting, but it's a possible. What did she tell the cops?"

"Her little brother used to be a hell-raiser—that's where she learned about neural blades. A while back he was persuaded by Bay PD to stay out of town. She had to pick him up from Harbor's ER. What do you think she told the cops?"

"Nothing."

"She's not that polite—anyway, I'm going to meet her after second mass. She attends Jude, same as I'm supposed to do." He yawned. "Sorry, long night. Actually it works out well for me."

"Going to confession?"

"I was able to have a talk with Sally Keller. Remember, she was the woman at the Blue Azalea who brought 'Angie' and thus got set up?" Danny stopped, looked at my crooked smile. "Sorry. I forget sometimes that you don't. Keller told me that her new novia had gone to a church here a few days before the action went down. But she didn't know which one. Now she told the cops the same, and I understand they've been having conversations with our local clergy. But when I was with her she happened to remember that she and 'Angie' had gone together into that UNI docudrama on the Hundred Years' War—the other woman's idea, Keller wanted to be in a flaming Regency—her new friend locked on to the part that dealt with Saint Joan and bonded heavily into that character's POV."

Just happened to remember. Danny Sullivan could get a tribe of leprechauns to happily tell where they kept their pots of gold. "Which means?"

"Which means—maybe—that the Erinyes number among them a person who sees herself as a leading figure rather than a member of a team. Who distrusts her allies. Who might, in other words, act from emotions rather than thought."

"Danny, I'm impressed."

He laughed loudly, scaring the hell out of a row of mopey

gulls. "I've had some practice, and I've been watching a real pro for years." He touched his cheek again. "Considering the lot of good the hand-to-hand training they gave us at Quantico has done me, maybe I should have been watching your other moves."

Roads taken. I said, "I'd be a lot happier if you managed to make that your last fight."

He lied cheerfully, "Whatever you say."

Danny, when this is over, missing you is going to be very hard.

He fished a planchet out of his shorts pocket. "I cobbled a quick backgrounder on Nancarrow for you."

"Thanks."

"No sweat."

"Really, thanks."

He started to punch my shoulder, stopped when he saw how fast my hand came up. "Hey, mate, relax. You got me. And I'm just getting started."

I took the data chip from him. "I know. Keep me posted. I walked away from him. I went back to my car on automatic, just concentrating on my breathing. It was too early for me to get this tense.

Inserted the file Danny had made up: "Jason Nancarrow y Balestreri. Age: 27. About 6' tall, 180 pounds. Brown hair and eyes. Right handed. No amps that I know of." There was a snapshot. Danny must have taken it with his camera ring, a souvenir from his days in the service. Nancarrow had long blond hair and an even longer expansive, tangled beard. Which made a provocative contrast with sharply creased slacks and expensive tunic. "Occupation track: none known. No arrest record— that I could find; seeing who his parents are, if he has a jacket, it's probably buried where the sun doesn't shine. Went to a small private school back East where I think he picked up his politics, and not much else. He's got perfect pitch, but if there are any other talents he hides them real good. Parents are David Nancarrow and Janet Balestreri. David Nancarrow is senior scientist for Iatrochemicals, she's a partner with Mason, Guthrie & Gurney; insurance defense specialists." (There were short sidebars on their professional histories: wealth, power, success, nothing remarkable.)

"I first got to know him through his mother. MG&G hired me for an investigation a couple of years ago. It wasn't the best beginning. Jason and his parents aren't on good terms—I'm trying for your flair for understatement, Gav. Actually I think they hate each other. Despite that, Jason lives in one of his parent's homes—he's only got a modest two hundred thousand a year—Jesus!—trust fund." A cam of the home: vastly oversized ranch house with a gabled metal roof, vertical redwood sidings, and large dormer windows. A huge solar greenhouse was attached to the right side facing. A long garage slanted off on the left. A text dot floated in front of the garage > "No cars—Jason prefers to ride his horses, or a bicycle; for distance, public transit. He's the type to be big on meaningless gestures." I panned the shot; saw only two doors to the outside, the front and one on the left side out of the kitchen to the stables. Went back to reading.

"Even with the bad reference I had vis-à-vis his mama, he sort of took to me. We've got some mutuals who told him what a great guy I was and all that mierda. The house has standard South Bay City wired security but it's usually left offline. Jason believes that the authorities can use a house system to spy on its inhabitants—he's paranoid, right? No guard dogs or cats, only Jammer. That guy's about average height, six and a fraction. Weighs in at two hundred and seventy, maybe more. A strong dude, has a hell of a punch and despite that heft, fucking fast. Maybe as sudden as you—watch it." There was a shot of the man leaning over a seated Jason. He was staring down the open blouse of a woman with a pinched mouth who was looking away. Had a beard just like Nancarrow's. Colorless, wide-spaced eyes. "Drives a big black bike—like, man, what else? If it's not parked on the grass in front, he's not there. Let's see; Jason can't stomach alcohol—that's a mod, his family has a history of trouble with that drug. He substitutes with synesthetics. When he's feeling his stones he likes to affect a braggadocio. Oh, shit, Robie. I'm beginning to sound like you. Seriously, Gav, if—when—you get past his pal, you should be able to roll Nancarrow like a tire. Hope it's worth the ride."

I started the motor and called up the map. We shall see, Danny.

CHAPTER NINE

JASON NANCARROW Y BALESTRERI LIVED on Northfield Road, a skinny two-laner lined with whitewashed rail fences and gnarly, surviving pepper trees; their seed droppings, red-green beads, crackled like tiny firecrackers under the Lotus's tires. The road wandered through real estate that could only be called Western Wholesome. The side streets had names like Ring Bit, Packsaddle, Maverick, and Wrangler. Nearly every house had a stable. The rolling landscape had been optimaxed to appear to be purely natural—you could hardly tell the real from the rebuilt.

As you would expect, there weren't any street or broadcast numbers, but Danny had included a gypsy bearing. The Lotus got its satellite fix and played a few flute notes—Jonah's sly programming. I parked across the road and watched for a moment. The long front of the Nancarrow property was bordered by a mixed row of wickedly thorned hedge roses, and flannel bushes—the latter called that because their emerald dark leaves feel like soft felt. The flannels, California Glories, had a little bloom left on them, a sprinkling of pretty yellow-red saucer-shaped flowers. Last election the Euphoria party put on the free ballot the proposition that we should make the Glory the state's plant: a boosted, sort of native,

Mexican-American hybrid. Takes a lot of abuse. Doesn't need any watering. Grows up fast, dies young. And at the roots—shallow. The motion got a fair number of votes.

It didn't pass, not because we've completely lost our sense of humor, but because of the others. The grizzly bear, the desert tortoise, golden trout, California quail—all gone. Our symbols of state have already done a good job of defining us.

As I was getting out, a black-and-white sunwing glided over the trees and came into view. It circled like a patient vulture just long enough to read the Lotus's license code and register my location. Then with a faint hum it soared off. The Pueblo de la Reina de Los Angeles only deploys sunwings for search-and-rescue missions in the canyons. The L.A. cops gave up on them for surveillance— home-built missiles. If what Danny said about Nancarrow disabling his house links was correct, the lad must be thrilled having the wings about.

It had gotten suddenly very warm. The old witticism about Gaia coming down with malaria—chills followed by fevers and round again—was too true to be funny. Neither was the added re mark that we were the guilty mosquitoes. I took off my coat, got my rattan cane from the backseat, and pushed the sleeves of the turtleneck up to my elbows. I entered through the crushed gravel driveway. Behind the hedge Nancarrow had let the front meadow go beyond benign neglect. A sea of yellowing crabgrass and foxtails was crowding out what were once neat flower beds. No sign of a bike. I bent down: some tread marks, weeds crushed within the last few hours. Neared the house and noticed that one of the windows was shattered; a fine spray of polarized glass lay on the steps up to the veranda. It seems I keep on missing all the fun parties. I was about to go up to the door when I heard a horse's unhappy neigh. I walked around the side of the house to the stables.

He was taking a young paint over a two-pole cavalletti. I saw why the mare sounded mournful. He was making her jump too high, as if she were going over six feet instead of just a couple, and he was sitting flat on his ass instead of rising. It pissed me off. Paints are wonderful animals—I grew up on one—but like almost all horses they aren't inherent jumpers. With a good rider they can learn to take a fence, but the way he was handling her, all he was going to end up with was a sour horse. I went up to the gate, climbed up, swung a leg over and shouted, "Try leaning forward from the hips."

He turned around so fast he almost fell off his saddle. A beginner. Well, he wasn't wearing a Stetson and chaps—and no holster. I gave him the best smile in my repertoire. "She'll do better if you keep your weight up and jump her lower."

Either the older I get the more harmless I look, or he wasn't quite as paranoid as Danny had briefed. For he trotted his pony over and in a not unfriendly voice said, "Who the hell are you?"

"I used to partner with a paint." I winked at the mare. She bowed her head and peeked up at me with shy blue eyes. Typical, a heartbreaker.

Nancarrow cocked his head to one side and did a funny thing with his shoulders as if trying to set his spine straight. "You didn't exactly answer my question."

Let's see, who was the Lotus currently registered to? I held out my hand. "Bill Delgado."

He ignored it. "What are you doing here, Delgado, besides telling me how to ride."

Despite the words I could tell he was interested. From the way the mare stood quietly, his free hand resting on the withers, he cared about his horse and she returned the feeling. I looked him straight in the face. "Why don't you give it a try?"

He blinked rapidly a few times as he thought about my suggestion. The fluttering eyes and unexpected docile manner made me wonder if he had a bit of residual chemistry floating about in his bloodstream. As if to confirm my guess he said, "You sound hazel," and turned his pony around. I called out, "Let her collect herself. She'll figure out the best stride." He didn't say anything as they trotted in a half circle, picked up a little speed, and went for the poles. It was a lot better. Going through a figure eight, they jumped again a few more times. He rode to the far fence, stopped, had his pony do a neat rear-hand pivot—somebody trained that horse well—and came back to me with a semiconscious grin.

"You're welcome," I said.

This time he shook my hand. "Thank you. Couldn't see what I was doing wrong."

"Next time you should try it with your feet out of the stirrups. That way you'll find the best balance."

He nodded thoughtfully.

"What's her name?"

He ruffled her mane affectionately. "Sunrise. Yeah, she's a shy one. Delgado, are you going to get around to telling me what you're doing here?"

"Hello there, Sunrise. Well, Mr. Nancarrow, I'm looking for a missing person and I think you might be able to help me."

As quick as the weather his expression changed. "Are you the police? Let's see some ID."

I waited a long moment, then forced the left sleeve of my sweater up over the bicep, showing him the wide web of scars that run around the muscle. It's not the worst one I have, but it's not pretty. "Do you know what a Texas handshake is?"

He blinked his eyes again and shook his head.

"It's razor wire wrapped around a heavy work glove. A country deputy gave me that greeting when he decided that I didn't look right." I waited until his eyes turned away and rolled the sleeve back down.

His mouth was a thin line; the sudden harsh testimony impressed him. Easy, way too easy. "Okay, let's say you're not," he muttered. Then louder, "So who are you, then, and what makes you think I know anything about somebody missing?"

I went with the second part of his question. "I heard that some friends of yours were involved in that fracas at the Blue Azalea last Friday night."

A frightened jerk of his chin. "And where exactly did you hear that?"

"It doesn't matter where, son, just that I did. It's true, isn't it?" His face said it sure as hell was. Ah, Danny, you sure don't miss much either. "Listen, I'm looking for some answers." I moved into a more comfortable perch on the rail. "Now, you're not the kind of man who'd ever need a bribe, and I don't think I could push you. So I guess that leaves me with only an appeal for what's fair."

Straight bull. I could see he liked it, but he shifted about in his saddle, and said, "I'm not a snitch."

"I'm not a cop and I ain't looking to get your friends in trouble. I don't care about that. It's about the woman being family, and I aim to find her."

That wasn't a direction he was expecting. "You don't look like her."

The news report didn't have a visual on Matthiessen. I laughed easily. "True enough. Siv's my cousin. Her mother's sister moved to the States and ended up married to Laughing Elk—my old man."

He said excitedly, "You're Indio. I thought so. What tribe?"

My hair is wavier, my eyes a bit too deep set, and I've got to shave very regularly. Outside of those minor details, if someone wants to, it's easy enough to confuse me with my grandmother's people. And the Native as icon motif is back in circulation. Again. Those of my cousins who bother to pay attention don't know whether to laugh or cry. For any sins I was going to commit I silently apologized. "Northern Cheyenne."

"Cheyenne, that's great," he gushed. "You know, I just finished reading Crowell's *Plain Souls*. Powerful book. Your people, they were the greatest; even the other tribes thought so. Called you the Beautiful People, didn't they?"

Except for the Arapaho and the Dakota, old friends and kin,

the others didn't use that term admiringly. The Cheyenne were taller than most, the women famous for their virtue and looks, the men superb hunters who had the most splendid ponies—many of which had been gleefully stolen from their neighbors. Envy and resentment are near universal traits.

But envy was the polar opposite from where Nancarrow was coming from. The dream of a people living nobly, simply, with themselves and with the earth. Not quite the bloody reality. Short-sightedness, deception, cruelty weren't diseases introduced by the Europeans along with smallpox. But still, there was just enough myth in the truth to keep on hooking many like Jason Nancarrow, youngsters searching for a better past. Was that why he was so ready to sing with me? I shoved down the burst of sadness. Played the game and corrected him. "Not were, are. And if you know any-thing about us you know we always look after our own, even if she is pale. . . . You gonna help me?"

He ran some fingers nervously through his beard. "You know who she works for?"

"Some big earth-ripping company. But taking her like that was wrong. Not the Path."

He stuttered, "I know, I know. But they keep on screwing us, telling us that we *can* supervise the land, that we really don't have to make any more sacrifices." He inhaled deeply and spoke slowly, his voice perfectly mimicking the reassuringly mellifluous tones of a school Desk: "Yes, undoubtedly tragic managerial mistakes were made in the past. But that was due to an incomplete understanding of complex, multifold systems. Today, human society has devel-oped far more powerful analytical tools and structural instrumen-talities. Given advances over the last quarter century, there should be no reason why the goal of re-establishing and maintaining a mu-tually beneficial relationship with the environment should not be successful. Beneficial—" The last word came out as a curse. He swung down off his pony, threw a stirrup over, and loosened the girth on the saddle. "You want to know what the title of that catechism is around here? 'All Watched Over by Machines of Loving Grace'—the chingas!"

Only poets should be trusted with prophecy, and irony. . . . It was a poem by Brautigan. Pretended not to recognize it. Wouldn't be right for my character.

"Manage. They can't manage not to fuck up. Sorry, hombre, if anybody should know what it's about, you should."

Try as we might, intentions good or bad, the cold sweaty memory of nightmare still on us, we still too often fall down. I had no fast and easy words for him so I went with the first part of the credo that once sustained me. "What shall we be, if we save the world only to lose our souls?"

Nancarrow stared at me. I had become something more complicated than a friendly stranger, a real live Indio. He squared his shoulders and said roughly, "It's a war, hombre. Sometimes the hard things have got to be done."

Hombre, you don't have any idea what hard is. "Maybe so. But you can pick who and choose how to fight. I don't see taking my cousin as anything more than jackal's work. They could have tried to do something hard like going after that company's Cores. But that would be hard, now, wouldn't it? Instead they went after someone they could give Custer odds—yeah, I know, he sure had it coming. It may have felt good but it didn't stop the dying. And Siv ain't the Seventh Cavalry, and hurting her ain't going to win any war."

He almost gulped his words. "Look man, I'm sorry, but they've got to be made to listen."

"Do you really think one more dead body is going to make anyone listen?"

"Red?"

I understood what he meant. "I expect that'll be the color of it. She's been put in the crossfire. People don't live long there."

I wiped some sweat off the back of my neck. Wished I had remembered to print out a photo of Matthiessen. Seeing a person's face, moving, smiling, can be a helpful nudge toward conscience. While I gave him some time I gently rubbed the bridge of Sunrise's nose. In the distance I heard what sounded like a bike coming up the road. Lovely. Glanced at Nancarrow. He was chewing on his lower lip. I didn't think he heard the motorcycle, or perhaps the noise came to him as a color on the wind. I tried to help him along. "You know, someone once said that you've got to have the heart of a hero to be a decent human being."

He stopped gnawing his lips. "You won't find her."

"Maybe not. But she deserves more than strangers, cops, who don't really give a damn, looking for her. She's kin, her family deserves more. All I'm asking for is a little help. A sign on the trail. You look like a good man; you understand." I climbed off the fence.

He walked Sunrise over to corral gate, opened it, and came around to me. There wasn't any swagger in his steps. He tugged at his beard as if it were a rein. "You really believe she's going to die?"

I nodded.

He didn't like it. That helped offset my feelings about his bathos. If he were ten years younger I would have had more sympathy. But he was grown-up enough, or trying to be, to think about consequences. While he reflected about ends and means I started counting down the seconds. "Mierda!" he said. "Okay. These guys I'm friends with. They move stuff around and do some protection work if you know what I mean. They helped get the— the people who took your cousin out of town."

"You sure?"

He got angry enough so that his pony pricked back her ears and shuffled her front hooves nervously. He snapped at me, "Yes, I'm sure."

Gave him a mollifying smile. "Easy man, I believe you. Who's the honcho of your band of friends?"

He paused. There was more than concern about being a snitch in his hesitation. The head guy must have a heavy thumb. "His name is Tyler; Warren Tyler."

"How many people does Tyler have?"

"I don't know. Maybe a dozen."

Great. "Where can I find Tyler and his pals?"

"They kind of scatter around, but Warren and some of the guys tend to hang out at a cabin outside of Fillmore; one-fourteen Sulphur Mountain Road."

"How did you find out about it?"

He huffed, "They told me. Like I said, we're friends. And they thought that my place might make a good way station—but they changed their minds. Your cousin wasn't here."

I thought, with a lot more pity than contempt, their telling you made you feel proud, didn't it? Like how you felt when they let you give them your parent's house as a transit center for their contraband. The outlaw life is so exciting. "Did you connect them to the Eye-rings?"

He corrected me absently, "Erinyes. No. I don't know how they got together. They could have met at one of my parties—I like to bring different people together, expand the awareness."

Smugglers, calico guards. I'll bet that set loves to have their awareness lifted. And when they finally get bored they'll gut your parent's house of anything worth taking. And if you are lucky, Jason Nancarrow y Balestreri, that won't include your life. There was the sound of a door slamming in the main house. Nancarrow heard it too. His hand tightened around Sunrise's reins. This interview was going to be soon over.

"You wouldn't have any idea of where they took her?"

"No."

A man was coming from the house in a hurry. Danny was right, he had to weigh in at about two sixty or more. Some of it was in his gut, but too much was muscle. He was wearing an intricately chained vest over a sleeveless red-on-black check tunic. Leather pants tucked into knee-high boots, the kind with metal heels and toes. Stomping boots. In his left hand there was a thick black stick about six inches long with a strap around his wrist. "Who's coming?"

His eyes had a mix of melancholy and something else as he looked at the approaching blade. "That's Jammer."

"A friend of Tyler's?"

"Yeah, he's part of the crew. My parent's insisted I have security. So I hired him. . . . He's okay."

I had heard the words behind the words before, often from people I pulled out of cesspools: I know what he is, but he's mine. Except that they rarely really knew what they had until it was far, far too late. Shifted my cane to my left hand. "Sure." I spoke louder, "You really should consider getting a jumping saddle, it'll bring your knees up more naturally—"

"Who are you?" If my voice sounds like gravel, then his had boulders. The timbre was so deep that it had to have been store-bought. I glanced at him briefly, and went on, "Jack McCallum—he's in Lorington, Kentucky—makes the best. You'll have to go there yourself with your horse for a personal measuring and then wait, old Jack's a fussy coot, but—"

"I said who the fuck are you?"

I finally turned around. "Name's Delgado." I didn't offer to shake hands.

Those strange, fog-colored eyes flickered over me. He didn't like what he saw. Most people at first glance take me casually, my best asset, but a few get by the front and see something else. Something in a dark forest. Something gray and silent. Something to avoid. It's not something I developed—call it a family trait. Usually when someone senses it I move far away, or they do. "You know, Jason, you could do with some home improvement. Good servants are easy to find." Before Nancarrow could stutter something, I started walking.

Jammer followed me. I increased my stride, hoping that maybe he just wanted to make sure I got off the property. No such luck.

He caught up with me in the front yard right by his shiny black bike—a replica Harley Panhead. I swung around to face him.

"You're a gazer, aren't you?" He was holding the black stick at waist level. I shifted my feet and let the cane slip a few inches down my hand.

I could have lied and agreed that I was with the DEA, but I didn't think it would make any difference. "Wrong call. I couldn't care less about what you're handling."

"Then who the fuck are you?"

I raised my cane and leaned it against my shoulder. "Sorry, fatty, I don't talk to the help."

He made a snapping motion with his left hand. A meter of blued steel telescoped out of the stick. Then he spun on one leg and tried to kick me. The foot blurred back before I could catch it. He danced forward, feinting quickly with the sharp tip of the baton toward my face, then whipping it toward my ribs. Instinctively, he raised his right fist. I stepped back and swung to his left, at the same time taking hold of his right wrist with my left hand. I pulled his arm across me and slammed into the elbow with the butt end of my cane. There was a horrible grinding pop. Twisted his wrist and pressed against the arm, trying to start him into a tumble. He pulled away. Off balance, in agony, he was still able to hit solidly at my waist with the stick. Got his wrist again, jerked up his arm—he sucked air explosively—and pushed him back on his heels. Released my grip and swept the cane across his face, ending the stroke with a hard downward chop on his right wrist. He stood rocking. I kicked away a kneecap. He fell. Lying on his side, his face full of tears and blood, he started moaning, "Jesus, oh Jesus Jesus."

I pulled the baton from his hand—he screamed as the strap came over his wrist—and threw it as hard as I could up on the roof of the house. Spoke down to him in a flat, indifferent voice. "Your elbow's only dislocated, but the wrist is badly broken. Don't know about your knee—I'm out of practice. Your face is bleeding a lot, but it's superficial. Are you hearing me? Good. Don't ever fuck with me again."

He got out a whisper through his pain. ". . . kill you."

I stepped away from him. Told him the truth: "No. Not today and not tomorrow, and that's all that counts."

Jason had made it to the scene. He stared at Jammer, at me, and back to Jammer again. The expression on his face helped wash down the heat. I said in the gentlest way I could, "After you get your friend to the hospital, pack a bag and go see Jack McCallum about a jumping saddle. Trust me, son, it'll do you a world of good."

I didn't give him a chance to say things I would regret.

CHAPTER TEN

I DROVE A HALF MILE down the Northfield road, stopped, and pulled the sweater up off my hips. The cloth had absorbed most of the blow's impact, hardening up the instant Jammer's stick had slammed into me. Still, the area around my kidney hurt like hell. Grimacing, I fumbled out the medic kit from the glove compartment and found the syringe that was preloaded with an antitrauma cocktail. Braced myself awkwardly against the door and shot up. Hoped I wasn't going to be passing red water for the next couple of days. Danny was right; he was fast and very strong. And I'm not as agile as I used to be. One of these days, assuming I'll be around for one, I was going to have to decide whether I was willing to pay the short-term price of intermittent muscle cramps, and then the long-term one of permanent palsy, for the speed given by a myoneural booster.

While I waited for the pain to dull I thought about the price I had already paid that morning. Since late last night I had started letting myself feel like a predator, letting the felling pulse work itself into my blood—I think that's what Jammer sensed, why he moved to attack. If you believe you're being stalked in the forest, flight or fight are your only options. He made the mistake of picking the wrong one. My mistake was in my pulse.

A blare took me out of my fugue. The ambulance swung past the Lotus and sped up the road. I remembered that Jason Nancarrow didn't own a car. Fast response, even for a high brahmin enclave. Started up the engine and drove as quickly as I could off the Peninsula.

I headed east, past the ring of slender, pastel office spires that rim South Bay like a wall of money. When I had gotten clear of SBPD's jurisdiction—that police sunwing may have witnessed the fight—I found an open-air hawkers' market and pulled into its small parking lot. I went searching for a public phone. They're as scarce as Republicans, but Bell is legally obliged to keep a few around and generally posts them in the poorer neighborhoods—corporate humor. The slums of Los Angeles were among the first areas in the state to go totally wireless. I found it by some overflowing cycle cans. There were a couple of rats trying to compete with the gulls; the rats were losing.

A small favor; the phone was functional. I used a traceless cashcard and called Eddie Yamada.

Eddie runs a small live courier service: biosamples, documents too sensitive to send by mail, fine jewelry, whatever needs hand work, Eddie and her crew will move it. Anything legal, that is. Eddie's straight—and she won't close her eyes.

However, she does know a fair number of people who are less scrupulous, and occasionally when money's tight, or if it's a friend asking, she's been known to make a referral.

The tiny bubble screen flashed Eddie's seven-arrows logo over the opening bars of Morrison's "Queen of the Slipstream," then like an image in a crystal ball her broad face glowed up at me. "Hi, babe! It's been a while. Don't tell me; the doctor left you again?"

"About two months ago."

She ran a finger over her lower lip. "That long. Looking for solace?"

The last time my mistress left me Eddie and I spent a strenuous weekend up in the Sierras. Strenuous as in both cliff-climbing during the day and within the tent at night. Often enough I've been in desperate fear for my life, but never in a sleeping bag. Eddie's a formidable free climber. "With you it would be a lot more than a consolation"—she blew me a kiss—"but I'm working and it's a case of *tsuki ni muragumo.*"

She translated slowly, "'Clouds over the moon.' Haven't heard that expression since I lived with my grandpa. Are you calling me about a misfortune?"

"Part of one. Warren Tyler."

"Who?"

"You got me. I know he's a delivery man, specializing in garbage. Possibly he's part of the local opiate pipeline. I'd like to learn more about his little operation."

Her eyes turned to slits. Even though L.A.'s a very tolerant town—mostly due to exhaustion—dexdiacetylmorphine, bright skag, new-H, blanco doña, by any handle insanely pleasurable and formidably resistant to every antiaddictive therapy, is way beyond our lenience. And even if it weren't, it would be for Eddie. She hissed, "Is it too unprofessional to ask why you'd be interested in that particular piece of sewage?"

"Yes."

For a second I thought she might cut me off. Wouldn't blame her. "Babe, it's amazing what you can do with a monosyllable. Forget I asked. Warren Tyler? Do you know his turf?"

"Ventura County would be my guess. He may be branching down into South Bay City."

She popped a piece of hard peppermint candy into her mouth and sucked for a minute, thinking. "I can try. Two hundred?"

"Four, by tomorrow?"

"Remind me never to lowball beaus—did I just make a joke? You know, babe, tomorrow could set off alarm bells. I'll be careful, friends of friends and so on, but if this guy finds out that a cit is looking in on him, he may go hunting himself."

"Can't be helped. It's rush job."

Her brows closed together. "Now, that is strange. You usually prefer playing with a slow hand—a very pleasing attribute, by the way. Your clients must really value their art."

I nodded, "They do. And in this case so do I."

"Then if I can learn anything it'll be Monday latest. I see that you're calling from a public phone. Any special number you want me to use?"

"Call my office. I'll have it random routed. Thanks, Eddie; talk to you soon."

Went back to the car, gave the kid watching it fifty cents cash— offered to go double or nothing but he wouldn't bite. Told him that worrying about losing was the short road to giving up on winning. He pushed the coins into the front pocket of his tight pants with nail-bitten fingers, and stared at me with sullen eyes that told me what he thought of a rich man's philosophy. My fault; should have known better.

After he left, I called Paul Thinh on my pad. Tried to, anyway. He was in a meeting, and could not, would not, be interrupted. A real surprise. Well, I'd had a pretty good run of getting hold of people. I was about to leave a message when I noticed the little mail icon. It opened up after I entered the historical date of when I was in a place that I wasn't supposed to be—charming. Inside was a voice-only note that the package I had requested from Madame Fouchet would be delivered to my house this evening at 8:00 P.M. So I changed my message to politely telling Thinh that I would very much appreciate it if he would be ever so kind as to bring it himself.

Called Liu, got past the greetings, and said, "I know it's Sunday but I'd like to work with you now."

"Something is wrong?"

"I almost lost a fight."

"Injuries?"

"Right kidney. I don't think it's serious."

"I am at home. Pick me up." The pad's screen turned to snow.

Llewellyn and Sulinn live on a little cul-de-sac called Chamoune Drive north of Sunset. It's right off the Sepulveda Pass. The Lius' house is a California contemporary; a good example of the gentle architecture movement: a low, squared-off building nestled deep into the side of a hill, large central greenhouse atrium, and a roof with long curving overhangs that were covered with dark turquoise-colored, spin-polarized photoelectric tiles. The windowless exterior walls that weren't hidden by the earth berms were painted a soft shade of grayed yellow-green. It didn't disappear into the landscape, but it did complement it.

None of the small herd of vehicles parked in front belonged to the Lius; Sulinn must be having a staff meeting. I pulled in behind a Pininfarina Cabriolet and a vintage Lexus 600 coupe. A reason to be in L.A.; it's one of the few places in North America where a Lotus can be considered an inconspicuous car. Gordie, Lew's houseboy and best student, opened the doors as I walked up the zigzagging path—ghosts and spirits can only walk in straight lines . . . in China, anyway. He bowed and spoke to me in Hakka, the archaic dialect of old Hong Kong. "Greetings, Mr. Robie. Master Liu will be with you shortly. I informed the Lady Sulinn of your arrival and she expressed a desire to have a word with you before you and the master depart. You will find her in the drawing room with her people."

For someone who would look just fine in a Highlander kilt, he managed the role of perfect Chinese butler very well. I gave a slight bow back, handed him the wrapped jar of Green Mist tea I had bought yesterday, and headed toward the drawing room and the buzz of voices.

Slid open the cardinal silk panel into an argument. Amid the welter of people, a gross of minisoltans with images frozen and moving were piled in the center of the room like children's building blocks. Someone, one of Sulinn's scriptdocs I think, was saying in a voice that would have been a yell, if she were ever to risk being that impolite, that the Mallory apov was plot essential if those of the audience that took him stayed until he happened to open the bathroom door. Someone else was replying that the damned bystander was too damned boring for anyone in the audience to bother staying with. All of the words were aimed at Sulinn, who sat in her favorite Morris chair in a corner of the room with a calm unflappable look on her face, playing with the end of her long braided hair. She saw me, tightened the belt on her morning robe, and rose smiling. "Keep going, boys and girls. I'll be back in a few minutes."

A half dozen faces glanced at me, registered that I was a vaguely familiar nobody, and turned—like sunflowers to the light—back to her. She frowned at them; they wilted. "When I return it would be very nice to hear a more orderly critique on the final cut for scenes nine forty-two through twelve hundred."

We went into the large kitchen. A maid was assembling a pile of dim sum. She glanced at Sulinn and left silently with the tray. Sulinn poured tea from a samovar into two large porcelain cups, cut and dropped a lemon slice into one of them, and handed it to me. I blew across the rim, sipped carefully at the scalding dark liquid, and asked, "Isn't it rather close to the brink to be making changes?"

She leaned against a counter and let her fatigue show. "Oh, Gavilan. *The House of Dust* had its last formal edit two hours before the premiere. It still managed to get Best Picture last year." She put her cup down and sighed. "You know, carino, life was a lot simpler when film was simply film and focus groups, and once you gritted your teeth and sent your print to the labs that was that."

"And now we're able to play with things until they go way past perfection."

"To use one of your favorite lines—yeah, something like that. Do you know I have more than twenty hours of variable story line, I'm overcovered from here to the O'Neill Observatory, and one of the studio corpses had the temerity to say that it might be too short?" She took a long pull at her tea.

"You might offer to throw in the Mahabharata as a filler."

Old joke, still good. If you haven't gathered yet, I'm particular when it comes to smiles, and laughs—Sulinn has a very nice one. She came close and rubbed her palms against my shoulders. "I'm so looking forward to seeing you on opening night. I don't know if Lew gave you all the details, but in case he forgot, I wanted to tell you that after the studio party and the interviews, we're going to have a few people, good company, here at the house. Nothing fancy, just some tea and that fantastic rum cake that Gordie's marida makes. And we'll all kick off our shoes and talk about anything else than"—she shuddered delicately—"the *Industry*. We expect you to come—we'd like that very much. It's been too long since I've had a chance to just be with friends." She shook her head. "Six months. It feels like six years."

Good company. Best compliment in a while. "I don't know if I'll be able to come to either."

She gave me a superbly baneful look. I stared at my teacup. No leaves to check my fortune. Sigh. I looked back up, and asked her, "You wouldn't poison me, would you?"

"No . . . definitely not. I would only poison my husband."

I checked to see if she was serious. I wasn't sure. "I'm on a job. It may come to a delicate cusp around that time."

She didn't face me when she said, "You don't tell us much, but we are not fools, Gavilan."

Softly: "What is this about?"

She put her cup down and looked at me over her shoulder. "God, your mother was a sublime actress—it's a shame she made so few films—and she certainly taught you well. But I have been around performers most of my life. And it is Sunday, Gav. My husband never works on Sunday. Whatever it is, it's bad, isn't it? You are sometimes the hardest man to read, but today it's written all over you."

"It's not your business, Sulinn."

That hurt her. "You are right, it's not my business. Mine is entertainment, about sharing and feeling, giving people a lift. Maybe helping some of the hurting ones feel that they are still part of the world. But you don't want that, do you?"

I stood close to her and wrapped my hands around hers. "I am sorry."

Sulinn pulled away from me. "So am I—I usually have more sense." She started for the doorway. "Tell Kit to call me when she returns."

"If she returns, I will."

There was no pretend in my voice. She stopped. "Don't worry, Gavilan. She'll come back again; she needs you too much."

"Needs me? Are we talking about the same woman? Katharina's beautiful, brilliant, and damned successful at anything she wants to do. I know, she knows, that she'll do quite well without me."

"You forgot to add temperamental, sweet, and sexier than any woman has the right to be without realizing it. God—do quite well!—do you think she's the kind of woman who would settle for just that? When she's with you—damn, I'm a director, not a writer—when Kit's with you she's *incandescent*. For Christ's sake, Gav, you're her magic." She stopped and looked at me sternly. "You've got a lot of limitations, carino, but you're the least blind man I know—don't you dare tell me you don't see that."

No, many things, but not blind. "So why does she keep on leaving?"

She replied with intentional offhandedness, "Maybe she's afraid that you'll be the only thing she can't be successful at . . . or maybe she's scared stiff of becoming a widow and not knowing why. I have an anxious staff waiting, Gavilan." She went through the swinging doors. And came right back in. "No," she announced, "it's not right." She took my hand and squeezed hard. She stared up at my face as if to memorize it. "When you're done with whatever mess you've gotten into this time, come and visit me. Please."

"I promise."

She slowly released me. "Lew says that coming from you that's never a line. All right, I will leave you to the tender mercies of my husband. Adios, Gavilan."

Magic. I grew up with it. Remember believing.

CHAPTER ELEVEN

Rinsed out our cups: they were the Spodes I had given them on their last wedding anniversary. I set them carefully on the drying rack and went outside to wait for Llewellyn. It's funny, Sulinn is like me, a blend of this and that tribe; I think her great-grandfather was Chinese. But as if they were Mendelian dominants, the Confucian concepts of *li* and *jen*—proper behavior and sympathetic attitude—run true through her like a vein of pure silver.

I massaged my eyes behind closed lids. If truth is silver, Sulinn had rubbed some of the tarnish off. While I sat on the Lotus's hood, I scrubbed at it a little more.

"If you won't promise me your life, can't you at least let me have your child?"

Why are there so many questions I can't answer?

I had remarkable parents, a loving extended family. They say that life recapitulates. It can. . . . My father had found his measure of peace with the unending gift of my mother's love. And in a late, unexpected affair with the innocent grandeur—the world seen afresh, seen as a moral force—that men like George Innes, Tom Cole, and Fred Church brought to him with their luminous eyes, their eyes to hands, hands to canvas, canvas to vision. But before he found what he needed . . . We share a history. Of darkness, competence, failure. Of watching others die because of our mistakes. Of worse things. No, not the same. He lived it unquestioningly for his country, I always had a choice. While he will always be part of me, I am not he.

What could I say? That I'm much too fond of children, that I've seen too many dead ones, watched too many die? We all have. That it wasn't the dead ones but the living, the babies held by children, standing over their parent's graves. What could I say, that some journeys are unfinished? That I haven't found my measure, my own way to a hush at Shiloh?

I said nothing to her. Instead, I had gotten out Jessie and played a slow piece by Bloch. Katherina didn't understand; I didn't give her a chance to. Not smart. Not smart at all.

Why are there so many answers that I can't give?

Llewellyn appeared before I could drag myself deeper into the morass. He carried a whisky tumbler filled with what looked like olive Jell-O. He put the glass down next to me, held my hands, and checked my pulse on the six meridian places on each wrist. He said, "Have you eaten in the last couple of hours?"

"A cup of your tea just now. But I took a shot."

"Whose?"

Closed my eyes and saw the label on the syringe. "Baxter's."

He took out his pad and short-handed some questions to it. Merck, or whoever's manual he was consulting, flashed back answers that made him nod. "That should not be a problem. Swallow this."

I sniffed first. It smelled like dog fennel. "What is it?"

"Site-specific evidentiary agents in a fast transport medium. When we get to the school I will do a thermoscan."

"Fine. Bottoms up."

Despite the color and smell, it tasted like liquid chalk—why does this kind of stuff always taste like that?

We drove to his school in silence. It's located in the colonia of West Hollywood, about a twenty-minute drive from Lew's house. The building was built right after Crazy Eight, very safe and very non-descript—lumpen functional. The school's above the Flor Harina bakery; one of the finest places in town to get *bolillos*. They've got the traditional brick ovens. After working out there for a few years I've come to associate the aching hours of our sparring with the innocent smell of fresh baked loaves. Wish I didn't; I like bread.

When we got there I parked in the empty back parking lot and we went up the aluminum stairs. Lew's school used to be a dance studio. He's kept the barre—it's useful for warming up—and all the mirrors; once a student complained about the multitude of images as being distracting, he added some more. Over the light ash hardwood floors he laid down a clear rubbery composite that gives about the same protection as an exercise mat. Great stuff. Wash it down every few months with a weak solution containing some nitro-oligosaccharides, chelated copper, a splash of potassium, and it grows up just enough to fill any scuffs or scratches.

"Do you want to do this in virtuality?" Lew asked.

"No, it's all right, I'm up to the real world."

He nodded, summoned his factor, and started giving instructions. I went to my locker, stripped—there was a four-inch-wide dark bruise above my hip—and changed. Lew had come out of his house already in his work clothes. I pressed the thirty-odd sensors and transponders scattered on the snug jumper against my skin. Stared at myself in the mirror. For a moment while I was dressing I had caught a sight of my bare back. If the scar on my arm impressed Nancarrow, what would he have felt on seeing the pair of raised ridges, soft mauve against the brown of my skin, that ran like a sinister bar from the lower corner of my left shoulder blade down and around to my right ribs? Should get rid of it. Don't yet quite have the nerve.

I met Lew in the center of the long room. "What kind of weapon did he use?" he asked.

"A two-foot steel telescoping baton."

He nodded, "A *tokushu keibo*. It conceals well; used right it is a formidable tool."

"He didn't bother hiding it."

Lew's face said, And you had trouble with him? He has little respect for the stupidly obvious. He sighed, went to the equipment rack, and took down a rod. "Is this close enough?"

"His had a wrist strap and no guard."

He looked at the weapon in his hand, and said, "I will imagine the difference." We bowed to each other and spent ten minutes in *wu chi*, the standing meditation. It was hard for me to flow into the bodymind. Too much residual adrenaline sloshing about in my bloodstream. I reached for a memory, a poem. *"Herons flying over a gray river, scarlet flowers dimpling the green hillsides . . ."*

"Now," Lew said, "show me how it went."

So I did. Each moment, each movement. As my father once told me, when it comes to combat, only amateurs wildly improvise. Professionals plan and practice for everything, especially the unexpected. My father didn't follow the Way of Tao, but he knew his zenjitsu. And he was right. What he taught me (my desire, not his), and what I learned later from others, has little to do with style, exercise, or sport. It has to do with staying alive—and making others wish they weren't.

It took around twenty minutes to relive a few seconds. Lew didn't speak, just followed my directions. Whatever thoughts he had he would save for the debriefing, or postmortem. From the look on his face I wasn't too sure which one I was going to get.

Afterward, I rested on my side on the massage table in the medicine room as the thermograph made its slow pass over my hip and back. Lew was busy running our reconstruction of the fight through his simulator. I could have asked the scanner to show me what it was seeing, but comical as it may sound, I'm squeamish about seeing my insides. Besides, I wouldn't have any idea as to how to correctly interpret what I saw. I can make a fair guess on traumatic injuries, set broken bones, been twice a midwife, stitch wounds as fast if not as well as any triage nurse, push pills down a person's throat without them gagging too much. But I leave real medicine to those who have the calling.

The scanner finally stopped, folded up, and pulled back on its retractable arm. I got back into the jumper and rejoined Lew in his office.

Music starting to play gently in the background. Think of the past and the universe accommodates. Mercilessly. Williams's "The Lark Ascending." My father loved it. So did my mother. It's what they played at their wedding. I was four; I remember.

I asked the factor to turn it off. Lew raised his head for a second and went back to what he was doing. In front of him there were two screens up, one frozen on the simulation, the other showing a bunch of charts and up its right corner a writhing reddish blob. I turned away and sat down cross-legged on one of the cushions and watched the pink-gold light filter through the window blinds.

Lew closed down the med display and looked at me. "It is not bad. The cortex and medulla are unharmed. The fascia—the connecting tissue—is bruised, but the medication that you took seems to be alleviating the swelling. The Desk's analysis is that you should be back to normal in a day or two." He came over and squatted beside me. "No, do not get up." He placed his fingers against my side. The pain flared, then faded into a coolness. He murmured to himself, "Two days at least." He returned to his cushion.

"Thanks."

He nodded, and said, "Now, given what you chose to do, let us see what you did wrong." He restarted the simulation.

In these matters I'm more low-tech than high. However, running a copysim—being able to redirect the movements of the little figures that were tenth-scale copies of Lew and me, getting direct tactile feedback—is one hell of an improvement over the old training videos. It also is one hell of a humbling experience. I saw, and felt, mistakes that I hadn't even thought of.

When we finished with the analysis we returned to the main room and went through the whole mess again. And again, and again, and bloody well again . . .

Lew looked up at me from the floor. "Well, Gavilan, if you insist on using that approach in the future I think it will end up easier for you."

Easier, a relative term. Easier to give nightmares, or to get them? Is there a difference? I bowed. "Thank you."

We shared a shower together, dried off, and got into street clothes. Lew went downstairs to buy us some *bolillos*. It was about noon; I went back into the washroom, closed the door, and called Danny.

"How'd it go, mate?"

"You first."

"It went nowhere with the priest. Hear no evil, see no evil, and let us discuss the meaning of evil." He cleared his throat as if wanting to spit. "I got no feel as to whether he really knew anything."

"What about the waitress?"

"Took a while, but I managed to help her remember a decent make on the character with the blade."

He is very good at what the French like to call the *chansonette d'interrogation*: patiently asking the same questions over and over, each time in a different way, and using a soft, singsong voice—a lullaby. Safer than drugs and often about as reliable.

"I collated what she gave me into my identikit; hold on, I'll send it to you." The transmission light on my pad came on for a few seconds. "There you go—you know, Gav, I've got a real itch about this guy."

A round face. Wiry golden brown hair, café au lait skin—heavy on the cream. Narrow bitter eyes and mouth. Was that factual or just an after-the-fact impression? I panned the body; about six four, maybe two hundred, two ten. His size wouldn't necessarily be accurate. Few people are trained like cops—or artists—to reliably make that kind of estimate. He was depicted as wearing a dark gray waist jacket buttoned with bright silver clasps up to his scarfed neck and navy blue pants—loose at hips, tight where they tucked in knee boots that matched the color of jacket. That part of the sketch should be right; when it comes to fashion women are generally far more observant than men—one of the advantages they have. He wouldn't have stood out in South Bay.

Unlike Danny I didn't have any particular feel, but I would consider passing him on to Paul Thinh—I don't completely believe in noncooperation. Possibly the guy had a traceable history.

"Okay, now your turn."

I said cautiously, "I think we may have gotten a bit of luck." I told what happened at the Nancarrow house.

His voice exploded off the washroom's tiles. "After you put him down, why the hell didn't you question him?"

"Practical ethics. People don't remember clearly when they're hurting. And with Jason coming on the scene the situation would have been too close to torture for my taste."

There must of have been something a little too loose in my voice, for I could imagine his hand on my shoulder as he said, "It's okay, Gav, sorry. It's your call."

I sighed. "Anyhow, I think Jammer's just muscle. Danny, do you know anybody at the DEA?"

"Let me think, there's been a lot of waves since I ran with that crowd. Afraid not; nobody I'd trust. Deputies and cowboys weren't getting along when I was with the Service. I don't think they ever did. They didn't like it that we regularly got more successful busts than they did." He laughed. "Remember that motto I told you about? 'Call us when you really *want* the job done.'"

As in the Warrant Apprehension Narcotics Team. From the stories Danny told me about some of the stings that he helped plan, they lost more than an outstanding officer when Danny left them. A sense of humor keeps people human.

There was a period when his becoming a deputy marshal had given us both a great deal of pain. I had grown up with stories about how the Marshals Service had acted as the gestapo for the feds on the rez. More than stories. There's a father and his son, my grandmother's brother, her nephew, buried in the memorial cemetery at Wounded Knee with the bullets that killed them after they surrendered during the Dakota March. It took a while, a lifetime of learning about sorrow and character, but eventually I came again to see the man, the good friend, and not that badge.

He asked me, "You're not going to give the cops what you found?"

It wasn't really a question, but I answered anyway. "I'll wait until I've heard what they give me."

"Planning to go after those guys yourself?"

I rubbed my side; it was beginning to ache again. "I sincerely hope not. What I would really like is to find out how they got linked with the Erinyes gang. I think the middleman might be a lot more informative."

"Is there anything particular that you want me to do?"

"Yeah, get some people to watch Jason Nancarrow—without him knowing."

"Surveillance?"

"Protection."

There was a long pause. I found some aspirins on a shelf and dry-swallowed them. He said ruminatively, "That's tough—wait, I got somebody; Henry Saltini. He used to be with State, their Diplomatic Protection Service. They're used to working at a distance. Foreign embassies get insulted if they think we don't feel that their home-grown security is sufficient. He's sort of retired, lives up in Madera County, but before he left the DPS he headed their West Coast detail. He knows South Bay and he's got a good rep with our local shields. There won't be a problem on that end."

"Will he do it no questions asked?"

"He's on a government pension."

You're getting cynical, Danny. "That answers that question. Get him fast."

"So you don't believe young Jason is going to take your advice?"

I thought of the look on Nancarrow's face as he saw Jammer bleeding in the dirt. "I hope so, but I wouldn't take it to the basket. As you said, he's young."

"I'll call Saltini as soon as I finish with you. Anything else?"

"Nothing special comes to mind. You've been doing great so far, just keep on trucking along—take care and I'll be in touch.

For Danny he said his last words very seriously. "Do that, Gav, stay in touch."

As I got out of the washroom Lew handed me a cup of strong black tea and a crusty football-shaped roll slathered with butter. I gulped them both down and offered to take him back home.

"No need. Gordon will come by later and pick me up. I want to study my game. My opponent has managed a new wrinkle with the Nimzo Indian which surprised me. We're playing closed pad. I did not think he was capable of it."

"Then I'll be going. Have you located the woman I asked you for?"

He shook his head and replied forbearingly, "Gavilan, I do have a *wais* out. There should be a response from the old-sensei stream soon. I did hear your urgency."

Lew has almost as much *jen* as his wife. I bowed and spoke in Hakka, "Sorry, I know you did. Thanks, Lew, and thanks again."

CHAPTER TWELVE

RUMMAGING AROUND IN THE WELL-COMPARTMENT between the seats of the Lotus I found a small paper tablet and a vellum envelope that once contained an invitation from the New County Museum for the patron's showing of last summer's Domhnail exhibition.

It was a rare night for her. Sulinn had been a little off; Kit does realize how she looks. I won't say that she doesn't use her beauty—you control it, or it controls you—but she's careful. She's never taken a theater class in her life, yet she knows how to use costume, makeup, her instrument—her face and body—to be, not ever plain, but simple. How to look only attractive enough to get a smile, but nothing more. She's very smart, and they grow up fast in the South. Even in Texas.

That evening she wasn't just pretty; she wasn't simple.

Because I have always been susceptible, I've learned how to detach. It's been a long time since I've been blindsided, by anyone. But that night I walked beside her shivering.

If she hadn't tossed her lace mantilla and kicked off her pumps as soon as we got home, and then run as lightly as a yearling into the kitchen to fix herself a huge bowl of fresh blueberries—I found her sitting cross-legged on top of a counter, the long loose folds of her gown bunched around her hips, her fingertips stained purple, her face as innocently gleeful as a ten-year-old—well . . .

I tore off a sheet and wrote a letter to Holguin—despite the Freedom of Privacy Act, he quite sensibly doesn't believe in the telcos' encryption systems. I'm sure for his link to the Electric Sea and the other oceans, rivers, and wells, he uses a secret line similar to mine. And even that protection isn't enough for him. Vladimir hardly ever leaves his house; when his clients wish to communicate sensitively with him they have to either send to him their own ciphers or use a live courier. Since I wasn't willing to give him one of the only two codes that I trust, I put pen to paper and asked him to find out in detail what significant acts of sabotage had been tried recently against the Congo Basin Project, and again to see what organizations, other than the enviros, stood to benefit the most if the project should fail or be canceled. I told him to send a courier with the data, but not before 10:00 P.M.

If Vladimir hadn't worked out what I was involved with by now I was giving him major clues. So be it.

I folded the message into the envelope, sealed it, and walked a few blocks over to the sprawling Cedars-Sinai hospital complex, the largest in North America. I know the place almost as well as UCLA—I can tell you how many tiles there are in the ceiling of the ER's waiting room. Casually I brushed some dirt from my boots and looked around as if waiting for a friend. That I work out at Lew's dojo is an open fact. If I was under close surveillance, it wasn't by flesh.

Reasonably satisfied, I went past the main entrance over to the taxi line. Most of them were cyberelectric runabouts. I was looking for a long-distance cab. I found one seven cars down. On its side, emblazoned brightly, was the name of the patron saint of cabbies, St. Fiacre. I opened the passenger door and slid in.

The young driver hastily took off his gameset and put on his company cap. Flashing prism canines, he smiled broadly at me, "Where to, sir?"

His accent was pure Ozark. Is there a universal law that says thou shalt not have any hometown cabbies? "Take me over to Wilshire and La Cienega."

His grin disappeared. "Uh-oh, sorry, that's a local. You've got to get one of the humps ahead of me or I'll be fined—city regs."

Floated a hundred down onto the front seat. "Don't worry; you'll still be going further on with a fare."

He picked the money up and gazed at it as if he'd never seen that large a bill before. Maybe he hadn't; Los Angeles has never been much of a cab town. He fingered smooth the corners of the hundred. It went into his front tunic pocket instead of the gratuity box. A free clue about his honesty.

"Are we going to pick somebody up, sir?"

I scribbled on the front of the envelope: "Holguin, pay the bearer one hundred dollars. Cash." I added the address and gave it to the driver. "You're going to deliver this." If the hundred was strange to him, the little gilt-edged envelope was a mystery. When he managed to read my horrible copperplate script his eyes danced. I asked if he thought it would be sufficient.

"Are you kidding? That's a six-bell ticket tops!" If he could have reached me I think he would have grabbed me in a bear hug.

"That's also to cover your turning off the tach monitor."

His glee went out like a match. "Whoa, now! Even if I could do that, sir—which I can't—turning off the tracker is a license buster."

I said in a pleasant, confidential voice, "I guess you've never deadheaded to Palmdale International for a big ticket."

The pink in his cheeks made his confession. "You sound like you drove."

"Only getaway cars."

He thought I was being funny so he chuckled politely and looked again at the envelope. One hundred and a hundred. Enough to pay for a month's rent on a two-room apartment, to buy a dozen games, or dazzle a novia, a sweetheart. "Okay, it's a deal."

I got dropped off on the corner and watched the cab speed down La Cienega toward the freeway. For a two-hundred-dollar jackpot, he was willing to pay the toll.

Started walking the half mile back to my car. On the way I stopped by a row of hawkers; they were all carefully standing by the curb. Beverly Hills aggressively bans them while West Hollywood is indifferently free market. On this stretch of La Cienega the city line runs down the middle of the east sidewalk. Every morning one of the hawkers lays down a fresh vermilion chalk stripe to warn the newcomers. I bought a small cup of cinnamon-laced Turkish coffee. Went up to the corner of Burton Way and La Cienega, sat down on an empty bench at the trolley stop, and slowly, morosely, drank the coffee.

Where's that careful, easy face, Robie? Where's that keen self-discipline? That life-long mastery that you believe has kept it a long life. Are we having another spontaneous existential crisis?

I finished the coffee, down to the gritty mud. All right, shove the bloody angst off—time's wasting. Time. On the gigs Ethan Hill gets me I usually take weeks, sometimes months, to work it through. And even with all that sweat more often than not it's hopeless. I had eight and a half days left.

It was so obvious it was hardly worth thinking about—if I pushed too hard, too fast, I was more likely to precipitate Siv Matthiessen's execution than to save her. And she would be executed—I wasn't doing melodrama when I told Nancarrow that whatever the outcome was, she would die. It might not be what Olivia Fouchet and GT might want—I wasn't sure how the freddies would feel—but it was in the best interest of the Erinyes that she not survive. She might give—no, considering what she was, would give—the authorities damaging information. And more importantly, their most recent previous actions were designed to generate fear. Maybe the Erinyes thought that they could stop the

Congo project, or maybe they were simply amending the soil for future victories.

So I stay for now with indirection. And that thought called up another avenue, a route that I had studiously not considered. If dealing with the Benevolences is like going down a gloomy alley, then this one could be like walking through a pitch-black one studded with mines.

Once upon a time when the last big dirty war was over, the concern of those brave warriors who had spent their careers behind terminals and desks became job, not national, security. So they became masters of competitive intelligence, getting the secret details of balance sheets rather than ballistic missiles. They got quite good at it. The tools, the techniques that they had developed, were easy to adapt to a different target. Swords into profitable plowshares.

Sometimes they used a web of shells, sometimes a partnership with firms that for generations had intimate ties to the community, developers of dark electronics and other sweet hardware. Those have always been government maridas, closer than lovers, less than wives. Until the income they were getting became a significant fraction of the money their particular agency was receiving from legal appropriations. And that was their downfall; the money got too large. Excess is the greatest danger.

The scandal stayed about as buried as that unit. The assets were quietly, painstakingly, sold off and a bunch of careers were scorched. And that was supposedly the end of that experiment in national security socialism.

Not quite. The scorching didn't burn all the cells. The survivors reconnected, regenerated, mutated. They learned from their mistakes; no official ties to any government organization, don't get too big, and don't do any domestic work.

So now they're one of the tight, almost invisible, players in the global marketplace; investing, providing black data for companies whose success is deemed in the national interest. And occasionally, if rarely, engaging in a strategic bit of wetwork. All in the name of patriotism—and profit. And very determined not to let the non-professionals know that they *are* in business.

As for the pros, well, the trend line has been toward privatization and nongovernmentals for nearly sixty years now. Why not let them operate, as long as they remember to be patriots and not merely condottieri—and should the day come when they forget, the scorching won't be metaphorical.

So how the hell did I come to know about their history, and more importantly, why am I still alive? A bit of synchronicity, eccentricity, and luck—bad and good. Hallmarks of my tradecraft.

I was on a regular job. An investment firm based in Santa Fe had bought some very high-grade artwork from a dead man's estate in Colombia. One of the paintings—a Modigliani—had gone missing. They asked me to look into it. I flew down to Bogotá. Nearly the first thing I did was make the obvious inquiries as to who else had made offers for the painting. Some collectors can't bear to be without. There hadn't been a lot of bidders on the estate, not because of the quality—the whole assemblage was very fine—but because the father of the man who had put it together had been a minor cartel lord; that made for some tricky legal as well as moral problems.

One of the offers for the Modigliani had come from a Brazilian holding company. I tried contacting them, but they weren't in an informative mode. So I asked the Colombian family if they had done a security check on the Brazilians. They were eager to help; the loss of the painting offended their honor, their hard-won legitimate respectability, and their bank account. Of course they had done a check—even without their family's history, the wealthy in Latin America have always had to be especially careful. And the Brazilians, it turned out, were a shell within a shell within a shell . . . and so forth. In effect, the buyer of the painting was a figment, and the Colombians decided against accepting the bid. It looked a little bit too tricky. I agreed.

My first obligation was to the people who had hired me, so I found the damned painting . . . no, not damned, it was a wonderful piece. One of those that are actually worth what the law of supply and demand pretends to dictate.

Then I headed south. It took me three months to get some idea what the hell was going on, and another month in a Sao Paulo hospital after they first tried to kill me. I broke a rule, and tried for a deal. I told them that we could be of mutual use to each other. The spectrums that we inhabited intersected at times, and cooperation might be beneficial. I didn't know what they really were about, and I was going on the assumption that the key to survival was value. I thought I had made a good presentation. It certainly had a lot more truth than lies. They agreed with my reasoning. And tried to kill me again.

The second time they sent two confident, local sicarios to finish me up close instead of another lased sniper. Always be grateful for small mercies.

Again I should have taken off. What stopped me was the realization that had come to me while I was healing from the first attack. I was at one of those cusps in my life. If I cut my losses and ran, I knew I would never do this work again. I didn't know then (do I know now?) if I could manage to live without.

There was also the other insight, the one I had faced up to a long time ago: Other people aren't the only souls I try to rescue.

So I stayed and broke more than a rule, I did something I swore I wouldn't do: I called in a debt that someone thought they owed to me from the days I was with the Committee.

At the time the man was a superintendent of the National Police. Fifteen years prior his sister had made the mistake of love and married a professor of communications who lived in a neighboring country that was busily rediscovering the myth of the savior-president. They were both arrested for sedition. He had slurred, to the wrong people, the name of somebody important: an apostle-general of the new order who had until then successfully hidden his greedy viciousness behind his country's colors. She insisted that she was an accessory to her husband's life. An extraordinary, foolish, woman. They would have no trial, and long before anybody could help them, they would both die. An accident, a prison fight, shot while trying to escape—pick a lie, the pack is full.

We got them both out alive. But it wasn't a good day.

Back then the man was a young police lieutenant attached to the Brazilian equivalent of the Border Patrol; somehow he found out that I was involved and what it had cost. He located and came to me—that was a time when luck rolled in every direction but mine—and said that whenever I would need it, I could have everything he could give.

A grand gesture, but he was a young man who believed in them. I told him it wasn't personal, that if he wished to help that he always had ARC for that. He understood—I heard that over the years he has been of considerable aid to the Committee—yet he insisted that it was also particular between us. At the time I looked at the strain on his proud face, in too many bloody ways a mirror, nodded, and went far away.

I called him. He wasn't young anymore, but he remembered his words. He was quite capable of ignoring his promise—I thought he might—but it was a debt he still thought he had to pay. Between us, we put the holding company, an extension of that semiprivate intelligence unit—call them Midas, the metaphor of that legend fits them well—into a very nasty vise. Their Brazilian concern was a sizable part of their operations. They decided to take my deal. I had it renegotiated a lot more to my favor.

Over the past four years I only once took advantage of that agreement, and then it was mostly to see if they would still keep to it. Don't use them for a lot of reasons; the easiest being that I know enough scum. And organizations like theirs, more para than nongovernmental, are too damned powerful for me to handle.

But even though they were a rogue outfit—I was pretty sure from a few other contacts that I have that they were uncoupled from the mainstream intelligence community—they had access to information that Holguin would never see. My gut said there was another critical player on the field; I wanted to know who it was.

I crumpled the paper cup and went for a three-pointer on the cycle bin. As far as I can tell, Midas still thinks that I'm part of his ministry's Special Investigation Unit. Part of the deal was that they were to do a back-propagation erasure starting with the preliminary dossier they had compiled on Calderon—sound familiar?—which reinforced the fiction. Another small detail, my superintendent, no, after what we did together, we became citizens of the same borderless land—call him a *companero*—made sure that my hospital records and samples disappeared.

Since, barring disaster, to them I was still Calderon, it meant I had to fly to San Jose in order to get a secure, safe link to Midas. Delta-Pacific runs a hypersonic route that loops from Taiwan to San Diego-Tijuana to San Jose, to Brasilia and then back again. If I could get a seat, I could be in San Jose by 3:00 P.M. and return before my 8 P.M. meeting with Thinh—if he showed up.

It was possible that Midas could be involved themselves. They are fond of playing the kind of game I suspected was going on— one of the bemusing twists in the chain of life was that a piece of false information they had on me had Vladimir Holguin's trademark analytical signature on it. Better than even money that they were among those of his clients that employed his strategic arts. The link worried me a lot until I realized that the origin point of the data had no connection to Gavilan Robie. Still, unless I misunderstood them, Midas keeps their active operations within our country's tenuous theater of influence: Latin America and the eastern Pacific. They had no serious stake in Africa—I hoped.

Took three coins out, tossed them on the bench and read what they had to say. Very well; San Jose it would be.

*   *   *

I called the airline as I walked to my car. For a full-fare executive-class passenger they certainly had a seat available. I booked it as Rafael Calderon. Went home, gave the genie some contingency options, changed into a fawn-colored lightweight suit, and opened the fireplace vault. I removed the small travel bag that has Calderon's details—passport and other ID, clothes with the right labels, the local brand of soap, etc. I also took out a thin wire choker: when wearing it I can adjust the sound of my voice to what it once was. A tool developed years ago by professional mimics to fool voice detection systems; possession is still a grade-two felony. It's uncomfortable to use for extended periods, and wearing something that looks like a slave chain isn't in vogue. Fortunately, high collar tunics—the old Russian style—are popular even in the tropics and I've learned how to live with discomfort. No one down there has yet heard my changed timbre and I didn't want to deal with explanations, or give Midas unnecessary clues.

I closed up the house, got into the truck, and rushed downtown to Union Station. I just made the Rapido. We pulled into the San Dee depot in under forty-five minutes. Jumped on the express trolley that ran out to the new international airport that straddles the border at Otay Mesa. Checked in at the viper lounge and boarded the giant arrowhead with five minutes to spare. As the seat thoughtfully buckled me in, I wondered how long after takeoff it would be before one of the attendants could offer me a drink.

CHAPTER THIRTEEN

THE BOURBON WAS PHONY, BUT the serving was generous. I stretched my legs and relaxed.

Worked on my drink. Somewhere I had read—or tried to—the classic paper that explained the mechanics of how alcohol affects testosterone levels, reducing it in men but increasing it in women. Since testosterone had long been known to be a facilitator in sexual arousal, the liquor combines were fast to rush new, improved versions of their drugs to the market. Recalled when it was that I had attempted to understand that paper, just after I met Kit; I was plowing through a screen stack of books and trade journals, trying to get a fix on what her other major passion was about.

Don't worry about it, darling, I've only the vaguest idea how you manage to get Jessie to sound so beautiful. Not really understanding doesn't always lessen the pleasure. She laughed low in her throat, patted the cushion next to her, and said with a twanging drawl, *Why don't you come here and I'll teach you some things you can't ever learn from a textbook.*

There wasn't a whole lot of reflection, but we both managed one hell of a gratifying response. . . .

Ordered another glass. Considering how feral I had been feeling, lowering my high-test levels was probably a good idea. Superb rationale, Robie.

Called Joaquin Figueres, my human factor in San Jose, and asked him to pick me up at Juan Santamaria Airport. Then I took a catnap.

Woke up to the plane's voice in English telling the passengers that we were beginning the descent. It repeated the message in Mandarin, Turk, German, Portuguese, Japanese, Farsi, and finally in Spanish—the world's current pecking order. I turned on the seat screen and looked below at the landscape.

We were still high enough to see all of Costa Rica. It looked like a rippling tricolor flag: the aquamarine green of the flooded Caribbean coast, the yellow-brown parched dead Pacific side, and in the center, the dark velvety green and black of the country's mountainous backbone. Holguin had been wrong again; the Transition had not been kind anywhere. But it was especially hard in the early years to Central America.

The Transition. One of the all-time great misleading figures of speech. One of those cache-phrases we use without thinking—but then, that's the idea. The media-doc who came up with it was a genius. She certainly didn't get it from the climatologists who were sitting mutely reading dataflows that said that the Industrial Optimum had decided to come to an abrupt halt just as the Greenhouse Nightmare started becoming true. The Earth couldn't make her mind up whether to get colder or hotter, so she became both. Throw in a, probably, coincidental spasm of volcanic eruptions on three continents . . .

Costa Rica did a lot better than her neighbors. A conscientious, capable government—a rarity anywhere in the Americas. A people who decided to take seriously what they believed their national character said: we're family, we are supposed to help each other.

Before the calamities, two-thirds of the population, five million, had lived in the highlands on the Meseta Central, a plateau that spreads like a large flat buckle in the middle of the mountains; now over eight million live there on the Meseta—and thrive.

After the local chaos settled uneasily, angrily, into its new forms, Costa Rica found itself with some compensation for being one of the hotter points on the Rim of Fire: a major increase in the amount of hydroelectric power it could generate and vast new geothermal fields. More than self-sufficient, they could now export energy all through Central America as far north as Oaxaca and south down to Colombia. And energy is—pardon—power as well as wealth. San Jose has become the unofficial capital of Mesoamerica.

Life's a balance. Sure.

As the plane twisted its wings down for its rapid descent, I turned off the screen and shut my eyes. I'm fine with takeoffs. Landings I have a little trouble with.

Being a national, customs went fast. I checked my wristband: 1:02 P.M. local time; the band had reset its chronograph on the country's master clock—not bad for a twenty-dollar Tajikistani copy of a Patek. Joaquin was waiting outside with a hired car—when they were pulling themselves back together they held a national resource referendum. Private ownership of cars didn't make the cut. "Hola, Rafael!" he yelled. He grabbed my travel bag off my shoulder with one hand and gave me an exuberant handshake with the other.

I managed to extricate my hand and smiled happily. "Good to see you, Joaquin."

He put the bag carefully on the backseat of the matronly Volkswagen. "Are we going straight to your apartment? Do you wish to drive?"

I looked at the key he held out to me and then at his face.

Joaquin loves to drive, rarely does, and consequently is quite terrible.

"Yes, the apartment. No, you drive. I want to roll down the window, lean my head out, and smell the land."

"Sí, it has been a long time. You must let the country come back to you."

The musky scent of the lava-rich earth, the as-yet only semiorganized landscape—it is a lovely country—did help take my mind off the haphazard seventeen-kilometer ride to San Jose. Joaquin's nonstop conversation helped too. He told me how it was with his wife, Maria, their two children, especially with their older daughter, Rafaella—only sixteen and already she's studying plant genetics at the university and doing well. The honors program, no less! The nursery was also doing fine, that F4bx Brilliantine had turned out to be a real winner; if I needed it, he would immediately transfer my share of the last quarter's profits to my personal account at the Banco de Cartegena. As we got off the highway and turned down Calle 42 he started reciting the latest gossip. I grinned a lot at him and periodically said, *"Buena nota."*

People hear that funny rapid-fire voice, see his puppy dog eyes, learn that he is a grower of pretty flowers, and then rarely notice how he stands around his family and friends, and how they stand when they're around him. How his thick peasant hands, so careful with a tender seedling, are so strong that they can bend rebars as if they were garden hoses. When he was twenty he served a hellish tour with the Blue Berets. A country without an army does not necessarily lack people of raw courage. Although I grubstaked him to the nursery, he's not a reclamation project—if anything, I'm his. When I first created Rafael Garcia Calderon I lived in Costa Rica for seven months, gestating, trying to pick up all the little details of what it is to be a Tico. To sink into my mind the cultural gestalt they call *la pura vida*. Joaquin Figueres, as employee, partner, compadre, made it a lot easier for me—and Rafael Calderon has helped keep me alive.

The best lesson I ever learned and too often forget: The key to survival is not in your value, or strength, but in the honor of your friends.

We came down to Sabana Park and Avenida Paseo Colón; they've relined the sidewalks of the Avenida with *pochotes*—a native hardwood that managed to make it. The government is attempting to replant them slowly down the western side of the country toward the Pacific. My apartment is in a six-story stone building near the corner of Calle 40 and Paseo Colón. I'm on the fifth floor; four spacious rooms with a view of the park and its Museo del Arte and the newly lush mountains beyond.

"Will you be staying long?" Joaquin said. "Should I ask Maria to set an extra plate?"

Maria's Sunday cooking; sometimes I think I should have offered to set them up with a restaurant, except that she loved the flowers as much as he did.

"I will only be staying for a few hours; then I must leave."

He shrugged. He is used to my coming in and spending just a short time in San Jose, although a few hours might be a record in brevity. He asked, "Will you need anything special?"—as in bodyguards, security devices, a manifest of currently bribable officials. San Jose is a low-crime town and the government is among the most honest in Latin America, but there are always cretins. Joaquin believes that I make a gray living, just below the salt of legality. He's a good factor.

"No, nothing special—wait, the thought of dinner by Maria has made me hungry. After you drop me off, can you get me a snack from Marcella's Sodas?"

"No problem."

We stopped in front of the apartment building, I noticed that the management had repainted the casements a dusky blue. A few strollers on the crowded street glanced curiously at the car. I got out the building's passcard from my bag and let myself in—that's all it took; I said it's a safe town. An unfamiliar couple were getting out of the elevator cage as I stepped up to it. They smiled at me and nodded politely; the handsome woman looked breathless and had slightly flushed cheeks. He was holding her hand. Love in the afternoon. I vaguely recalled doing that once upon a time.

The building's housekeeping staff had dusted, switched on the environmental systems, and turned down the soft cotton covers on the bed. Joaquin must have come to the apartment before going to the airport; on the table in the sitting room in a plain glass vase were a dozen fresh roses the color of burnished gold.

Opened the windows and took in the view. Kit would love it. A good place to spend some years. The San Jose University Hospital was far smaller than UCLA's but it was first-rate and they would literally fall over themselves to get her on staff. As for myself, there were a number of pleasant, innocent things I could do here and there. I wouldn't get bored. ". . . And leave the world unseen, and with thee fade away into the forest dim."

Not a bad idea, assuming that Kit comes back, that I'm willing to change my life, that I wouldn't be dead this time next week. Large assumptions.

I left the window, went to the desk, and turned on the apartment rig. Entered the figment I had brought with me, "George Estaban," and told it to nose around for any tidbits on Warren Tyler and some relationals. Left the Digest and had my business program bring me up to date. I keep a little ongoing activity in this country, nothing much, just a few thousand colons worth of transactions; that's about six thousand American. Most years it covers my local expenses and gives anybody curious a solid, dead-end trail.

I was back sitting in the chair going over my accounts when Joaquin came through the door with my food; Marcella's is a good five minutes away. He gave me the paper sack. Inside were seven cheese-filled tortillas, a large pile of *patacones*—slices of plantain deep fried like chips—and two icy cold bottles of tamarindo. I cocked my head at him. "Thought I asked for a snack."

He tsked. "You look thin. Maria would be terrified to see you."

I closed the rig and crunched down on one of *patacones*—delicious. Marcella makes the best. "Perhaps you are jealous of my waist."

He happily patted his wide stomach, "Why should I be jealous?"

I popped the caps off the bottles and handed him one. Took a long swallow of the tart juice. "You are right," I said, "there's certainly no reason to be jealous."

He sat down next to me and looked at the tortillas. I pushed them to him. "Como quieras."

"Gracias."

For Maria's sake I ate as much as I could. If you are old enough to remember how bad the Hunger was in some places in the South, then you'll understand why Joaquin was kidding on the square when he said that Maria gets scared when she sees people she cares about looking skinny.

I finished off the chips. I looked at my wristband; it was twenty to the golden hour. "We leave now." I stood up and reassuringly I asked him to drop me at a certain cantina and wait for me around the corner, if he didn't mind.

He looked offended. "Jefe, your time is mine." He held up a scratchy book. "I came prepared."

The Laird and His Lady. A romance. At least it was an improvement over the Westerns he favored last year—those almost made me blow my cover. I glanced at the cover illustration. The laird looked nothing like a Scottish baron, and I've known a few. The lady, on the other hand, looked like someone I would certainly like to know.

I frowned at Joaquin and teased. "Is Maria aware of this?"

He replied with unthinking sincerity, "Maria is aware of where my heart lies."

"I'm glad she does." He gave me a puzzled glance. Returned it with a momentary smile. A fractional life. Damn.

*   *   *

My Midas contact address was a hole-in-the-wall bar. On the way four Exiles, a bottle party, perked up as I passed them. I wasn't dressed for this scenery. I started singing a song in patois about a man, and a gun, and a posse. They decided to return to lounging.

Thank you, Sara Michele of the plain dark face and bright hazel eyes, for that long summer we spent together, and for the patience you gave someone who needed both badly. A man who was luckier than he deserved to be.

In the nameless bar I ordered a Stripe and told the bartender in the same patois that I would like to see a person if that was okay with that person. He served my drink, took my money, and heard my message as if it were as natural as seeing crap in the gutter outside. It probably was, in this neighborhood. Joaquin had given me a glance when I gave him the address. The plastic countertop had a fine patina of grease. I kept my sleeves away from it, drank my beer, and thought about how the sound of my old voice singing had startled me.

He came back in two minutes and told me in better Spanish than I'll ever speak that the person was available to see to me. I was to go in the back, by the unisex washroom, turn a corner, and wait.

I did what I was told. The washroom was rancid, not to my surprise. I turned the corner and found myself in a dimly lit corner with a sloppily bricked-up doorway; presumably the original other loo. Then the bricks swung away, and I found myself staring into the snout of a very large shotgun, poking out of the dimness. Then it swung away, and a light came on.

The Midas contact—the name I had was Veloso—was waiting for me in a tiny compartment. He looked me over, waved me in, and closed the wall. He was sitting on a plain metal stool closely surrounded by massed banks of displays that danced colors against his matte white skin. There was barely enough room for me to squeeze in.

I could hear the sound of a heavy-duty baffler coming on.

Veloso focused his eyes on me. "Who are you?" he asked in Portuguese.

I gave him the trivial bit of data that identified me.

"What are you buying?"

"A panel discussion."

"What are you selling?"

This was the hard one. They didn't whore themselves cheap. "Next month there's an auction at Hancock's. A supposed copy of a Carel Fabritius taken after the master's unfinished *Lamentation*. One of the few paintings he did that wasn't a portrait. Catalog number four-eight-four-six . . ."

He yawned behind a slender hand. "Yes?"

"It's not a copy done by his brother Barent. It's a much earlier version that Carel had started."

Veloso dropped his shades over his eyes. Going over catalogs and references. When he found what I was talking about, a quick intake of breathe, then silence. Undoubtedly calculating costs and profit. A real Fabritius, regardless of quality, even though it was more a sketch than anything else, would go for ten, maybe twenty times what the ersatz copy would bring at auction. Carel Fabritius was a pivotal artist; besides the superb quality of his own work, he was Rembrandt's best student, and he helped shift the focus in Dutch painting from his teacher's incredible study of the soul toward an objective realism that was different but equally profound. There's some reasonable speculation that he taught Vermeer.

Carel Fabritius died too young, killed when a gunpowder factory explosion blew up his Delft neighborhood. Most of his paintings went with his body. There are a dozen or so for-sures, and another half dozen maybes. A piece, even unfinished, that was truly, or even just arguably, by his hand should go for about two and a half million. The profit after the wild bidding war that was sure to erupt—the syndicate had spent dearly to set up a fake provenance and wasn't going to lie down—commissions, and some unavoidably complicated expenses, would be about a third of that.

Even for Midas a very tidy sum. Veloso wasn't going to ask me for proof; I had already demonstrated to them that I wasn't an idiot.

He no longer looked sleepy. "Conditions?"

"That the discussion prove as fruitful to me as owning the painting would be profitable to you." And if it isn't, Samantha Jardine-Wilcott, Hancock's senior in-house expert on the seventeenth-century Dutch, will learn the truth and become very embarrassed and very pissed that I didn't inform her sooner. I had figured that I would tell her—just before the auction—even though one of the conspirators was a man I once respected, but then I got called to this particular foxhunt. The hospice that thought they were selling off a minor bequest was going to be screwed, but not nearly as badly as they originally would have been. As for the people who had set up the elaborate graft, they were going to be very upset, but they were only rich amateurs, playing at corruption as much for fun as for profit. They earned their loss. And they didn't know me.

"Agreed."

"A stipulation."

"What?"

"Donate it to the National Museum in Brasilia. They can offer a straight two-for-one write-off. And it will make certain people grateful."

"How grateful?"

I shrugged and arched my hands away from my wrists.

A very long pause. Then, "It's unclear whether we can do that. However, we can offer you the condition that the National will be able to purchase the item at the most favorable price. Satisfactory?"

I had to try. Jardine-Wilcott, I was told by the man who had sold me the truth, had thought long and hard before sighingly agreeing that it was by Carel's brother—the painting actually could be authentic. Modern attribution methods may be a wonderful blend of knowledge, intuition, and technology, yet even for the best it's difficult to know for certain. I nodded and sighed inside. At least, unlike the sculpture that Holguin was trying to un-load, there was a good chance it wouldn't disappear behind a steel door. I leaned against the wall. It was common brick, on both sides, though Veloso's side was a good deal cleaner.

He moved his hands over a control panel; some of the displays dimmed down to standby. What he did next was utterly undra-matic: he didn't install headgear like a crown of thorns, or pull away skin from his forearm, exposing a neural socket and plugging in. He simply pushed the cuffs of his shirt away from his wrists, exposing flat gray-black bracers that glittered as if they were dusted with mica, and put the heels of his hands against the hol-lows of his temples. He squinted for a second and closed his eyes. I waited for the panel to assemble.

Electronic telepathy; a great invention. A wonderful way to reintroduce the world to what senile dementia and acute schizo-phrenia looks like. Even a junkie like Holguin knew better. What was Veloso, and the others he was linking to, getting that could possibly be compensation? Maybe, predictably, Midas had in-duced them to believe that their minds wouldn't eventually turn to mush.

Veloso opened his blank eyes and we began to talk.

CHAPTER FOURTEEN

IN SAN JOSE, JOAQUIN DROVE: he may be erratic but he's fast—and at that moment an accident would almost have seemed a kind act of Providence. He sensed my mood and was silent as we got on the highway and went back north. When we pulled into the airport we stopped in front of the new main terminal The walls are faced with lava rocks, a testament to the country's ancient eternal enemy and friend. A few brief words about business, a gentle handshake and hug, and he was off. As I said, Ticos are almost all pure Spanish and like their Iberian ancestors they know how to combine warmth with reserve.

I had a little time to waste before my flight back so I went into one of the gift shops and bought a liter of Salenica rum. Purchase in hand, I wandered over to the statue of Santamaria, the national hero they named the airport after.

Juan Santamaria. The nineteenth-century drummer boy who volunteered to torch the building that William Walker— one of our earliest all-American freebooting imperialists—and his gang of invading adventurers were holed up in. A suicide mission. I looked up at the thinly handsome, determined face the sculptor had given the boy. An optical trick perhaps, but I thought he looked back. I hate obvious omens.

There weren't any convenient distractions on the hyperjet. I didn't have much choice but to think about what I had learned from Midas. What they fed me as information was a dinner of suet and gristle. I had learned too much of what I didn't want to know, and not enough of what I needed. I couldn't fault Midas; they had amply filled their part of the deal.

Item: Midas had some surplus Eurocash. They had been interested in the Congo basin bonds—until they found out that a "money society" based in Chongqing, the capital of Sichuan Province—more populous than Germany and almost as wealthy—had been secretly shorting the bonds, betting that their value would seriously decline over the next eighteen months. It wasn't the gamble that the Chinese syndicate was taking that warned them off, it was the fact that the Sichuanese had as an investment partner a certain Chao Wen, the procurator of External Security (Africa) for the Chinese Realms.

Chao Wen. For a few years the Committee attempted to compile files on certain individuals likely to rise in their professions—certain political individuals for whom the term "civilized murderer" wasn't an oxymoron. The undertaking didn't get too far. Too hard, too expensive; resources were always limited and there were too many possibles. But before the project was cut off, Chao Wen had made the list.

Knowledge itself is power. Bacon's words are the axiom of our age. But knowledge doesn't guarantee anything. The man who had taught me Mandarin, Wu, the Hakka dialects; the man who wrote beautiful, poetic commentaries on the I Ching, died with his team in a trap set by Chao Wen. A mission I had designed.

Synchronicity, coincidence, karma—I'm not stoic enough to let those words gentle me.

Item: A covert delegation from the CR had met with certain members of the ruling council of the Equatorial African Community in Huambo, the capital of Angola; agenda unknown, but some of those members were on the oversight commission set up for the Project.

How did Midas glean that bit of data? Angola and Brazil share a language and history. Even though the former was a member of the Southern African Union, Brazilian business interests had more than a toehold there. Midas's Brazilian company was a player. And where Midas plays, even if it's a small game, it keeps very keen eyes open—and it happened to own the hotel where the conference took place.

Item: Also in attendance was a female executive whose last name was MacKenzie, as in MacKenzie-Rao, one of the Southern African cartels.

For the last forty years or more, the SA cartels have regarded Africa south of the Sahara as their exclusive playground—at least they've tried hard to ensure that was the case. For most of that time none of the other globals cared to argue the point. Africa to them was like deep space, a profitless desert. (Did racism tinge their judgment? Of course not; the marketplace is always rational.)

A lovely thought came to me: If anybody had clout over the West Coast Benevolences, the Chinese Realms working through the mainland's triads—extinct, of course—would.

Item: MacKenzie-Rao has used on occasion the services of a certain Chilean moneycenter. Said bank was founded by refugees from Hong Kong. Said bank was known for its willingness to facilitate what is euphemistically called extralegal enterprises.

I knew something about that bank's North American operations. It had the wrong kind of friends.

And I had a story of my own about MacRao.

Item: The bank—its name was Hsin-min—the "New People"—had profited from the demise of a specialty chemical producer. Profited in both deaths—the firm, and its owner, whose untimely departure removed a serious impediment to a major business venture they were backing.

There was a sardonic coda to that story. It seems that the senior executives of the company actually didn't know about the dumping—eventually most volunteered to undergo the local version of a TruthTell exam. The renegade operation was done by a handful of employees, all of whom had disappeared. Midas was amused. It had the sweet smell of an elegant set-up. They doubted whether the avenging angels—their term—knew that the owner was innocent. Yet, as one of them commented sourly, "For fanatics ignorance is not an excuse."

Unfortunately, but not unexpectedly, there wasn't any certain—to Midas—connection between the group that had its revenge and the Chilean moneycenter.

There were some other items, but they were part of the smoke and mirrors that I tried, however feebly, to confuse them with.

I took a sip from my second round of bourbon. If some part of the CR was involved—despite the reach of Midas's datacore I don't accept anything I'm told by anybody until I've verified it with a second source and preferably a third as well—then finding Siv Matthiessen was a puzzle grown exponential. And lethal.

Damn Groupe Touraine for coming to me. Damn me for giving a damn.

I mentally shook myself, like a dog who had finally remembered to come in out of the rain. I was nearly fifty and still alive, today, and with luck, tomorrow. I had Thinh and Holguin to fill up my plate. Perhaps I would enjoy my supper better than my dinner. I turned on my seat screen and leisurely finished my drink, watching the world go by.

I made it to Los Angeles and home in time to rinse off the tropical sweat, shave, and change into slacks and a long-sleeved knit shirt. Eight P.M. and no Paul Thinh. I spent half an hour letting the house read to me a monograph on the unintentional, aesthetically driven, sociological characteristics to be found in the paintings of Charlayne Sahm—the dense paper was as humorless and meaningless as Muzak—while I went through my ordinary correspondence. Eight-thirty-one, still no Thinh. I took a risk and called my office, retrieving the "Estaban" I had sent out earlier.

It had some news. The Privacy Act has a big hole when it comes to convicts. "No agency, public or private, shall obtain information on the *lawful* activities of a citizen without freely given consent." "Freely given" and "citizen" being the other big cracks. There were four individuals named Warren Tyler—or close variations thereof—that had done time during the last twenty years in a state penitentiary. The one that seemed most likely my Tyler, still alive and registered in Ventura, had spent a full nickel for gunrunning. Some of his time was done in Grover Bay; one of the special prisons where convicts that are very difficult to handle are sent—unless they voluntarily opt for reconstructive chemotherapy. Few do.

I built a small fire in the hearth and stared at it for a while.

As I was beginning to think that, Madame Fouchet's assurances to the contrary, I was going to obtain from GT the indifferent cooperation that a shark gives to a pilot fish, the house told me that I had a visitor. At nine-fifteen. Paul Thinh showed up.

He came in wiping his face with a handkerchief with one hand. It was pouring again. He was carrying a lightly wrapped package under his arm. I walked him down the main hallway—his eyes widening at the sight of the blazing tiles—to the living room. Offered him some coffee. He told me tersely, no, thanks. While I was undoing the package he looked intently around. Not much to see: two comfortable loungers along with a scarred mission-style coffee table in front of the fireplace; at one end of the room a wet bar tucked into a small alcove; at the other, by the curving windows that faced the canyon, a timeworn Bechstein grand. When it comes to furnishings, less is more. He didn't seem to be interested in whatever the room revealed about me. He was focusing on the walls and floors. Maybe he was an admirer of the fit and finish of impeccably crafted joinery; the color and grain of woods that are either nearly extinct or can only be found as biosynthetics. Or maybe he was just trying to see if he could spot my defensive systems.

There were three datablocs in the package. Two buff colored, the other chartreuse. It had a golden caduceus on its top that looked like it had been X'd out with black thermo-ink—somewhere in Paris there was a demonstrably unhappy psychiatrist.

What there was of the house's defenses settled down and I offered Thinh the other chair. He shook his head, and said, "This will be brief."

I shook my head back at him. "No, it won't."

It wasn't a contest of wills. I had too good an idea of how tough you have to be to hold the job he had. But he had come in person, he had been given marching orders, and he knew well who had given them to him. What is it in the Gallic character that makes their women so formidable?

He took off his charcoal gabardine topcoat, folding it across his lap even though it was wet, and sat down. He stared for a moment at the tentative flames licking at the logs in the fireplace and stretched his legs. "*Bien,* what do you want to know?" His words came out weary but not too impatient.

"First I have something for you. It's not completely concrete but it might be useful. A man named Warren Tyler runs a freelance gang of smugglers and thugs working out of Ventura County—that's the department north of L.A. He may have provided the first vector of transportation for the Erinyes group."

He looked up with interest. He may have seen me as one of those pilot fish, picking debris out of the shark's teeth, but he had read the dossier that his firm had assembled—the one that hung over me like a pendulum ax—and if they knew a little bit of truth about me, it was that I rarely gave the authorities anything, but when I did I didn't feed them *mierde.*

"Your government's agent in charge believes that they were aided by one of this city's crime syndicates."

I said something a little revealing that he could add to my file. "Arthur Cormac is an effective asshole, but he's got a mind that always seeks the most common denominator. If a Benevolence was involved they wouldn't put themselves right up near the firing line. Either before or after."

His dark eyes confirmed what the Padrino had told me about others asking for help. It wasn't his fault, he was obviously tired— so was I, but I had centered, readied myself, and when I'm ready, I don't betray. He pushed himself upright and took out a leather-covered pad. "Details?"

I reached over and closed its lid. "No details, no recordings."

Thinh took his instrument from under my hand. He said caustically, "And for you, details, recordings?"

I got up. "Yes, I'll want the second-level data, but I don't keep permanent records. I think that's fair enough seeing as I didn't ask for this gig. I'm not a soldier, I didn't volunteer, and I've never been a mercenary. I'm the bloody conscript, the specialist that WOTAN said had the right tools for the job—if it makes you feel better I think the damned machine was wrong too." I stopped and shifted my voice to a softer tone. "I just want to get back some privacy in my life and I want to help bring the woman home—don't you remember? That's the point of this miserable exercise. That matters. I'm sure you're doing the best you can. So am I. You read my file, you decide. I'm going to get something to drink, *un petit verre de vin.* Want some?"

He put his pad in the breast pocket of his coat. *"Oui."*

I planned to give him enough time to scan the living room with the instruments that he had stashed in his jacket and verify that there weren't any active overhears. While I uncorked a '31 Stony Hill—an austere wine, fitted the mood—and brought out some self-chill glasses, I thought how well I shaded my inflections during the brief soliloquy. Conviction is easy, convincing sincerity is hard. My mother would have been proud. Maybe.

When I returned to the living room Thinh was standing up and listening with a startled expression on his face. "What is that?"

From the arroyo behind the house there was a diminishing echo of a howl. E-flat, a key they like, and why they sound so lonely. "Just a coyote."

"A what?"

"A coyote." I pronounced the name the way I heard it growing up: ky-oht. "Sort of like a little wolf . . . in a sheepish kind of way." I could have sworn somebody pinched my ear hard—go away, *yayo.*

"A little wolf," Thinh repeated slowly.

"Actually the urban subspecies genetically has as much wild dog in as it does the original Canis latrans; they even look like feral Alsatians. But they're not a serious problem around here. They've got the excellent sense to stay out of harm's way." I put the tray on the table and sat down. "There's a saying among some of my people, that next to God the coyote is the smartest person on earth. Seeing how well they've done compared to everybody else, that may be true. Have a seat, Thinh. All the ones I've run into are tough hombres, but very shy."

He struggled with his embarrassment for a second, folding and refolding his coat. Then, with a stone-still face, sat back in the chair.

I brimmed our glasses with the wine, and he filled me in.

Not much luck on tracing the gang's movements after they took their hostage, excepting that, based on a handful of witness sightings of their original vehicles and an exhaustive analysis of all the monitored traffic flow, there was a moderately high probability that they had headed north, at least initially. Sounded reasonable. The counties immediately north of L.A. have a lousy grid infra-structure. Problems with funding, maintenance, and a lot of local anarcho-conservatives who delight in monkeywrenching the system, makes that span of the Californias from Big Sur down to Oxnard a happy zone for people who don't want others to know where they are and where they're going. And it was Tyler's home turf.

Cormac had sent a squad up to coordinate a search with the welter of police jurisdictions in that area. That was going to be slow, painstaking work, both in the search and getting the effective cooperation of the local cops. The lack of fraternal love between local, state, and federal law enforcers has been the salvation of many a criminal. The engineers have yet to isolate the gene cluster that produces politics.

A pleasant side note was how Thinh, in response to a delicately phrased question, described Cormac's and the South Bay police chief's barking confrontation with each other. The head of security for Groupe Touraine had an appreciation for the theater of the absurd.

There was a make on the original escape car and the motorcycle; the Koten limousine had been purchased for hard cash from the back lot of a Westside used car dealer (an only-in-L.A. kind of transaction). The ID given for registration was the kind you can buy from a clever fifteen-year-old on the street, convincing only to a salesperson anxious for a commission. If anybody human at the DMV had checked it would have held up like the proverbial wet tissue, but since the system didn't flag it for violations, why should anybody bother? The bike, a BMW-Honda, was stolen from outside a dance hall in northern Texas.

Thinh had discreetly contacted various enviro NGOs that might know something about the Erinyes. Apparently Groupe Touraine was as sensible a global corp as they come. Over the years it had tried to cultivate a frank if not friendly relationship with those that opposed it—not unlike the private dealings between America and Russia during the twentieth century. And some of the nongovs nowadays have almost as much clout as those old great dinosaurs. By the nature of the contacts his firm had, he was pretty sure that they wouldn't be taking the story to the world media—at least not until the deadline had passed.

The people he had spoken to were appalled by the kidnapping. Besides the heritage of nonviolence that runs through most of those organizations, kidnapping an executive was, hardheadedly, in their eyes a moronic no-win strategy. Notwithstanding that general good sense, I gathered from his voice that some of them had barely bothered to hide their gleeful sense of schadenfreude—there's nothing quite like the pleasure gotten from the discomfort of your foes. None had any information that was worth a damn.

Trying to get more details from and about the people who were at the Blue Azalea that night had been even more frustrating. The club management was willing to cooperate up a point—it was after all a major felony investigation—but only up to the point where it wouldn't compromise their business. They were already damaged by the fact that a kidnapping of a customer had occurred; revealing too much of what they knew about their patrons would be the kiss of death for the club. The management's ability to be stubborn was backed up by the might of those patrons.

A few, just a few, of those who had not been questioned on the night of the crime had come forward. However what they had to offer were only sense impressions. I thought that the investigators weren't weighing that information very seriously. I did. The chemistries enjoyed at a Flower club include some of the most effective perception enhancers available. I asked Thinh to offload those interviews for me. He glanced at me oddly and complied.

"How well do you know Siv Matthiessen?"

He pursed his lips. While he sorted out obligations about loyalty and instructions, I took my pad out and short-handed some guidelines of my own concerning the patron interviews.

"I know Mademoiselle Matthiessen well enough to say that those who try and typecast her are wasting their time."

"How so?"

He looked briefly at the fire before saying, "They see her beauty and intelligence, her position in Groupe Touraine, and her relationship with Madame President. And they make assumptions, mistaken ones. The stupid ones think her job is a sinecure—a place to conveniently park a lover." He snorted. "Neither Madame nor the young lady are fools. The smarter ones presume that she is simply a siren scheming to reach the top. The wiser ones, those that have felt her . . . her potency, expect that she has already achieved that goal. That she is the Richelieu of Groupe Touraine. What they all see is what they wish for themselves—their own fantasies projected. None of them see her for what she truly is."

"And that is?"

He silently held out his glass. I poured him some more wine. "You've read Vasari, yes, of course you must have. While your father was primarily an expert on the Hudson School, he did write that article that many consider to be one of the finest meditations on Varsari's writings. I understand that he saw it as, how do you Americans put it, 'a quick knockoff'? Impressive." I said nothing. He looked away from me and slowly tasted his wine. "Pardon, that was unnecessary. Let me start again. The work, the regular work you do—they say that one of the reasons you are good at it is that your knowledge of art isn't merely professionalism. That you care deeply. That it matters to you. Yes?"

"It does."

"Then imagine what it must have been like to be Giorgio Vasari. To have known Michelangelo, da Vinci, Raphael. To have lived in their midst, been in their company, been a friend . . . Did Vasari write about their hunger for power? That given what glory they had in their eyes and hands they would care about . . . If you wish to learn more about her I suggest that you use the files I brought."

Do you think that a chief of security wouldn't have read *The Lives of the Artists*? Couldn't have walked through cathedrals and galleries and been stunned by a greatness that can't be measured by wealth, knowledge, or by power? Then you're making the same sort of mistake that Paul Thinh had damned.

And if it was an act, then he was better than I was. There was sufficient finality in his last words that I didn't hesitate in returning to the police report.

The best, if not the most immediately consequential, news Thinh had was that they had identified one of the primary abductors. They got on to her largely thanks to Vassey—moribund though she was. They had retrieved a few threads of yarn and some cells from under the bodyguard's nails when she had briefly grappled with the other woman. The federales, doing what they were superlative at, had forensics run a makeup on the threads. As the media constantly tells us, one of the great advances of modern fabrication is the ability to profitably make micromini runs of differing products—mass production is becoming as quaint a term as workers' rights. What they usually don't mention is that most manufacturers automatically send a template sample of everything they make to police datacores. Makes it easy for lab smiths to find out where a particular item was bought or ordered from. In this case the curly silk threads came from a yarn called bouclé. It had been specified by a small Quebec fashion house. The jacket the woman was wearing was sold only by a few Montreal clothiers. They sent the DNA sample extracted from the cells to Quebec's Bureau de la Protection, and fortune struck. The Bureau had an established file keyed to her code. The folder on one Chloe Rogen had come in early this morning.

Rogen had made the kind of small, careless, mistake that solves more crimes than the cops like to publicly admit. Still, being imperfect doesn't always count.

Thinh got out his pad again and asked me for the room's frequency. I told him (recalibrating is easy), he linked; the big eighty-inch Soltan rolled out from its corner niche and positioned itself so we could both comfortably see the datastream.

The conspicuous points were highlighted and the synopis referenced: Subject was born Chloe Alis Rogen on June 10, Year Thirteen, at her mother's home in St. Jerome, Quebec. She is the daughter of Anne-Marie and David Rogen. Race is Euro-American and she is chromosomally female [REF102A: attached file of comparative genetic analysis between birth print and current sample shows only standard postnatal modifications]. Public Health records show her parents as legal cohabitants at time of birth. Her father works as a self-employed paralegal, her mother is a chapter chair for the Sane Society [REF217G: medium-sized nongovernmental specializing in providing alternative modes of mental care via community-based group homes. Political influence: mild. Subversive rating: very low.] Anne-Marie and David have no other surviving children.

Subject comes from a family of political activists. One of her grandfathers had been an American war resister that had fled to Canada. I glanced at Thinh to see if the tenuous connection between his past and hers had any impact on him; nothing showed. Subject's primary and secondary school records showed an excellent but not exceptional student, popular with her fellow students, somewhat less so among her human teachers; a little too much argumentativeness. She was on her secondary school's lacrosse team; worked part-time for two years at a local veterinary hospital, and briefly at one of the Sane Society's hospices [REF388C: attached note: unsubstantiated data, level 3 probability, that subject and an attending medication nurse engaged in unlawful drug experimentation].

Sometime during her adolescence subject began going rapidly through a string of lovers. Her lycée psych counselor noted that although the behavior pattern wasn't unusual for her age cohort, the numbers of lovers was high given the subject's macrocultural milieu: rural French Catholic. (I smiled. The counselor couldn't have been country-raised herself. City folk have no idea).

However, when subject went to college [REF719A: subject's track was nurse practitioner; list of courses, grades, and professors

appended. Successfully completed program in Year Thirty-three.],
subject got involved as a sophomore with a graduate student
named Valere Lavour and became monofocused. Lavour was a bio-
geologist, specializing in the tundra. [REF842B: dossier on Valere
Lavour is White: no significant data].

During the Easter break of subject's final term they went up-
country together on a vacation/field trip. Lavour had gone into the
town of Missirou apparently for some additional supplies when the
Grand Ney Dam collapsed. Her body was one of the several hundred that were eventually recovered.

Chloe Rogen was safely in their camp to the northeast when
the slaughter of the waters came to Missirou.

Subject returned to school, finished out the academic year,
then vanished.

The dossier was started four years ago on the subject when she
was identified by an informer as belonging to an ad hoc terrorist
band that kidnapped the long-retired head of the State Utility
Board, and then drowned him. Slowly. An arrest warrant was is-
sued, but as of this time there has been no apprehension of the
subject. The Bureau pour la Protection de la Constitution would
appreciate being informed of her whereabouts.

There was a graduation photo of her. Light brown hair,
medium blue eyes, a pretty twenty year old. Thinh waved his hand
like a showman; a second image came up. This was of a woman
some years older and very, very beautiful. A cascade of dark hair
and eyes like the finest emeralds. Too stunning to be natural. He
merged the pictures. You can do a lot with surgery, but you can do
more with an FBI differential graphic analyzer. It was the same
woman.

"I didn't think the clubs allowed anybody to take shots of their
guests."

"It was their mishap," he said, meaning the Erinyes, "that one
of your cinema's brighter stars had dropped by the club that
night." He continued, "As you would expect from someone who

would go so far as get a bodyplant, her friend is a photographer enamored of the spontaneous. The guard who was running the entrance scanners that night was willing to overlook the body camera the friend had. There isn't a satisfactory explanation as to why."

"Could be the guard was too embarrassed to admit that she's a fan of the star. Got blinded by the klieg light."

He pressed the palms of his hands down so hard on the arms of the rocker I thought he was going to crack the wood. "Whatever. Rogen and Matthiessen happened by when the photographer decided to take a shot of her friend dancing." He shrugged. "She couldn't resist capturing Rogen's face."

"Let me guess. The reason this data wasn't in the preliminary report was because the star's friend didn't want to reveal that she had sinned."

Thinh nodded dispassionately. "Besides her moral qualms, the star is supposed to be happily married to another."

"What made her come forward?"

"She didn't. After a day of reflection the club's entry guard informed us. The police contacted the photographer, and under the promise of confidentiality and immunity from prosecution, she agreed to release to them the photos she had taken that night. As for the guard, she was an off-duty sheriff's deputy. She has been dismissed from one job. I suspect she will soon find herself completely unemployed." He stopped and added coldly, "When you accept responsibility for others there is no acceptable margin for incompetence."

His anger wasn't only with the club. "I know."

The genie informed me that I had another visitor. I excused myself and answered the door. The courier from Holguin. Ten-oh-six P.M.— well, it was raining hard. I put Vlad's databloc in the study and went back to the living room.

We resumed the conversation, mostly from his side. I didn't

ask how his internal investigation as to how the *otriad*—Thinh also used the same term for the Furies as did Madame Fouchet—had obtained a copy of Matthiessen's personnel folder, and he didn't volunteer. I also decided not to tell him about the possible that Danny had gotten from the waitress; I wasn't sure why. What Thinh was willing to talk about were the tiny bits and pieces of data being strung together, the various avenues they were exploring, scenarios that were being simulated on both GT and the fed's part. As I suspected they would, they were still laboring on the straight-ahead approach. More perhaps because of Cormac's insistence than Thinh's preference, but he was handicapped by the fact that this wasn't Europe, where being chief of security for Groupe Touraine would have given him far more power and leeway in how the investigation would proceed. He didn't say so, but frustration was there in his hands and at the corners of his eyes. I tried a small test. "You know the best way to catch a wild horse? Build a fence around it."

"Vous avez raison, mais je n'ai pas le temps."

We were finished. I got an umbrella and walked him to his nondescript gray Ford. He still wasn't thrilled to have me involved, he had told me a few lies, but he said good-bye cordially enough. I watched him until he had safely made the first hairpin curve, the sulfurous street lights turning on and off as the car slid past them, then walked slowly back up the steps. He was right, there wasn't enough time to build a corral, but I didn't see any other way.

INTERLOGUE 2

MONDAY, OCTOBER 25TH

PATIENCE, ANTON REPEATED TO HIMSELF, patience. "They that wait upon the Lord shall renew their strength; they shall mount up with wings as eagles; they shall run, and not be weary; and they shall walk, and not be faint."

Calmer, he finished his coffee and raised a finger. He was sitting alone at an outside table of the café. Watching the Seine irritably lapping the edges of the reinforced embankment, wondering how much higher the river would go. Paris lived nowhere near as precariously as London, or as fatally as Amsterdam or Hamburg, but, despite the best efforts of the hydroengineers, twice in this decade alone the old center of the city had been flooded, the waters cresting four meters over the ancient streets. As he did every morning when he was in Paris, he wished the river *bon chance*.

The *garçon* came by with a fresh espresso, deftly marking with black chalk on the edge of his plate that it was his third cup. It then abruptly spun on its wheels and rolled away. The machine's mannered behavior amused him. Only the French would replace their waiters with robots and then program them to act as if they were human.

His contact was late. He dismissed the urge to look at his wristband. Instead he pondered the koan: "If fear is banished, where does it go?"

The woman finally arrived. Her head and shoulders were covered with a heavy fleece-lined cape and she was wearing across her face the opaque half veil that had recently become popular with some of the younger Europeans. It was supposed to be some sort of statement—what kind, he had no idea. Even though his persona was an artisan, the politics of fashion wasn't a subject that he could persuade himself for the sake of the role to be interested in. Still, as she made her way across the wet street he spent a moment wondering. It could be about privacy, or modesty, or gender impartiality—a sharp wind blew and winged out her cloak; underneath it she was wearing a clinging, thinly cut slip of a morning dress better suited for an intimate conversation in a boudoir than a public café. No, it wasn't about the latter two. He dropped a cube of brown sugar into his espresso. Then again, maybe it was. After spending so many days and nights with Teresa, a woman in fascinated denial of her sexuality, he thought he had come to a small understanding of how some women live with their contradictions.

"Hello, have you been waiting long?" She had a southern accent, Toulouse or perhaps Avignon. His was Walloon, the legacy of a Belgian nanny.

"No, not long."

She sat down and moved her chair so that she could see him and both sides of the street. She glanced at the markings on his saucer. Her eyes smiled at his little lie. "That is good. I am afraid I found waiting for me this morning some communiqués that had to be addressed immediately."

"I understand." The *garçon* returned. He could see the loathing in her light amber eyes as she gave the machine an order for a small cognac. He smiled and thought, "We are indeed strange bedfellows." Her people saw instruments such as the servitor as the great threat. His saw them only as mere extensions of the blight.

After it left, the woman took from her suede purse an eight-sided gold cylinder engraved with black-lined palmettes. She laid the tool beside her on the table and pushed sideways at its lid. There was an all but inaudible hum from the amulet. The café on the Quai de la Tournelle was popular with senior bureaucrats from the Ministry of Extra-European Affairs, and the management had invested in the best contrasurveillance and neutralizing equipment. Which was why—besides enjoying the allegory of the lion's den—he had chosen it as a meeting point. But a dose of extra precaution was always an excellent idea. He followed her lead; his fingertips touched tiny indentations on the engrailed wires embroidered into his jacket's shawl collar.

She rested her small manicured hands on the table, and said, "As a matter of fact, one of them involves you. I am informed that there was a small handling problem during a shipment transfer. The package wasn't securely wrapped up."

An incorrect use of the past tense. The trouble had occurred during the shift to the seaplane. Anton poured a tiny dollop of cream into his espresso, stirred, and took a sip. "I hope there wasn't any damage," he said as if he didn't know.

"The package got a little wet, but the carriers say that there wasn't any harm done. They tell me it is securely on its intended route."

Even if someone were able to listen in on their conversation, it would seem innocent. The woman was the licensed representative for a noted gem dealer; the brooch pin that held her cape together at her throat had tiny emeralds that picked out the logo of Handley et Frere. He was a lapidary with a select, appreciative clientele. They were talking about a legal if surreptitious business deal involving stones. They both worked in an industry known for circumspect speech—a deliberately selected convenience for both of them.

Matthiessen had tried to escape. Chloe was right to be suspicious of the drug's efficacy on the woman. Anton had worried about it too; the particular medication they were using wasn't very effective on him. He had never told the team that he was also a *beneficiary* of one of the major psychobiologicals. When he was a child of two he had been diagnosed as having Rashnoff's syndrome, a rare form of autism that wasn't then, or now, treatable by conventional gene therapies. His parents had taken him to Geneva and had him undergo what at the time was an experimental program. Turning him into a freak. Like they were turning all of God's creatures into. He wasn't a monster like Matthiessen—the effect on him had been milder. But he couldn't tell them. They would be understanding. Another word for pity.

"I'm glad to hear that; I am anxious to get to work on the stones," he said. "My client has been pressing me." He spread his fingers and curled them toward him. "One of those who have all the impatience that wealth can buy." Meaning: our mutual ally is anxious to receive their payment, the information that they believe Matthiessen holds in her beautiful but monstrous head.

Along with his fellow Furies he had deep misgivings about the bargain they had struck, but no modern guerrilla movement ever succeeded without outside help. And that help, particularly the intelligence provided, had been essential. But Erinyes also knew that believing the enemy of your enemy is your friend was a snare and a deadly lie.

Her cognac arrived. She waited until the servitor had gone away, daintily lifted up the bottom of her veil, and swallowed the brandy in one gulp. "And they always buy as much as they can. . . . You like to listen to music while you work, yes?" Anton nodded. She fished around in her purse and retrieved a planchet. "I have the latest by Damaris." Her voice took on a warm bubbly tone. "It is a prerelease; a friend of mine works in the maestro's studio."

Without expression, he took it from her hand. Her warm fingers lingered on his palm. Embedded within the music on the coin-sized disk would be additional material their ally wanted Anton to extract from the prisoner. A refined, if not foolproof, method of encryption. Decoding would involve doing various key changes—a pattern he had memorized. Anton had retained enough of his sense of humor to be amused by the joke. But he wasn't amused by receiving supplementary instructions. He didn't give a damn for the profits their backer wanted to gain out of the Erinyes' action. He laughed silently. He was the one who had to constantly remind the team that moral acts are still legitimate even if they do materially benefit the actors or their allies. He kept his hand on the table. Her nails drew lazy, meaningless circles on the fleshy pad, the mount of Venus, beneath his thumb. A warm shiver ran up his arm. It was a moment like this that in the end had tipped the balance when he had decided not to take vows.

"When you've finished the work may I see it before you deliver it to your client?" she asked sweetly.

He pulled his hand away. "I do not think you would care for it. I am creating the tiara in a chinoiserie style."

"I see."

He didn't know whether she was more displeased over his denying her group the information, or what she considered to be a blatant breach of security. The shadowy ally of their ally was not ever to be mentioned, however obliquely. He didn't really care. As much as he enjoyed her flirtation, it would only be that. Her group of desperate populists were of no importance. They were generations too late—and whether they admitted it or not, they knew that. It was the cause of their desperation, their despair. The greater part of the people, the masses, had been scourged enough by pestilence, war, famine, and death so that they had become numb to the coming real Apocalypse. As for the remainder, they had been seduced into indifference by a tenuous balance that they thought was salvation.

Her band wasn't going to change that—ineffectual Mensheviks, that is how his ancestors would have cursed them. But he didn't despise the masses either. They weren't the ones who had loosened the reins of the Four Horsemen. Who so cleverly hid the fate of the world with their patina of techno-management the same way an undertaker hides the ravages of death with wax and glue and paint from the bereaved. But those who had, those who hid, they were the ones who would be punished, forced to change. So that maybe, maybe, there would be a little bit of a true salvation finally for all of God's creatures.

He collected his thoughts and tried to ease the sting of his rebuff by saying, "That was not polite of me. I am sorry. But my client was very specific about not showing the piece to anyone else. I believe there is intent for it to be a present, a surprise anniversary gift."

"Yes. Clients must always come first."

He ignored the bitterness that coursed under the words like a stream of sulfuric acid. "If one wants to prosper, yes. When do you think I might be able to take delivery of the stones?"

"I am not positive. There may be a delay at Customs, but certainly within a day or so."

Forty-eight hours until he rejoined the team. There was a soft pang underneath his heart. In another life, another world, he would never have associated himself with them as individuals, but together, collectively, they were brethren, closer to him than his family ever was, and he missed them. Still, it would give him time to finish purchasing on the black market the ingredients necessary to culture the bacterion whose blueprint he had acquired a few days ago in Marrakech, the designer's paradise. Although he was only an amateur when it came to neurophysiology—and he had factored that along with humility into his analysis—he felt confident that however strangely kinked Matthiessen's peptides were, the microbes would find for them the right keys. The keys that would open her mind, her treasures.

He put the planchet in his billfold and removed a five-ecu note. In the distance, church bells pealed the hour of terce. He stood up, leaving the paper money sticking out from under his marked saucer. "Well, thank you for coming personally to tell me about my shipment."

She remained seated. "It was nothing," she replied glumly.

So it was his refusal to share data. He understood. "On the contrary. It was very reassuring."

She rolled the small tulip-shaped brandy glass around in her hands. "Oh, there was something else in the communiqués that I suppose I should tell you. Another buyer has expressed interest in the stones."

Anton sat down. "I have already paid for them."

Her veil didn't hide the pleased twist to her mouth. "That is understood, but this individual is very persistent."

"Do I know him?"

"I do not think so. He is a very private person. We ourselves believe that we know less than nothing about him. An enigma. From what I have heard that gap is true for most everybody in our field. However, since these are exceptional stones I made an effort this morning to find out how serious his interest might be." She shrugged very slightly and put her glass down. "My attempt was fruitless." She looked at the table and touched her amulet. "Whoever he is, he has a marvelous collection of nightingales."

The woman opposite him had a deserved reputation. A series of warning systems that were too difficult for her to slip past. Under the table Anton's hands tightened on his thighs. "Part of a syndicate?"

"As I said, he is an enigma. But no, I don't think so. . . ." She rested her cheek against the palm of her hand. "However . . . I was able to reach a friend of mine in Pamplona. He is a connoisseur of connoisseurs. He did know a little more than nothing."

He refused to get angry over the way she was teasing him. He had learned long ago that it was wise to let others have their small pleasures. "Yes?"

"My friend said that there are those who have a great deal of respect for him as a collector. A respect earned in no small part by his willingness to pay a special price for his purchases."

That was the second time she used a phrase that wasn't in the ordinary vocabulary of their public lives. This bit of information that she had withheld from him until the last moment was something she considered very significant. He took several long, slow breaths and then thought over carefully what she had said. A man who appears to operate alone. That was unlikely. Much more probable was that Touraine had contracted with an agency that was exceptionally good at keeping their operatives covered. A special price. A man who was willing to risk everything. The most dangerous kind of opponent, a man like the Furies.

He studied what he could see of her face; her brow, eyes, cheeks, the tiny flaring of her nostrils. She had something more about this man. Anton shifted his mind to a place where he could review events, plans, the time frame that had been so purposely selected, as if they were a virtual topographic map that he could run eyes and hands over.

Except for the difficulty during the transfer that she had told him about, there had been no mishaps—that worried him some; perfection can be a trap. But he couldn't see how the man, a fool, or a nightmare, could disrupt the action. The time frame had been constructed to handle unexpected variables. He returned his awareness to the café and smiled at the woman. For her there had only been a brief moment of silence between them. There were some advantages to being a freak. "Regardless of what he might offer, I have already paid for the gems."

"Yes, he made his bid too late. There should be no problem."

"Of course, no problem at all. But thank you for bringing it to my attention. I will mention to my client that it is getting a very desirable item." He stood up again.

"I expect that you are going back to work?"

She was asking whether he was going to require another meeting. His answer had only partly to do with the language of subterfuge. "Not right away. First I must go to mass."

CHAPTER FIFTEEN

GRABBED THE DATABLOCS THAT I had gotten from Thinh and Holguin—along with the half-empty wine bottle—and went upstairs to the bedroom that Kit had converted into a study.

I paused for a second at the doorway. There was a barrenness to the room. Kit had emptied out most of the shelves, cleared off her heart-of-pine secretary—I went over to it and rubbed my fingers over the soft pale gold wood. Richard, Leah's fiancé—a quiet, solid young man, he had held up well in the witness box under close cross-examination—had built it for Kit out of lumber he had salvaged from a two-hundred-year-old Maine farmhouse. Gone were the things that usually crowded its top: yellow paper pads; a scattered heap of pencils and various antique fountain pens; the crystal acorn paperweight that her father gave her as a going-away present when she came out West to attend Caltech; her aquamarine blue water pitcher and glass; the photo of me at the helm of *Shiloh,* grinning like a jackass, while we were running in a force-eight sea. Kit said I looked irresistible; I thought I looked terrified. At least she had taken the photo with her—unless of course she had shredded it and dropped it in the compost drum as she left. She's tidy that way.

What she had left behind was her rig, simply because it's too damn big. I had to take out a foot-thick wall to install it—a sweet job. Even so the machine fills up a third of the room's floor space. So far, she never left long enough to find a suitable place to put it, not to mention the expense her department would have installing a new hard-link cable. So I get custody.

(I could say that there are other motives for her leaving the rig behind, but I lack the thousand hours or so of a psych rotation to argue the point.)

Thinh's databloc had a red light over the port. I touched it and Madame Fouchet's voice said, "Before you left Monsieur Robie, what did we talk about?"

"About a Guarneri cello." The light changed to green. So Olivia Fouchet had faith that her conversations were private. I surely hoped she was right.

I fired up the rig, married it with NPI's jumbleplex, and loaded in Siv Matthiessen's files; I didn't have an ethical issue with using Kit's equipment, she had freely given me the keys to her kingdom. She may have complicated feelings about what I do, what she thinks she knows that I do. Even so, she's never lost her trust in me. I wasn't about to poke around in hers or anybody else's personal files, I was only going to use one of NPI's more arcane experimental programs.

Factors, figments, strategos, genies, Desks. For over a generation now we've been creating instruments that when properly tweaked can pass an as-if test, yet they still fail to resonate as being sentient, self-aware. A lack of intuitive reasoning, emotional insight, a tragic sense of time? Pick your rationalization.

One thing I'm sure of, despite Kit's best attempts, is that I don't understand the explanations as to why. If you want to know how come Mozart is too easy for children and too difficult for adults, the various ways that you can try to stop a gun from being pointed at you, why Joseph Mallord William Turner is the greatest painter of the last three hundred years, how to lie well under pressure, then I'm your man. But when it comes to the philosophical sciences, my mind drifts right off its mooring into a fugue state: psychologically and musically.

I suppose that's what I get for not going to college. Yet, despite the general failure, the ceaseless war between the intuitionalists and the epiphenomenologists—I do hear a few things before completely going out to sea—through unexpected avenues, acts of creation, there have been for brief periods of time entities that have grown into what's been called, for lack of a better term, a heartfelt consciousness. From those ephemeral experiences, hope sprang.

I don't have a clue when it comes to the metaprogram I was intending to borrow. Kit—innocently overestimating me—had laid out a few of the thematic underpinnings: The University of Florence's fifty-year investigation of artistic mentation; Wolfram's rules of evolving logic; the Edinburgh School's attempted resurrection of general semantics; Sonya Zetbegovic's work on topological wave structures, the final thesis she managed to finish while dying in a concentration camp; the personality template system that the University of Minnesota created for the State Department (and for our less public executioners of foreign policy); and a radical Ph.D. dissertation that an Israeli neurolinguist, Sara Ladri, wrote on notational rhythms and interpretative intuition—or to borrow someone else's words, why we seem to *over*hear poetry and music.

Kit told me that Ladri's study had originally been kindly but summarily rejected. Apparently her dissertation had strayed too close to a current black hole of cognitive study. Every field has its borders that young researchers are warned to stay away from, or risk never getting a career. It took the enlightened self-interest of the very important international consulting firm that the Israeli woman had joined after being jilted, to bring the possibilities of her research forcefully to the attention of the doyens in her field.

I had listened attentively. Read and reread the materials she had bookmarked. Some of it was beautiful, much of it was incomprehensible in how it could possibly lay a—I didn't get it.

Anyhow, from those conceptual backgrounds and much more—and with the implementation of some esoteric hardware that I don't even pretend to fathom—came offspring that could, sometimes, conjure up a psyche, an *entirety*. . . .

I was going to try and see if I could get Siv Matthiessen to help me find her.

How I can get access to one of the most shielded parts of the UCLA/NPI jumbleplex is a secret between Kit and me; it's going to stay that way.

The chance that someone might find out that I was utilizing the 'plex was slim. First off, Dr. Seferides has the privileges granted only to NPI's not quite official but very real core of elite. Second, they call it a jumbleplex for a good reason. Over the decades ambitious young researchers and engineers kept on throwing every exotic and/or interesting thing they could into the systems, until it grew so chaotically big that its admin no longer can monitor everything that goes on. From stories I have heard, it's a problem that has become endemic in the academic community. Rumor has it that Caltech's system makes this one look as organized as an accountant's wallet (Kit refused to confirm or deny, just looked at me with the sly corners of her lovely eyes and giggled—Techies.) About all the sys can do effectively is maintain a *cordon sanitaire* around each part so that the whole doesn't become infected—some lessons are learned.

Actually, I should give Kit the credit for my plan. Three years ago I was the negotiator for the ransom of Davila's *Tolerance*. The Browne Museum had called me in when the thief, a man named Alan Labensohn, said he would only talk to me. We had done business before—Labensohn was a man devoted to his vocation; he thought I appreciated that. It was tough. Labensohn was very erratic and had wired explosives to the sculpture. One mistake in judgment and two hundred marble pounds of a masterpiece would be powder. His financial demands were far beyond the capacity of the museum to satisfy, and his additional requirement that they burn all the Degas pastels they owned was insane—he wanted the drawings destroyed not because they were by Degas but because they were of ballet dancers. Go ahead and envision dealing with that bit of logic. He wasn't the most irrational person I've dealt with, but he ranked up there on the bizarre scale. Twelve days of talks and I was getting nowhere. I offered to try to steal it back, but the Browne was too scared to go for it. Called Kit and told her that I was getting ready to quit. That shocked her into suggesting that I might try rehearsing my conversations with Labensohn, practice a little psychic judo. And then she told me about the NPI entirety program. After making a crack about holodecks that she didn't get, I agreed to give it a shot. Through the museum's very brahmin board of directors and the Chicago police's Fine Art Squad, I was able to get a lifetime's worth of files on Labensohn—he had voluntarily spent unsuccessful years in and out of various psychiatric hospitals, and some involuntary ones in prison.

Despite her training, she was a little disappointed when Alan Labensohn turned out to be not some glamorous dashing cat burglar but a confused, somewhat dull-witted, pathetic little man who simply had some luck and a small talent at evading museum security systems—an idiot savant of theft. Like most cits, she used to live under the influence of a century's worth of bad and worse movies. That truth—with very few exceptions—is that criminals are banal, stupid, brutal. People that I have spent far too much time with. One of the not so minor reasons I didn't tell her much about any of my work; one brooder per household is enough.

At any rate, what we got wasn't really the man, but it was essentially close. Working with the persona seemed to do the trick. For a few thousand dollars and the promise not to chase him, the Browne got back its treasured Davila—they found it under a pile of pig manure on a Wisconsin back road. The Fine Art Squad caught up with Labensohn a few weeks later.

Not with my assistance.

The rig–plex interface would take a number of hours; how

many was variable, but generally less than twenty, as the metaprogram evolves its gnostic circuits—Kit swore those are the proper technical terms. Theological engineering; why not? It suits the age—and then builds a personality around the schema of a life. In addition to the huge amount of detailed information in the blocs— Lorca's children are carefully observed, and anyone who is close to the center of power is watched—I entered some specific impressions of Siv that I had culled from witness statements given by the patrons of the Blue Azalea. Finally, I worked with a playwright sub, creating a fiction that would be securely embedded in the entirety's memory; a story that would explain to it why it was sitting in a strange room talking to a strange man. We settled on a post-break interview; the playwright's editor found a history of two previous events that Matthiessen had experienced during her late teens. I would be an L.A. clinical specialist in transient psychic traumas. Matthiessen's well-being was a high priority for Groupe Touraine. And it was a role I figured I could handle.

While I waited for a confirmation that the first-level integration was successful—the program's quirky as well as unstable—I activated Holguin's databloc.

"Really, Robie, a handwritten message? Besides being absurdly archaic, isn't it a bit unhealthy, passed from hand to hand? I do not wish to even discuss the bacterial swamp that constitutes the paper cash that you wanted me to give to the driver. Happily, Jordan was present and she was willing to deal with the situation. By the way, since you are so fond of the antiquated, I shall say that you've made yourself a conquest there. She could hardly contain her interest in you, asking all sorts of barely proper questions. Don't be concerned, I fed her your favorite lies."

He stopped to open an enameled, mother-of-pearl box and do a pinch of black snuff. "Since the information you requested was so ancillary I have decided not to charge you for the service."

That was Vladimir, courage in the remote. He rubbed his right nostril vigorously and continued. "Acts of sabotage: There has been only a little preliminary work started on the Congo Basin Project itself; it has taken almost a decade of survey and analysis for the consortium to even design the enterprise. Therefore opportunities for dislocation have been few. During the past ten years some of the key personnel involved in the blueprint phase of the project were either hired away by other companies, or suffered fatal, or near fatal, accidents. No apparent pattern, and the numbers were not too far off the statistical norm. Unless the project heads had other suspicious evidence I would suspect that they didn't make much of it, although the effect was to delay the work for up to six months. However, my instrumentalities are more finely tuned; there is a 59.25 percent chance that a systematic attack is going on. A rather skillful attack   in spite of my best efforts I was not able to discern the motive. I am sorry. You know, Robie, I do try my best even with lightweight requests." Holguin actually managed to sound apologetic: hurt professional pride.

"I do have something more concrete. Early this year an almost completed specialty steel mill outside of Bangui, the capital of the Ubangi-Shari Republic, was wrecked by a series of massive explosions—perhaps you scanned it. The steel mill was being built expressly for the purpose of providing materials for the Congo Project. The authorities blamed it on a radical fringe element of the Miners Union. The government made some arrests, followed by the usual lockstep convictions.

"I examined the government's case. Although the people they arrested appear to be quite guilty, their investigators had brushed aside the problem of where the saboteurs had acquired the explosives. An inventory taken of the regional mining companies showed an insufficient amount of missing dynamite. Fortunately, there was an accessible record of all the raw evidence gathered at the site of the destroyed mill. A trace of a chemical compound had been detected at some of the initial blast points. It didn't fit any known explosive or combustible and was dismissed as a sensor error. I ran the structural formula through one of my libraries and found that a South African company used a very similar isomer in the explosives that they had developed in-house. They do not sell that product to anyone else. Provocative, both in light of what I found out later, and in the failure of the Ubangi police investigators to discover what I was rather easily able to."

I froze the lecture for a moment and bought myself a little time by pouring some more chardonnay. Don't trust anything unless you hear it at least twice. Holguin was giving me a confirmation that I wished he hadn't.

I felt a dull twinge in my side and cursed. I summoned the phone and called Eddie Yamada. Her house told me that she wasn't available. Since we weren't close enough for me to know her override, I had to settle for giving her genie a high-priority note saying that she should immediately stop making inquiries for me—she would be paid anyway. Eddie doesn't take foolish risks, but someone like Warren Tyler who had been running guns—and sinners tend to retrace their footsteps—and was now into drugs, was far too dangerous for her.

I was cold angry with myself for not calling the moment I got the input from my figment. I'm not supposed to make that kind of mistake. I've been at this sort of thing for almost thirty years. I was tired. There were complexities running around my head, but those things had never in the past clouded my judgment of a situation. That's what earns my goddamn keep. Judgment and reflexes. I was furious, but I wouldn't, couldn't, let myself give in to it. I took slow breaths until I could count my pulse going back down to a steady fifty beats. All right, maybe the anti-T shot I took had a mildly dopey side effect that I hadn't noticed, maybe my subconscious mentation had worked out that there was less jeopardy to Eddie than I was certain of at that moment. I would figure out my error later.

I turned Holguin back on. "Some other damaging events have occurred. Those are difficult to assess as being acts of sabotage or simply the kinds of accidents always attendant with a large engineering project. I can attempt a richer analysis if you wish, though I will certainly require more time."

He shrugged under his cashmere shawl and took a sip of water. "Parties that might desire the failure of the Congo Basin Project. That, Robie, is a truly open-ended question. After some thought about the vectors you seem to be curious about, I decided to limit my artistry to those that have an immediate relationship with Equatorial Africa and then to only those organizations that have the potential capacity to injure the Project to the degree I believe you would find interesting."

Would find interesting. Holguin, why do you so want to impress me? I know you are a wizard, one of the best of the digerati. I'm sorry, but I don't think you can ever make me believe that you're a man.

"I started with the nongovernmentals. I eliminated those who are overtly enviro. That left over five hundred NGOs, domestic and foreign, that are involved in the region and have an active interest in the success or failure of the Congo Basin Project. However most, eighty-six percent, dance to the tune played by the Global Association for the Preservation of Natural Resources, the GAPNR." Yes, Vlad, like approximately 78.9 percent of the human race I know about GAPNR—oh, cut it out, Robie, you were taught better than to mock the pathetic. And for all you know, his precision is justified. Your life may seem to dance on the edge of chaos, that doesn't mean that everything else has to.

"Principally because their African branch has the most money and influence on the continent, also because it has the probity of Caesar's wife, the Congo consortium wisely labored hard to win GAPNR approval." He started to go into the intricacies of the relationship of NGOs and the political economy of Africa. I thumbed the fast-forward switch. ". . . the remainder of the NGOs fall into three groups, those who firmly adhere to nonviolence, those whose status in the region is fragile and would therefore be unwilling to jeopardize their own projects, and those that mistrust any government enterprise and feel that while Caesar's wife may have been the essence of virtue, she still slept in Caesar's bed." He smirked briefly at his own wit. "The latter might have the will, but their prejudices make them terribly inefficient.

"While all of them undoubtedly have individual members who are significantly unhappy with the Congo Project, as possible organizers of sabotage I found them to be low-probability candidates.

"Regional politics: the Equatorial African Community currently enjoys the system of authoritarian democracy, similar in many aspects to that practiced under de Gaulle in France during the middle of the last century, by Mexico for nearly a hundred years after the revolution, or by—" I fast forwarded again.

"Nguza Karumi, the former presiding president who initiated the contract between his Community and Groupe Touraine, endeavored to see that the numerous sectors of his ruling party would be satisfied. Karumi's efforts were considered successful, at least publicly. In private, a number of concerns are still being unhappily voiced, most strongly by the region's newly rising industrial barons, who object to the degree of economic penetration they see that the outsiders will be allowed. Their arguments have some sympathy; even without any secret codicils to the agreement, the Europeans will get tremendous access to what has been a fairly closed market. But their cry of recolonization, dredging up the horrors of an earlier era, seems to have little impact on the cadre of decision makers who are fully aware that their citizenry's hunger for some prosperity is powerful enough to have forced the creation of the Community and might well be strong enough to replace its leadership. Besides, they knew that what those industrialists really wanted was time to build their budding business empires into the kinds of massive cartels that effectively run the economies of their southern neighbors.

"At least five of those barons have a secretive relationship with the MacKenzie-Rao combine, which owns the company that manufactured the explosive that the miners used to blow up the mill that Groupe Touraine built."

I applauded silently. Congratulations, Vladimir. I sighed, and put my wineglass very gently down on the secretary. I instructed the pad to extract from the remainder of Holguin's lecture the data he had obtained detailing the relationship between MacRao, as most people who know the company call it, and their Equatorial African novitiates.

The rain was drumming a tattoo against the leaded window. I went over and opened it, cupped my hands until they filled with water, and washed my face.

CHAPTER SIXTEEN

I INSTRUCTED THE PHONE TO call Eddie every ninety minutes until she became available, and went back downstairs. Got a fresh bottle of chardonnay from the wine closet and headed for the living room. Lifted the top of the Bechstein on the short stick and sat down at the keyboard. I needed a little music—my mother used to say that life would be a lot easier if there was a soundtrack to cue us. She was right. The way I was feeling, Jessie would be a little too overwhelming. Fortunately, she's willing to forgive my indiscretions with a piano.

My hands went where they wanted to, drifting along for a while, floating over keys until they found a complicated knuckle-busting sequence of sevenths. I stayed with it as long as I could, then crashed into a reef of chords. Not pretty, but pretty good.

I rested my hands and considered the economy of Africa. By no stretch would I call myself an authority on the real workings of the New Randlords, the label tagged on the Southern Africa combines by the media. Yet the involvement of one of them in a kidnapping didn't feel right. There's a prevalent fantasy that the great corporations routinely behave much the same way governments do, i.e, engage in premeditated covert violence against their peers.

From my unpleasantly not so limited encounters, that isn't how they usually play their politics.

Violence, wealth, and information. The first is effective, but limited, and has great potential of incurring negative feedback—a fancy way to describe the old adage about living and dying by the sword. Money and knowledge are both safer, and in the end more compelling. The men and women who run the world's great businesses have all been indoctrinated since childhood in the twin disciplines of risk management and cost/benefit analysis—not much of a substitute for a code of ethics, but it keeps them wise enough to stay away from the killing fields.

Usually. The exceptions come when they get desperate or crazy. The Randlords are far from being in dire straits. For almost two hundred years they've enjoyed the kind of success and influence that most of the other globals couldn't even begin to dream of.

At one time the largest of the Randlords, the Anglo-American Corporation, by itself accounted for 16 percent of the old Union of South Africa's gross domestic economy; over half of the companies traded on the Johannesburg Exchange were controlled by Anglo-American. Altogether, that one combine alone ran over thirteen hundred good-sized companies. When Mandela was released from years of imprisonment, among the very first white men that he wanted to see was the head of the AAC.

Through apartheid, postapartheid, civil conflict, and Gaia's convulsions, Anglo-American and its smaller cousins—originally five all told, later the list grew to nine—were careful to only use the golden velvet glove.

In some respects they are international paragons: thoroughly multiracial, minimalist corporate bureaucracy, fair if not generous employers. From pariahs to role models, a remarkable achievement. But that glove maintains a tight grip on the economies of the dozen member states of Southern Africa. Like any honest capitalist, the Randlords believe that monopoly is the best of all possible worlds—and woe to those who challenge that belief.

I didn't have to consult the *Times* for details on MacKenzie-Rao. My interest in them came from two old loves.

MacRao controls Assagai Transport, the company that builds and operates a good deal of the private space fleet; they also own the largest stake in the solar power station that provides energy to the cislunar factories. When I was a kid there was a time when I thought that the best job in the world was being an Assagai pilot. I grew older, and vectors changed. Still, a company that puts aside 5 percent of their net profits for pure space science was one that I had a soft spot for.

The other love gave me a more sober perspective.

In an interregnum between my lives, I spent a summer on a hiking tour of the western Pyrenees, looking up distant relatives, practicing my rusty Basque, searching for a way out of the labyrinth I had constructed inside of me. On a climb I met a woman dangerously stuck underneath an overhang. I helped her make it past the rock, and she helped herself to me. Chenna.

She wasn't beautiful. She didn't have a brilliant mind. She had no particular genius or talent.

I won't lie and say that those things don't matter. Except sometimes they don't.

She first told me simply that she was from Bangalore. Then as our nights, and lives, slipped into each other, I learned that on her mother's side she was closely descended from the rulers of Mysore, once and now again one of the largest princely states of India. Her family and MacKenzie-Rao had long been allies in business together—Bangalore is the principal aerospace manufacturing center for south Asia. For her family that alliance was of critical importance. And so, when the offer came, despite the caste differences, there wasn't any hesitation. They married her to a Rao. They weren't cruel, they did ask her. But she was Chennamma Nayaka, the namesaked many-times great-granddaughter of a woman who was as great a poet as she was a queen. Romance and duty, the worst mix. And beyond the burden of a name there were the simple facts: she was twenty-four years old, with sisters younger and older all married and as far as she could know, happy with their husbands, their children, their lives.

She said there had been a few miracles. The son who got her spirit and not her husband's, and that she had been able to see, before it was too late, the bars that kept out the light. After a twenty-year war in which she had only one trump, that she was the mother of one of the principal heirs, she had finally won the right to have for the first time in her life a ration of freedom.

I added to that allowance by giving her the pleasure of living for a while without the pack of watchdogs that MacRao had surrounded her with.

We shared with each other the tricks that prisoners learn in order to stay sane. She was delighted at how easily I managed to get her a false passport. She would gently, amusingly, correct my English grammar (I can entrust my heart, but not my life—and she never asked me to). I taught her how the night could be a joyful promise, not a dutiful sacrifice. She taught me little of what I didn't already know, only what men and women can always teach each other: the importance of paying fierce attention to the fragile notes of life, and the consequence of failing to do so. . . .

The gifts we give.

Passion fades, memory doesn't. I miss her face. The smell of her skin. The sweet puzzle lines that formed between her brows when she didn't understand me—which wasn't very often. The clear clean excitement in her eyes as we traveled and climbed from the Pyrenees to the Carpathians and then down to the Balkan crags. Places where we were strangers, or if not, where I knew a priest; a scholar; an old man with a number tattooed on the inside of his lower lip; a lonely artist; a farmer whose son lived with him with a body that was once crippled and whose soul was healing. Places where any other strangers would be noted, where they would be talked about, where I would hear.

Just before they were able to find her, she went back. We knew she would. We were lovers. We weren't children. The morning she had to leave she wrapped herself for the first time in a sari that hovered like sea mist between blue and white, and held for a long time my right hand against her heart.

"You are my last miracle."

"That's the first cruel thing you've said."

"I know. But I don't believe in mercy."

I see the tears that refuse to move from her eyes. "Neither do I."

She takes my hand away and twines our fingers together "Liar."

We haven't seen or talked to each other since. We won't.

About the corporate workings of MacRao I learned from my time with Chennamma only a little more than what any news Well can provide. Even if MacRao wasn't a part of a present she wanted to forget, she had the deep, abiding discretion of her place and class. Still, I got a whispery hint, as much from what she didn't say as from what she did, of what it is like living at the frozen apex of power.

What anybody can know: MacKenzie-Rao was one of the newer cartels. Prior to the nineties, the partnership of Vishwanath Rao and Theodore MacKenzie would have been both illegal and unthinkable. Two geniuses, one in aeronautical engineering, the other in finance. Together, against anybody's odds, they built an aerospace company to rival Boeing, Eurobus, and SkyNippon. (In a way MacRao was the counterpart of Groupe Touraine, relative newcomers that had achieved astonishing results in their provinces.) And they went further, emulating the vertical integration of the other Randlords, through purchase and cutthroat competition, they created the largest air carrier in all of Africa, and one of the biggest in the world. Then, down the chain of production, they took over most of their subcontractors, the manufacturers of speciality materials, the mines that produced the critical ores needed for modern aircraft. There was also the fourth-largest private bank on the Indian subcontinent—the Nayakas were the next biggest stockholders; the third largest insurance group in Australia; the company that maintains most of the software for air-traffic control in the world, and so on. Not quite thirteen hundred companies, but not far from it. And all of it brilliantly done while using manners better than any British aristocrat—and the determined ruthlessness of a mogul.

With my left hand I ran chords up through the sharps. Anglo-American had its wellspring in the gold fields, MacKenzie-Rao had its from a gamble: they provided the venture capital for the company that developed the first geomagnetic drives. MacRao holds 27 percent of the patent rights.

The JPL grant, Matthiessen's section. If the research that Groupe Touraine was financing leads to a way around that curtain wall of patents then MacRao could find its cash cow as dried up as the Kansas desert.

A blizzard of lawsuits, industrial espionage, bribery, those tactics were the kind of response you'd expect, but kidnapping? For all the reasons I knew, and more, that was too risky for them, too stupid.

Unless . . . There might be an untethered piece of MacRao. The combine was certainly big enough for a part of it to have stepped over the edge without the family board noticing. Corporate schizophrenia. Desperate or crazy, I would bet on the latter.

That possibility, even with all the assumptions that were hooked on to it, actually cheered me up. You've been in a great mood, Robie, when the idea that you might have to rub up against a variant of Midas lifts your spirits.

This is not how it's supposed to go. The words of the Tao chided me; I was guilty of trying to understand running water by catching it in a bucket. I was looking for specifics, while what the piano—or some reaction of my subconscious to the attempt to make music—was providing me was an informed dissonance. A gentle, strophic prod toward swimming in new streams. I eased myself into deep waters, and focused without focusing.

Hard work.

It was four o'clock when I found something I wanted. A pattern that showed a way to build a piece of a fence. I needed some tools and lumber and then all I would have to do is persuade Olivia Fouchet to spend a lot of money. Easy.

I stood and stretched up on my tiptoes. Felt sated, the way I do when Jessie and I manage to come together, when she's no longer lacquered wood and strings, but as much of me as my skin.

Jessie, it was her time. I started to get her when the phone told me that it had connected with Eddie Yamada.

Her voice was whispery, "Babe, I've got a B-and-E in progress at my office."

"You there?"

"No, I'm home, I'm monitoring it on my rig. They just got through the first security level; they think they're clean. Listen, one of them actually said out loud, 'I'm in, Ty.'—what jerks— looks like your message was a little late." She sounded more tickled by the burglary than pissed.

"Called the cops?"

She shook her head. "Just about to. I thought I'd let you know first in case they were working on your office, too."

I was going to have to withdraw, temporarily, my gift to Thinh. I owed Eddie what I tried to do for Jason Nancarrow. And since he insisted on being nosy, I wanted to get some answers of my own from Warren Tyler. Sometimes you can pick and choose your targets, sometimes they choose you. "If they are they'll be wasting their time. Eddie, don't call the cops, I'll handle it."

She stopped sounding amused. "Don't be a stupid cock, this is what I pay taxes for."

I was changing into my sweater and jeans. "Taxes won't protect you. These guys smuggle for a living. They've got to have at least one lookout and a fast getaway. They may be inept burglars. That doesn't mean they're lousy coyotes. They've made you. And they're anxious. If the cops don't get them, the next thing they'll ransack won't be your office, it'll be your body—and after you tell them what they want to hear, they'll be coming for my hide."

Eddie had the good sense to believe me and to be afraid. "I don't want you to chance it. Let the cops chase them. We can get protection. Babe, my second level is telling me that there are three of them in the office."

I was downstairs opening the vault. "Come on, Eddie, you know better. Even the best protection's no guarantee, and anyway that's not a life worth living."

Her words came back sharp as a nail. "I've never asked for guarantees and living with the memory of a dead beau won't be much fun either."

I stopped by the front door. "All right. Let me put it this way. We've climbed together. Think about it. How often have you seen me back off?"

"Plenty of times when you thought you couldn't—you're telling me you're sure you can."

I heard the skepticism. Eddie and I have slept together. Occasionally we share a climb. She likes the fact that I made the time to teach her how to play stride piano. She's aware of what Kit means to me. She knows how I make my living, and that I've got an undue familiarity with the crime spectrum. She thinks we're friends. She doesn't know one important thing about me.

"I'll have help. And . . . let's just say that I'm a lot worse than my reputation."

CHAPTER SEVENTEEN

RELINKED WITH EDDIE IN THE truck. "Details."

Her voice was taut. "Like I said, babe, there're three of them in the suite. Two are in my inner office, one's in the wait room."

I instructed the Cruiser to take the fastest route to the road that leads to Eddie's office building. "How are you reading them?"

"Thermals and motions off the third level. I killed the over-hears as soon as they breached the first—I thought that live mikes would be a giveaway that they had screwed up."

"Good move. They're still searching for the second?"

"Yep—I guess they're not total jerks—and they're going to find it. But the third's pretty well hidden." She allowed herself a dry chuckle. "I'm not sure I could find it and I did the installation myself."

"Once they have number two down, how long before they can break into your files?"

"Even with a clumsy smith, twenty minutes tops. Gav, they took ten to find and get through the first, the next should take them about the same, maybe a little longer—that gives you thirty minutes or so before they're out the door, which I guess isn't where you want to meet them."

She may never have worked as a control before, but for an amateur she was quick. And right. I told the truck to ignore the speed limit.

Eddie's business suite is located in a three-story Italianate. Some architect's impoverished idea of what the Medicis would use for their offices if their game had been moviemaking and not loan-sharking. It's just over the hills from my house. Right by the Forest Lawn Cemetery and the complex of movie studios the players call CinCity. When Eddie moved there from her old digs in Culver, she joked that she was going to the dead end of imagination. Although a lot of her courier business comes from the industry, Eddie doesn't have much respect for those clients—I had passed on to her Sulinn's nickname for film execs . . . corpses. She thought it was about as apt as it was funny. While the truck swayed around the corners and I went over my options, part of me was hoping that when the sun came up that description wouldn't literally apply to yours truly. Not a lack of confidence, just the certainty that there was always the chance.

Practice helps the odds, and that was also one of the reasons I was going. I don't have the facilities—real or virtual—of Quantico that the FBI's Hostage Rescue Teams enjoy. If the Erinyes were as good as I figured them to be—and as stubborn about letting Matthiessen go as I suspected—then I was going to need all the damn exercise I could get.

I asked Eddie, "Has your landlord improved the building's security system?"

"Nope, it's got the same biometric locks on the front and rear gates. Just the minimum insurance requirements."

Retinal scanners, as Danny and I had discussed ages ago, are no longer difficult to get past, if you've got the desire and the money. To be fair to the owner, Eddie's the only occupant of the building that had any need for additional protection, and he had been willing to subtract from her rent her cost in putting in the suite's security system.

I thought about how I would get in.

The building is constructed around a cobblestone inner courtyard. Eddie's office is on the second floor, west wing. Once you get past the gates, there are ordinary elevators and stairs that lead up to the colonnaded walkways that line the inside of the building. Someone posted on the walkway could see anybody entering the building. However, the stairwell on the northeast corner goes up to a little open tower, and the door at the top only has an electro-mechanical lock. Okay, assume some professionalism. Say two lookouts, one to spot trouble coming from outside, one on the walkway. A getaway car in the alley behind the building with a driver and a backup. I could reach the roof without the car seeing me or the guy watching the courtyard—Eddie and I had done it a couple of times for her idea of fun. What about the outside spotters?

I called up the Thomas Bros. mapbase. The display gave an excellent three-dimensional view of the area. Her building was freestanding, sixty-foot meadows on each side covered with mossy Korean bluegrass—not the easiest surface to run on, but a hell of a lot better than the vegetation called ice plant. The other structures on the curving block were depicted as also being office buildings of similar design—but several stories higher. Good, along with it being exposed, that meant that the mock watchtower would be a poor vantage point. Across the street on the northwest corner was a fuel station, a good place to park a bike and watch. From the pumps you could see almost all of the road going down the hill—the route the police would take if they dispatched a vehicle. Considering that up the hill were only the indifferent dead, the odds were low that a patrol car would come from that direction. I rerouted the truck.

"Gav?"

"Sorry, I was thinking. How are they doing?"

"Still working to find the second."

"What did you learn about Warren Tyler and company?"

"And I thought I was going to make you a happy puppy when I got around to calling you this morning. Oh, well . . . My sources in Oxnard knew a fair amount about Tyler and were only too happy to offload. He's not a popular cock. You were right about the drugs. He's a wholesaler for a crowd of small-time operators along the central coast. Tyler's pretty marginal himself; his outfit's got no more than eight or so members. I was told that he's ambitious, but frustrated; he doesn't have enough capital to expand. He's supposed to be smart, claims he went to New Stanford. Anyway he likes to hang around what passes for intelligentsia in Ventura. They probably think he's some street-tough poet, that kind of mix of rough muscle and sensitivity turns some people on. Oops, no offense."

There was something approximating a smile on my face. "I didn't know you thought of me as rough muscle."

"If you weren't, would you be going to my office? You can be as sweetly polished as they come, but I've had my hands on your back, babe. I may have been distracted, but I felt those nasty scars. Didn't think they were just tribal decor."

Maybe she does know a damn thing about me. "What else did you find out?"

"According to my sources—mierda, I'd love to know who ratted on me—during the last couple of months Tyler's boys started spending more cash than usual for them, buying toys for their bikes, hitting on some of the more expensive working girls, that sort of stuff."

"Any word on whether he's been moving people as well as skag?"

"There was something about him being recently involved in smuggling illegals in, but that doesn't make much sense. At his level there's no profit unless you move numbers, and there's too much guard-monitored traffic off the coast where Tyler works. It's not a great entry point for heavy cargo."

Not if the cargo wasn't bulky; a handful of people in and out.

Outlaws, not illegals. Use somebody experienced in moving merchandise, but with no rep in moving the human kind. A clever touch.

Eight or so. Three inside and then add the support troops. It was a good guess that he had committed most, if not all, of his crew to this gig. Until that point I hadn't been sure that he was actually on the scene himself, but you don't send that many for a simple burglary and you don't—not if you're planning on holding their respect—send an invasion force without going yourself.

On a straightaway the truck swung narrowly past an early-bird shuttle for the Burbank heliport. One of the pinstriped passengers flipped me the finger. It would be one of those lovely backspins the universe is so fond of if the supposed good guy got himself into an accident before he could do any good. I kept a closer eye on the road while I asked Eddie about the layout of her office and the building, going over the precise location of everything, whether there had been any changes during the last few months. As she spoke she periodically updated me on the progress of the break-in. It took a little under fifteen minutes to arrive at the point where I would go in on foot.

"Do you want me to try and put some roadblocks in their way?"

"No, if I were their smith I would be keeping a sharp eye out for a dataleak. Sending-in would increase his chances of finding your seam."

Speaking of communications, I put a bud phone in my ear—I've had too much nonelective surgery to want to voluntarily go under the scalpel just for the benefits of a cochlear comlink—and tuned it to the Cruiser. Eddie's voice came in clear and plaintive. "What about your chances?"

"Well," I drawled, "I guess I'd rate it a five-four on difficulty." I parked and put on my work belt. As I slipped out of the truck I attempted to reassure her one last time. Being a control is the worst job there is and I needed her to be focused. The bud is very sensi-

tive to bone vibrations. I could speak below a whisper. I said with
as much conviction as I could project: "Damn it, Eddie, I wouldn't
begin to try this if I thought the prospect of success was low. Remember, I don't pick places to stand unless I like the footing."

Silence for a second, then, "Okay. You want me to tell you if
any of the three leave the office?"

"You got it. Unless that happens, don't speak until I do." I took
quick breaths, oxygenating my blood. The cool air smelled wet and
green. It reminded me there were reasons to be alive. I squatted,
pulled a balaclava over my head, got on a pair of superfine gloves,
rubbed crystal chalk on my cold palms, and looked through a
night scope at my target. Nobody in the tower. The rangefinder
gave me eighty yards. Then a forty-five foot wall with plenty of
handholds. The crux of the climb was going to be getting over the
eaves. I moved.

Four minutes. The hardest part turned out to be the roof itself.
Rain had made it treacherous. I slipped and started rolling off the
eaves. Jammed a hand hard into a gap between an overlapping row
of tiles and hung on, my feet pushing against air. If I were thinking, I would have cursed the ironic stupidity. Instead I pulled myself up and crawled to the tower.

It had been an almost noiseless stupidity, thanks to a gyro with
a faulty muffler that had flown by on its way to the Burbank 'port.
A piece of semiluck; heard it coming. I waited a few seconds, listening to the night. Quiet. Eddie didn't call. The lock looked easy,
but I was still careful on how I picked it—learned that rule from a
guy doing ten to whenever in a Bolivian jail.

I was inside the stairwell. Time to make a decision. Intuition
and experience said that if they had an inside watcher he was on
the west side; the two gates to the outside are the north and south,
the stairs and elevator on the east, west was the best spot. The
question was which floor? The third was least likely; worst line of
sight. The ground floor had the advantage of allowing for a quick
escape via the back gate, the second put him close to the rest of the

crew. What was he into, fight or flight? I remembered how Jammer had gone after me, that Tyler had been sent to Grover Bay Prison because he was constantly making trouble.

Got to the second floor landing, went past it and sprayed superslick on the descending steps. Went down on my belly and wriggled my way onto the walkway. The walkways have a solid four-foot balustrade. Made it to the railing, willed myself to be invisible, and followed it around to the west wing. At the corner I stopped and heard the faint regular scraping of a boot; the sound of a man shuffling in place, consciously or not, trying to work off his nerves. Half rose into a crouch.

"Gav, one of them's moving to the door!"

I sprang down the walkway. The bravo turned too slowly, putting his Bowie knife out in front of him. I stepped past him and threw him over my hip, the long knife flying from his hand, going over the railing—a break that never happens by design. He fell smoothly and attempted to get back up. My knee met his jaw. He was gone. The suite door was opening in. I slammed my shoulder into it. The man behind the door stumbled backward into a row of folding chairs. I followed him. He had a double-edged hatchet. I hit him twice, once under the armpit, my knuckles crushing up against the nerves, and once under his chest. He crashed down. I did a half pivot, keeping my face away, and hurled a flasher through the open door of the inner office. A couple of million candlepower worth of photons exploded in the adjoining room. Crushed an exposed ankle, and went into the afterlight.

One gray-haired man was sitting in front of Eddie's rig, groaning, his face in his hands. The other, tall and very thin, was standing in the middle of the room by the desk. He pumped a few rounds into the ceiling from his silenced .45 as I squeezed his wrist with the fingertips of my right hand while my left wrapped around his throat and pushed him down onto the desk. The gun fell from his hand. He tried to break my grip. I smashed his head a couple of times against the fake wood top of the desk, and said to him, "Give it up, fucker; a broken windpipe is a lousy way to die."

The guy at the rig started to get up, so I added, "Almost as bad as getting your goddamn head blown off. Sit down, asshole." The man abruptly dropped back into the chair.

The guy I was holding, Tyler, started to laugh. It worried me. I looked down at him. The pupils of his eyes had almost disappeared, but the irises were that strange colorless shade like Jammer's. "Did you laugh a lot when you vacationed in Grover?" I twisted his neck for emphasis.

I didn't think it was possible for his throat muscles to tighten further. ". . . Not a cop." His voice sounded nearly as bad as mine.

"Your fucking lucky night. We prefer to handle things personally."

He didn't like hearing that. "Who are you?"

My voice came from one of my nightmares. "Don't be more stupid than you have to be. This is going to be simple. We can kill you"—he struggled briefly, his heels banging louder than his gunshots against the side of the desk, but I had all the leverage—"That was a question, asshole. What's the answer?"

He screamed "Fuck you!"

Called him a worthless piece of offal in French and punched him in the groin. He gagged on his scream. Green spit.

Waited until he was capable of hearing me again. "What's the answer?"

"Fuck you!"

"Nice to see a man with stones, but, Warren, I said this is going to be simple. The next strike is going to be your eyes, not your balls. I'm not going to bother talking with what's left after that. Do you fucking understand?"

". . . Yes."

"Good, you are smart. You had a gun. A jury would consider burning you right now to be justifiable homicide. But I'm the forgiving sort. Why don't we pretend that we've just run into each other and are having a polite talk."

He thought about it. Almost blinded, his henchmen either dead or gone, for all he knew I had a heavyweight wrecking crew backing me, his gun hand nerve dead, and he was a finger twitch away from having his larynx broken. He actually thought about it. I could see why they had shipped him off to Grover. Stones. Between his blinks, I touched his right eyeball softly with a finger as rigid as a steel spike.

"Shit! Okay, okay!"

Felt a spasm of relief, buried it. In French again I said calmly, "Target taken, interrogating." I was only seeing him with corner vision, but I thought that the man at the rig tilted his head slightly like he understood. Good. I switched back to English. "Okay, Tyler, let's start with your telling the smithie over there to call your outside boys and tell them to stay put—and smithie, please fucking remember what I said about blown heads."

Tyler croaked, "Do what he says, Frank."

While the smith relayed the order I tapped my phone off with my free hand. Eddie had already learned too much.

I said first to the smith, "Kiss the screen and keep it there as if it were your last lover. Then put your hands behind your back and grab your wrists." He leaned forward and did it. "Now, Tyler, you'll find this an old, familiar script. I ask questions, you give me the right answers. We're both going to work at doing it right. Got it?" He managed to jerk his goateed chin a little.

"Fine. And after we're through, we'll discuss your brave new future."

He tried to breathe. "Let me up?"

"Sorry, not until we've finished our conversation, unless you're prepared to die tonight and you're one of those blades that wants to go on their feet. Are you?"

He was quicker this time. "No."

I eased off his throat a little just to see if he clearly understood the situation. He seemed to. The harsh moaning sounds coming from the waiting room probably helped him see it clearly.

I studied his face. I could feel his pulse pounding weakly under my fingers. "Okay, then. Let's start by getting some of the trivial crap out of the way. What the fuck are you doing here?"

"The bitch's been asking about me. I wanted to find out why."

Tightened my grip. "You haven't figured it out yet, have you? You don't have the right to be rude to that woman. You barely have the right to air. Understand?" He gagged a yes. "Now tell me why her asking is so important that you'd make it a personal trip?"

He was getting back some of his sight. I shook my head in warning. He decided not to move. "I got word . . . word that some ogres from the Midwest were thinking of relocating into my territory. Somebody, somebody I know told me that the bit—the woman—was crosslinked with them."

"Somebody who?"

"Soares."

"Soares who?"

"Just Soares—he's a mule driver."

A dispatcher for drug runners. "And you believed him?"

Tears running down his cheeks. "He's never fucked with me."

"What, he doesn't think you're pretty? But in this case he did fuck with you. The woman's clean on that score—and more importantly she's got coverage. Comprendo, amigo?"

"Yes."

I said in a friendly, conversational tone, "*Dieu!* You are a pathetic high-test piece of shit. Aren't you?" He didn't say anything. "Tyler, questions, remember?"

"Yes!"

"That's better. Let's move on to more interesting shit. You helped a gang kidnap a woman from South Bay. Where did you take them?"

He didn't show any signs of confusion about the change in subject and he didn't hesitate. Appreciated that. "We took them to Pinckert's Cove."

"And where's that?"

"About an hour north of Morro Bay, up in Slo."

"You left them there?"

"Yes."

"So how did they get off the beach?"

"I don't know."

I banged his head again, not too hard, hard enough. His eyes rolled in his head. "Tyler, I'm considered easygoing."

"I saw them leave in a seaplane."

"Did the kidnappers tell you who they were going to get?" I had to repeat the question.

"No."

"Tyler, like you noted when we first met, I'm not a cop. I don't have their patience."

"The man who put us together told me."

"Who's the man."

"Carlos Chou."

As in the Carlos Chou who is one of the three principal officers under the Padrino. I owed Arthur Cormac a very small apology—one that I didn't plan on ever delivering. Chou was the main liaison man for the Mid-City Benevolence. Sort of a roving ambassador at large for the syndicate. Right now I would bet he wasn't in North America, nor would he return soon. Giving Tyler a name was part of some kind of setup. The Erinyes would never reveal their quarry to an outsider before the action went down. Something was going on, but I didn't have enough time to work on guesses.

"How many people did you move?"

"Five. Two men and three women, including the snatch."

"What was the name of that place you took them to?"

He answered without a trace of surprise at my asking him again. He knew the drill. "Pinckert's Cove."

"Where did the others go?"

"Others?"

"The other people involved in the fracas."

"Don't know any others."

Not lying. "How'd they pay you?"

It was funny, he had a harder time responding to that then telling me about the connection to the Benevolence, more concerned about his money than the possibility of a visit from troopers who wouldn't bother asking any questions. I didn't need to know anything more about him. His life was an accident waiting to happen.

"Some cash . . . and a line of credit."

That made an appealing intersection. "Let me guess; with a pipeline bank?"

"Yes."

"My arm is getting tired. I really would like to finish this."

"The Banco de San Marco."

Nice. "Now tell me something, anything."

"What?"

"Be imaginative. Make me decide not to tidy up."

"Motherfucker—"

I closed his air off, saw the panic, smelled the piss as his bladder went, counted to five, and let up. "Yes?"

He gagged, trying to clear his throat. "Please man, don't. . . . Comlink chatter, something about storms and turkeys—strong blockers, too much static. Enough?"

"Yes. Thank you. Now let's talk about what is going to happen." I spoke quickly, I wasn't sure about the guy I had taken outside the door—I may have left him with a concussion and a broken jaw, or maybe not. It's hard to apply just the right amount of force, and when I make a mistake it's usually in the other's favor. He was wearing armor under his pullover sweater. He may have reacted a little too slowly but the way he fell told me not to underestimate. If he came in it could get stiff. "Besides having my organization to deal with, you've got another problem, Tyler, you've been made—man, did you think this was going to be a fucking walk in the park? It's a goddamn political kidnapping, asshole. Once they know you're involved they won't stop looking until they find you. Your only chance is to get out of the country right now—try Bolivia." I forced him to see my eyes. "And forget about unfinished business. We won't be having another conversation."

I've looked into a few faces—I've been where he was—I was satisfied. What he had lost might come back, but it was going to take a while.

I let go of him and scooped up the gun before he could sit up. "You're going to stay for another ten minutes, no less, no longer. Don't think of touching anything here; people are watching." I looked over at the smithie. Through all of it he had kept his back to me, the only one of them with any sense. "And then, get the fuck forever out."

I got back to the truck the same way I left it. Not exactly—I broke a couple of bones on the way out. Insurance. Called Eddie, told her the immediate problem was over, but she should still get some protection for the next few days. If things were tight I would cover the cost, and also that of some unspecified repairs to her office. She heard it well. As for security, she named a couple of Samoan brothers who were friends. Seven hundred pounds between them and the speed of pass-rush linebackers. I said fine.

Touched the bag on my belt where I had stuffed Tyler's gun. My hand didn't tremble. It should have.

She asked a question, waited, then asked another. "Did you kill anybody?" and, "Would you have killed him?"

I hardly heard her. She was calling to me from a far distance, a bleak wind blowing. "No."

CHAPTER EIGHTEEN

WHEN DANNY ASKED ME WHY I hadn't questioned Jammer, I had told him it was a matter of ethics. So what justified what I did to Tyler? That there were no innocents in that room? That the process of interrogation was designed to produce more than answers? Because I was trying to make sure that a good person wasn't going to get hurt? That in this case the means justified the end? Maybe.

But what alibi differentiated what I had just done from torture? That they had the chance to defend themselves? Now, there's a real specious bit of logic.

Means. Sulinn called my mother a sublime actress; she was more than that. She could stop a hysterical colt from hurting itself trying to break out of a stall, keep a grizzled tomcat purring while she cleaned out his battle wounds, coax a too-silent child into telling her what was wrong. She had taught me how to use the power of the voice, how you could drive words past the best defenses. I don't think she ever conceived of the uses I would put her training to.

My father on the other hand had a perfectly clear idea of what he taught so regretfully: how to stay alive, how to hurt.

Regret is wrong. Despair is closer. Truer.

But they both had tried to give me other things. From my father I learned what honor was supposed to be; from my mother what conscience is.

What I had done I did precisely, dispassionately. No anger, not much fear, and thankfully, no pleasure. I was doing a chore. I had over thirty years of training and experience, a body that still had a hell of a lot more quickness than most, the advantage of surprise, specific tactical information. I could have gotten into lethal trouble, but as someone very smart once observed, luck is the residue of design. And I felt nothing, except tired.

And that scared me. When you become indifferent to your actions, that is the moment you start living your death.

On the way home I left a note with Thinh that the tangibility of Warren Tyler being involved had grown exponential. Omitted details, but unless I read him wrong, I figured that hearing twice from me on the same tip would cause him to push the matter. I got in, sprayed a strong analgesic over most of my muscles, made myself a cup of hot chocolate, swallowed a mel tab, and went to bed. Before I drifted off I thought a little about Tyler's and Jammer's eyes. Were they brothers? Or a new riff on the tribal tattoo? I filed the questions away in a mental cubbyhole for future inquiry. Curiosity may kill cats, but it can keep wolves alive.

The bed massaged me awake. The house told me I had slept four hours and there were two messages: a follow-up per my request from the *Times*, and an MBI. Did I want them now or after I took my shower? I told it afterward. I staggered to the bathroom, stared blearily at the meter—still green. Since Kit left, it's been easy to stay within the allotment. Got into the stall and ran the water this side of scalding. When my body finally said hello to my mind I set it to cycle down to cold. For a long time I stood under the spray, letting the icy water guide me into Wu Chi—I needed to wash my psyche as well as my skin.

Afterward, I went to the kitchen and fixed myself a rancher's breakfast: two thick chops, half a dozen eggs scrambled with salsa, pan biscuits, a slab of butter and lemon marmalade on the side, and a small bucket of coffee. I took the mess outside to the paved terrace. The sky was a clear, virgin blue; the color Turner used in his Venice paintings. The morning sun was casting shadows as sharp as a pant crease across the arroyo's declivities. The air was hushed; the only bird call, a crow's faint, disgruntled caw.

Turner. I had the rare pleasure of a dream during my sleep. I was in a painting of his: *Rain, Steam and Speed*. Through the distant grayness I see the brilliant red fire coming from the locomotive's stack. I'm standing by the tracks that run past the edge of the painting. I can sense the train's hurtling approach through the soles of my hiking boots. The air feels as cold and still as a high-country lake. I don't feel worried or impatient; I'm just waiting.

Well, kind of obvious. Still, it was nice to know that my unconscious was doing its best to lend a hand.

"Let's have the messages, order received."

The first was from Sophie. Told the genie where it could find the Bonhoeffer—when it finished decoding and encoding it would automatically forget the location of the encryption routine. Sophie was brief, simply telling me that the operation I had requested was successfully launched. I sent a note back thanking her and Lila, and asking that her niece gently sniff around trading in Congo bonds and where Groupe Touraine stood in relation to the Southern African combines.

The next one was from Paul Thinh. Technically that was a violation of our agreement. I was to contact him, not the other way around. It had come in at 8:36, a little less than an hour ago. He'd taken me seriously. The Ventura County Sheriff's Special Crimes Squad had raided the hangout of Warren Tyler. They were eager to help. Tyler's gang was a well-known, and until this morning, frustrating irritant. Getting a fed warrant and a chance to squash that crew made the crash squad quite happy.

They caught four men, three injured. Thinh was meticulous in his gratitude, he included names and descriptions; two of the injured were my handiwork, the third was the sheriff's—a by-product from having to blow in a steel-plate door. They were in the processes of rounding up three others, including a Jammer Jacobson. Unfortunately, Tyler and one other, a man named Francis Laffray, according to information volunteered by one of the captured men, were heading somewhere north into the Santa Lucia Mountains. Supposedly planning on getting out of the country. Given that Tyler had access to a number of smuggling routes that the rest of gang didn't know about, the sheriffs were doubtful they could catch up to him. No mention of what had happened five hours ago. If Tyler wasn't caught then perhaps, just perhaps, the fracas would go down as an inexplicable occurrence. I crossed my fingers.

Swift work. About what I expected if Thinh had really been paying attention to me—and if Cormac was willing to pay attention to a foreigner. Whatever feelings I have about the police don't interfere with knowing how efficient they can be. I forgave Thinh for calling me.

Tyler heading out of the country with his smithie. Maybe he was smarter than I was willing to give him credit for being. I almost laughed: it would be really funny if the real honcho of that gang turned out to be quiet Frankie. It would also be real nice if he managed sometime to pass along the story of being attacked by a French wrecking crew. A small thing perhaps, but everything helps.

Thinh had something else to say: Marguerite Vassey had died this morning at 1:45 A.M.

I pushed aside the remains of my breakfast and knotted my fingers together. More people die between the hours of midnight and dawn than at any other time. That's why it's called the graveyard shift. She wouldn't have died alone. With the criticals there is always a Sitter to wait and watch and say the last farewell. A good custom we acquired along the way. A very good custom. Yet, I hoped there also was a friend, someone who had listened to her late at night, laughed with her some bright morning, standing by as she went into the wind.

Some say it really doesn't matter . . . that rituals are only for the grieving; the dead don't care. They don't know.

I gave Vassey, that smidgen of what I imagined I knew about her, the last moments of her conscious life when she tried to do her job as well as she could, a few minutes of complete attention. Then I put her away. Into a crowded box. Unless I was to hear or see her name, I wouldn't think of her again. Can't afford to.

The *Times* follow-up was on the wave of European bank bombings that I had flagged. A source in Europol had leaked to one of their reporters that the group known as the Moutons Enragés—the Angry Sheep—were believed to be responsible. The article cautioned that there as yet had been no media announcement from that para.

Unusual; most action groups love publicity. It helps them get recruits and assistance, and when you spend your days in chronic anxiety and frequent failure—the revolution always seems to be the day after tomorrow—the fame soothes and strokes the ego. Only a few try to avoid notoriety, like the Committee, where anonymity works in its favor and the careful avoidance of glory is its pride. And groups like the Erinyes, who only care that those who really wield the power know, and feel, and hurt.

I pulled myself back to work. Okay, if the Angry Sheep were on the same team as the Erinyes—could be a careful long-term campaign, like a chess game played by mail. Lots of differing pieces, lots of motivations, a tricky game to play. I wondered if Holguin knew any of the coaches—it had occurred to me when he had suggested that the Congo Project was under systemic attack that he might be one of the sideline coaches himself. It was his kind of game. No, I've made a point of learning how his body betrays him. I didn't believe I was being overconfident in thinking that, so far, he wasn't lying to me.

I didn't care about the game or its outcome. I just wanted to sneak onto the board and pluck one of the pawns away. But finding my way past the players and the other pieces wasn't looking terribly good, even if I could pull off a little gambit. Then I never thought it did look good at all.

Sometimes Kit uses a telling nickname for me: Outis. The name Odysseus gave up to Polyphemus. He blinded the Cyclops and got away. I could use the Wanderer's luck.

And his patient Penelope. But then, the husband she never stopped believing in did manage to find his way home. . . .

Instructed the house to up the flush rate on the current interest files. It complained that it wouldn't be as efficient. I told it that efficiency—in this, and only this, particular case—was an overrated virtue. There was a long pause, an EI's version of shock, then it acknowledged.

I finished the coffee and went back in to put on some grease paint. I gave my eyes a heavy lidded look. Added a few more age lines around my neck. My hair had enough shots of silver through the gray black. The mirror showed me how I would begin to look in a couple of decades. About right for my character—I tried not to grin until the organo-cosmetics set. Cleaned up and then got dressed: sapphire blue silk tunic and scarf, solid dark charcoal vest and gabardine slacks with a matching lightweight cape, wide snakeskin belt, handmade black oxfords on my feet, thin gray gloves, cherrywood walking stick, and a pair of don't-even-think-of-bothering-me shades. The clothes were expensive and had the worn appearance of having been owned for years. My character was definitely not nouveau. I checked in on Kit's rig to see how the program was evolving. I got an estimated completion by late afternoon. Good. I went to my office.

No signs of an entry, forced or otherwise. All Tyler probably had gotten from his snitch was Eddie's business address. Lord, how stupid he was! I loaded and started to launch Goddard and Kohler; "she" was to go sight-see the banking industry (across the cube ran the dry comment: "Thank you, that type of assignment is such a delight."). Kohler was to try to find that elusive Interpol entity. At the last minute I changed Goddard's appearance, made her closely resemble Siv Matthiessen—I was curious to see if that stirred anything up.

Went to the piano, butchered Scriabin, and wondered about tempests and Turks. Stopped in mid-discord and asked the office to throw up Reuters's weather report for the New Turkic Republic and its hegemonic clients. The display showed scattered showers around Istanbul and points south, no storms. I ran the weathermap backward and forward over a three-week span. Cold but clear weather throughout the time frame.

When I heard the all-clear from my figs I locked up the rig; nothing fancy, just basic black-ops field security. Anyone who plays with it gets one chance to guess the password, otherwise the rig spits sparks and becomes disposatech. I headed downtown to see a man about money.

N. W. Palmer is a dealer in all but worthless currency. There are always nations and private-issue banks that manage to trash the value of their money, and companies that get stuck. Lovett buys the notes, real or electric, for fractions and sells them for a fraction more. He does it in sufficient volume to own a good part of a floor in the Bunker Hill Mercantile Guild. I didn't know him personally but I knew someone who knew someone who did know him very well, and I had learned some revealing things about him from down that line.

One of the excuses I have for living in L.A. This city has always run on contacts. From the days of the little black book, to the Rolodex (that's a spindle that held a bunch of paper data cards), to bases, to multiphasics, to power taquieras, Los Angeles has been a city of who you know and who they know. It may be a megalopolis in irreparable decline, but it's still one of the great personal information nexuses of North America.

I walked over to the Vermont substation and took the train to downtown. No tail. Got off at Third Street and entered the rococo ziggurat (Versailles colliding with Babylon, not a fortunate encounter) that flows over Bunker Hill. Went through a security check by the guards who were as efficacious as Groupe Touraine's, and rode the glide escalators behind a young woman who never took her attention away from her pad—which allowed me to politely admire great calves. She got off on the fourth floor, I went on up to the fifth. Stood through another careful survey—there's more actual cash in this building than most banks—and then I was allowed to pass through bronze doors.

There was a human factor sitting behind a solid Adam-style table. The woman rose with a half-puzzled smile. She was wearing a metallic, dove gray cheong with a modest slit. She might have originally hailed from somewhere in south Asia—her face had been obviously sculpted to the Hindu-Islamic ideal. Oversized gazelle eyes above high cheekbones, full lips, her smile showing teeth like matched pearls, a strong yet slender nose. All of it framed by a perfect oval. She brushed a jet-black wing of her bob cut away from her face, and greeted me. "Good morning, sir. You have an appointment?"

Her accent had the breathy, slightly overpolished enunciation of the new elite. Mine was from a different, older class. "Good morning to you. No, I'm afraid this is an impromptu visit to your firm."

Her smile faded. "I am sorry, sir, but Mr. Palmer does not see anyone without an appointment."

"Let me give you my card. Perhaps he would be willing to make an exception in my case." I took from a vest pocket an identity planchet, unlocked the bank access codes, and handed it to her. She assessed me silently for a moment, then inserted the chip into her minitel.

The Mercantile's security had run my bonafides. I was a citizen in good standing. In a little while she would find out how good.

She kept her smile and her eyes on me until the datastream flowed across her hidden screen. She glanced down, absorbed it in a few seconds, then said, "Please have a seat, Mr. Kenmar. I'll see what I can do."

James Alexander Kenmar. A name chased by a slew of archaic initials. A real person with very robust real assets. And a history gratefully doctored by old friends in His Majesty's Armed Forces. He took his mother's Breton name when he emigrated to North America.

The bulk of those assets are held in a confidential, irrevocable trust. It's safeguarded well enough to be all but impossible for any-one without a court order—and try to get one in Scotland—to dis-cover that the large income, filtered through various channels, goes mostly to support an Irish medical research center, the remainder for art scholarships at the University of Edinburgh, a few other good schools, and for miscellaneous good works. When I was old enough to understand, he told me about it and gave his reasons. The way it's set up he, and now I, can make suggestions as to how the money goes, but no control, no back-door "honorariums." I was raised with people who understood what could be bought and what couldn't. No complaints.

But when he saw the road I had taken . . .

I enter the sweatlodge with Joe Irons. Cold air following us like a curse that's echoed loudly by the men already there. While I'm shut-ting the door, Joe brushes ice from his beard and says to them, "Four feet five." Some nod, some groan, nobody disagrees, Joe always wins bar bets on how high a snowstorm's fall will be. We strip. The men, friends, cousins, see the new scars on my chest. They're silent. Most have ones of their own; ranching has never been safe, and some have done the Sun Dance—gone through pain to vision—but none of them have mine. I sit across from my father. There are expressions that can be read but shouldn't. . . .

I rubbed my chest absently. Those scars are gone. They weren't worth keeping. I got something else from them. My father's old persona. Carefully, brilliantly, altered so that I could use it as mine. So far it's never been breached, even by the cleverest. The British used to be legendarily lousy with their security. Not anymore. Not his people. I don't bring it out very often, and I try very hard not to stain it. Not always easy.

A diminutive young man with flowing light hair came to me and asked if I would care for a refreshment. I took a glass of ice water. While I waited, I tapped the Central Library, removed my shades, and read some Neruda. Fifteen minutes later, the woman told me that Mr. Palmer would be pleased to see me.

CHAPTER NINETEEN

NATHANIEL WALTER PALMER FACED ME half-naked across the wide expanse of the room. A grizzled black man was deftly helping him out of brightly lacquered Kendo sensarmor. The trader appeared to be in his early thirties. He was a handful of wiry inches shorter than me. Ginger haired; velvet eyes fringed by almost black lashes; strong chin and nose; and a splash of freckles across the back of his smooth arms and muscular shoulders. The knuckles of the servant's hands were swollen with heavily built up cartilage, a boxer's carapace. Palmer undid the last of the ribboned knots and smiled at me apologetically, "Awfully sorry about the informality, but it promises to be a busy day. Monday, you know. I am absolutely squeezed for time and my physician says that I must have the exercise."

A Brit, great. That bit of info hadn't been passed along. One of life's backspins. I told him I understood. The servant glanced at me briefly while he stored the pieces of armor in a tall Hepplewhite wardrobe. I finally recognized him. Calvin Renshaw, many years ago the eighth-ranked cruiserweight in an outlaw sport. I hadn't seen him during his ring days, but some years ago he taught part-time at UCLA —there was a fleeting revival of interest in the legal version of his trade. I had unofficially audited one of the classes.

Even though it had been twenty years since his last pro bout he was still remarkable—we've had such a long running affair with Asian fighting techniques, it's easy to forget that a talented practitioner of the old sweet science is quite capable of annihilating you before you've gotten off your first *kata*. Skill and speed always matter more than style. And to get to an eighth ranking in barehand boxing took a powerful amount of both. Renshaw then, or now, wasn't somebody I would want to rub up against. He might have remembered my face. Luckily, there wasn't a real name to go with it.

A first-class, if elderly, bodyguard. The man went with the furniture and the extravagant amount of office space—I doubted Palmer had more than seven or eight people working here for him, including servants. Trading money is not exactly a labor-intensive job. But then, what is?

He had been getting his workout solo. I suppose if nonboring sweat is all you need, virtuality will do. But when the object is to survive, my experience is that the haptic modalities are misleadingly dull. Useful maybe for gunplay, useless for close work.

Renshaw closed the armoire and left noiselessly by a sliding side door. Palmer wrapped an apricot kimono around him (he hadn't bothered to add inches to his height, but almost unquestionably had added some to one feature of his anatomy—I stopped myself before giving an amused shake of my head; fetishes really don't die). After waiting for me to take a seat, he placed himself behind a wide horseshoe sweep of laminated ebony.

He followed my example and took a few seconds to examine me. Except perhaps for my frame, and an occasional bit of touchiness, there's not much Scot in me. But for His Majesty's sentimentally loyal subjects, ever since Richard took a caramel queen, race is an indelicate subject. "Kenmar . . . I know the Kenmars of Dundee, a marvelous family. Are they relations of yours?"

I answered smoothly. "Quite distant. My people are from Glenmerle."

He straightened up. Must have Burke's on permanent recall. If there's a Somewhere, my father is letting loose that great laugh of his.

"I am afraid I have never had the privilege of being acquainted. I must say it's a privilege to have the honor of serving you."

Unctuous as a Balmoral butler. It wasn't just the number of digits in the Kenmar accounts. You'd think that meaningless mystique would have evaporated a couple of generations ago. Maybe the backspin could work in my favor. He was waiting expectantly: my cue. I looked past his shoulder to the wide clear window behind him. The tops of the San Gabriel Mountains were faintly dappled with snow. "Actually . . . I am not sure that you can. You see, it's not a matter of exchanging some paper." I managed to seem mildly embarrassed.

If he was puzzled, it didn't touch the outskirts of his face. He moved an antique gold letter opener precisely three inches to one side, and said, "How then may I help you?"

"It has to do with a South American investment I'm considering. A friend of mine suggested that you might be especially able to assist me in determining the wisdom of pursuing it."

The room cooled a bit. "What sort of investment?"

"Oh, just a bit of arbitrage involving a Chilean bank that I've heard might come into play. I've heard—sub rosa, you understand—that a certain French holding group and one of those big Johannesburg outfits are both interested in expanding into that part of the world."

He frowned slightly. "I see. I am afraid, sir, that I cannot be of assistance. I deal strictly in currency and equivalents, not in advice."

Confused: "That's not what Tony Chotiner told me."

"Sir Anthony Chotiner?"

Tony to Tonya back to Tony again; the only thing Chotiner was ever indecisive about was gender. "Yes, ah, terrible about his dying like that."

Officially, the inquest determined that Sir Anthony had died by overdose six months ago in his little castle in Portugal. Unofficially, Tony was hotshot—an involuntary lethal dosage—by persons unknown that he undoubtedly cheated. He always cheated, once too often.

He moved the letter opener back to where it was. A minitel disguised as a Fabergé paperweight glowed. "Terrible, yes," he said absently. "Would you give me a moment, sir?"

"Certainly." I got up and went over to the mirrored fireplace. Above the mantel in a place of pride was a two-meter-wide Elul. The air filled with the soft opening strains of the second movement of Beethoven's Seventh while Palmer got his bafflers up and placed his real calls—the tel's glow had been timed just right. I stepped back a few feet and enjoyed the painting. Most artists who experimented with smart mediums ended up producing works that looked like nothing more than finger paintings in progress; Elul was a happy exception. Took a closer look. I didn't recall his using that flowing shade of madder. Thought about it. Elul had been strongly influenced by Anselm Kiefer, especially by the objects Kiefer did around themes based on the Kabbalah. Examined the shifting figurative elements of the painting . . . A fake, albeit an excellent one. I glanced back and smiled approvingly at Palmer.

Whoever he was calling to find out more about James Kenmar than could be found in the scant public record was going to come up dead empty, particularly in regard to a link with Sir Anthony Chotiner. Tony had been a stellar tournament bridge player, until he got caught; a raiser of champion Sealyham terriers, until it was found out that he was playing around too artificially with their genes; and a swagman who specialized in the most expensive hard-to-move items, until . . . Not somebody a Kenmar would know.

There should be no making me—not as Kenmar, or Robie, or Calderon, or any one of a multitude of others. Although Tony and I had conducted a lively correspondence, business and otherwise—as man or woman, Tony was an endearing rake; it got him past seventy-five, no mean feat considering—we never saw or talked real time to each other. Not that he didn't try hard to find out who was his anonymous Stateside contact, but he never was able to get past my barrier of honest lies. And I had another bit of insurance. I learned of his business connection to Nathaniel Palmer not from Sir T but from another informant.

Tony . . . His laconic obit in the British edition of the *Times* had kindly focused on his extremely valorous actions with the Scouts during the Second Balkan War—*"Garbage, dear boy, garbage. We simply had the misfortune of being the rabbits that ran the wrong way."* Yes, Tony, that was why they awarded you the Cross. No doubt at all.

I wouldn't have been surprised to learn that it was he who sold Palmer the phony Elul as the real thing. Bless the poor conniving bastard. His dying was terrible. . . .

And vengeance is not yours, Robie. After this morning, I was going have to put him back into that box.

I thought about aimless things. Like the fact that, except for Renshaw, all of Palmer's employees that I had seen were shorter than he. That the environmentals were pumping in an almond fragrance, not my favorite pick-me-upper. The orchestra playing the Beethoven sounded like the Berlin being led by Weber—great musicians, terrible conductor. That the fireplace was actually a gas burner. Now, that's rare. That he had positioned himself so that I couldn't lip-read him off his reflection.

He called me back to business. "Sorry about that interruption. Where were we—oh, yes. Whatever the late Sir Anthony might have told you, I am afraid he was in error. As I said before, sir, I am a currency trader, not a financier."

I looked at him, and said lazily, "Tony never said you were a *financier*—God knows I have the devil's purse of those—only that you were a purveyor of sound advice."

His skin flushed to the color of his hair, but he replied steadily, "Sir Tony was wrong. I am only licensed to be a dealer." He rose politely. "Now, if you will please excuse me, sir, as I said, this is a very busy day for me."

I joined him in standing up. Time to toss a blatant bit of chum. "Yes, the world of commerce and all that. A shame to have taken up your time so fruitlessly. Pity . . . Tony really thought that you might be of some aid, your having considerable experience in Chilean businesses and all. And I distinctly recall him saying that you were very knowledgeable about the Hsin-min—is that how you pronounce it?—Bank of Santiago. It wasn't like him to be wrong about something like that. Despite his, ah, lamentable reputation, when it came to this kind of matter I always found him to be quite savvy and reliable."

This time it was a little twitch of his manicured hands that betrayed him. He shook his head and repeated again, "In this case he was mistaken. I am sorry, sir."

So was I. A half-decent performance—triumph of inflection over appearance—but a lousy audience. A properly careless, aristocratic look. "So am I. Should you reconsider, you may reach me through my solicitors. Their number is on my card. Good day."

The good-bye smile on Palmer's factor's face was strictly perfunctory. Besides being audited, audioed, and as far as I knew, olfactoried—you can learn quite a lot about somebody from how they smell—the woman unquestionably had been listening in, analyzing, taking mental notes, using trained intuition that still, so far, works better than the best inference engine.

I got out of the building, walked south a few blocks, and then cut into a narrow alley. Nodding habitués propping up the walls with their backs gave me cop-fear eyes. At the end of the alley I turned right and crossed the street at an angle—a delivery van braked hard enough to bounce awake its dozing driver. I was through the door of a beauty boutique before the teamster could think of the right adjective for me. Flashed a don't-mind-me smile at a young technician doing something creamily intricate to a customer's face, and went out the back exit into a small parking lot. Turned left, went around the block, and backtracked to the Third Street Station.

I did a peripheral sweep. Thought I might have been followed. Possible, not certain. The few people around were busy walking away from me. No loiterers. I took the steps down into the ground two at a time.

I looked up at the fixed security camera that watched over the entrance. Noticed it had been vandalized when I arrived. It still was. The next camera down the line didn't have an overlapping field of view with this one. Fine. Waited to one side of the stairs. If a bird dog came sniffing after, he was going to become suddenly unhappy.

No one came down. A train rolled in, then out. The subway's got its faults, but unreliability wasn't one of them. The stops are scheduled at fifteen-minute intervals during this time of day. If there was a watcher still upstairs he would have to figure that his quarry was gone—even if he was unfamiliar with the routine, you can hear the whooshing rumble of the trains from the top of the station. I relaxed and thought about some other tracking.

When Palmer and his factor checked, they were going to find that the Kenmar Trust had a fair amount of holdings in Chile, commercial real estate in Valparaiso, part ownership of a coastal freighter line, and many, many Neuvoines in the glacial Magallanes region of southernmost Chile (my old man had spent some of his adolescent summers working on the funda, the family's endless sheep ranch. A long way for a Scotsman to go to learn the sheep business, but he wanted the adventure, and in a completely unexpected way it helped much later when he acquired a Spanish Basque father-in-law). But the Kenmars had no dealings with the Hsin-min Bank.

Not that there necessarily shouldn't be. When the handbasket went merrily to hell, the Chileans smartly took a leaf from the West Canada handbook and welcomed a number of skilled Chinese refugees from Hong Kong and Indonesia; an investment in compassion that paid off heavily. The new immigrants made a respected place for themselves.

The Hsin-min is a well-regarded regional bank; they can handle everything that involves capital—except for insurance; Chilean law—and manageable risk. That they manage deposits from the scum of the earth is not thought about at all. Rumor, the slightest ripple on the darker waters of the Electric Sea, has it that the Chilean authorities know, but chose for various reasons to let them continue to operate below the line. "Sanctioned" is the term they like to use in the trade. The rules are that they keep the dirt offshore, and don't harm the local civilians. Classic behavior for most governments, regardless of their configuration, since money got married to power.

The Banco de San Marco that Tyler had been given a credit line with is a wholly owned subsidiary of the Hsin-min. And the Hsin-min was the bank that Midas had told me about.

Sheep. Odysseus got out of the Cyclops's cave by clinging to the underbelly of a ram. I was doing something I usually have the better sense to stay away from. Edging too close to the giants, not to mention the possibility of dragons. If I made it through the next few days, there was a dusky hope hiding in the back of my head that I might get away with being looked on as nothing more than a stupid, scraggly ruminant that only wants to get back with the flock, not worth the slaughter. How's that for optimism?

A wheezing west-bound train pulled in, most of the cars empty. Local folk prefer taking the trolleys and having sky overhead, even though the underground had been ironically one of the safest places to be. Found a seat near an exit and rubbed at my eyes.

The surgical maneuver with Palmer had actually gone pretty much the way I had expected it would. I had sliced into him a little bit—his connection with Hsin-min—and dropped into the cut the inference about Groupe Touraine and the Southern

Africans. He might be out of the loop but everything I had heard about him said that he was a prudent man. He would make inquiries with his home office. And unless I was being totally off they would be concerned. The big question was would they play passive, waiting to see what happens next, or would they get back to me to do some exploratory work of their own.

I rested my head against the pole next to my chair. The problem with this gambit was that it was going to take time. To switch metaphors and borrow a chess analogy from Lew: at the upper reaches of the spectrum the players prefer the classic Russian style—build up your strength, carefully probe your opponent for weakness, and then methodically, steadily, grind him down. The Hsin-min could afford to wait. I couldn't. But I didn't have the pieces to rush them.

I got out my pad and started rummaging in my mental—yeah, Rolodex. Not encouraging. I may have a healthy backlog of favors, but most of the people who owe me don't float around the level I was heading into. I was thinking about people my debtors might know, when a text-only note dropped into my mailbox (Muchas gracias, PacBell, for dumping cellular at last and going mesonband). I turned on my shades and read it off the glass. "Lucy Gorelik."

Come again? A warning, a death threat, I could see, expected to see, coming in my mail. But a name from a long-ago finished case?

I don't forget much, but I remember my wins the best: she was twenty-four years old then—that was twelve, no, thirteen years ago—working as the ground crew for a small shipping company based out of Birmingham, Alabama. A fuzzy blond, classic peaches-and-cream complexion: very lushly attractive, all natural. She wasn't happy with her work, had just gotten a queasy divorce. Parents dead, no siblings. Lonely. She had decided to take some accumulated vacation time and went off to visit some friends in Detroit, no names to coworkers. She never got there.

The police investigation was only a bit more than cursory—she didn't owe anybody money, no signs of violence, there was evidence that she had planned to move from Birmingham. That she wasn't generating any traffic didn't mean that she was in trouble—people walk away from their lives all the time and when they do they often stay off-line for a while. Over a hundred thousand people disappear every year. Alabama has its share. The State Police had more immediate problems.

Someone thought she hadn't walked by her own choice. Ethan Hill, and then I, agreed.

I found her in a brothel outside of Santo Domingo. The house's security was muscle and one level of electronics. I'm not much of a smith but the latter was easy obsolete junk. The former was lazy—the management had been too successful with their bribes; the troops never got challenged. The greatest difficulty turned out to be that during the five months Gorelik was there, her "owners" had been chemotroping her into a willing acquiescence. A hitch that almost got me killed.

Well, nobody died, no critical injuries (I ran my tongue over a set of regrown molars) and I got to torch the slave quarters. There can be a whole lot of satisfaction in arson.

Slave brothels? You don't believe that kind of horror still exists in this hemisphere? In this century? You're right, of course; they don't.

A successful gig with, as far as I knew, a happy ending. There aren't that many. At best, things work out about a third of the time. Unlike baseball, being a .300 hitter isn't a cause for autumn joy. Though, being able to hit safely at all when the opposing pitchers are trying to pass fastballs between your ears isn't something to be ashamed of either.

Baseball, surgery, chess, and the Odyssey—nothing like discontent to bring out the metaphoric in me. Something to do with a displacement mechanism. A useful trait.

Lucy Gorelik. The last I saw of her she was being carried unconscious, wrapped in a rain-soaked, feces-smeared blanket, onto one of the small swift hospital ships that the Sisters of Grace operate in the Caribbean. A few days later Ethan told me she was probably going to be okay. A year after, he added a final one-word coda: Yes.

It's not a game and only children keep score.

Back to the mystery. Why had someone dumped her name, just the name, in my lap?

Options: Ignore it. If somebody was trying to tell me that they knew secrets about me, hell, at this stage I wasn't sure who didn't. Remote chance it's a start-up for a payback—no, too long ago as a percentage play. Pepper on the trail? Come on.

Secondary issue: How the hell exactly did Gorelik and Robie get connected? On that job I was Jacques Condé, survivor of St. Barts, French national, professional gambler. I was wearing a different face and my skin was the right shade of mahogany—not too far off my natural color—and my cover had been solid down to the bone. And I killed off Condé years ago.

Related to Siv Matthiessen? The Gorelik case had been about sex, perversion, and greed—mundane things. The Furies play on a different level. The people behind that Hispaniolan brothel had powerful clients, and a silent partner in the head of the local branch of the Phalanges, but they weren't the type to be involved with the game I was getting a blurred view of.

Call Ethan to see if he had an update on Gorelik. There's a three-hour time difference. Courts are closed on Mondays in New Brunswick; I could find him at his club Ethan's a squash fanatic. It was way out of our routine for me to check on cases after they're done—does somebody want me to contact Ethan? If so, why? I sighed. Paranoia is corrosive.

Got off at Hollywood and Vermont. Took the stairs slowly.

As I went through the office door the phone informed me that Danny was calling. I told it to put him through. The cubes's black wait-state flared briefly violet; Danny was running a prelim bug tracer. The phone's diagnostic display told me it wasn't the kind you can buy at your friendly Peace-of-Mind Shoppe for $29.95. In fact the phone had no idea what type of debugger it was. Danny left the Service with a few exotic toys. None of which he was willing to let me copy. That was all right; I do have some idea about the ambiguity of ethics. But his using a tracer implied that another sort of quandary had come up.

His image appeared in the middle of the office. I said, "Como 'sta. I wasn't expecting another call from you so soon. Got something?"

He was frowning as heavily as he's capable of. "Yeah, but it doesn't have to do directly with the case, and I don't think you're going to be happy—I'm sure as hell not." He rapped his knuckles nervously against the arm of the patio chair he was sitting in. "It's like this: yesterday afternoon I got to thinking about the niches in the Bay where I don't have so many connections. So I called Nell Carval. Remember her? No? That's right, she joined us on the waves after you left. A fine surfer, but real aggro. It took a while for her to settle down but eventually we got to be mates." The frown slipped into a brief smile. "She used to call me her best straight boy. Anyhow, she moved up to the Northwest some years ago— she's an organizer for the IUW. Man, now, that's what I'd call a tough track. But she comes down every now and then, and she's got strong ties to her community.

"So I called her for some leads—told her about the kidnapping and that I was covering the insurance carrier's ass on possible collateral liability—that's legit, by the way; Tom Philips came through. I got arched brows on that, so I threw in that I was also interested in the ten K ratbait the city's put out—odd that the woman's company didn't match it. Anyway, while I've got the feeling that she thinks I've got some extra juice for the case, she didn't push it. She started telling me who I could speak to that might be willing to speak back, when I happened to mention that some of the domestic cops were into a flame conspiracy regarding the kidnapping—the guy the chief assigned to head our hometown investigation detail is a real prize. When Nell heard that piece of crap she told me that she was coming down to lend me a hand.

"Seems her people forced her to take some leave. The woman hasn't had a vacation in six years, but all that was doing for her was making her stir-crazy. She ran the red-eye from Portland and hit the Bay ready to take no prisoners. Someday, you two have got to meet—I'd love to find out who's got the harder stones. I managed to ease her off a little, told her to remember that the best rides come from feeling your way through the flow, not fighting it. Reminded her, in case she forgot, that's what I used to beat the pants off her on the waves."

I grinned. Danny wasn't joking. While he had no use for competition on the waves—it's *not* a sport for him—there were times when a friendly conversation with a newcomer didn't cut it. The drawback to being a legend while you're still young. So when a stubborn challenger showed up and insisted, Danny would set a wager that taught a lesson· losers had to forfeit their wet suits—right there on the beach. That the woman took the bet, lost, and became his friend afterward, was a testimony both to her confidence and her good sense.

He continued, "She agrees to go soft—for starters—and goes out to mesh with her friends. And practically right away she finds that there's a South Bay cop in civvies making the same rounds. No surprise, right? Except that this cop's been asking about me and someone who, nine points to the abstract, matches you."

"Give me a second, Danny." I closed my eyes and drew some sloppy Venn circles. Looked at what I got: South Bay PD shouldn't have an undercover asking about us. With the feds all over their turf, if they had a problem with Danny they'd have him in a room with the environmentals turned off and some pros asking him some serious questions. They're not exactly the most subtle force.

The cop was hooked. Thinh's people might have bought a local, but they shouldn't be wasting their resources on scoping me. Thinh wouldn't. Zealous subordinates? I saw no reason, yet, to believe that Olivia Fouchet had broken her promise to me about only Thinh knowing I was working for them.

The Mid-City Benevolence. They don't do business in South Bay. Too far west, too expensive a turf for their operations, but they like to buy little edges into the neighboring power structures—corrupt a cop or a city clerk. Call it their form of liability insurance. Again, using a hook is a waste of resources—unless there's something in South Bay that they're worried about. Or . . . Carlos Chou telling Tyler things the smuggler had no business knowing (and the nagging thought in the back of my head as to how Jason Nancarrow knew how Matthiessen looked). Unless there's something they want me to find. Using the hook as a trail marker? Could be. And Danny, thanks to his friend, found out sooner rather than later. But a marker to what? And why?

The latter might be relevant, and it also might just be a throw-off; pepper on the trail.

"What do you know about this cop?"

"Nada. It's a small force but not that small. She doesn't surf, she's not on the Property Crimes Squad, and she doesn't hang around the cantina. Sorry."

"Don't be." We both saw the problem. Cops can't be touched. The cardinal rule of self-preservation. When it comes to retributive violence, the State wins the prize. Usually. "This cop's flame?" He nodded. "Can your friend run a community backgrounder on her?"

"Nell's already on that. Her idea."

"Good. Have her ask some questions about cash flow. Also, what was the cop's vector; who'd she speak to first, where does she hang out, and so on."

He scratched an ear. "Money. A hooked cop?"

"Ten bloody points to the abstract."

I didn't think his frown could deepen. Danny doesn't take that kind of information easy. "You think she knows something?"

"Maybe."

"Nell wants to talk to her."

On a maneuver like that I would normally wait a week or so, reckoning out the best angles. "Can she handle it?"

"Yes."

No equivocation. Good enough for me. "Here's a name for her to play: Carlos Chou."

Danny repeated the name. "Timing?"

"Her discretion."

He nodded. Pleased. I asked, "What does Carval know about me?"

"Not much. The description the cop was putting out on you rang some bells for her. You may keep clean in South Bay, but people do tend to remark on you now and then. But outside of the fact that you and I were fast, and that screwing with you can be a quick trip to the hospital, I don't think she knows anything else important. So far she hasn't said anything. If I were to make a guess I'd say that she thinks that you're working for me on this gig."

"Sounds good. Let's keep it that way. Anything else come up?"

"Nope. I've heard a lot of opinions but nothing worth pursuing. It's been over two days, and there's a tight lid on—local gossip's beginning to fade. It's going to get harder to stir the mix. You know how it is. Do you want me to cool off?"

"No, keep on. But you and Carval, watch your shadows." Watch closely, Danny. I crossed my fingers and hoped my risk assessment was back up to speed. He signed off with a wave and a comforting smile.

From one friend to another. I punched through a cross-country call out to Fredericton.

Ethan looked less like a Roman emperor than a sweaty, sort of happy centurion who just managed to beat off a horde of youthful Germans. "Win your game?"

"Yes. How are you, Gavilan?"

"Tired. Too much work and not enough sleep—how are you doing in that regard? Leah told me you've been having some insomnia."

"Nothing more than what comes with age. There are compensations. My study looks cleaner than it has been in ages."

"Now, that will shock Ann. How is she?"

"As happy as any oceanographer can be these days. None of her equipment has broken down lately, and some of the data is beginning to make some sense. She's also as unhappy as a mother can be, not being here for Leah."

"But she'll make the wedding?"

"I have the word of a heartsick commodore, and that's a powerful combination. She may have to land on the church's meadow in a navy skycar, blowing snow from here to Halifax, but she'll be there." He shook his head, smiling at the thought. "Now, will *you* be able to make the wedding?"

"Count on it."

The smile left his face. He placed the palms of his hands together and nodded wordlessly.

"Besides just to say hello," I said, "the reason I called is because I'm thinking of taking a vacation. Have you ever been to Kiev?"

He leaned against a marbled bar and took a long pull from a stein of beer. His eyes never left me. "Can't say that I have."

I glanced down at the phone's display. My toys may not have been developed by the National Security Agency but they're not bad. Clear. Probably. "Haven't been there myself, but someone told me recently that I should pay it a visit. And it wouldn't hurt for me to brush up on the icon trade."

His shaggy brows lifted. "I didn't think there was anyplace that you haven't been."

I laughed dryly. "There're still a few. I was wondering if you could ask around your firm for some names and introductions—you know, the sort of oil that lubricates a trip."

He took another sip. "Hmm . . . I'll call Warsaw. Stefan Ulrich, he oversees the firm's business in Eastern Europe. I think he might be able to come up with some nice Ukrainian contacts for you. When you planning on going?"

"Not right away, but I would like to get a head start on my itinerary."

"I will see what I can do."

"Thanks, Ethan. How's Leah?"

"Delirious. Half the time she's thirteen, the rest she's thirty-three going on eternal."

"Hard on you, old man?"

"As hard as a feather."

Leah was an unexpected child. The archaic cancer treatment that took Ethan off the bench should have sterilized him. He hadn't put away any frozen sperm; he was too old, Ann's career was beginning to accelerate. The little boy they lost to one of the meningitic plagues. Reasons. Then Providence decided they deserved better. Want to see pure happiness? Mention his daughter's name. Ethan thinks that I'm the one who has the patent on courage. A decent man, a fool. "Thought so. Thanks again, Eth. I hope we'll get a chance to talk again soon."

"Yes, let's. Stay well, Gavilan." His image dopplered away.

Vacation for "I need to know about the past;" *Kiev* for a "young, brutally victimized woman;" *Icon* for I'm talking about "an old case." *Warsaw* for "I will check her out." *Eth* instead of Ethan meant that I would call him back in twenty-four hours, and so on. A simple code, only to be used when there might be civilians around. Judge Hill designed it himself. He read too many spy novels when he was young.

I looked in on my figs: Goddard was getting nowhere slowly; there are a remarkable number of moneycenters operating simultaneously both above and below the line. You'd think that they would be happy making profits the old-fashioned gouging way. Kohler had been sidetracked into a long-abandoned Mud that featured nubile metallic-skinned fifteen-year-olds. It took a while to perform the extraction; the scummy wizard who designed the space had installed a clever tollgate. I finally managed to pull "him" out and booted him back in the direction I wanted.

Waiting is the second hardest part. Not knowing if what you're waiting for will be of any use is the first. Took my jacket off and cleaned my face. Did Tajji movements with an imaginary sword. Stood across the room and snapped playing cards through a four-inch ring. Opened up the piano and tuned a few keys. Rented and watched a vid of the great Bahian artist Belos Leao demonstrating *capoeira* moves. Tried a hands-free back flip. Almost broke my neck. Fixed myself a stiff gin and tonic and thought about what I was going to say to the entirety that was slowly waking up in my house. Avoided thinking about Kit, mortality, failure.

Three o'clock, I was about to head home when Kohler came through. I separated his memory, strip-searched it, put it into a safe box, and played it back:

Hazy blue air, no, water. Kohler, a dolphin, except that there are hands at the ends of the fins. Through his eyes seeing some kind of aquatic butterfly, translucent webbed wings of purple and black. Read the stippled patterns on the wings—Enbright, the person with the Interpol ear. Yes.

They are floating around each other. Below them a huge pink coral pyramid with a long boulevard running away from it into darkness. The street was lined with bone white Doric columns, seaweed growing like clotted pale green ivy around the stones. One of the abandoned Atlantis playgrounds. A nursery for the mind. The speed was good, but the background matte was showing slight fractal edges. Somebody's forgotten engramic junkbin.

ENBRIGHT
So what is it that you are looking for?
KOHLER
What can you get on the Angry Sheep and the Erinyes? I want to know about their finances. Also, especially possible conjunctions between the two groups.

ENBRIGHT

I'm not certain I can be of much help. My source's antiterrorism section specializes in helping suppress mass-destruction acquisition—they have ever since the god Shiva incarnated over Delhi.

KOHLER

Do not be coy with me. Interpol gets a heavy feed from over two hundred countries. They will have dirt.

ENBRIGHT

It's a bit risky for me to spend too much time searching for answers—and expensive.

KOHLER

Will five thousand ecus cover your costs?

ENBRIGHT

For five I'd let you embrace me, for ten I'm willing to risk a disease.

KOHLER

For ten I will also want a name inside the New People's Bank of Santiago. A name that can be cashed.

ENBRIGHT

(Long abstracted pause, probably checking with its creator.)

That bank? Hmm, looking to move across the spectrum? I'm impressed—might there be any play for me?

KOHLER

I've changed my mind. Seven is as high as I go.

ENBRIGHT

(Grimacing.)

Would an apology for my indiscretion bring back three? No? Seven then, and a name in that bank, if one can be found. But this time I wish to be paid in NT lira instead of ecus.

KOHLER

(Thinks for a moment, working out the currency exchange rates between the New Turkic Republic and the European Union. The bastard was going to get an additional five hundred and forty-six extra. He agrees. His programing is to be hard and cheap, but not too cheap.)

ENBRIGHT

Excellent. When I'm ready I will leave a find-me for you at DX97392/ap9.

KOHLER

Auf Götterdämmerung, Enbright.

(He and the imaginal dissolve, fading like an old black-and-white photo in the sun.)

Playback end.

It went about as well as I could hope for. If the real Enbright decides to fulfill the commission, if there's anything worthwhile from Interpol, if I hear about it in time. A lot of ifs for a hope.

Enbright was getting greedier. A sure sign of incipient failure. I was planning to cut off contact with him, or her or it, by December—that would have made it four years shy of a few months since I had first linked up with whoever, whatever it was. And four years is about the life expectancy for sellers. I want to be far away when he goes down.

Kohler had functioned satisfactorily. A well-designed figment. Summoned Goddard back—no sparks off her new appearance, put her and Kohler away. I headed home to deal with something, someone, far more potent than what I could carry in a pocket.

CHAPTER TWENTY

KIT'S RIG, WITH A TINGE of impatience—an echo of its mistress—
informed me that it was running through some final diagnostics
and would be ready in a few minutes. I checked the sensor array I
had gotten out of storage. The eyes, ears, and noses responded correctly to the stimuli tests. There wasn't anything I could do about
taste or touch. To seamlessly incorporate those sensations would
require hardware far more elaborate and subtle than I own. Supposedly, they wouldn't be necessary. The metaprogram had a way
of inducing a form of cognitive dissonance that would keep their
absence from the entirety's attention—sort of the reverse of phan-
tom limbs. It isn't aware that some things are not there. Just as it
would also make sure that the sensors and projectors would be
edited into invisibility.

I placed two chairs near each other by the open window. The
one in the shadows would be for her. I put my drink—just tonic
water this time—beside me on the wide sill, sat down, and told the
rig to bring up Siv Matthiessen.

In the beginning there was—in the beginning there was the
deed. This was Faust, not Genesis.

Like a painted dream of a flower greeting the day, she bloomed into the chair.

An extraordinary program—about as large an understatement as I've ever made. It not only composited all the images it had of its subject, it tried to be more than accurate. The program attempted to show how its creation saw itself, what it saw in the mirror.

And if that were true . . . I had called her *une belle à se suicider.* I was wrong. She was not to die for, but to live for. Her beauty was more than just a property of form. What she possessed had a claim of its own. A mystery that promised that there was a purpose, a meaning . . .

It was only particles of light. And I had seen that radiance before, lived with it twice. I could guard myself with my past. Do it all the time. I took a careful swallow from my glass and concentrated on the present.

She was wearing a loose-fitting ribbed sweater the color of aged ivory, and wine-dark leggings. Like the sculpture of hers that I saw so long ago, only certain aspects were emphasized. Her head, her hands, the swell of her breasts. I drove my nails into my hands. She looked about for a moment, then rested teal eyes on me.

"*Bonjour,* Gavilan Robie."

I have been with ghosts all my life. Their intimacy doesn't scare me. This time I came very close. My name—oh, yes, that familiarization routine Kit had created to ease the birth process. I had clear forgotten that was still installed in the front-end buffer. I felt more relieved than I should have.

"Hello, Siv Matthiessen. I'm glad to meet you. Are you comfortable? Would you prefer speaking in another language?"

No incongruity tremors. She tucked her legs underneath her and leaned her head to one side. A small smile. "Nynorsk?"

"Sorry, I never got around to that."

"No matter. I'm fine with French, unless"—the smile grew—"do you know Italian?"

"Not as well as I would like, but I can struggle with it if you wish."

She closed her eyes for a moment then laughed. Incredible. "Not that much of a struggle."

I shrugged, waited a moment then asked, "Why Italian?"

"Ah, the first why. *Molto bene.* When I was a child my parents and I would spend the winters down in Sicily with good friends of theirs who were artists. They lived in Taormina. My mother used to say that when I was four I spoke Italian better than Norwegian. My parents were happiest there, then. . . . So, you see, Italian makes me feel warm, *comfortable.*" She ran a lazy finger along the high demure neckline of her sweater.

"I see. Do you like the room's fragrance?"

She inhaled and murmured in faintly accented English so softly that I almost didn't hear her, "'When lilacs last in the dooryard bloomed.'" She paused, then spoke louder. "It's a delightful scent. *Grazie.*"

Now, where did the Whitman come from? While the Europeans are as fond of poetry as we are, old Walt was too idiosyncratically American, too full of life for most of them. Was it a true memory, or some random associative flotsam that had drifted in with the tide of data that the jumbleplex used to cover and support the metaprogram? I remembered the poem. It wasn't a pastoral. I leaned forward a little. "But do you *like* them?"

She ran her hands through her hair. "You *are* a psychiatrist."

I thought I had set myself against the unexpected. "Why would you think I wasn't?"

She said dryly, "I've known a few. You don't have their varnish. No . . . you look like a man who I would enjoy sharing a late afternoon espresso with at that café just off the Piazzale Michelangelo. You must know the place, you sound very Tuscan. We would watch the sun go down on the Duomo—God, is there any other city that drinks color in as if it were the face of her last lover? You would be a man who would tell me interesting, strange, stories. You must love playing the cello, or is it perhaps the bass? Those are very deep grooves on your fingertips. It must be a *violon d'Ingres* for you, a hobby of the heart. Please don't be offended, but you also look like a man that it wouldn't be smart for anyone to get to know too well." She folded her hands on her lap. "Have I passed your tests?"

Kit had said that in a way one of the major advantages of working with the entireties was their weak ego states—that they seemed caught fast on the line that separates "becoming" from "being." A consequence is an inability to realize what they actually are. I threw away my mental check list.

"You know."

Her words came gently. "That I'm not really me? The explanation that I woke up with about why I am here talking to you isn't terribly convincing. You will have to work on that. No, I don't believe that a better story will help. You see, the woman that I have come from, she has—I'm not sure I can explain it—she has an awareness of herself that goes far into many different directions. I *know* this, yet I don't feel it. Yes, Gavilan Robie or whoever you really are, I know."

This conversation wasn't being analyzed, monitored, or cammed. And if Dr. Katherina Seferides should ever find out about what had happened here, forgiveness would not be the issue. I looked at the image sitting patiently in front of me and felt a loss that I couldn't explain.

She said, "You're going away somewhere. Please don't. I can still be of some help to Siv—funny talking about one's self in the third person."

Some help? "Why do you think you're here?"

"I imagine this has to do with my therapy. Some new technique, a way to safely try new avenues before springing them on the patient." She grinned wickedly. "Pauline would love to do that. She finds me difficult."

No fooling. "Knowing, does it bother you?"

She shook her head slowly. "Strangely enough, not at all. Have you ever done any high diving?"

"Not voluntarily."

"I was right," she said musingly, "you do have some interesting stories."

"Not a word I would use."

"Would you hold your hands up in front of me?"

I raised my arms cautiously, afraid that she would try to touch. Without moving, she examined my hands painstakingly, then said, "Thank you, and you're right—interesting is the wrong word."

I leaned back, sticking my hands into my pockets. "You were saying something about diving."

"I was trying to find a way to tell you how I feel. It's like coming off a ten-meter board doing a three-and-a-half reverse. The world is spinning, yet it's not; there's a kind of symmetry, an equilibrium between you and the sky and the water that's coming up so fast to kiss you—does that make any sense?"

"Some."

"Well, it's like that. I know everything's wrong, but I don't feel off-balance by it." She laughed again. "That may be a handicap for your experiment. I don't think that the real me is normally as composed as I seem to be. No, I don't believe she is."

"You're not here as a therapy tool."

"Then why . . ." She looked at the clenched fists in my pockets and took a heavy breath as if it were her last bit of air. "I said you were a man I shouldn't want to get to know too well—unless I was in a lot of trouble and then I would pray devoutly that you cared. Cared a great deal. Is it that bad?"

Complexity has a high drag coefficient, and thinking fast is not just a matter of processor power.

"Yes."

"Tell me?"

Her "memory," by the strange virtue of its interweaving nature, is supposed to be shielded in a way that denies access to anybody else. On Kit's word, I took the freedom and told her just about everything.

Her image wavered a bit as the projectors adjusted for the changing play of sunlight and shade. I believe that's what it was.

"What day is it today?"

"Monday."

She sighed. "About seven days. How long will this I exist? Longer than myself?"

"Probably not."

"Why?"

"Your platform is unstable." I lightly rapped my forehead. "Even in this shell we're damned precarious. In your form—" I knew then what it was like to be a physician, having to discuss the mechanics of death with a terminal patient. "From what I can understand, it seems that your adaptive systems will rapidly develop stress points that they can't handle and they start folding down."

Detached, cool. "You cannot just save and reset me?"

"It would be a cold resurrection. Each time you would be starting fresh with no memories of the past yous, and you wouldn't even be exactly the same—the matrix that's built up always varies. Is that what you want?" I thought: And if you say yes, does that shard of honor bind me to make it so? This wasn't a fig, a construct crafted out of imaginative, interpretive libraries, this was . . . She spared me.

"Not really. It sounds like the kind of reincarnation that the Hindu believe in. I always thought that idea of eternal life left too much to be desired." She ran her hands quickly through her hair again. "So, am I to be a Norwegian Ophelia, before the end of the play going mad and drowning myself in a cybernetic creek?"

At the end everyone died. "No, the people who designed your particular platform are humane. Before the stress points start to bend the program will instantly terminate."

Her shoulders fell, but she nodded her chin. "Better like that."

Her expression suddenly became stiff. "And that is what the real Siv would want, too. "

A grim note came to me. *Thou shalt not suffer a witch to live.* They wouldn't—if not her body, then her soul. I turned away and looked out at a vista that she could never see. It didn't matter that she was imaginary, transient, I didn't want her to see my face. *"Capito."*

"And?" As stubborn as Kit.

"It won't come to that."

"I can't tell if you're lying—one of the things that I seem to be missing—but Siv isn't a fool or an infant. And *if* it comes to that?"

"Then I'll decide."

"You've done it before."

Computers are incapable of hunches. But then, no entirety ever came out of someone like Siv Matthiessen. I gave her a stretch of silence.

She waited until she understood that it wasn't going to go any further, and said, "So it's going to be like that. All right, Gavilan Robie, you can look at me again. Your hands told me how capable you are, how hard. Now I will try to be the same. What do you want from me?"

Wanting and giving, the only meaningful dynamics of life. I brought my eyes back to her. "For starters, could we tone down the seductiveness a bit?"

She rubbed her knuckles against her lips and grinned impishly behind slender fingers. "How far down would you like it to go? Sorry, it's not Siv's, my, our, normal behavior. I'm not a tease. It's just that sometimes we like to run our own sense of reality tests. I'll stop. Promise."

I wasn't about to ask if I passed. Another subject: "How extensive are your factual memories?"

Her lips moved silently, like a child adding up sums. Perhaps she was. After a while she said quietly, "Pauline had me start a life journal after our first session. It's quite a detailed multiplex. I seem to be a bit of an obsessive stick. I can recall practically all of it, rather more so than what I suspect I should—is that what you used to raise me up?"

"Actually I didn't look at most of the template data. I'd expect so."

"You're puzzled."

I sure was. Why a life journal for someone who had so strong an inner life? Except for some specialized knowledge about certain drugs, I'm not up on the current practice of clinical psychiatry—*pace* Kit—but unless they've changed the guidelines, my understanding of a journal is that it's supposed to help facilitate the process of self-discovery. And thanks to the power of modern rigs it's much more than a structured diary. From the multimedia libraries and personal cams you can incorporate a lot of the sights, sounds, and yes, smells, that affected you during the course of your days. If you have the discipline, it's a powerful tool. But whatever Siv's problems were, and I could guess at a few, her working on a journal sure as hell sounded like a case of shipping iridium to the moon. "What reason did your therapist give for having you keep a journal?"

"Oh, I see where you're going. I've been in therapy ever since I hit puberty—I started skewing off far more than could be explained by—Do you know about the treatments I got?" I nodded. She inspected my face for a second and continued. "Along with having to deal with that torrent, I was being swamped by a deluge of emotions that were far more than the usual glandular flood adolescents suffer through." She paused and looked longingly at my soda glass. Intimate conversations with strangers can be hard on the throat. "I didn't ever really grow out of it. Chemo mods only feed logs to the fire or they just don't—Do you know that I am impervious to lithium carbonate?" She stopped, started to smile, and changed it into a frown. "Excuse me, that was unintentional. I think. Anyway, Pauline thought that if I had a journal that recorded how I was feeling, and what was the outside gestalt, she might be able to detect an underlying rhythm to my occasional storms. Also I imagine she wanted to use it as a partial veracity check—a problem with too many years of therapy; you learn where all the strings are."

"And did you pull them?"

She laughed again, ruefully. "Sure did, when I was a kid. I thought I was being so clever. Until it came to me that there wasn't much point in therapy unless you're willing to be honest." She pulled her vague legs tighter under her. "If you're thinking that she is linked to that Erinyes *otriad,* you're wrong. Olivia had Pauline carefully vetted before I started therapy with her. Olivia. Have you spoken with her? How is she doing?"

The glow, the concern, in her voice when she spoke her lover's name; an ache passed through me. A reminder of how Kit used to sound. "She's scared."

"Oh, Livy . . . She loves me, she loves Touraine. It must be her worst nightmare. It is going to be terribly hard for her to weigh her responsibilities. You don't know her very well, do you?"

"No."

She said with seriousness tinged with something else, "That is what drives her. Responsibility."

"I did get that impression."

She nodded. "She doesn't bother to hide it. Letting people know how committed she is gives her a great deal of respect . . . and what helps her, helps Touraine."

"But it can be wearying sometimes, especially to those close to her. Especially to those who are young."

"Please, Gavilan, don't do that. People have been asking me leading questions most of my life. Just ask."

"I was curious whether that was the reason why you were at the Blue Azalea."

It was her turn to take her eyes away. "My recent 'memories' don't extend past last Thursday . . . perhaps." Her face returned to me and glowered. "Or maybe it was because I was horny and I was looking for a quick fuck."

"And it's easy for you to be irresistible, isn't it?"

She clenched her hands faster than the program could compensate; her fingers went through her palms. She didn't look at them, she looked at me. Her hands slowly unfolded. "You are that capable. How did Livy ever manage to find you?"

Wish I bloody knew. "Well?"

"Yes. If Siv can, she wouldn't hesitate to use it on the Furies. I doubt it will stop them from . . . from destroying her, but it may slow some of them down while you try to get her away."

If this was anything near what Matthiessen really was . . .

Time for a tack: "Thank you. What do you think of the Congo Project?"

She took a long time answering. Her face gradually took on some the sorrow of her Pietà. "A beautiful design coiled around a tragedy—a necessary one. God, that sounds so horribly cold even if it is true. There are still too many of us suffering. We've created a Procrustean bed of our lives, of our world. We have no choice. We have to cut and shape. We have to."

"But you don't like being connected with it, even obliquely."

"I can't help wondering what my grandchildren will say. Or, worse, that they might not even understand why I feel the way I do. How can you miss what you've never had? If they are lucky they will grow up in a garden. A gracefully designed garden, with graceful, designed people. But a garden no matter how beautiful isn't nature, a garden isn't free. And if there's no freedom without, how long can freedom survive within?"

A few months, a few years, depending on who is running the prison. Didn't share the thought, wasn't necessary.

She twisted her palms against each other. "By the way, Livy agrees. That's why she had me start up a team to explore the prospects for deep space resource development. If we can take some of the burden off the planet maybe we can leave enough room for—I know, it's an old fantasy." She sat up straight, a flush of excitement on her cheeks. "But the time may have finally come. The sciences we've evolved over the last forty years, the efficiencies we were forced to craft—when we started combining those tools with the incredible amount of neglected data that has been collected, along with some of the proprietary tricks that the Groupe has developed, we came up with some wonderful scenarios." She suddenly scowled so hard it cut like a razor. "I hate this!"

"What do you hate?"

"The gaps. Siv knows why she's excited. I don't. She's censored details of her work. It makes me . . . it makes me feel like a puppet."

The sad irony didn't escape me. I tried to touch the only way I could, with my voice. "It's all right."

Whether it was because of the familiarization routine, or that the talent my mother gave me could carry across the light electrical, she heard me. Her face relaxed. "It seems that I am acquiring some of our temper. Interesting . . . There was something else I wanted to say that felt relevant—oh, yes, the only real bottleneck we're facing is still the problem of transportation."

"The JPL grant."

"That's only one of the avenues we are pursuing. We're also looking at new drives—damn, another gap." She rubbed her brow as if that could bring memories back. She shook her head as she said, "However we do it, if we get past that last hurdle, Olivia's willing to commit Touraine to going out. To finally build the road." The admiration in her voice was almost luminous. There are many reasons to love somebody; some of them aren't mysteries.

She put an elbow on the chair and rested her chin on her knuckles. "You weren't thinking that I might have somehow collaborated with my kidnapping?"

A steady half beat ahead of me. Lord . . . "It's happened before."

"It wouldn't happen with me."

I looked at the image sitting so determinedly in front of me. She was only a portrait of Siv Matthiessen, brushstroked in by a machine. A trompe l'oeil, an illusion so strongly done that at first you don't know if it's real or just a representation. Yet, I know a bit about art, and a little less about people. I took a chance and believed her.

"What about opposition within the Groupe?"

"I can't recall any—and I don't think that's a gap. If there were, Olivia would be dealing with it, not Siv. Hmm, does Paul share your suspicions?"

"He might."

"Are you not working with Paul because you want to keep a multipath going, or is it because you don't trust him?"

"Something like that. Why did you refer to the Erinyes as partisans?"

"So you *are* an American. Is your accent really that good, or is it something the machine is giving me?"

"It's real."

"Truth?" I nodded. She gave a sigh of relief. Inside I joined her. She may have said that knowing what she was wasn't bothering her, but if doubts started to creep in—a hesitant diver is a dead one.

She went on to answer my question. "We call them partisans because it's apt. Despite everything, you persist in the view that all terrorists are crazed criminals, pure and simple. In Europe we have a different perspective. We know how often that isn't the case. Most of them see themselves as soldiers, fighting with the weapons that are available to them: a bomb in a building, a plane dropping incendiaries over defenseless villages. The difference lies only in what nations are willing to consider legitimate acts of horror. Using that name doesn't mean that we approve, or respect, what they are doing, but it does help us understand. And when you comprehend your opponents you have a better chance of defeating them." She paused. "You know this, don't you?"

"Yeah . . ." I finished the last of my drink and stood. "I'll be back in a moment. I'd like you to think about possibilities while I'm gone. Like who you might have spoken to about your trip to Los Angeles; did anybody suggest going to the Blue Azalea? The members of your research team; could any of them have had contact with MacRao? And any other vectors along those lines you might come up with."

She nodded and half closed her eyes. I went down to the kitchen, started to pour some more tonic, said the hell with it, and got out the leftover bottle of Stony Hill. I filled up a fresh glass and waited, reestablishing my own equilibrium, while it cooled.

Despite her assurances, I put her psychiatrist down as a strong possible. Setting up a honey trap for someone like Siv Matthiessen wouldn't be easy. If she were a man, well, men in heat are generally as discriminating as a machine gun. But I've never met a woman who wasn't conditional about her lust. I didn't think Siv was the exception—on the contrary. They had her Scherzi matrix, the most sophisticated, so far, measurement of emotional intelligence. It could have given them a road map to her id (*pace* again, darling, I do know the danger of using the simplistic when it comes to souls), but it requires years of sensitive training to properly interpret a Scherzi. One of the Furies might have the expertise—no, that didn't feel right. Nor did the likelihood that they would have given the matrix to an outsider. They were too tightly wrapped up. And I didn't think that Siv would be sufficiently revealing about her drives, to a casual lover. That left the shrink. Unfortunately, I would bet that Thinh had already moved in that direction. Even if he didn't know about the journal, he would be running double-checks on anybody that knew Siv intimately. And my asking for her psychiatric history very likely had resulted in Siv's therapist taking a country vacation—chaperoned by some handpicked people from Groupe Touraine.

But I did like the journal angle. Siv may have been careful to keep out politically sensitive material, but if she was as much a stick as she called herself then there could be enough—correlated along with other sources—to draw some inferences about Groupe Touraine's future strategic plans. Strategies that someone in MacRao might be very interested in. I shook my head; it was only conjecture. The lip of the glass had turned dark; 60 degrees. I took it and myself upstairs.

Her face had gone back to the controlled grief that she had given to her sculpture. I sat down and waited.

She rubbed her hands against the arms of her chair. "Wine? I wish I could have a sip—several sips. Large ones."

"What came to you?"

"The woman assigned as my bodyguard, Marguerite Vassey. *Hun er min venn.*"

I didn't have to be fluent in Norwegian. *Min venn*, "my friend." There are a few things worse than betrayal. I'll be damned if I know what they are. I waited, letting her have the time to figure out how she wanted to talk about it.

She started speaking in a low monotone. "She's been with me ever since I started working for the firm. Marguerite's more than a friend, she is, was, my ally, my confidante. That went both ways. Together we made our lives within Touraine easier for each other. When I started sharing Olivia's bed that life got complicated. It made me need her even more. Her position in security went from minor to very major. I saw to that, one of the few things I forced. We covered each other's backs. And she would help cover for me when I went off on a brief fling—I wasn't hiding them from Livy, she knew that they were going to happen even before we joined, but I didn't want to *inflict* them on her. It was Marguerite who suggested that we go to that club." She laughed briefly, painfully. "I thought it was a marvelous plan. I love to dance almost as much as—she organized it all: getting the incognito passes to the club, arranging for a hired car instead of one from the company fleet—" She dropped back into Norwegian. What she said next doesn't need any translating.

I hadn't told her that Vassey was dead. Not because I was worried about her stress points. If she couldn't handle that sort of news then she wouldn't be of any use. But because no one needs to hear that someone died on account of them. I put away half of the wine.

So, that explained some things, although I still didn't like the flamethrower. I asked her, "Could Vassey have gotten access to your psych files?"

She shook her head. I marched on. "Do you think she knew you well enough to help make someone into an object of desire?"

Her fair skin flushed, not from excitement. "She was my friend, not my lover."

"Friends usually know more than lovers."

"Oh, Gavilan, that is very sad and cynical—perhaps you would be more comfortable speaking French."

Now, why did I think that was a carom shot? I smiled apologetically. "Does Thinh know the extent of your relationship with Marguerite?"

"Of course. But how helpful she was?" A thoughtful pause. "I suspect he knew only what we let him know."

No doubt.

"What are her politics like?"

"I have no memory of us ever talking about political matters. Which doesn't mean . . ." Her face said that she was wrestling with an unwillingness to believe something. "I do have a strong recollection of how much she admired the Fouchets' chateau. It is by Chinon, near the mouth of the Loire. Livy had to spend a fortune reclaiming the estate. I thought it was a fascinating project. Just the desalting problem alone—well, Marguerite wasn't interested in those details, but she couldn't get over how beautifully the house and grounds had been restored and how much it must have cost. Marguerite admired expensive things—" Her voice rose almost faster than the speakers could handle. "Did she sell me for money?"

I shrugged. " 'The gray wolf of greed.' It licks the hands of a lot of us."

"Then I hope she stays in the inferno!"

Dante's Hell and the photos of Vassey's incinerated flesh. I felt sick. Not her fault; I had told her that her friend was hurt, not how. While my stomach settled, I thought of different lines. Thanks to the Erinyes, that direction was lost and not to be refound, not in seven days. I said mildly, "It's not that simple. In the end, she did try her best to protect you. She may have been just operating on deep training, she may not have known that she was hooked—engaging someone without their being aware is a cultivated art in some circles. Or maybe, it was that at the last moment, when everything you are becomes a fixed point, she remembered that you were her friend."

A trace of tears in her voice: "Do you think so?"

"I'd like to believe so."

She hunched her shoulders and stared at the dark mahogany floor. Faintly: "Thank you."

"I hope to hear that from your other you."

She looked up, pushing a wisp of hair away from her forehead. "Yes, of course, I almost forgot. You want to know what else I was able to think of." She sat back. I absently noted that the chair legs should have creaked. "I do not have any references to MacKenzie-Rao, except for meeting with some of their technical people at various conferences over the last year. Siv didn't record what the conversations were about—I can't lay my mind on *any* meaningful specifics about her work. Am I that scrupulous? But she felt that they were conceited, patronizing, and remarkably stupid." She managed to smile at herself. "Apparently I can get very angry at other people's arrogance. After the conferences would let out I would find the hotel pool and swim a thousand laps. But there was one person that she made an unusual entry about—"

She froze. Rather, her image froze. I jumped up and turned on the rig's analytical display: operationally everything was running smoothly. I glanced over my shoulder, still rigid. I didn't have a clue as to what was going on. The Labensohn persona had gone exactly as I had told Siv she would, in a flash, no lingering, and no locked-up sequence. I told the rig to give me immediate change in internal status reports if they came up and returned to my chair. How the hell do you administer CPR to a metaprogram?

The minutes dragged. Watching her so still I realized how much of her loveliness came from movement. That other time, with Labensohn, I had hesitated, afraid I was crossing too important a line. I had spent a restless night on it and in the morning I had talked with Kit about my uncertainty. She had taken my hand and looked at me in a way that took me too long to understand.

In the end I decided that if I couldn't trust my sense of ethics, I could trust hers. I wished she were here. I wasn't happy about what I was feeling. I don't delude myself about my virtues, but I usually do know what is moral, and what isn't.

But Katherina wasn't here. The odds were that she would never be here again.

I started going over everything Siv had said—asked the genie to give me a short background on lithium carbonate. About halfway through I saw the joke: *impervious*. The mod affects cell membrane permeability. So she doesn't normally do puns. Or at least obscure ones. I managed to smile. Good for her. I thanked the genie and went back to worrying.

Twenty-two minutes, fifteen seconds. The image vanished, then reappeared standing three feet away from the chair. "Gavilan?"

"I'm here."

She turned around. "What happened?"

"I was hoping that you might be able to tell me that."

Without any sense of her realizing it she moved through the chair and resumed her curled-up position. "I was thinking of my journal entries and then I started thinking about how my memories of the journal come from the journal and—that's it! I must have been caught in a Marikawa formation."

"A what?"

"Uh, how is your math? Are you familiar with PKT—protothetic knot theory?"

Lord, how many goddamn cognitives of hers had gotten enhanced? "Never mind. Do you know how you got out of it?"

"Not really, and even if I did I'm not sure Italian is the best language to explain it. I'm not sure there is any in which I can. I do know that at one—twist?—I thought of you, and the formation started to ravel in very odd ways."

Humor's a good cover for relief. "I'm flattered."

She ignored me and spoke as if to herself. "It probably had to do with your not being in any of the preexisting memories. An inadvertent leak into another sector, sloppy design"—she grinned quickly—"for which I should be grateful."

"How do you feel?"

"Tired, like I've just done those thousand laps I was telling you about." She snapped her fingers soundlessly. "And I was going to tell you something interesting before my mishap."

I stopped her. "Are you sure you can continue that line?"

"I think so. I know what I need to stay away from—after years of therapy I've gotten good at that. Let me tell you before I get too tired. One of the people from MacRao wasn't patronizing, he was very curious—and frightened. At the time it made me feel very confused, which is why I wrote it down for Pauline."

"He was afraid of you and he shouldn't have been?"

"That's right. I hadn't said or done anything at that conference that should have made feel him feel that way. I usually know if I'm being scary. And he was the only one that had reacted to me that way."

"Do you have his name?"

She pursed her lips. "No, I only enter initials. His were S.B.

However I might be able to . . . can you get me a sketch pad and some chalk?"

"I don't know. I'll see what I can do." I got up and went over to the rig. She shifted and turned so she couldn't see what I was doing. Did she feel the same way I did about viewing one's gizzards? I hand entered some queries. There was a carrel that could be integrated in. It was going to be difficult, but if I augmented with the house systems' secondary graphics—yes, that might work. I gave the instructions and returned to my chair. "It will take a few seconds."

She nodded. "Black or red?"

"What?"

"The chalk."

"Oh, black, I think."

As she was shrugging, the sketch paper and chalk appeared in her lap. She whispered to herself, "It's one thing to be in a virtuality, it's another to *be* one." She took up the stick and began drawing. Her hand moved swiftly, unerringly over the paper; she kept her dark blue-green eyes looking off into the distance. She whistled silently. "I think this is what he looks like."

Three-quarter profile, as if he were looking at you but not quite. Craggy face, a Teutonic cast. Thin lips and deeply focused eyes. His long curly hair was richly detailed, almost obsessively so. Except for that, it wasn't a good or bad drawing, just ordinary. I was glad. I had been staggered enough. Still, I memorized the sketch beyond its utility. It wouldn't survive her.

"Thank you. Was that conference tel or live?"

She "put" the sketch beside her on the floor. It faded away. "Live. Siv is convinced that virtual conferences are mostly a waste of time. They mostly end up being a—" She made a jerking motion with her hand. "Is that the right gesture?"

Thank you, Siv, for making me laugh. "What about the name of the conference?"

Her brow furrowed. "Nothing, only that it was last spring and it was in Dresden."

No problem. I would get the name, and if there was anything else worthwhile about him, I'd get that too.

She stretched her arms wide, the sleeves of her sweater rode up a little, showing me strong forearms. Thousand of laps. I said, "You are tired. Why don't you go to sleep?"

Her face registered some panic. "Can I?"

I spoke to her as soothingly as I could. "Close your eyes and count backwards from ten."

"But, isn't there more that you want to know?"

"Yes, but we both need some time off. Close your eyes."

She nodded and followed instructions. I pressed the bottom on the remote in my pocket that put her down into a low-level wait state. It was getting dark outside. I thought of the poem she had quoted. . . . "Lilac and star and bird twined with the chant of my soul/There in the fragrant pines and cedars dusk and dim."

I closed the windows.

CHAPTER TWENTY-ONE

IT WAS POSSIBLE THAT S.B. was only an ordinary man who had been
not so inexplicably intimidated by Siv Matthiessen. But I had two
hunches, hers and mine. I was willing to take the bet.

And assuming that he hadn't used an alias, finding him
shouldn't be too difficult. No need for subterfuge routines; I told
the house's data retrieval system that I wanted a simple boilerplate
kind of agent and gave it a basic stack: start with the Dresden
Chamber of Commerce; go to the listings of live tech conferences
held in that city during the last year; see if it could find, and buy
its way into, the archive files that contained the names of the participants and start sorting through with the keywords: MacKenzie-
Rao and all of its space/engineering subsidiaries, Groupe Touraine,
Siv Matthiessen, geomagnetics and other space propulsion systems. Maybe he was the head of his company's delegation, or a
speaker, or sat on a panel. It didn't matter, as long as he wasn't just
an anonymous face in the crowd.

At the same time it was to bud off some tendrils; one to access
the University of Alberta's International Business Database and go
through its global Who's Who, focusing on MacRao, et al., execs
that are involved in space R&D. In case S.B. wasn't a corporate

viper but a staff scientist, another tendril was to scan authors in the appropriate abstracts for a strike—yes, I knew the last would take some serious time. And as long as it had the time, it was to take a sweep through the major news combines for pertinent articles. Finally, concurrently, try the graduation yearbooks—starting since MacRao became a major player—of the National University of South Africa. That was really pushing it, but it was worth a shove; for extracurricular operations most companies like to harvest talent from their domestic base. Less danger of unfortunate misunderstandings—such as betrayal.

If the agent found Siv's S.B., it was to look for a public biography on him; there might very well be one. Auden labeled his times the Age of Anxiety. You could call ours the Age of Ambivalence. And prominent on the list of our personal inconsistencies is the fact that as much as we say that we treasure our privacy, too many of us still want the shiny coins of prestige. Speaking of coins, I moved a thousand from a numbered account I have with a Liechtenstein bank into ready cash—even boilerplate inquiries aren't cheap anymore.

Over the years we've been together my DRsys has gotten nicely fine-tuned as to how I prefer searches to be conducted, and it's gotten very good at developing extended lists of wheres. It asked a few clarifying questions, then got to work. During the free-range years, the hunt would have only taken a few minutes, but now, with barbed-wired protectionism the order of the day, I would be lucky if I got any answers in a few hours.

I shouldn't complain. That barbed wire helps protect my land. Helps lengthen my life.

I got Jessie and brought her with me into the conservatory. Tuned her, took up the bow, and did a sight-reading of Sibelius's *Malinconia,* the house playing the piano part—perfectly, impersonally. I refuse to let it use samples.

It was a luscious piece with a faintly bitter, plaintive undertone. (Critics say that Sibelius only wrote well for the orchestra.

Guess they haven't been informed that tone deafness is easily curable.) The old girl was in a mellow mood; she took to it. Sibelius composed it soon after his daughter died of typhus. I sat still for a moment, thinking about that, then went into my reduction of Debussy's *Pavane.* . . .

The last strains faded as soft as a cat's breath into the corners of the room. I put the bow aside and rested both of my hands gently against Jessie's neck. My hands. I put one in front of me. The entirety that was Siv-not-Siv had read it and said that I was a man that she would not want to know too well. What did she see? Many calluses. Fingers long enough to span twelfths; no sign of how often they had been cut. All the scars gone, except for the missing nail on my right pinkie, and the knuckles and sides of my left hand that were grazed from my rooftop mishap. A life line as jagged as a California seismograph, a love line—well, I had one. Hands that nearly strangled a man yesterday. It didn't require any special magic to decipher what they were capable of. I was glad that gloves were back in fashion.

Thought about secrets, and luck.

I once spent a long weekend with Sophie in a hillside house near Trabzon that overlooked a fog-shrouded Black Sea. We were being briefed by an Albanian who had been a colonel-superintendent in his country's penitentiary system, before his superiors found out that he was taking a cut from the inmates who ran a drug smuggling business in and out of the prisons. He wasn't arrested; it wouldn't have been politically expedient. But they forced him to hand over nearly all of his wealth—the penalty for not sharing his profits. For only a bit more than thirty pieces of silver he was willing to deliver over useful information about the prisons he had overseen; their exact layouts, vulnerabilities in their security systems, which guards could be hooked, even a backdoor pass into an archaic computer that handled some police work.

After filling our plate, he offered as a dessert what he claimed were some rich trifles about the narcotics industry that he had obtained from some of his prisoners. Sophie wasn't interested. She told me it was going to be a waste and left. She was right; I spent the last night listening to useless gossip while slowly becoming numb from the fumes coming off the *yesca* blunts the man insisted on smoking as a celebration. But one of the stories he told me was so unbelievable, and he was so unimaginative, that it passed over into truth.

He claimed he got it from a man who had worked as a pharmaceutical technician for one of the principals. That a space transport company had agreed to ship up an automated drug manufacturing microfactory hidden inside a private, retrievable research satellite. The factory was to produce an extremely purified variety of argent *lody*. With a potential 2,000 percent profit margin, it was worth the up-front cost to the syndicate. Bringing the parties together, handling the finances, that was done by certain officers of the Hsin-min Bank of Santiago. Impossible. Near space is powerfully policed. Except that transportation and cover were provided by Assagai.

It was almost a twenty-year-old story; it might be worthless, it might be gold. Luck.

I tried to get Jessie interested in some Bach. If it's possible for a cello to sound coldly indifferent, she did. She's never been much for her contemporaries. Jessie has given me so much that I suppose I shouldn't mind. But I do.

In 1989 my father was on detached duty, posted to Berlin. A day or so after the Wall came down, he happened to be at one of the old crossing points when an old man with a cello and folding chair came quietly to the square in front of the checkpoint. The man opened the chair, sat down, and began playing. Word spread faster than the sound of his music; women came running with flowers, men came with tears. And Mstislav Rostropovich played Bach by the broken Wall, with perhaps the greatest passion of his great life.

Until that day my father had never been particular about music.

He didn't tell me the story until I was almost grown. He never tried to persuade or force me to do anything. Before I was born he had put those parts of his personality into his mind's version of the drawer where he put his broken watches, solitary cufflinks, expired passports, medals from forgotten, useless wars.

So for him it was just one of those lovely serendipitous moments when, as we strolled back together to the train station after seeing a performance of the Denver Symphony, I stopped and informed him, with all the solemnness and intensity that a five-year-old could muster, that I wanted, that I had to have, that big fat fiddle you could hold between your legs. The one that was beautiful.

Year Ten. Sitting on the bench one of my uncles built for me under the oak that bent lazy boughs over the creek. The air summer soft. The smell of the smoke from the spring fires all but gone. My mother and father lying close to each other on a picnic blanket, he resting on his elbows, she with her head on his chest; listening together to Bach's Suite in G Major. Listening to their son . . .

I tuned Jessie back. I was going to see if I stood a better chance with Villa-Lobos—if I couldn't have Bach, maybe the melodies of his best spiritual descendent would do—when my pad chirped. Somebody had just dropped a note in my postbox.

"San Pedro de Macoris." The port where I had handed Lucy Gorelik over to the Sisters. I groaned wearily. It was going to be that kind of game. Okay, I'd ante up. Entered the date of when I was in San Pedro, tagged it to the note, and left it in the box for whoever had managed to get that number to read. You've got me, now come on out and we'll find how much it is going to cost both of us for you to forget about me. I felt relaxed as I put away the pad; I was getting tired of juggling balls. I took my bow up again and played with Jessie music whose only complications were technical.

And when we were done, the agent told me that it thought it had found my S.B.

Sebastian Broder, age sixty-seven. Born in Pietermaritzburg, South Africa. Bachelor's with first honors from the National University, two years of military service, then a doctorate in engineering physics from MIT, followed by postdoc studies at the Kadohata Institute. After the Institute he spent twenty years at various universities and research centers—never longer than the standard two-year contract. Considered a leading expert in electrostatic systems as applied to GM drives. A number of citations. The last seventeen years he has been a senior scientist with MacKenzie-Rao's Center for Strategic Innovations. Married and divorced twice, there was no available information on his ex-wives or children if any. The only address for him was the Center. The second week of March of this year he attended the fifteenth annual Scherling Conference on space engineering where he was on a panel that discussed new ideas on alpha particle shielding. A delegation from Groupe Touraine also attended that conference. The group leader was registered as S. Matthiessen.

A blowup from a group graduation photo at MIT showed a face that in the essential details matched the drawing that Siv had done.

Sometimes you get noise, and sometimes you get a chord. Now, if it only connected to something.

Broder had spent twenty years on the academic road. Easy to explain if he was mediocre, which he apparently wasn't. Maybe he got bored staying in one place too long, and that changed when he passed fifty. Hitting the halfway mark will do that to people. And maybe being a traveling scientist is about as good a cover for gathering information as being a journalist. Better; hardly anyone trusts journalists anymore.

Speculate a scenario: Broder gets recruited early in his academic career by—I looked over the slim details on his career during that time—the hunch was MacRao, not his government. For having to bounce around tenureless he receives a steady deposit of cash as compensation, maybe the occasional access to the firm's datacores—that gives him a track edge over his less well connected colleagues, or maybe it's something else—there are many different kinds of price tags. He does his twenty years in the field and gets as his reward a position with the company's distinguished think tank.

Could be he's retired from the espionage side and is devoting himself to deep thoughts about his specialized branch of knowledge—or shallow thoughts while he counts away the days, and dreams of his mistress—whatever. In which case his reaction to Siv is weird but not important. Or he's still involved, a section head, or a member of the firm's competitive intelligence committee—now, that would be nice. He meets Siv at the Scherling and is spooked either because A: He knows what is planned for her and running into a victim, having to see however briefly their humanity, will set most off. Or B: He's been away from the playing field for too long, and is unnerved when she says something that's a threat. Or it could be something else entirely. That's the problem with these kinds of constructions. Too many unknown variables.

"It is a capital mistake to theorize in advance of facts." So said the Great Detective. But then Holmes always correctly interpreted his facts, and studiously ignored any alternative explanations. I have always wondered whether Doyle hadn't been slyly pulling his audience's legs through all those books. That his protagonist only pretended to be logical, window dressing to hide the fact that in reality he thought with his gut.

I paused my thoughts and played a series of semiquavers, an aimless melody going nowhere.

A wise man knows when it's time to trim the sails and run like hell from the storm. If I was sensible I would assemble a folder, go to Thinh and say to him, "Listen, this is too much for me. WOTAN had it wrong. It was basing my chance of success on the small private gigs that I've done. This is far too difficult for a solo operation. Here's what I've put together. It's not much, but you might be able to use some of it. Good-bye and good luck."

The problem is that I am not a sensible man.

Alone, oh, Robie, you are always so reckless. . . .

Yes, because there's only one life I'm willing to lose.

And so on into the breach . . . There is a directory, available by special subscription only, that lists and independently rates private investigation firms around the world. I've used it now and then for regular jobs; their evaluation of quality is very good. I told the house to fetch me the volume on Africa.

Located a suitable outfit: small, independent, no known history of involvement with the Randlords, four stars for efficiency and integrity—not an easy combination. There is a ten-hour differential between L.A. and Johannesburg. It was seven o'clock here. I had three hours until their office opened. I spent them doing minor chores: trying to persuade my body that it was thirty again; reading as much background material as I could absorb on the political economy of central and southern Africa; converting some more assets to cash; and mulling over how I could get MacRao to betray the Furies.

The operator of the agency was William Mpondo. We thrashed through the problems of establishing my credibility. Liked the fact that it wasn't easy. Finally, he said "Let me see if I understand you correctly, Mr. Giancarelli. You wish me to undertake a vetting of one Sebastian Broder, who is employed at the Center for Strategic Innovations. And furthermore you want me to send to his postbox at the Center a series of anonymous notes every four hours."

I'm not too proud to plagiarize. I nodded at his image. Mpondo had a trim beard running along his jaw line and tightly chiseled features. Phones can be made to easily deceive—the image he was receiving from me certainly was—but there was no reason for him to play tricks with a prospective client, so I figured he was about my size, my age.

"That is correct. Will a transfer of funds from my account to yours constitute a contract?"

"It will."

"Thank you, Mr. Mpondo."

INTERLOGUE 3

TUESDAY, OCTOBER 26

AS SOON AS THEY WERE aboard and secure, the first thing Thomas did was head down to the engine room. He could have run his status checks through the bridge, but his teachers at the polytechnic had drummed into him the importance of a hands-on inspection of machinery—cybers were clever, but they weren't perfect. Besides, he loved being with motors, the sight and smell of equipment doing precisely what they were supposed to do. "Look long on an engine. It is sweet to the eye."

He could never understand why there were so many who couldn't see that it wasn't the fault of the tools that the world was being devastated. Before the *satai* found him he had gone to meetings where angry voices babbled the old retrograde bullshit— lumping together the immorality of behavior with the joy of creation. He wasn't the sort to stand up and argue. The words were there, but he knew that all that would come out would be stammering half sentences interspersed with "Can't you see?" and they would either laugh derisively or ignore him. He could take being disregarded; the cold sniggering—especially when it came from the young women whose bright eyes he wanted so much to look into, whose perfume made him miserable—he couldn't.

The Furies weren't like that. They knew that evil didn't come from the hands but from the heart.

Thomas made his way into the bowels of the ship. The light bars came on slowly; the vessel was just coming out of its standdown state. From his bag he found and put on a pair of thermogloves and went over to the HYCOS system. He carefully examined the four hydride tanks. They seemed to be okay, although he didn't like the look of the seal on the outflow valve on the LaNi container. It was too hot—228.2 Celsius, seven degrees too high. Even though it was well within tolerances, nowhere near a failure point, the right thing to do would be to shut down the system and replace the seal, but that would take too long. He thought about it and decided that three layers of Friglex wrapping would do the trick. A sloppy solution, but it couldn't be helped. Just to be sure, he double-checked the pipes on the others: the calcium, the vanadium, and ferrocarbon tanks—their seals and joints registered the right surface temp.

Next came the fuel cell. The hydro/air mix was right on the mark. That took away some of the annoyance he felt about the seal. Whoever the previous engineer was, she knew how to keep old machinery running smoothly. The seal probably had just started degrading. Thomas carefully brought up the cell: plenty of current.

He went around the room examining the various subsystems, whispering notes to his pad on things he could improve, upgrade with the few pieces of equipment he had been able to persuade his team members were absolutely essential. Overall, he liked what he was seeing.

The fire-fighting system was linked to the enviromentals. A practical bit of engineering, piggybacking the sensors. It was the kind of cost-efficient utilization of resources that Groupe Touraine was so good at. The three months he had spent working for them taught him more about field work than he ever learned in school. If only they weren't indifferent bastards. Zombies. Hooker's term was dead on. Dead on—he laughed briefly at his own joke. Hmm, he could separate the systems; no, it wasn't necessary, the ship had manual overrides on the bridge and in the engine room. He moved on with his inspection.

Finally, like a kid saving the largest birthday present for last, he trod across the narrow gangway over the driveshaft to the engine. It was, in its own oily, dun-colored way, a brawny, no-nonsense beauty. Originally a Perkins marine diesel, it had been successfully converted to hydro about eighteen years ago according to the ship's log (he had spent happy, absorbed hours on the flight going over the ingenious work done on the refit). Fifteen thousand horsepower—it gave him a kick to think of energy with that term; the image of a huge herd of wild mustangs thundering across a vast golden plain. It made him dizzy just to imagine the sight. According to the specs, the Perkins could move the ship at a steady eighteen knots just about forever. He shook his head. Forever wasn't in the cards, not for the ship, not for the human race.

He didn't have any delusions of some great victory. The final triumph of Mother Gaia—battered, bleeding, but still alive—over deathgreed. Some of the others might dream otherwise, but he saw the creeping abyss and knew that there wasn't any bridge that could span the coming inferno. The only future he saw for himself was the one that faced the Spartans at Thermopylae. He just hoped that he and his friends would give as good an accounting as those brave warriors had for the sake of their beloved land.

Although his parents were Greek Cypriot, they had been too tired trying to survive to teach him anything about his past. That bit of imagery was the byproduct of being a scholarship boy at a mediocre public school run by a headmaster infatuated with the Neoclassical movement. Once he had thought it a joke, a waste of time; now he was glad that he had gotten an education in the heroic.

Hooker called him over the comlink as he was about to run a quick compression check on the huge cylinders. "How does it look?"

"Looks real good, *mon capitaine*."

"Hah-hah. Placed the explosives yet?"

"No. Not yet."

"Do you want Knut to come down and give you a hand?"

"I can manage it."

His comlink tended to sound flat, but Thomas was sure he could hear Hooker trying to be as consoling as possible. "It's okay, man. We know you can handle it."

"Yeah. Listen, I've got a lot of things to do here."

"Right. Call if you need anything."

"I will." The comlink hummed its sign-off.

He took out the two bombs in his carry-all. They were his design, but when it came to assembling them his hands had trembled. Knut had seen what was happening, moved him aside, and done the work, skillfully following Thomas's hoarse-voiced instructions each step of the way.

It wasn't because of weak guts—he had long proved otherwise on that score to Hooker and the rest of the team. It was because the bombs *were* his design. And he had dreamed of being a builder. . . .

They wanted weapons. The little gang that ran the street where his parents and younger brother lived. They wanted guns. So he made them. In the machine shops of the polytechnic—the security alarms were as run-down as the rest of the school. Working metal and diode. Guns, small, easily concealed, powerful enough to penetrate the cheap body armor of their rivals. And when they came to him for his tribute, when all of them had one of his guns in their hands, he squeezed the trigger in his pocket. The shaped charge that each gun really was blew into their faces and throats. He was good with bombs.

It wasn't good. But the *satai* needed his talents. And for their sake he would do anything, as he had for his family. He put the first bomb down in the dry bilge under the driveshaft. The second went next to the liquid hydrogen bulb—the ship's emergency fuel backup for the HYCOS. The bombs had multiple triggers, both internal and external. The latter were hardwired. After he finished his inspection, he and Knut were going to spend most of the day running and then hiding monofibers to strategic points on the ship. He had considered installing a dead-man switch, then rejected it—too great a chance of an accident. The bombs were supposed to be a final resort. That's what Hooker said.

He agreed, but it still hurt.

*　　*　　*

Teresa came down as he was finishing with the engine. She waited until he wiped his hands clean and then offered him a large sipper. "It's a fruit cocktail. I found some bananas and mangos and a ripe papaya in the galley's fridge."

He reached for the jug. "Thanks, uh, gracias. Uh, is there any . . ."

"There isn't any rum in it. Come on, Tomacito, I know you don't take alcohol." She gave him a teasing smile.

He didn't understand. He hadn't been that miserable young man for some time now. There are some compensations for living a rebel's life. Women who got wet at the thought of sleeping with an outlaw. He had enjoyed his share. *Kanena provlima*. Except when he was with a woman he knew and liked. And he wasn't even in lust with her. Not that he didn't find her attractive. She had the thin lips, large breasts, and the precise 350mm differential between waist and hip that he had established in the lonely frustration of his adolescence as his all-time favorite measurement. But while she was desirable, when he looked at her all he saw was a sister. So why did she make him feel clumsy?

As he sucked on the cool sweet juice, Teresa walked over to the bomb that was magplated to the liquid hydro. Something floated across her face. He asked shyly, "Is there something wrong, Terry?"

She twisted her body halfway toward him and ran her fingers through her hair. "Wrong? No, nothing's wrong. I was just admiring your handiwork."

For a moment she had looked so dejected, so lost. But now he understood. She was feeling sad for him. For what he had to do for the mission's sake. He went to her and clasped a hand under her elbow. Her hand clasped his in turn. Yes, a sister.

CHAPTER TWENTY-TWO

TWO A.M. IN THE SAN Gabriel Valley. I found him on my fourth stop: three cantinas and finally the only all-night diner I knew of that served fresh orange flan. He was sitting in a booth near the kitchen door that allowed him a view of the entrance and the front windows. He was lost, but not that lost. He saw me come in and ignored me.

I slid into the bench opposite him. "Hello, Harry."

He looked up from his pudding and said in a soft, slightly wavering voice, "Hello, Gav, brought me a gift?"

I placed the package next to his plate. He stared at it pensively. "Long, round, and narrow. Promising."

"Salenica rum."

His eyes brightened. "Why, Gav, that is splendid of you! Can I offer you a piece of flan? They make it here with real sugar and flour."

"No, thanks. How's your new pancreas?"

He put his spoon down and jerked his head to one side. "You really fucking well know how to give with one hand and take with the other. . . . It's gone cancerous again, just like the last two." He touched briefly his right shoulder. "Maybe I will get some joss, the wheel will turn in my direction and I'll get a transplant next time instead of a stem clone." He held out his arm showing me his wrist monitor. "See, my residents are still compensating." He smiled thinly. "If I have got to live under an indeterminate sentence, then I will be damned if I am . . ." He pulled his arm back and looked at me from under scared brows. "Come on, you know what that's about."

"Yes."

"Fine. Then you'll let me finish my food in peace and then we will go for a drive. Okay?"

I nodded. He leaned his elbows on the table and ate with silent concentration. The three remaining fingers of his left hand trembled slightly. A resting tremor. He could have the nerves rewired but he doesn't bother. He's had enough operations. Harry's old, very old. He told me once that his mother gave birth to him during the firebombing of Tokyo. Among his many tattoos there's one of a rising phoenix, on his right shoulder. Wish magic. Then again, perhaps not. If a fraction of his legend is true.

He's not a chip—I will not use that term again—any debts that are owed come from me, not him.

He cleaned off the dish, carefully scooping out the last of the apricot glaze from around the plate's rim. Fished out some coins from his tired flannel vest, dropped them by the plate, and stood, tucking the rum under an arm. "Let's go," he said.

I pulled off NCH and parked by the Zuma wall. He handed me the bottle, but he wouldn't let me help him clamber up the concrete boulders. It was as black as the night gets around a city. The moon had set, the nearest house was hundreds of yards away, and clouds hid all but a determined handful of stars. Far off in the distance there were the faint twinkling green running lights of a freighter, heading north by northwest. Harry found us a dry place to sit. The wind was sluicing down from the canyons at our back. Our conversation would only be heard by the sea. I twisted the cap off the bottle and poured some of the rum into two paper cups. He took one from me with his good hand and swallowed. "Now, that's good. Salenica; it's from Costa Rica, isn't it?"

"Uh-huh, by way of Barbados. It's made by a family that resettled after Zenobia stripped their island out."

"When was that? Year Nine?"

"Ten."

"Yeah, I remember now, eight class six monsters in a row. A bitch of a year."

I sipped the heavy rum. A comforting fire ran through me. "We've had a few."

That was the observation that never needed a comment. He held out his cup for a refill. We sat there for a while, the surf sluggishly collapsing below our feet.

In a voice just above a whisper he said:

Break, break, break
At the foot of thy crags, O sea!
But the tender grace of a day that is dead
Will never come back to me

I said, "Poets are the only real prophets."

"What's that?"

"Something I was thinking a little while ago."

"Well, now, maybe that's why they have gotten so back in favor. You are going to need all the beacons you can get."

I shifted. I could barely see his lean face. "You've heard something."

He took the bottle from me and helped himself. "I heard you went to Mid-City for aid and he turned you down."

After Harry's Yakuza got wiped out, he landed a job as a mediator between the Pacific Rim gangs that were attempting to recreate the Pax Mafiosi that had made the underworld from the eighties to the teens the largest and most successful business alliance on earth. He was respected enough that when he wanted to retire they actually let him. That had been so long ago that most of the lords had forgotten about him. But he hadn't forgotten about them. He still has some unfinished business, and his memory is damned near as good as mine. "You know what I am working on."

"I know what and who, but I don't know why, nor much of how. Take it easy, Gavilan, have some more of that rum. They do not know much either. That could be the reason they've let you run free." He shrugged his too-thin shoulders. "Or it could be that they are too busy beating off the dogs."

"They're getting that hard a press from the feds?"

"Nothing that they don't seem to have anticipated, but I think it is tougher than they expected. It's caused the Padrino to decide to take a vacation, nobody knows where. In the old days—" His laugh sputtered into a long hack. I reached out to steady him. He waved me off. "No, I'm okay. I was going to say that in the old days they would have been smarter than to get involved, but of course they weren't any wiser then. None of us were."

"How involved are they?"

He didn't answer me right away. There were pebbles in between the stones. I pried a few out and flicked them into the ocean.

"They are working it as a favor," he finally said. "For the Sing On tong."

"Don't know them."

"They were a triad that had enough karma to survive Hong Kong, but there wasn't any space for them to go overseas. So they moved inland to Nanchang. Had a hard time getting established even after eliminating the local amateurs. The provincial governor then, he belonged to the New Scholar school; the Sing On tong had never run into someone who was both virtuous and efficient."

His voice had taken on a musing yet withdrawn tone; a retired colonel sitting in a lonely library talking about old, distant battles.

"What happened?"

He moved his thin legs about, finding a more comfortable perch. "Oh, they tried killing him and his family a couple of times. They got one of the daughters. Mailed her heart back wrapped in red parchment. A stupid maneuver, they should have—" He hissed slowly through his teeth. "Forgive me. Well, afterward, what was left of them hid, became inconsequential, until the governor retired at last and somebody less effective took over the local reins."

"How consequential are they now?"

"Let's say they've become prosperous shipping merchants, mostly in dielectric synthetics, gold, and high quality *lody*."

"Besides drugs they handle real gold?"

"China's the biggest market. The trade is supposed to be regulated—you know what that invariably means. Do you find it interesting?"

If those unspecified mineral rights the GT consortium supposedly were given included a gold field, then—no, wrong direction. "Not really. Do you know if they have ever been in the production side with ice?"

His shook his head.

Too many lines to pursue. If you're not careful, Robie, you'll find yourself wasting time trying to untangle knots that you have no business touching.

"Why do you think they asked Mid-City to assist?"

"If you are asking for a fact, I have none. If you're seeking an opinion . . ." He rolled his cup awkwardly between his hands. "They have no politics. Despite their rituals, their plans, they have no past, no future. They are ex, exis—what is the word I am looking for, Gav?"

"Existential?"

"Yes. They only exist. They see the world the way a maggot does, just a body to feed on, to burrow into. Listen to me! I should talk. . . . I would guess they are involved purely as a service in turn for somebody else."

The thought came: Arthur Cormac knew some of what Harry

was telling me. The Justice Department may have the devil's own time fighting the Pacific crime kingdoms—even if they are on the wane—but that doesn't mean that they don't occasionally succeed at getting good data. That was why he was pressuring the Benevolence so hard. The notion brought back my conversation with Warren Tyler. "You don't happen to know if there's a mule-driver named Soares on Mid-City's payroll?"

"A Soares on the drug side? Let's see . . . there's a Martin Soares, but he is a lab boss. Highly thought of, a master cook. I understand he studied molecular engineering at a university somewhere. I doubt he has ever worked the streets. No, I can't think of anybody else."

Well. Another alley that I didn't really have the time to explore. I had another route that felt more promising. "What do you have on the Hsin-min Bank of Santiago."

He hummed softly to himself. "I hadn't thought . . ." He watched the surf, then said, "Understand, it has been many years since I worked at that level, so what I say may no longer be true. . . . No, the details may have changed, but no matter what pretty blossoms they have grafted on to themselves, the root stock would be the same." His voice got back that old colonel. "They have always been a reputable family, one that could stretch hands in both directions. North and south. Do you follow me?"

I nodded. He continued, "Besides laundering money, they also served as a conduit for companies that wished to utilize the resources of the syndicates. Sometimes it would be for something as simple as acts of sabotage against competitors or to help neutralize unions; sometimes it would be more subtle. Say an ambitious company developed a product that a government ruled unacceptable. Rather than shrugging and writing off the costs, they would turn to us—through the New People—to see if we could make a market for them." He paused to replenish his cup. "From what I understand, the kidnapping was done by people who are not part of our spectrum. Is that correct?"

He wasn't asking a question that revolved around legal semantics. "Yes."

"Yet it seems that they may have the right connections. And the connection that you might find most intriguing is that back in the old days of Hong Kong the family that founded the Hsin-min frequently employed the Sing On tong for *special* situations."

Intrigued? You could say that. Now, if only I could figure out a way to break in to the bank. "Have any idea how well the Hsin-min are covered?"

He sighed. "It has been too long for me to know that kind of detail. But no one is invulnerable. And in their case, they may be more exposed than they realize. I only dealt with them a few times. They were very good at maintaining face, but underneath I could sense how tightly stressed they were, standing on the knife's edge between the worlds. It occurred to me then that they might not be able to stay there for much longer. That tension always leads to poor judgment—and you know where that leads to. But I must have been wrong since they still seem to be managing." He briefly put a hand on my knee. It wasn't meant to be comforting. He said, "Even if they are weak, going in that direction wouldn't be a smart idea unless you prepared for a war."

I smiled sincerely. "Harry, I wasn't planning to go that far."

"No, of course not. You are wiser than that."

I wasn't positive, but it didn't sound like irony. I took a long pull of rum. Had another direction that might result in a more immediately difficult decision. "Does the Benevolence know something that's actually worth the press they're getting?"

There was another long wait. This time it didn't feel like he was running calculations. He rubbed wearily at the bridge of his nose. "How much money does it take to disappear?"

"That depends on who might be looking for them."

"Say someone like Carlos Chou."

I took the time to slow my pulse. "If they knew how to vanish and they were smart enough not to look back . . . fifty."

"Do you have fifty thousand dollars, Gav?"

"I can get it."

"There is a woman. She is in San Francisco now."

"His first woman?"

"She is not that far up the hierarchy; she's only a concubine that is beginning to age. Now you will ask me how has she acquired anything of value, and I will tell you I do not know, except that she does know more than she should, and her master isn't aware."

"And she wants to leave."

He said simply, "She is tired of her life."

I didn't ask why she didn't go to the police. "Guarded?"

"She left ten days ago accompanied only by another of Chou's personal women. They're staying at a small hotel. If they are being watched over it is probably by a local affiliate." He shrugged. "It should not be significant coverage; she isn't important."

She wouldn't be. There are some women in the organizations— like the one assigned as a perimeter guard for the Padrino—but there aren't many, and I've only heard of four who had risen above the street. Mostly the syndicates see women the same way they see the outside world; with utter, brutal contempt.

"What's her name?"

"She lives by the name of Rebecca Donovan. I don't know the name of the other woman. They are staying at the Bennington."

Chou scattering his household. Like throwing aluminum chaff in the air to screw up radar. "How will I know Donovan?"

"Call the Colorado branch of In Our Hearts. Ask for the Jean Rawlings file."

A runaway. Who ran into something she couldn't run from. She wasn't that important, unless she tried to leave without permission.

I had the sense, and the respect, not to ask him how he knew about her. So I asked him why he had hesitated.

"I have no idea as to what she can tell you. It may be an irrelevant tangent, in which case all I am doing is providing a time waster."

"That's not all."

He rubbed at his nose again. "We see each other so seldom, I forgot how good your ears are. The other reason: if it is not a clean operation, then you will have to vanish yourself. I don't want you to completely disappear on me, Gavilan. I have a favor to collect from you. Should you or I die before then, well, that is our karma. But if we are still alive when the day comes, I want to be able to find you. Do you understand?"

I nodded. He was a *yurei,* a dead man staying around to settle a bill. Not the first one, and probably not the last one I'll know.

"Good, then let's drink some more of that beautiful rum and discuss poets and all the other unlucky bastards."

So we talked, until the night was no longer black. Two gray men.

I dropped Harry off at the Santa Monica trolley terminal. I have no idea where he lives. Safer. There were several messages waiting for me on my pad. One was from Danny. I told the truck to head east on Sunset Boulevard. I opened the mailbox up and listened to him.

"A couple of things have come up that I thought you should know about. First, an update on Jason Nancarrow. Seems he went to the hospital with his friend and then returned to his house alone. Saltini arrived late Sunday night and has been on him, without any trouble, until yesterday afternoon. Then the cops arrived. Nancarrow's been taken in as a possible material witness to a major felony. Saltini says that he is being held in voluntary protective custody. His parents showed up. Jason wouldn't see them."

Did his name come up during the questioning of Tyler's crew? Or did he call the cops himself? If Siv dies, in all likelihood he was going to get charged with being an accessory after the fact. We lost our patience a long time ago. The average length of time in the Californias between a homicide verdict and execution is now seven weeks. Swift, if often unsure, justice. No, wrong. It doesn't have anything to do with justice. Even if Jason's only crime was knowing and not saying, there was a good chance that he was going to face not seeing sky for a long time. Unless his parents were able to bend their will on the district attorney. Unless he was willing to let them.

I turned Danny back on. "I told Saltini to hang around for a few days. Reckoned it wouldn't hurt to carry some extra insurance. Next piece of business. Nell had her conversation. She started by playing it friendly. A sisterly talk about the community's image and how it could be hurt. Just easing into what was going on, when, out of nowhere, the cop got egregious and threatened to pull her in. Nell just smiled and said that was fine, she would wave for a fast truth test and then a talk with the woman's lieutenant about how to file a false arrest complaint. That got her a hard knock down they were talking alone in a back alley. Nell got up faster than the other woman expected and told her that she could see that the woman was new at this and she should be more careful not to leave any bruises."

Danny paused, and added thoughtfully, "I know it sure sounds like Nell was running on high-test, but from the way she told it to me I think she's been on that wave more than once and had a good balance on what she was riding. A union organizer, sweet Jesus. Anyway, the cop swore at her a bit, then suddenly left. Nell's puzzled, and so, mate, am I. We can't figure out if the cop's hooked or just plain dumb. Nell's still checking with her friends on the cop's pattern. If she finds anything that makes any sense I'll let you know. That's about it, Gav. Sorry I can't bring you more. Keep hanging."

I was a bit confused too. Well, South Bay was Danny's show and I didn't call him in just because he was a friend. I went to another piece of mail.

Ethan had forwarded a pair of legitimate job offers (a basic rule of life, always try to appear normal). One was from an ergonomic instruments firm headquartered in Boise. A Rodin *Hand* had been taken from their offices. For some unspecified reason the sculpture was grossly underinsured. And there was a sidebar: the piece had been bought by the founder when the company had its first real profit. His children were on the board of directors. They weren't happy.

The other was from Germany. A private collector I had helped some years ago was going to donate to a Nuremberg museum his greatest prize, a Dürer engraving of which there were only two other known copies. But before he did so he wanted me to test their security system. Any way I could. It sounded like someone had made an almost fatal flaw and let slip some arrogance about how safe the Dürer would be behind their walls. The man had made his fortune betting that other people's assumptions were wrong.

They were both gigs I would have seriously considered. I marked off on the first one and returned it to Ethan. For the other I sent a personal note apologizing and suggesting another examiner, a woman I knew who would give the museum a good scare—among her many skills was the ability to make a weak link out of the strongest man.

The last message was: Gorelik. UCLA, the hospital's sand garden. Eight P.M.

Considerate. The garden was a lousy spot for an assassination. So, would I go? And what do I do about Rebecca Donovan? And what . . .

My body finally took over. I rested my head in my hands, told the truck to deposit me at my office, and stopped thinking.

CHAPTER TWENTY-THREE

BEFORE I FELL ONTO THE office couch I forced myself to make two calls. The first was to Colorado. It took the In Our Hearts factor a few long seconds to find and send me the file on Jean Rawlings. When she had turned twenty-one the documents had gone into automatic storage. Then I called the San Francisco office of Hardesty and Sons. The line was a little shaky; I got Michael Hardesty's warm tenor a second before his visual: "Hola, Gav! Man, you look like the stuff my dog likes to drag in."

Mike's got an exuberant retriever that thinks anything dead is worth showing his partner. "Remind me not to ever lay down on your porch—I'm fine, just low on sleep. I have some work for your firm."

He nodded. "Fee or split?"

On the West Coast the Hardestys are becoming to detective work what the Rothschilds used to be to banking. Marilyn Hardesty adopted six boys, all out of various hellholes from around the world. Each brother, except for the youngest, who's studying to be a veterinarian, runs a different regional branch of the firm. I've worked with them a number of times on art thefts and related cases. We already have mutual trust.

"Only a fee this time. I'm not getting a percentage—and the way it's going I'm not likely to even see much of a profit. It's proving to be an expensive gig. And what I need from you is going to add to that. I'd like a round-the-clocker on a woman staying at one of your hotels. Starting now."

His handsome face looked a little disappointed; the last time I had called on his firm they got half of what I was paid—they earned it—for helping me recover from some hard SOBs one of the few privately held Innes's (maybe the best painting that odd man did in his old age. A book my father wrote on Innes used it as the central motif. Won a Pulitzer. One of the sons of bitches had read it. Said it was a motivator. Still don't think that's funny.). At the thought of how much my request could run he put away his letdown and grinned. "Pas de nada, you called at a good time. I've got a sharp crew of Watchers sitting around on idle—you know how they can get when they're not working." He shook his head ruefully, "Why is it that the best people at stalking have to act like crank freaks when they're not in the field? They've only been off two days and they're already getting on my nerves. All right, is she a primary or a secondary?"

A light came on warning me that he was recording. "A secondary. I think she can be a source, if I can get to talk to her." I paused. "That's the complication. She belongs to a power in one of our Bennys."

He scratched the deep cleft of his chin. "Aha . . . You want to find out how strong her protection is?"

I nodded. "That and a breakdown on the hotel's security. I may want to make an unannounced visit."

"Anything else?"

"If it works out, I'll also need an E-ticket for two."

"Your slang's getting old. We're calling it an 'Eve Ride.'" He looked at me curiously for a moment, then said formally, "I think we can arrange an evade and escape."

The advantages of having a strong, competent organization.

But there are some disadvantages. I thanked him and gave him what I had about the target.

Michael ran his eyes over his paper notes—like Kit he prefers to jot stuff down with an antique ink pen—and said, "Okay, I don't see any trouble getting an estimate on her cover. We know all the local hires, and if they sent any troops up one of my Watchers is a phenomenal reader—I don't think there's anybody he can't pedigree. If they're holing up in the hotel—the Bennington? Classy, which means they've got a large live staff, and that means I can put somebody inside. Hunh . . . You know, if she's not impor-tant, the only guard may be the other conk. That would make things easy, wouldn't it? If they aren't under orders to bunker down then it shouldn't be too hard to arrange a separation. Sounds good?"

"Sounds good."

"Now, this Rawlings file, I see that her image has been age-enhanced, but do you know if she's had any sculpting since then?

Jean Rawlings at her imagined majority was a nice-looking young woman: triangular face, high cheekbones, large hazel eyes, soft, undefined mouth. Except for erasing some baby fat, the graphic program had decided that she must look much the same as when she was a fifteen-year-old runaway. The IOH bulletin didn't speculate as to why she left her family, only a note that there wasn't any criminal abuse report on her parents. Going from high school to a harem—don't say it's better than ending up being dumped cold dead into a back-country arroyo. Sometimes it is, sometimes it isn't. "Sorry, I don't."

"That's okay. Unless she's had some truly radical work done, making her won't be a snag for my crew. If she's still at the hotel, they'll have her."

"Good. I don't know exactly when I'll be flying up. Let's say sometime over the next forty-eight hours."

"Do you want stat briefings?" he asked.

I fought back a yawn. "Not unless anything unusual comes up. I'll call you before I come up, for details."

"Got it, and Gav"—he stared at my face—"go get some sleep. You run too fast and you'll find yourself ahead of the wind."

Just as long as I don't end up on a dead run. "Thanks, I will."

I was driving down to Compton feeling refreshed, and stupid. After I finished my nap, I had sent Kohler off to the void meeting place on the off chance that Enbright might already have extracted some of the data I was looking for. There was something: a hexadecimal kiss-off note.

>*I do not have anything to give you. I do not want anything from you. I do not want your attention. Go away.*

Clear and succinct. The Interpol files on the Erinyes and the Angry Sheep had been radioactively fortressed by someone very massive and menacing. Our government, the French, maybe Groupe Touraine. Whoever it was, they were powerful enough to scare Enbright into not even trying to salvage part of the deal—that name in the Hsin-min Bank. I had deluded myself, been naive in thinking that I was quicker with my intuition than teams of intelligence experts backed up by arrays of dedicated EI's. Had allowed myself to forget how formidable my not so friendly competition was. That, compared to them, I was only running a sideshow.

My competition. I had heard Olivia Fouchet tell me that I had a much better chance than the intelligence resources of a global corp allied with at least two heavyweight governments. Part of me had wanted to believe WOTAN's analysis; I got caught just when I needed to hear that kind of flattery. Did Fouchet lie to me? A bit of honey to go with the vinegar so I would make more than a half-hearted effort? I wouldn't put it past her. Might have done the same if I really didn't know what I was about.

So what was I about? How about running out of rabbits to pull out of my hat? I had an iffy maybe in Sebastian Broder. A who-knows in Rebecca Donovan. Danny sifting through the sands of South Bay hoping to come up with something that wasn't pyrite.

Sophie and her niece fishing in Paris. Goddard and Estaban knocking on some doors in the Sea. Kohler was deconstructed history. No opening into the sweet line that the Chilean bank could be. Not bloody much.

If you are not good enough to have doubts, then you are not good enough to do this work. I shook my head. Wrong context, Enrique. This is about means, not motives.

I was on my way back to my home when Llewellyn called and told me he had the sparring partner I had requested. Would five o'clock today be convenient? I said that would be fine. He asked about my kidney. Lied easily and told him that it wasn't bothering me.

Took the steps up to Liu's dojo two aches at a time. They were stretching together at the barre. Her back was toward me. She was wearing a plain black leotard. A heavy mass of hair pinned up into a bun the color of coffee. A slender body with extremely long muscular legs, one of which she was pointing up almost vertically.

Lew nodded at me, and indicated the woman. Without lowering her leg, she pivoted in my direction.

He said, "Gavilan Robie, say hello to Helena da Silva Carvalho."

She smiled seriously. "Nell will do—*Robie?*"

I couldn't help it. I leaned against the doorjamb for support and started to laugh in great gulps.

Lew left the barre and hurried over to me. "Are you all right?"

I got a hold of myself and knuckled tears away from my eyes. "Sorry," I coughed, clearing my throat. "It seems I just got blindsided there for a second."

From behind Lew she said, "Do coincidences always affect you that way, Mr. Robie?"

Lew was doing his best not to be baffled. He gave up. "What am I missing here?"

I said to him, "It seems the lady and I have a good mutual friend. Danny. He was telling me about her only a little while ago." I looked over his shoulder. She had lowered her leg and was narrowly staring at me. "And no, doña. Not usually. Only the ones I don't expect."

Her smile grew less serious. She came forward with her hand out. "As I was saying, Nell suits me fine."

Her grip was firm and dry. "Gav," I replied. I paid attention to her face. It was squarish; a strong jaw. Her skin was darker than mine with more cinnamon than bronze. One of her parents must have been an *acastanhado*. Her eyes were nearer black than brown. There was an amber fleck in her left iris. Her nose appeared to have been broken once. It hadn't been resculpted. Indifference or remembrance? A wide mouth, lips neither full nor thin. Her eyes reminded me of Sophie, but the way she held her head, the tilt of her chin—Olivia Fouchet.

Be careful, Robie. You already have Kit and Siv to complicate your life.

We let go of each other's hands. Lew looked at us and decided to ignore what he didn't understand. He commented, "My wife tells me that coincidence is bad theater. Audiences become restive when they are reminded that life is full of flukes. Well—since introductions do not seem to be necessary, shall we get ready?"

She nodded, and asked me, "I was told that this was to be a serious match. How serious do you want it to be?"

"Full contact. I'm going to try and take you out as fast as I can." I paused and glanced at the small iron ingots she had for biceps. "But I would like to avoid broken bones or blood—have you worked with force-reflection suits?"

"A couple of times; they won't slow me down." Her eyes flicked over Lew and me. "No blood, hmm. Then I guess I won't need these." She reached into her bun with both hands and removed a pair of straightedge razors.

It was quiet. Then Lew said smoothly, "May I examine them? I am not familiar with that particular design. I think you will find a suit that should fit you in the third locker on your right. The keys for it are on top of the stall."

She wordlessly handed him the blades. And kept her deadpan expression on as she started to pull her leotard off her shoulders while walking past me to the locker room.

I looked at the razors in Lew's open hand. "Don't say it," I muttered.

He didn't, instead he grinned and stropped the dull end of one against a cheek. "You did say you wanted a formidable opponent."

Needed. Wanted is altogether another verb. "Yeah. Where did you find someone like her?"

"With difficulty. I ended up having to go so far as trying Brazil. The Leao School in Bahia. One of Belos's sons told me about her. She had been a prize student there a number of years ago—I hope her being near forty is not a problem—and last year she had returned for a refresher. From what I was told, she hardly required one. She had left an address for them at the school. The son was kind enough to provide it. When I called upon her she was initially reluctant, then she changed her mind—I did not mention who you are."

Maybe she has a frustration or two to work out. Like having to take a hit from a cop. I had noticed the ugly bruise on her shoulder. "I don't think her age is going to matter. Thanks, Lew; I appreciate it."

He bowed slightly. "Go and get dressed. I will get the arena ready."

"I'll wait until she comes out."

He had started to move away. He stopped and looked back at me. "Really?"

"I don't want to scare her with my scars."

"Of course . . ." He put on a sorry Welsh accent, "She is a splendid lass, isn't she?"

"Not her type."

"If you say so."

He didn't believe me. He's a gifted man, but he's not always smart. I went over to the shrine and lit a joss stick—suspected I would need the luck.

The FR suit she found did fit her, except for being a couple of inches short at the ankle and a little too wide at the shoulder. She was barefooted. Large feet, ugly stone-hard calluses.

I asked, "Can you fight with shoes on?"

She looked puzzled. "Yes, of course. But I wouldn't be at my best. Is it important?"

Would the Fury be barefooted when, if, I met her? I shrugged. "Probably not. I'll be with you in a moment."

As I was changing, music came in on the speakers: Drums, something that sounded like a bass flute, and a stringed instrument I didn't recognize. *Capoeira* music.

It is difficult to describe with words the martial art of Brazil. I could say that it looks like a cross between tae kwon do and floor gymnastics. But the analogies wouldn't let you see what a terrible beauty the art is.

There's a story that it originated in Angola and was brought to northern Brazil on the slave ships—that might be true. The area around Bahia, where the art is most intensely studied, was settled by a lot of Angolan slaves. Another version has it that it developed locally, the slaves using their energetic dancing as both a foundation and a cover to create a system of self-defense.

My guess is that it's probably a blend of both stories. The Angolans do have a number of moves when they fight that look like some of the basic plays in *capoeira*. But it took the impetus of the rack and the lash for it to become a coherent, powerful system. The art can be done in two ways: as an entertaining sport—dancing on the edge of violence—or for serious combat. The Leao School instructors—all sons and daughters of the founder—teach both, but they are famous for the latter.

I pulled on the head covering and spent a moment centering myself. I had easily half again her mass and a much longer reach. Amateurs, and not a few pros, would presume that it wasn't going to be any kind of contest at all—but they didn't know how exactingly Lew takes my requests. I had asked for someone who would be up to taking me. Had a feeling Helena da Silva Carvalho was about to make me very miserable. I closed my eyes and released myself to my body; it knew what to do.

When I was ready, I activated the suit and went back as silently as I could into the main room. Lew was hovering by his monitors. When he saw me he reached out to cut the music. I shook my head and watched her. She was spinning low on the floor with one leg straight out. She touched the floor with a hand and suddenly sprang into a cartwheel across half the room and then into a backward flip. That's when I attacked.

She saw me rushing her in the mirrors. She turned ready to leap aside at the last moment like a matador with the bull and then strike me down with her feet as I passed. Instead, I dropped and slid into her, heels up, aiming for her shins. She jumped up into the air. Rolled to my feet before she could land on me. Hurled into her, shoulder to her chest, not trying for any strikes. Just wanting to knock her on her back. She tried to hit my throat, but I had my chin tucked into my chest. We went down together. A scrabble of arms and legs. She did something with a hand at my crotch that, even with the protection of the suit, hurt like hell. The jolt of pain slowed me enough so that she could use her knees to heave me off her. We both whirled away and then came back to each other.

The rest of it lasted too long and hurt too much. I threw her across the room a few times—once so hard against a padded pillar that I thought I had overdone it; she kicked me in the head when I went up to her. She mostly used her legs on me, concentrating on my ribs and face. I was glad there weren't razor blades between her toes. I don't remember much of the end of it, only that I couldn't take another breath, there was blood running from her mouth, and she was holding on to her right knee as if she was afraid it was going to fall off.

Lew turned off the music. Through ringing ears I heard him say, "That was entertaining, but I believe it is time to take a break. Gavilan, can you make it to the tank? Good. Nell, would you come with me. I want to take a look at you."

I stumbled to my corner and slipped the oxygen mask over my face. Cold heaven. About the only thought that managed to surface was that the cop who had knocked her down was awfully lucky.

They returned too soon. Lew leading Nell with a professionally friendly hand on her shoulder. She wasn't limping much. That was good. He asked, "Are you ready to listen, Gavilan?" I took the mask off and grunted.

"Excellent. Now, I would not dream of telling this woman about her technique—except to say that I noticed that she used some tricks that I believe properly belongs to Gracie jujitsu."

She worked her jaw a little, and said, "Gracie has better counters against choke pins."

"That may be, but do you know many who are skilled in both arts?"

Her cheeks darkened. Lew has the politest way of embarrassing people. "I'll try not to use any jitsu."

"As for you, Gavilan," he said quietly, "I have a few comments."

He did. His few comments ran for about three minutes, or six times longer than the fight. At the end he switched briefly to Hakka. "Do you really need this?" I answered with a hand sign: a wagon going off a cliff. He shrugged in a way so that only I could see it, and turned to Carvalho. "It may take some time, but with your consent, doña, I would like to see if we can't create something better here." She nodded.

A good length for a concerto is about four hundred bars. I didn't total up all the moves and countermoves but it sure seemed as if they came near that number. It wasn't a concerto, more like those extraordinary pieces that Evans composed; structural improvisation, formal jazz. Applied to violence.

Carvalho was a trouper. I'm used to Lew's method of choreography, but it can be abysmally hard on someone who's never worked with him before. She listened to him less with her head than with her body, as if this were a ballet studio again and she were a member of the corps rehearsing her first pas de deux. Or in this case, a *pas de guerre*.

I had learned what my best chances were against someone as good as her. If the Fury was better . . .

We showered together. I was past caring about my scars, or much else. She didn't say anything when she saw my arm and back. Afterward she dressed slowly, thoughtfully, in loose white cotton slacks and a black jersey pullover. When she was done she turned to me, and said, "If you have the time I would like to buy you a drink."

I looked at the wall clock. I had ninety minutes until my meeting. "Sure."

CHAPTER TWENTY-FOUR

NELL HAD COME UP FROM South Bay City on a scooter. Told her to follow me and headed to Westwood. There's a small bar about a mile due south of the campus that doesn't cater to students—its clientele runs toward Near Eastern 'emigres' who either aren't Muslim, or if they are, have long since lapsed in their faith's stricture against alcohol. She parked her bike between two decaying cars in front of the bar and waited while I found a spot. When we came to the bar's entrance I stepped in front of her and pushed open the swinging door, holding it ajar. She was startled for a second, then amused. Could have told her it wasn't ancient gallantry—I like to be able to see who's in a dark spot before I go in.

There were a few solitary drinkers at the bar, and a small collection of men gathered around the bar's wall video. The sound was muted: gunfire across narrow streets and an ululating wail coming from somewhere off screen. The men were speaking in desultory tones to each other as they watched. Their Arabic had the flavor of the upper Nile. As we sat down at a small table near the door I caught fragments of their conversation. Their homeland was apparently practicing the opening chords for yet another civil war. Another opportunity for their river to run red.

A sour-faced waiter left the corner of the bar he was resting against to take our order. He ogled Nell briefly with habitual Mediterranean maleness. She touched her mouth and asked for a daiquiri with a straw. I settled for a small brandy and coffee.

"You understand them?" she asked, nodding toward the cluster of men.

"They're worrying about the friends they left, and wondering why cousins have to kill each other."

She murmured in Portuguese, "Because they can't dream of better alternatives."

I quietly gave her Mel Neto's poem. The one about the worst fear: the final dream.

She fingered her throat, and said, "That's not necessary, Robie. You've already made your impression on me."

"Sorry about that—the quote I mean. It's a bad habit of mine, no, it's more than that. Sort of a safety valve."

She glanced at me thoughtfully. "Somehow I can believe that. . . . How many languages do you speak?"

I folded the paper napkin the waiter had left into a tight triangle. I picked from the air some random numbers. "A few. Seven pretty well. I can figure out what's going on in another half dozen or so."

A passable imitation of a smile crossed her lips. "That is quite a few. Is English your first tongue?"

"Yes, of course. Why?"

"The way you talk. Sometimes you sound some of your vowels like someone who studied their English by listening both to the BBC and CNN—and ended up somewhere in the middle of the Atlantic."

Another inheritance. It comes out when I'm very tired or not thinking. "And you sound like a teacher."

A flash of a complicated something crossed her eyes—anger, regret. "That's because I was one for a while."

"And now you're an organizer for the IWU."

"So I am. What are you, Gavilan Robie?"

Not who, what. I folded the napkin again in half. "Nothing special. Genetic male, pushing fifty. A child of the millennium. A friend of Daniel Sullivan."

"Please, I've known that you two have been best mates since I was thirteen. Which government agency do you work for?"

"I don't work for the government."

"Of course you don't. You speak more languages than anyone needs to unless they're a scholar or a deep field operative. You fight like a man who—"

The waiter came by with our drinks on a worn brass salver. He set them down and waited for me to pay. She had a card on the tray before I could reach my billfold. He blinked and removed a cash wallet from his apron, ran her card over it, handed it back to her with a minimal bow and retreated.

She stirred her daiquiri with the straw while watching the waiter return to the bar. He and the keep exchanged a few low words, they glanced in our direction and laughed softly. "Great place," she muttered. "I hope we came here because no one knows you."

The world, people rotate at different speeds. For some the ancient is still new. . . . "You were saying something about my fighting."

"Liu told me while he was treating my mouth that he had never seen anyone hold you to a near draw in a serious bout before. The sensei is so precise in his work that I doubt he was being polite in not saying that he had never seen a woman match you."

"He's an honest man."

"I think so too. . . . I also got the impression he was offering me a very large compliment." She jerked her head as if shaking off sweat. "Undeserved. What we did, it put us together like this." She clasped her hands tightly. "We may have been wearing armor, but what passed between us went right through my skin. I'm not a psychmet, but I learned about you. . . . You could have killed me without trouble."

"That's not true."

She slowly freed her palms and took another sip of her drink. "Which part? The killing or the trouble?"

"Both."

She leaned back in her chair and stared at me with narrow eyes. "Given your occupation, I should expect dishonesty—but I damn well don't like it."

Her face started to show disgust, then changed. She said quietly, "You're a polyglot. You fight like a professional, practiced killer. You're involved in a political investigation. You lie like you attack: no hesitation, no betrayal, no *effort*. I don't make quick assumptions." She stopped to take a deep breath. "The reason I came down here wasn't just because of that bullshit story Danny fed me about the community being scapegoated. Do you know the Stockmann Well? Thought you would. I went under it. I know why that woman was taken and by whom." She crossed her legs—ankle over femur, not knee over knee—and paused, waiting for my reaction.

The Stockmann. One of the samizdats. On top it's a somewhat self-righteous documentation backbone site for health issues, industrial and environmental, that are conveniently neglected by the media combines. But deep underneath it runs a strong river, the Kreisau. Named after a group that in the heart of the last century's greatest horror came together out of love for their country to try a moral path out of madness. They were aristocrats, thinkers, theologians, not fighters. They were all hanged. Their namesake dataflow deals with a number of subjects. What they have in common is matters involving the destruction of not just lives but spirits.

Once upon a previous life I had access—no, she wouldn't be able to find out anything important about me there. The Committee's housekeepers are among the tidiest around. There wasn't any point in wondering how she had earned the right to go under. That river doesn't have any wardens, there's hardly any formal structure at all, but somehow only those who have the need and can give the trust are able to pass through that gate. I hadn't thought of looking there. Hadn't occurred to me that they would be interested in a small skirmish amongst the blind. And perhaps because I didn't want to know if I still could get entry.

Even though it would probably increase her misunderstanding about what I was, I decided not to hide the fact that I knew exactly what she was referring to. "And what did Usna's children have to say?"

Her eyes drifted over my face as she took her time in answering. "Enough. Siv Matthiessen was taken by an enviro action group. They call themselves the Erinyes. They claim they took the woman in order to put pressure on Groupe Touraine to pull out of the Congo Basin Project, but that's only an excuse, a cover. They're not stupid. They know that their action has about a zero prob of success. But then, they're not involved with justice, only with punishment. With winning battles and not caring about what the war does."

"Why is that important to you?"

"Important . . . Do you know anything about the IWU?"

"Not much. Only what I've seen in the media."

Her eyes said, Well, that's real sad. "Then you probably don't know that Lionel Akawa, the man who founded the International Workers Union, was trained as a social ecologist of the Kyosei school. Unlike Araiza-Unger, Akawa and his colleagues refused to believe that we are cursed by our heritage to dominate and desolate the world. Where she saw invariable equations, they saw incomplete theorems. Akawa particularly felt that the status paradigm, the obsessive drive for wealth and power and prestige, is predicated far more on culture than pack evolution. Our obsessions are a taught behavior, and we can teach ourselves how to behave differently. . . . Where he agreed with Araiza-Unger was that the 'wise use' philosophy that our rulers have been selling for the last fifty years is only a smoke screen. Optimax technology, Dia! Optimal performance—guess who gets to underwrite the definitions; maximum efficiency—and who gets the profit?" She twisted her lips. "It's amazing how easily we can be conned."

The Holocausts, the Virals, the Southern Hunger, the Transition. We have to forget, we've run out of the strength to live with our memories. It's hard, too hard, to accept pain as a permanent inhabitant of our hearts. We aren't being conned, it's just that we'll take the first painkiller, the freshest paregoric, that seems to work. We've never been wise, only human.

She relaxed her mouth and took a sip of her daiquiri "I'm lecturing. Sorry. I guess you're not the only one with old bad habits."

And the need for safety valves. "It's not as bad as some. Really, go on."

She spent a minute working on her drink. "I said that Lionel Akawa had been trained in the Kyosei. That school specialized at developing macrobehavioral techniques that would strengthen the cooperative impulse against the competitive. The Lion—Akawa—thought that by using the ethics of Kyosei, especially the concept of using equity as a social operant, we might be able to restructure the paradigm. Institutionalize fairness. Make it a first principle of formal relationships. All of them, including our relationship with Gaia. The problem he faced was that ethics by itself can't be sold. It has to be a dimension of a larger object. One that people can give their hearts as well as their heads to. He was too honest a man to found a religion, so . . ."

"The labor movement was about fairness, justice," I said with just a hint of irony.

Her voice turned harsh. "Until they were corrupted. Ever wonder why companies and the government constantly turned a blind eye to union graft? Those that didn't lose the loyalty of their members got destroyed in the name of a freedom that always ended up being about the weak one against the strong many, or turned into castrati, singing the corporate bel canto. We won't let—sorry, it's an irrelevant sidebar. The IWU's commitment to justice for nature—for our homeplace—as well as the workplace is central to what we are. It's what defines us, it's our faith."

She was the one who had brought religion in. "And the Furies are heretics?"

A glance at me to see if I was being mocking. "I hadn't thought of them that way, but yes, they are. They've taken a belief and twisted it terribly. They've substituted revenge for justice. And their actions will only end up being snarled around and used against us. And in the end the earth will be a factory—I know, a quaint metaphor, 'dark satanic mills' and all that supposed obsolete history. But it works. A place that manufactures, that is filled with products, made things. But by that time the term *human*made will be a meaningless proposition. And so will the difference between virtual and real. The world, the people will only be bits of data to be manipulated. And those who do the manipulating will think that they are alive only because they control the flow. . . ." She laughed, softly, bitterly. "You know it just occurred to me that the Erinyes, whether they know it or not, are part of the blueprint. That their actions are part of some corporate Lord's design."

If my speculations weren't totally wrong, she was close to guessing right. I tore the napkin in half and wadded it up into a ball. "The barn's door is open. Whatever happens to Siv Matthiessen, the Furies have already done their damage."

"That's true." She ran a finger around the edge of her glass.

It took me a while. The most subtle things are the simplest. If you want to build a bridge, do an unexpected favor. It works more often than cynics imagine. "The IWU has something going on with Groupe Touraine?"

She briefly gave me the kind of grin that a good teacher gives a bright student: enough to praise, not enough to let the kid get too cocky. "Not yet."

"So it's about politics."

"Yeah, well . . . And maybe it's about Matthiessen being a sister."

I didn't know her. I wasn't sure about her. She had hurried through those last words matter-of-factly, knowing it was a cliché. But I heard the underlying strain. She might be a good actress—I was willing to give her the benefit.

She went on, "What I'm trying to say is that I want to help. I would just appreciate a little honesty about who I'm working with."

Honesty, truth, gifts. I said, "Come sit beside me." Without hesitation she stood up and moved her chair next to mine. She didn't flinch when I put my hand over hers, bringing our palms together, but the muscles of her face were taut. I moved my head until we were only inches apart. "What passes through the skin—I am not and I've never been a government agent. There are other places and motives to acquire the skills you so succinctly listed. I'm involved in this because the woman who is the head of Groupe Touraine, and the lover of Siv Matthiessen, asked me to and I said yes. Not for money, not for politics, not for the salvation of anything, but because I hate thieves who steal lives. Do you really need to know more?" She kept bottomless eyes on me as she pressed no against my palm. "*Obrigado*. I can use your help." I took my hand away. "I'll tell you why. Because you are not my friend. Do you understand?"

She touched her cheek. "*Sim*."

I pulled away from her and opened the fist where I clenched the napkin. I unfolded it into one whole piece. "One other thing. You're right, I do lie well. The trick is to shade it with some truth, and never show everything you're doing. Still want to work with me?"

She shook her head, not to the question, but to me. She took the napkin and began smoothing the creases out of it with her blunt hard fingers. "As long as we do not become friends."

I didn't smile. "I'll do my best."

The silence between us wasn't awkward, but it wasn't comfortable either. We were two people who had entered, precariously, into a relationship that we had no idea where it would lead. A sudden impulse: I told her about my meeting at UCLA and asked her to come along.

"Do you think it has anything to do with the kidnapping?"

A good question. One that I hadn't taken enough time to look at. I went away for while, then came back. "It might."

As if it were the easiest thing in the world she said, "Then I'm with you. What do you want me to do?"

"Act like you're a visitor, an unhappy one—your sister is at the hospital, she tried to kill herself. Touch your face with this napkin. Walk around the second floor, there's an open balcony that runs around the garden. When you're done, go into the ladies' room by the hall on the east side of the garden. Inside write down what and who you saw on the napkin—you're carrying a pen?" She nodded. "Good, then put the paper in your left pocket and leave the rest room. I'll get it from you as we pass."

I knew how well she could fight, now I got a good guess as to how fast she was. She took the napkin and tucked it away. She didn't ask for any more details, instead she asked, "And if there's trouble?"

"It's a public place and there's a lot of hospital security. Not a good choice for an abat."

That got me an owlish stare. If I wasn't some kind of undercover cop I certainly played the jargon, and the techniques. I sighed and went on. "Actually, picking that spot for a meeting is sort of a good-faith sign. Whoever wants me there isn't looking to start a war." At least not right away.

She nodded indifferently and worked on her daiquiri. I am not sure what quality in me inspires confidence, but it seems to be there. I just wish I could internalize it as easily as I seem to project.

They say that the only optimistic people left are the Brazilians and the Americans. Who knows why. Maybe it comes from having started off with the promise of endless vistas. Maybe it was combined with a congenital shortsightedness. Or maybe it was just a confidence that wouldn't be denied. Whatever. She might have a storm boxed inside of her, but behind her words, her gestures, her eyes, was a sparkle of light that said that she believed in the possibility of hope.

She reminded me of Siv, of Katherina. Of what I didn't have.

I glanced at my band. "Time to go."

Nell stood, stretched her arms, and cracked her knuckles. Lord, I thought, have pity on anyone who gives her trouble.

I bumped into her as she left the ladies' room. A tiny grin crossed her solemn face as I removed the balled-up napkin from her hip pocket (I never said I was as good as Sophie). Her note said there was only one person in the atrium, a black man in a long gray coat and felt hat sitting on the bench facing the entrance. No one on the balconies. I went into the atrium.

Perfectly raked white sand, perpetually held in place against the wind by a sprayed molecular attractant; two gaunt black granite boulders representing islands in the sea. A tranquil Zen meditation. They say it's good for the patients, even better for the visitors and the staff. I've always found it depressing, foreboding.

He stood as I walked along the pathway toward him. I said, "Good evening, Mr. Renshaw."

His eyes searched the space behind me, he didn't offer his hand. "Evening, Mr. Kenmar."

I sat down on the stone bench and crossed my legs. "Well, how do we begin this?"

He remained standing, looking down at me. "For starters, let me tell you that I'm not here for Palmer. It's because of Lucy."

"Who?"

Scarred hands tightened into fists. "I'm not here to play games."

"Could have fooled me."

He looked at me balefully from under the brim of his fedora. "Fuck you too. . . . Lucy Gorelik. The woman I know you got out of a chinging whorehouse in Santo Domingo."

A wind came over the surrounding building and dropped a load of cold air like a suffocating pillow on the atrium. I didn't need the accent mark. "So I did. That was a long time ago. What does it have to do with us?"

"Yeah, it was a long time ago. . . . I was there, with some friends. We were all set to go in and get her when the fireworks started—shit, we didn't know for sure that you had gotten her out safe for two days." He pushed his hat back and suddenly sat down beside me. "This is a thank-you, man."

"Why?"

He reached a hand slowly toward his breast pocket. "I've got a pipe in there. It helps my conversation, okay?"

It was the way he asked that question that made me decide that I wasn't going to have to hurt him. "Go ahead."

He nodded gratefully and brought out a long-stemmed briar and a chamois pouch. While he packed the bowl with a Cavendish cut, I laced my fingers together over a knee and wondered if he was going to be a boon, or a thorn. He got the pipe going with a no-glow hot-wire lighter. There was an insignia embossed on its gunmetal surface.

I waited for him to settle into his smoke, then said, "Force Recon."

He looked briefly at his lighter and put it back into the tobacco pouch. "Yeah. I wasn't a golden boy; I didn't find boxing until I was in the army." He took a deep puff and exhaled. I had a taste of the sweet-sharp cloud and stopped breathing until it passed by. Not one of my current vices. His voice dropped a little as if he were talking as much to himself as to me. "Started too late, that's what everybody kept telling me. Guess they were right."

"Were your friends also army Specials?"

"Mostly. Those that weren't were 'bout as good. We were going to cut into that shithole like a hot knife into a slab of butter."

Not butter, flesh. I asked him again, "Why?"

He cupped the pipe between his hands, letting the heat off the bowl warm them. "When Lucy was taken she was on her way to Detroit to see my brother. They had met a few months before and got crazy on each other. Crazy . . ." He glanced up at the fluorescing rails around the atrium and fell into an embarrassed silence. We were sitting in what tries to be a peaceful siding, surrounded by the debris of humanity's soul wrecks. He moved his head slightly. "When she disappeared with nothing, not a word, that pretty much described what happened to him. That alone would be enough to go looking for her, but . . ." He cleared a knot in his throat. "Bobbie had CP I figured any woman who was still willing to care is someone I just about had to find."

Calcutta polio, a cousin of an enemy we had almost forgotten. We don't make that particular mistake anymore; all you have to do is see someone shambling along on exoskeleton legs and remember that summer. Renshaw's brother must have been one of the unlucky ones who were too scrambled to be completely repaired.

"That's my reason," he said. "What was yours?"

"I had some time on my hands."

He moved down the bench. "You got a problem with me?"

"I have a problem with this."

"Yeah, I got it. You don't want nobody to know nothing." His voice suddenly relaxed. "Okay, I'll tell you how we got here." He took a puff from his pipe. "I wasn't sure it was you when you came to see Palmer. I had a description from Lucy before you knocked her out—by the way, she felt real bad about tearing up your face— she thought you were a blackman. A redbone maybe, but surely black—now where did a well-brought-up little Georgia girl learn that tired expression for a light brother? And afterward, we tried some backtracking. I'm sure you understand us wanting to do that. There we were all primed and pumped and somebody who doesn't have anything to do with anything comes along and does the entire show. Solo. I mean, who the fuck were you? Anyway, we got some bits an' pieces of how you looked an' who you were supposed to be. Jacques Condé. You did that dude real well. We got more 'huhs' and 'mind your owns' than we could stand. My friends packed it in, but I kept at it for a while until I could see the trail going nowhere. So I put it away; didn't forget, just put it away. Then when you came into Palmer's office some of those pieces fell out again. It seemed real close, but I couldn't be sure." He snapped his fingers sharply. "Then it clicked."

"What clicked?"

"Wasn't much, something about the way you move. Like you're carrying no weight. It didn't fit who you said you were, but it did for a man who ghosted his way through Santo Domingo."

Before you start learning your lines, learn your body. Posture portrays character. All right, I embarrassed a great teacher. Another bloody thing to work on. "So you jerk me just to make sure. And you decided you had to see me in person to say thank you. Very well. You're welcome."

"What is it with you, Kenmar or whoever the fuck you are? Gratitude gives you the runs? I'm here to give you a present. Palmer, you want him? I'm going to give you the stick."

Unexpected favors. As Lew said, coincidence is bad theater. For some, maybe; I just worry about the actors.

Palmer was the West Coast comprador for the Hsin-min Bank's illicit operations. It's about as hard to keep secrets from a bodyguard, or a lover; a reason not to have either. . . . Renshaw could be for real, and he could be bait. I was having difficulty reading him. I moved my eyes slightly to the right side of his face. An old simple trick they used to teach fighter pilots—when there were fighter pilots—to heighten awareness; register with the left eye so that the primary dataflow goes to the right, intuitive, side of the brain. "You left something out. How did you get my number?"

"Palmer's got a gadget that can pull it off a pad."

The Digital Collective had passed the rumor of that new wrinkle along to their customers a few months ago. They promised that if it were true, they would have a blocker ready—hopefully. I made a note to give them a cheery call. The pad's number is listed to a shell corporation that is owned by another and so on. It would take Palmer and his people a couple of years to get past the web of contracts I had paid handsomely to prevent people from learning who the number really belonged to. And who says that nothing good ever comes from lawyers? I took my hands off my knees and folded them against my sides. "Okay, talk to me. Tell me why I need a stick, and if I do, what do you have?"

His eyelids had been half-closed, he opened them wide. "Decided to stop sounding like a Brit. Guess that's supposed to tell me something." He took his hat off for a second and ran a hand over his bare skull. "I was listening in. Not supposed to. Palmer's got himself a body alarm and his office is a class-four defense installation—he's got the lethal response permit. Inside the Mercantile I'm around mostly for decoration. And I'm only his office sentinel. The rest of the time he's got two boys that he thinks are better."

"Sure."

It came so fast it caught him off-balance. He smiled. "Thanks. I was saying that I wasn't supposed to be listening, but as I learned in the army, and even more in the fights, if you've got to deal with shits, you better have a good idea how deep the pile's going to get."

"So?"

"What I heard sounded to me like you were looking for a buy-in to the Hsin-min's wrong side and he wasn't selling. Now, if it has to do with,"—he deliberately stretched his vowels—"wasting time, then—"

"What if it doesn't?"

"Don't matter. Bobbie got a few years with his woman. . . . I don't give a chinga why, man, I only care about giving you how. Now, do you want it?"

"What is it?"

"Palmer's been sharing a pillow with Natalie Orloff."

I didn't hide the fact that the name meant nothing to me. "Natalie Orloff," he repeated slowly, "she's the niece of Pyotr Orloff." I shrugged. He threw me a you-really-don't-know look. I shook my head. He scratched at the side of his neck with the stem of his pipe, and continued, "This Orloff, he's sort of like my boss. He gives advice, makes connections, monitors business arrangements for a Russian investment group. But unlike Palmer, he's a lot closer to the streets. And he's a man with funny rules about his family, like even if his niece has got three ex-husbands and so many boyfriends that her mattress has been pounded into a futon, she's supposed to keep her hands clear off people he does business with. The funny part is that if he catches her breaking his rule, he doesn't touch her, don't even raise his voice. He has the guy erased instead—personally. You'd think people would be upset—shit, it just adds to his rep as a righteous hombre. Man, somehow I can't believe you've never heard of Orloff."

The Russias, Greater and Lesser, were never part of my bailiwick in any of my previous lives. And I've been lucky in not having to play more than very peripherally with the North American branches of their criminal Organizatsyias. I didn't want to start now but, if Renshaw wasn't blowing me into the wind, it sounded promising. Sledgehammer moves, about the speed I was up to. "So you think Palmer will turn around just because I waltz into his office and clip him with a threat?"

He reached into his coat and withdrew a long plain envelope. "Here's some ammo for your clip."

I took it from him, pushed open the loose flap, and looked inside. Some action Polaroids and a planchet. I randomly picked out one of the snaps: Palmer standing behind a flushed-faced brunette. They were on a terrace draped with scarlet trumpet vines. She was arching her back and had one hand twined into his hair. He had his hands moving slowly over her heavy breasts and his mouth was on her neck. There was a little distortion, some perspective cramming in the lines. Must have been one hell of a long lens. I asked him, "How long have you been putting this together?"

"Pretty much since they first started playing hide the sausage, about two months ago." He looked down and polished the rough surface of his briar with his thumbs. "Palmer's got me with some heavy paper—a couple of years ago I managed to get myself debts no honest man can pay. When I found out what he was about I decided I needed some righteous protection. Until this came along, I didn't have anything worth shit."

Debts no honest man can pay.

"Where can I find Palmer this evening?"

"Tonight?"

"Why not?"

"You're sure not a caution, are you?" He gave me a long, speculative look. "Yeah, I can see how it works for you. Don't know his schedule precisely, but I can find out."

"Why don't you do that. I'll get us some coffee from the machine."

CHAPTER TWENTY-FIVE

Renshaw was finishing his call when I returned to the atrium with two cups in my hands. I set one of the coffees down beside him and dumped packets of sugar and cream bulbs out of my pocket. He put his pad away, knocked the dead ashes out of his pipe, and picked up his cup. "Thanks," he said.

I tore open five of the packets and poured them all into my cup. "Wait until you've tasted it."

He blew over the coffee, took a sip, squeezed his face into a grimace, then rapidly followed my example with the sugars. "What did you find out?" I asked.

"He's finishing dinner at one of the Mercant's restaurants, then the game plan is to go over to the Scarlet Swan. He does that a lot; it's where he likes to relax. You play at being a Brit; know the place?"

A pub, as its familiars like to call it even if most of them have never set foot on England's soggy soil. It's located next door to the Sacker Center for the Human Arts—a software baron's memorial to his tie-dyed grandparents in their old Topanga neighborhood. The gesture hadn't been applauded, the canyon had changed from being pleasantly, if wealthily, funky to being only about money; and artists, unfamous ones, aren't good for property values. Then came the Great Fire of Nineteen and the only structure that was spared in the lower canyon was the Center. Nobody would say it, but there was a sense that Somebody was making a point. Topanga got rebuilt, one of the first exercises in optimaxing, and the SCHA keeps on plugging along. About a dozen live theater and dance troupes share, with lots of energy and squabbling, the pretty little block of buildings. The baron's endowment covers their performing expenses and some walking-around money, much of it spent at the Swan.

There was a period when I wasted some happy hours there myself. An actress who had a little talent and a lot of enthusiasm. I stopped dropping by when we decided that the afterglow of lust couldn't hide anymore the fact that I wasn't going to be an asset to her career. It's been a few years but I strongly doubted that the layout of the bar had changed since then. A small, helpful detail.

"I've been to it."

"Thought he'd prefer a hellclub or such? Not Mr. Palmer, he likes to think of himself as a principled man."

Common delusion. "Who's going with him?"

"His two regulars and Tyra."

"Who's she?"

"Tyra Ganyang, his assistant. You met her when you came to the shop."

I remembered. Poise, aesthetic efficiency, graceful hands, fast eyes. You'll find her type, like bees drunk on nectar, dancing around the angiosperms of power. Some hope, scheme, to get a permanent seat at the center, some are content to just be close by for a sip now and then. Both kinds can carry powerful stings. "Is she his beard?"

"His what? Oh, got it. No, he moves in public with a couple of steady ladies. Tyra's with him because he doesn't like to stay too far away from his business on weekdays—she's wired to be his portable office."

"How long is he likely to stay at the Scarlet Swan?"

"Until midnight at least. He likes the scene and the folks there like him. Being a real Brit kinda authenticates the place for them."

"Tell me the important things about his bodyguards and Ganyang."

"You really going to hit on him tonight?"

My decision had come partly from not having the time to be as devious as I would have liked—blackmail is as tricky an art as disarming a bomb—and partly because in the back of my head the proverbial bells were ringing, the kind they hang around the neck of Judas goat. Rushing the moves seemed like the best way to upset any carefully planned ambush.

I shrugged noncommittally. "Now or later, I'll need the information."

He yawned suddenly and frowned a little himself. I snuck a glance at my wristband. If I had judged the dosage right we would have about ten to twelve minutes. He might be an ally, and he might be bait—wittingly or not. I didn't know. Which meant he had to be out of the way.

Before he slumped against me on the bench I managed to extract some useful data. I called Nell and when she appeared we got him to his feet. I adjusted his hat so it blocked easy view of his slack face, then between us we "walked" him to the parking structure. Thought there might be a problem when a duty nurse glanced our way, then glanced again. But no troopers showed. A drawback to working in a place where unusual behavior is the norm, you can forget that it really isn't.

I try damn hard not to. Which is why I was carrying, mixed and disguised in with the usual bindle of pills that nearly every citizen carries, some quick fixes.

After we got him into the truck, Nell asked, "What now?"

"First a small hotel off the Strip where the night manager is professionally blind, then my place."

While the truck drove us east I alternated telling her a bit of what was going on—more than I thought I would, it surprised me—and periodically checking on Renshaw's condition. The drug I had stuffed him with had as its far distant ancestor methaqualone, a sedative hypnotic. Besides inducing extreme drowsiness, it blocks the nerves that control the vocal cords, and inhibits short-term memory. It's supposedly a rip-off from one of the government hot labs; FBI, DEA, NSA, one of the alphabets, the man who had sold me the formula hadn't known. But it certainly read like a succubi-spawned child of National Security. I had run it positively through a long series of sims, got it synthesized, tested it on myself, used it successfully on occasion on other involunteers, but I still wasn't happy—the population is too variable, and while the results are simple, the coding on this pharmaceutical was complex and that always guarantees a chance for error. Renshaw had been a Special, and even though it had been a lot of years ago, the military were early hit-and-miss pioneers in the art of multivalent defenses. I was crossing my fingers that the soporific wasn't going to compound somebody else's mistakes.

Whenever I use this kind of tool—let's stay away from euphemisms—this weapon, the chemistry that passes for my morals leaves me with a lot more than residual guilt floating in my bloodstream. Should be grateful, stops me from being a complete hypocrite.

Speaking of being unhappy, Nell was. Very. She had grown tense when I told her about the people Palmer worked for and the line that stretched to Southern Africa (a thin line, a gossamer. Yet it felt as strong as whiskered titanium). But it wasn't the politics that was setting her off. She didn't care for my plan or that I was censoring. The truck had turned onto Sunset Boulevard, we were a couple of blocks from the hotel. I touched manual and pulled over at a corner. "*Muito bem,* I'll drop you off here. You can catch the trolley back to the campus and get your scooter. Then you can go back to South Bay, or wherever."

She switched to English, "Don't be a cock, Robie."

Deliberately harsh: "And you said you don't make quick assumptions."

She raised her hands, looked at them as if they didn't belong to her, then returned them to her lap. "When I said I would help you it was with the idea that I would be more than an after-the-thought accessory. I may not be whatever the hell you are, Robie, but most people think that I'm quite capable. If you're not willing to listen to me, then how can I help?"

Being worried is no excuse for stupidity. Being alone for too long makes me forget how easy it is to fall into the gutter of arrogance.

"I'd like to get this man to a safe place first. Then I'll listen, okay?"

With a face that could have been cast in bronze she silently agreed. I started the Cruiser up again and drove on to the hotel. As I figured, there wasn't any difficulty in checking Renshaw in. The Strip is filled with rip joints and bars; it wasn't unusual to have a semicomatose man brought in to sleep off the poison of his choice. And I paid in cash. For a few extra Kennedys I got the Medwatch turned on in the little canister of a room. Hand-entered the variances it was to be on particular lookout for. If there were complications there would be a first-rate EMT from Sinai in the room within minutes, one of the reasons I picked this particular place. Nell helped me get his clothes off and watched expressionlessly as I searched through them. I copied a few IDs onto my pad, checked the slow, even beat of the pulse at his throat, ran a hand gently over his bald head, watched him, then carefully block printed a couple of words on a card I left in his trousers pocket: SORRY. HAD TO.

We were coming around the Hollywood Reservoir when I turned to Nell, and said, "Okay, now."

She had been watching me with puzzled eyes as we climbed into the hills. You ride alongside of someone who keeps on showing you different faces, being perplexed should be the least of your reactions. But her voice was calm. "Are you sure his information is real?"

"I know, I know, damned near anything, everything, can be faked. But as a setup it doesn't make much sense. And the man had . . . he had the right bonafides." And should I be on the bad end of a coincidence and Renshaw was paying off his debt to Palmer instead of to me, the fact that Palmer wanted to get me meant that he had something I wanted.

Nell shrugged. "All right, let's say it is real. This guy you're going to try and shake down, what kind of man is he?"

I told her. When I was done she had learned some things about Palmer that I doubted even a man as observant as Renshaw knew. The advantage of sensitive ears, and money.

She shook her head, and said flatly, "Then you'll fail."

"Why?"

"Blackmail's tough work." The way her mouth moved it was plain that she wanted to use other adjectives. "With a man like him, with his position, it's impossible. If it was only about money, maybe, but you're threatening to compromise not only his safety but his place in the world. You'd be wounding him too much. He can't let you succeed. Oh, I'm sure he will believe you if you tell him that you've got a deadman's switch on the deal, that if anything happens to you the information goes to the worst possible places—you were planning on doing something like that?"

"Yes."

"It won't be enough. He'll still have to take you and try and squeeze everything he can to disarm you. It may not work, but he wouldn't see that he has any choice. It's too risky for him otherwise. And whether he succeeds or not, you're going to be dead."

"I can make it so that taking me triggers the switch."

"Do you really think that will stop him?"

I doubted it. But it wasn't certain that would be the way he would jump. Nell's analysis of Palmer's response was colored by her own dynamics. There were other possible scenarios. Under crunching stress people react in a lot of different ways. But it was plausible, very much so. And if he was able to take me then he would get what he wanted. It would only be a matter of time. When it comes to that kind of questioning, bravery, character, will, they're all immaterial. People don't die rather than talk. They talk, and then they die.

"I think that I can't let him have me."

"Maybe we can prevent that from happening right away. But failing once won't stop him from trying again until he succeeds. Unless he's dead."

I noticed the "we"; I didn't know what I wanted to do with it. "Not an option."

"What, did they revoke your license?"

"My license?

"Never mind . . . Palmer, he doesn't know much about you?"

"I don't believe so."

"Then if I were him I would first string you along, agree to whatever you demand, and try to delay the payment until I was sure of what you were about."

"I was going to try and hustle him along."

"And if he balks? What will you do? Try and bluff him that he's not that important? What if he calls you out?"

"Then I fold my cards and try another table."

"Which will only give him more time to track you down and kill you."

I didn't say something stupid like, Well, he can try. "Nell . . . the best approach would be a faceless encounter, but this isn't the usual extortion game. I'm not after his money, I want a meeting with one or more of his bosses, and they won't deal with shadows. It has to be face to face, real time, all the way through." And then if everything goes well, if I'm alive when it's all over, odds are that I'll have no choice but to construct another life. Maybe it's better that way. Maybe.

She studied the side of the road. "You're certain."

"Yes."

"Then I guess we'll have to figure out an alternative to folding your cards."

There was that plural again. I closed my eyes. What was driving her? She had given me reasons. But I had opened the door a little bit, enough for her to get a glimpse at what kind of terror might be waiting on the other side. She might be a stone woman, she wasn't a fool. Then why was her body, her voice, telling me that she was throwing herself into this with the kind of passionate intensity that reminded me, painfully, of Kit?

As sharp as one of Nell's razors came the memory of the shower we took together. Her slim body covered with skin that glowed under the water like toasted cinnamon, her boyish hips and taut buttocks, her womanliness . . . There was a way out of that hormonal loop. I laughed.

She turned abruptly in her seat, startled as a fawn—cut it out, Robie. She asked, "Did you find something funny about this?"

Nell was wrong, lying isn't completely effortless for me. Hell . . . "Yes, me. Know the song 'Forbidden Fruit'?"

She looked at me with large eyes. "Oh . . ." She groaned faintly. "For the life of me, I'll never—are you serious?"

"I did laugh."

"So you did. . . . . Gavilan, I thought that you'd, I mean I'm not prejudiced, but—"

"You don't have to worry about it. It isn't a problem for me and it won't be one for you. There are men, and women, that are stupid that way. I'm not a moth." I paused, looking at her in the dim salmon glow of the truck's instruments. "Nell, it's not completely about sex."

"No?" She was still for a long moment. "Is it natural, or did you learn it like that trick with the napkin?"

"Learn what?"

"How to be so dangerous."

It was my turn to be quiet, letting my feelings turn from a

major chord to a minor. Finally said, "We better get going. There's a lot of work that needs to be done tonight—you were saying something about alternatives. Why don't you think about them?"

She didn't say so, but I saw the muscles against her neck go down. She was as relieved as I was that I hadn't answered her question. "Okay, so what are you going to do?"

I pulled out my pad. "Hopefully, learn a little more about what we're walking into."

"*This* is your place?" Nell was standing at the threshold, staring down the long main hall. I was just inside the doorway checking with the house if anything unusual had happened while I was away—I wasn't putting much faith anymore in discreet warning signs carved into doors. The house was murmuring to me in slangy Basque—it goes to that format whenever there are strangers around—that except for a game of tag some masked bandits, the family of coons that have made mia casa theirs, had decided to play on the terrace, nothing eventful had occurred since I left. I told it to run a time-sequenced incongruity audit; selective amnesia is even easier to do on machines than on people. I glanced at Nell absently.

"Afraid so."

"So you're rich." She made it sound not quite like a felony accusation. I gave her my full attention, and replied, "It's worse than that. I work for the rich."

"And here I was willing to give you the benefit of the doubt when you said that you didn't work for the government."

Humor. Encouraging. Except that considering who she worked for, what she believed in, it was a scorpion's tease. I said, "I'm a detective of sorts, a specialist. I recover stolen works of art. Most of which are owned by the rich." I massaged my eyes, weary. Weary enough for a soliloquy: "I'm an eccentric. I believe in the lines that hands can design, in the mystery of color . . . and legacies. I said the rich own the art. They don't. No more than anyone can own the past. At best they're only the trustees. I like to think that I'm one of the stewards who tries to see that the inheritance doesn't get lost. And since most of the rich insist on equating value with money, I get paid a lot for my service. Who I am, Nell, that's what I do in the real world. Are you willing to put me on probation?"

"Bread and roses."

"Come again?"

"'Hearts starve as well as bodies; give us Bread, but give us Roses.' I guess you don't know all the songs. All right, probation. For the moment."

She was right, I don't know all the songs. And sometimes, stupidity wins over memory. "Why don't you go into the living room, it's through the first archway on the left. There are a few things I need to check on."

She nodded and started to walk past me. Then she turned, and asked, "No servants?"

"I know how to cook and the house manages to keep itself clean—I know, socially irresponsible of me."

There's a phrase in Portuguese that doesn't translate with any flavor. Something about stuffing things. She tossed it at me as she left.

Careful Robie, probation is a delicate state.

The *Times* database didn't have anything beyond the superficial about the *vory v zakone*, the "thieves within the code," as the Russian alliance of gangs liked to refer to themselves. A code . . . it's funny how even the worst of us seemed to be compelled to set up rituals and rules, however perverse, to govern our lives. The Mafia, the Yakuzas, the Triads, the Tanzeens, the Kaliyatas, the Blitzvolk, the Organizatsyia, and so on down a long nasty list, they all have their creeds, their mock honor. Perhaps it was because they understood, as violent people have always known, that in order to have people act and face the consistently horrendous you must imbue them with an esprit de corps that submerges the urge to feel—that humans have to be structured into collective monsters, that the capacity for group horror isn't bound in some yet unknown way, deep within the recess of our helixed souls.

I returned back to the material that I had skimmed. The *vory v zakone* has existed for centuries. One of their "heroic" folktales claims that they were used by Ivan the Terrible as a spy network. They were almost destroyed by the last czars of the Communist dynasty, as the Italian Mafia was almost crushed before the Second World War by Mussolini—not from any abhorrence of their crimes but because they were too competitive as predators.

The Soviet Collapse didn't come in the nick of time to save them—the Russian gangs had gotten very good at survival—but it did suddenly create extraordinary opportunities. More than any of their countrymen, they did just fine during the post-Collapse era of laissez-faire thee well. The borders open, the KGB in chaos, they exploded over Eurasia. Isolation, poverty, and the harshness of their rulers had forced a kind of natural selection upon the *vory*; they were among the most ruthlessly efficient pack of beasts on that list.

And they were smarter than most. Perhaps because they had always been a loose coalition rather than a monolith, they were good at diplomacy. They found it easy to form strategic alliances with the more powerful syndicates in the outside world. Their most famous joint venture allowed drug profits from the Western Hemisphere and Southeast Asia, laundered by the Sicilians and Corsicans, to buy whatever it wanted to in what was once the Soviet Union. The dollars and ecus that the Organizatsyia got as middlemen bought a lot of the rest.

As for the weaker syndicates the Russians encountered in their move out—obliteration is a precise term.

But that is all supposed to be old news. Immense prosperity on one hand and the revival of police despotism on the other fist caused them to decide that the best course was to become as legitimate as the Latin cartels. The only *vory* gangs left are no more than unstable isotopes, an insignificant, if regrettable, side effect of a fluid, complex society.

That's what the *Times* said. And they only print the facts.

There were only two snips about Pyotr Orloff, both from the financial archives. One identified him as a recent major investor in a string of gaming halls spread around the Great Lakes region; the other listed him as a member of the board of directors of Suratov Ltd., a smallish merchant bank that dealt with Pacific-Siberian trade. No bio, no pictures, no history. Lucky man.

I went upstairs to my bedroom. After I closed the door I woke up the rig that's separate from the house systems. I gave it the parameters to create a daemon—a slash-and-burn agent—that would go hunting for any data it could find on a relationship between the Russians and the Hsin-min. The most useful nodes would of course be completely sealed—spy hacking is a nearly dead art—and the public streams would be about as useless as the *Times,* but there are a few gray zones remaining, shadows in the detritus of that once great river of information, places where the dams haven't completely bottled up the flow.

Rivers and dams, information and power, the Congo . . .

My daemon was going to wake up the Listeners, government and private, that wait patiently in the crevasses, waiting for fools. But hell, I could smell the burning bridges. Still, before I set my torpedo off I sat on the edge of the bed and ran through some of my own diagnostics.

If you feel it's right, cara, then it is. You never went wrong when you trusted yourself. I never went wrong when I trusted you.

On my whisper, the house launched.

I came downstairs with an armful of woman's clothes. After Kit left I had gotten out a chest of things that I had accumulated for earlier friends who might need a quick change. Always be prepared. I guess in my own way I'm quite the Boy Scout—the absurdity of that image made me laugh a little. A good sign. There was a time when after hearing that voice I wouldn't be able to feel anything decent for days.

Nell was sitting at the piano. She was playing slowly with her right hand on the black keys. An unfamiliar tune. She stopped and looked at my arms quizzically. I said, "Folks at the Swan like to dress up, dramatically, you might say. I thought it would help if you blended in."

"Okay." She stood and took the clothes from me.

"There's a powder room at the far end of the hall."

She nodded and started to leave the room, then turned and said hesitantly, "I had a thought."

"About alternatives?"

"About that too, but . . . do you see Siv Matthiessen as a masterpiece in the making?"

I'm not the only one capable of doing homework. And the Kreisau can be a very helpful tutor. "That's part of it."

She nodded to herself. "Thank you."

Watched her walk away. Nice walk to watch. I shook my head, closed the lid, and headed for the bar.

While I waited I poured myself a couple of fingers of bourbon and called from the library an audio copy of Chekhov's *Three Sisters,* a lesson about people who can't hear—a little positive reinforcement. But I listened to it for another reason as well, it confirmed something, my Russian was *strashny:* terrible. I turned it off. Well, can't always have an edge.

The genie finished its internal inspection and informed me that it was clean. Just in case, I told it to start running nonperiodic z/K-wave sweeps through its storage architecture. Another trick I got from Kit; an anomaly search method developed by neuroengineers. If there had been any skilled tampering, the wave had a fair chance of finding echoes of their work. The genie displayed for me the signal's parametric formation, as if I would understand it. I grinned and told it to go ahead. Then I checked on flight schedules to Chile, looked at various mailboxes, ordered my broker routine to start liquidating some securities—my working capital was starting to get seriously depleted.

I called Ethan. He was in his study. The lights were low. The dark bags under his eyes looked especially heavy but there wasn't a glass in his hand. Encouraging. I held up my right hand and shook my wrist: I was pressed for time.

He nodded. "Lucy Gorelik. She's living in Ottawa, working as a cargomaster for a small spacefreight company called Paterson Logisticals. My friends say that she saw a good clinician after you returned her. She seems to be doing fine."

"Is there a Renshaw in her life?"

A good judge never lets a jury see his reactions. Ethan Hill, before he retired, had been voted trial judge of the year by the North American Bar five times in a row. He hasn't lost his talent. "She was married for a while to a Robert Renshaw. He died seven years ago, complications from polio, I believe. She changed her last name to his." He smiled briefly at the thought of that. He added, "That was after he died." Not a surrender, a keepsake.

In music, in love, in hunting, timing is damn near everything. "Did the name Calvin Renshaw come up?"

"A *Calvin* Renshaw, I don't think so." He glanced at the console by his chair and touched some screen keys. "Nothing on that name. Is he related to her late husband?"

"He's supposed to be." I sent over the IDs I had gotten off Calvin. "Take a look into it will you?"

"I will. . . . Going well?"

Ethan usually doesn't ask questions, but then I usually don't have this much contact with him once I've started working. "About as well as I expected. I'll call you soon." He saw my gesture. We broke the connection simultaneously.

Nell had returned in a dress and with her composure back. "It's been a while since I did chic. Will this do?"

A long gown of rose-colored velvet embroidered with quicksilver stitching. Snug to the waist, loose below. Right shoulder bare, the left covered by a thin apricot shawl. The tones brought out the red in her mahogany skin. The dress hadn't turned her into a beautiful woman, just a stunning one.

"I think so."

"I would have preferred something with more movement but you didn't have anything that would have worked any better." She pushed at the folds of the gown, the gore seams were slit on each side nearly up to her hips. Razors come in handy for a lot of things. "I did a quick alteration," she said apologetically. "I hope your lover doesn't mind."

Katherina's about as slender as Nell, and they have the same length of breathtaking leg, but overall Kit was at least four inches taller. The hem of the dress would have come to midcalf, not Kit's style at all. "If I had one, I doubt she would mind."

"No?"

"No. So what alternatives have you thought of?"

She came over to the bar, casually helped herself to my glass and finished the bourbon. "I've got two ideas. They're not really different options, more like variations on the theme. I don't know if you'll like them, or even if you do, whether they can be implemented—"

"I didn't change my mind about listening."

She let herself breathe. "The first is simple. Promise him that if you or yours gets hurt, he dies."

A mad tactic, as in mutually assured destruction. History says it's a good gambit, if both sides are at least borderline sane. Even if I could vouch for Palmer's state of mind, I wasn't about to use it. I didn't cut her off. I wanted to learn how she thought.

"Of course you would have to convince him that it's a real threat," she said slowly. "For obvious reasons it would be preferable if the sicarios weren't local. I know some people in Bahia . . . the kind of people that always fill their contracts. It would be expensive, but that's not a problem, is it?"

"No, that wouldn't be a problem."

She didn't appear to be thrilled either, but she went on, "Fine. If you want to use them I think I can make a contact tonight."

"Who are they?"

"It would be better if you didn't know."

Her familiarity with an assassin guild didn't come from her work with the IWU. The Kreisau and sicarios. Does she know what she sees when she looks into a mirror? "What's your other idea?" I asked.

She looked relieved and got out a small grin. "Persuade him that you *are* a government agent."

I repressed the urge to smile back. "Go on."

"It's simple. If he can be made to believe that you belong to the government then he'll know that there's no chance of his winning. Killing you would be irrelevant at best, suicidal at worst. Dia! The best he can hope for is that you'll be willing to protect him against his superiors. The problem is convincing him. Palmer's going to want cold proof."

I took out another glass and splashed some bourbon and seltzer into it. "I think I can satisfy him."

"Can you? That fast?"

"Probably. Can you let your accent slip in?"

"My accent—you work for Brazil?"

Sometimes people think so hard you can hear the engine running. "I said I didn't belong to any government. It's a coincidence, that's all."

Her fingers were tight against the rail of the bar. "Yes, it must be."

Why did who I was, or what I was, tear so much at her? Occupational paranoia? I knew the disease. She wasn't showing the right symptoms. Reminded myself that we weren't supposed to be friends, shouldn't be friends. I emptied my glass. "I have to make some calls. I'll need about twenty minutes."

"Okay . . . I'll find your kitchen. Want anything?"

"No, thanks."

She nodded, I think, and left. I went over to the Bechstein and softly played back the tune she had been doodling. Tried changing the tempo—Chopin's E-minor Prelude? No, the opening chord sequence was similar, but . . . I closed the lid, went to the conservatory, summoned the phone, woke a man up.

I had to tell him more than I wanted to. And I had to promise that if I should find out certain things he was to be informed—he hadn't forgotten his honor, but he was after all a cop. But he came through, and more. The fiction that Midas believed (hope, always hope), that I was a special investigator who reported personally to the now Senior Deputy Minister of Justice of the Republic of Brazil, would hold for Palmer and his bosses. The more was part of his country's files on the Hsin-min Bank and certain safe-conducts that would expedite the daemon's hunt. It was a lot to give—but then, he knew what it took to ask.

There was enough time to recall my agent, glean the slim data it had acquired, and add the passes. I made two quick mail calls, Johannesburg and San Francisco, asking for updates. Nell, toasted sandwich in hand, found me watching my plants.

She stared at the conservatory's two-story-high centerpiece. "*Meu Dia!* Is that a mimosa?"

"You know your trees."

"I used to date a dryad." She took in the crowded mass of greenery, and commented, "Not many flowers."

"It's autumn. Most of them are past their season."

"Hmm, still it's very pretty. Are they all originals?"

"Most are, some are faux—sort of like people."

She broke off a corner of her sandwich and swallowed it. "Is that another bad habit?"

"Sporadic."

"You got your badge, I take it."

"Gold plated." I told her who I was going to be.

She looked at me with flinty eyes. "And they gave it to you just like that."

"Just like that."

"That kind of power must be wonderful."

"Nell, I don't have the time."

She put down the sandwich and wandered away from me. She tried to put her hands in pockets, when she realized she had none she folded them under her arms and averted her face. I waited.

"That bush over there, the one with petals that look like cherry blossoms, I've never seen anything like it. What's it called?"

"That's an imperial peony. Its name is *Hana no Kumo*, 'Clouds of Flowers.' Almost as old as I am." And still flowering into the fall—more than obstinate. "Sit down, Nell. Let's talk about how we're going to do this."

She came back. The flint was gone, but it wasn't replaced by anything particularly soft. I started by giving her my notions on the approach. She had some improvements. We got to an agreement and then went over the technical aspects. I found a light pen and drew diagrams of rooms and the ideas we had agreed to on the stone floor. Discussed timing and safety signals. Some of it was new to her, but it was all based on common sense. Finally we were both reasonably satisfied. I stretched my back a little, and said, "One question. For you and me. Okay?"

"Go ahead."

"Blackmail."

"You want to know why I know so much about it?"

"It's your answer."

"It's one of the favorite weapons used against us." She looked at me incredulously. "You don't believe me?"

It was nice to know that she was capable of misreading my face. "On the contrary."

"Yeah, well. I should have said that it was something they liked to try. Most of the time it doesn't work. We're pretty much nonhierarchical. Cutting a piece of us may cause bleeding but it doesn't cause us to die. But we have, I suppose you could call them, pulse points." She lost herself for a moment. "I guess it isn't important now. . . . There was a woman, a friend, a special friend. No, she wasn't my lover, although I would have. . . . She was very eloquent. She knew how to help others fight fear and stupidity, She was a threat. The company whose slow-death plantations she was trying to organize knew that. But the way things were going they didn't want to risk making a martyr. So instead they found out something personal about her, something they thought they could break her with."

She looked at the peony again and bit gently on her lower lip. "No . . . it's not important. When she was fourteen years old she had a child, a boy. Her homeland had a government that claimed to be progressive, they were sending out mobile health clinics up to the hills where the most destitute lived—it was really nothing more than a pacification program. She went to one, the first time she had ever even seen a doctor. They ran a genetic scan on her fetus—one of the big biotechs had donated a bunch of their latest analyzers, a cheap way for them to have it field tested. It was supposed to be just the usual automatic defect check, but something caused the attending doctor to take a closer look at the chains. My friend's baby had the Russell metanormal set. Genetics one of your skills?" Shook my head. "Me neither. I looked it up. Like all the other metanormal sets the relational structure of its registers doesn't make any sense when described in a three-dimensional causative space. Escher would have loved it. The Russell's one of the rarest, about one in three hundred million. And most of those who possess it don't seem to have anything extraordinary about them. But three of the greatest mathematicians of the last two centuries had the Russell. . . . I suppose we're lucky that the engineers don't have any idea of how to duplicate those metasets, otherwise we'd be well on our way to rolling Alpha pluses off the assembly line—who came up with that utterly arrogant term?"

"It's from *Brave New World*. Huxley, I think. It was supposed to be a warning."

Nell knew that. She needed the delay. "Another one of the Cassandras. Another one who saw the Factory coming . . . Anyway, while the government might have been playing at being compassionate, the doctor had his own agenda. And the right contacts. An offer was made to her. Not an opportunity to raise her child in a way that would allow him to have her love and still have a chance to achieve whatever potential he was capable of. They weren't interested in her. She was husbandless. Her parents had died from cholera the year before. She had a younger sister and brother who needed—can you understand? She came from a place where family, children, were all anybody had, were all that mattered. She had to decide. . . . She did. She sold her baby."

Sometimes the only way to help someone with pain is push on. "So this company used her shame."

"No, she killed herself."

I waited a while, then said, "With deliberation. In order to win. She left a note telling everyone what had been done to her, by whom, and why. The company ended up making a martyr after all—so much for deep profile analysis. And the workers won."

Nell looked at me as if I had slapped her. Then it penetrated. Not what I had said, but how. No sarcasm, none at all.

She thought about what she wanted to say to me, then settled for: "You got it right. We won. And I set about learning all I could about blackmail and how to fight it so that maybe we wouldn't ever have to win that way again."

We sat silently. Not too close, close enough. I said, "Your turn."

"Not now. I'm not sure I'm ready to hear your answers. Understand?"

I stood up. "I think so." I left her in the conservatory while I went back upstairs to change. Found a richly inlaid silver Zuni choker that I thought would go well with her outfit. One of the links was weak, the choker would break if anyone grabbed it. Spent a moment deciding which suit I wanted to wear, avoided thinking about Nell's story. There is so much I don't know anything about. But I know how some people die.

CHAPTER TWENTY—SIX

WE DROVE TOGETHER BACK DOWN to the flats. The plan was that she would take a cab to the Swan while I followed a little later with the Lotus. I had called ahead to the bar to make sure that one of their private back parlors was free. Didn't make the mistake of asking if Nathaniel W. Palmer was there. If he wasn't I had a fall-back plan—the daemon had gathered up some reasonably useful bits of data along with the usual set of lies, half-truths, and who-knows. More deadly than the bytephages are the land mines of convincing disinformation that are strewn throughout the rivers. But the other maneuver would entail a confrontation on his personal territory. I was crossing my fingers.

Beside me Nell was sitting quietly, looking more relaxed than she had ever since we left Lew's dojo. I asked her, "What did you find out about that South Bay shield?"

"Oh, her. Not much, some hearsay, a few stories. Her name is Patience Lark. That's some name. She's in her early thirties. Comes from somewhere in southern Missouri. Her father was a deacon in the NewMorning Covenant—one of those sects that took credit for Dia's decision to postpone the Apocalypse. Great people. My aunt would have called them the kind that could see evil in the crotch of a tree. Lark claims that she's always known she was flame. Must have had a wonderful childhood. . . . Anyway, she came out here a few years ago from Kansas City and joined the SBPD. She doesn't have many friends either on the force or in the community. One of the women I spoke to who knew her a bit said that the only reason Lark was able to get into the local department was that she was willing to take a hefty reduction in grade. Seems she had been a deputy investigator with the Missouri State Police." Nell absently rubbed the backs of her bare arms and smiled scornfully. "Another woman told me that she thought that Lark was a shield only because it turns some of the brides on."

"The brides?"

Nell stopped smiling and shook her head. "Stereotyping—I'll have to remember to put a quarter into the lame box. . . ." She glanced at me. "Brides, a not very flattering term that some use to describe women who are addicted to extremely butch lovers."

"How does she do for money?"

"Cops have the last strong unions in North America—funny, isn't it? She does okay. Nothing fancy. Lives alone in a three roomer in Hawthorne. The apartment building's sort of a police dorm— you know that South Bay requires its cops to live close by, just in case. She may have had some sculpting, she looks a lot like an actress that was an Incomparable a few years ago—Marla Cirreli, remember her? She doesn't do no-trace chemicals. She doesn't have any idea how to swear right. Her only hobby is doing twenty-K runs. Her only apparent vice is taking vacations out of the country when she can snag a—a sweetheart."

Overseas vacations. A cover for discreetly spending, or hiding, payoff money? If there were time, I would have wanted to find out exactly why she left KC, what squad she had been assigned to when she worked for the State Police—there were some rumors that I had heard about infiltration problems that they've had with their officially-don't-exist local versions of our Benevolences. If there was time. "No encounters or anything since you had your brush with her?"

"So Danny filled you in on that? No, nothing since we played that little skit."

"You think it was purely an act?"

"I don't know what it was. And I'm not sure that Lark had any good idea either."

"Odd."

"Cops."

It became so frosted you could have skated on the air. "I wouldn't say it that way around Danny, he's sentimental."

"Daniel's a great guy, one of the nicest men I've ever been friends with. He's . . ."

We turned onto Vine. I downshifted. "Yes?"

"I was going to say that he's a part of why I'm sitting here. I know what he thinks of you."

"But you'd be here anyway," I said.

"*Sim,* but I'm not sentimental."

I switched the conversation to the roles we were going to play. Even if it was going to be a short, not too complicated performance (my fingers were getting numb from being crossed), I wanted to be sure that we would hit our marks at the right time and not step over each other lines.

Vine becomes Rossmore and the neighborhood abruptly changes from rim village to high-brahmin enclave. I skirted around the invisibly, but extensively, fortressed colonia. Headed westward on quiet Melrose to La Brea's art row. The galleries were featuring this season's discovery—like the fashion lemmings they are—photonic steel assemblages that transformed their discreet fronts into stained glass cubist fantasies. Then a short jog south to Sixth Street and west again, slowing down to the mandatory five miles per hour as we went by the topless pylons of the Memorial, one rough-hewn pillar for each of the thousand dead—our spirit poles.

Went past the soaring frescoed walls of the new County Museum—yet another fortress—to trolley-thick Fairfax and busy Little Bombay. Then the run southward to the Douglas District, the light auto traffic falling away like fearful leaves. No one following. Dropped Nell off three blocks from the King's Boulevard and a busy cab stand. There's a jazz club on the corner that only a handful of pigment-impaired outsiders are willing to make the pilgrimage to. We were taking advantage of the fact that we can't ever seem to get blind enough to really see. Around the club Nell wouldn't stand out in that dress—if anything she was underdressed—and she had enough of the right look and coloring that most would think that she belonged.

Chose a leisurely, circumspect route to Topanga. Wanted Nell to have sufficient time to do some pioneer work before I went in. I put my pad on the warm seat that she had left behind and listened again to what my torpedo had struck.

The Swan hadn't changed. Across the long side of the main room there was the stand-up bar with a pewter countertop. The herringbone parqueted floor was covered with innumerable scratches. Heavy blackened oak beams on the ceiling. Opposite the bar was the twenty-foot-long digipainting of Ariel Thornton—the titian-haired, fabulous, turn of the century prima ballerina the tavern was named after. This cycle she was being portrayed with the vibrant color and line of Ting Shao Kuang. I once had a skilled acquaintance insert a virus into the display that turned her from Tchaikovsky's heroine into Daffy Duck and then in rapid succession into various other cartoon fowls, no disrespect to Ariel, but digipaintings are to real art what sampling is to real music. The gag got a standing ovation from that night's crowd of regulars; even the help clapped. The pub's architecture might be affected; the people weren't.

The rows of trestle tables were filled with noisy, happy men and women—the sad ones usually stayed at the bar, close to the taps. At the far end a few steps led up to a gallery with several booths; that was where, according to Renshaw, Palmer held his court. That choice spot must have made his other bodyguards uncomfortable. There wasn't a clear view of the entrance. I had come in with a group. They made their way shouting hellos to one of the tables. Saw Nell halfway down the bar—she held her drink up in her left hand and smiled broadly at no one in particular—and slipped into a side door.

Gave the manager—a new man, he didn't know me from Adam—a twenty for the private room he was holding and told him to send along right away a bottle of Buchanan and two glasses. He smiled knowingly. I smiled back. The hallway that ran past his office led to the parlors. I had the one with its own exit out of the building.

A quick check of the room: about six yards across, low ceiling, ox-blood red carpeting, pearwood paneling on the octagonal walls, a small couch facing a fire screen, and a round table with a green baize top big enough to handle a full crew of poker players—not a metaphor, that's the second most popular activity in the Swan's back rooms. Five card draw or impromptu couplings on the loveseat, both games of chance.

I opened the back door, counted off how many yards it was from the alley to the street, then closed it and stuck a sliver wedge under it. Unless someone did a search at eye level to the floor it should be invisible, and the slight signature noise of its circuitry would be hidden by the normal electronic ambience of the room's antisnoop shields. It was my own bit of handiwork; the block was going to hold that door shut, unless I called out a command word, then it would blow itself off with a loud, very distracting bang. Insurance. Being reckless doesn't mean having to be completely stupid.

A waiter came in with the scotch and the glassware. Tipped him and asked him to tell a certain lady that I was ready. He smiled with better manners than his boss. After he went out I opened the door to the hallway and sat where someone could see me as they came to the room. Everybody was going to be nervous; I wanted to minimize if I could the odds on an accident. I looked at the whiskey, left it sealed. Put a unifield D/J on the table, rested my hands next to it in plain view, and thought of nothing.

Fifteen minutes. Then a flyer whirred cautiously through the open doorway. The detector, and experience, said it was a wizard's eye. One of Palmer's men must have sent it ahead. Off eye contacts, or shades, he was seeing through the tiny bot's pin cameras. A straight-out-of-the-manual tactic. It came closer, circling. I left it alone. The flyer finished its reconnaissance and landed on the table, wings beating feebly. A useful tool, and cheap. Pity that they have only a short range, and a duration that makes mayflies seem like Methuselahs. I brushed it off the table. A couple of minutes later my party came.

First one of the bodyguards. Flaxen hair cut close to the skull, not tall, very wide. Hershel was the name Renshaw gave me. Carried a Sig with pulseshot loads in a hip holster and a pair of throwing knifes coated with a simple and nasty curare derivative sheathed behind his neck. Better with the knives—if Renshaw was telling me the truth. He came slowly to the doorway, ran unblinking eyes over me and stood at an angle so that he could see everywhere inside. He didn't say a word. A dozen steps behind him was Nell, purse in her left hand. So far, so good. Next the factor, Tyra Ganyang, dressed in a yellow silk chemise, gold at her neck and wrists; no smile, unreadable expression, but the fact that she was along was revealing. Then Palmer. His eyes were big, they had started getting that way the moment he saw who exactly was waiting for him, and had grown larger as he got closer. The other bodyguard, Springer, he was wearing shades, stayed ten feet back in the hallway, watching everything.

The D/J's display said there was a wide-band probe in operation; coordinates placed it on Ganyang's head. She touched the amethyst-jeweled circlet that crowned her black hair and nodded slightly at me.

Hershel moved on silent feet into the room and stood between me and the back door. Nell went to the opposite side of the room and watched him; the table wasn't going to be in her way. Ganyang and Palmer stopped together at the open door. "My word, the Right Honorable James Kenmar," Palmer drawled, "Really, sir, blackmail. How gauche."

I twisted the cap off the bottle and poured amber into a glass. "I agree, but sometimes in my work that is all you're left with."

He waited for me to say something else. I held the glass up, swirled the liquid, examined the color and viscosity, then tasted the scotch appreciatively. Eased back into the chair, and counted the beats of a waltz off in my head. An unbecoming flush came and went on his face. Finally he asked, "And what kind of work is that?"

"The other side of your coin, Mr. Palmer." I grinned. "The side that in the end always comes out ahead, the side of justice."

He looked at me sharply. "Are you trying to tell me that you are a police officer?" I shrugged. He smiled broadly, and said, "Oh, dear, I haven't had a cop try and shake me down in years. Tyra, darling, what is the penalty for that?"

She managed to speak with hardly a movement of muscle on her smooth, perfect face. "Penal Code five-twenty-one, as amended by statute on August thirteenth, 2023: Extortion, commission under color of official right. A convicted officer shall receive a sentence of not less than ten years; neither parole nor pardon shall be permitted."

Ganyang was his factor. Also his consigliere? I dropped all accent from my voice. "Very good, doña. And what is the penalty for someone who holds a diplomatic passport?"

A satisfactory bit of silence. Then he chortled, "Oh, how dear! Next I'll wager that you are going to say that you are a Special Branch DCI direct from Scotland Yard."

"He's witty," Nell said in Portuguese. "You didn't say he was witty."

Something flashed in Ganyang's eyes. Not humor. Renshaw said that she studied Hapkido; he didn't have any idea of how good she was. Hershel was still by the back door where he had clear lines of fire. Nell made a tiny geometrical adjustment in her stance. Otherwise she was doing her best to look both assured and slightly bored.

As for Palmer, there's a Cantonese proverb that goes: Never trust a man who doesn't laugh with his belly.

I answered him diffidently. "Not a bad guess. Right occupation, but I'm afraid you got the wrong country. I have the honor of representing the Federative Republic of Brazil."

He had been in the process of leaning comfortably against the doorjamb. He stopped.

I put my drink down and steepled my fingers. "Oh, and the name, Kenmar, that is only a goodwill loan, a figment in the flesh if you will, extended to my government by the kindness of your former government. You may call me Meireles."

Harry had talked about the knife's edge. How hard it is to straddle two worlds. The way most go about it is through a fierce self-confidence; an internal mantra that says that you're too smart, too clever, too whatever, to fall—not off, but worse, right onto the blade. Break that assurance, and you have the man.

When I saw the flyer come into the room I knew that the hardest part of this was over. Nell had gone to Palmer's booth with only nerve and a picture and a story. She had to convince him that it was in his best interest to see a man, now. The only weapons she had were what cold iron she could put into her voice, and two names: a certain powerful police official in Santiago who was uncorrupted, unafraid, and had a long-standing professional interest in the activities of a certain bank. One of that paragon's duties involved working liaison with elements of the Brazilian equivalent of the FBI—not quite equivalent, the Brazilian agency's charter is broader, their rules of engagement looser. The other name was that of the man whose job with the Hsin-min was being its senior regulator; the man who made sure that the bank would be kept out of embarrassments. A few terse remarks in a file indicated that the regulator's reputation didn't include forgiveness as a character trait.

Palmer was smart—redundancy, damn near everybody's smart—but he had too many things thrown at him in a few seconds, psychic judo. He should have rolled with it and backed away. But he had chosen to believe in what had gotten him as far as it had. Luck. Maybe.

Before he could respond I glanced at Nell. She said to Ganyang, "You've got uplink capacity?" The other woman touched her heavy necklace of thick braided gold set with pieces of lapis lazuli shaped into rosettes, and nodded. "Here's a series of entry codes." Nell rattled off the address and then the short alpha sequence. "Use whatever cross-check tools you want, but don't take too long to confirm. The window won't stay open too long. Understand?"

A brief glance at her boss before she spoke. "Yes."

He was still standing in the doorway, trying to wash confusion from his mind. He said to me, "What do you have to do with—"

"It's simple, Nathaniel; my portfolio covers quite a bit of territory, all of it outside my country's official jurisdiction. So I have to use whatever resources I can acquire."

"And I'm to be one of your acquisitions."

At least he did me the courtesy of not playing the cry-innocent game. I reached for the bottle of Buchanan and answered him carelessly. "Only for one small task. Then you can go back to being your normal sack of shit."

Off to my side I saw Hershel tensing. I tightened my grip on the bottle as I said to Palmer, "Loyalty is a wonderful thing. But for all our sakes it would be wise if your man avoids the urge to scratch the back of his neck."

It was Tyra Ganyang, coming in a flash out of her subaudible reverie with the Brazilian Justice's core via that department's Fast-Sat, who raised the two fingers that caused Hershel to wind down. I kept looking at Palmer. "My apologies. That was uncalled for. This is business. Nothing more."

His voice dropped an octave and became distinctly and more harshly North Country. "I don't consider having blackmail attempted on me business."

"Of course, Nathaniel. You're just here because you're a charitable man."

He pulled his lips back from his teeth. "I don't care if you are who—"

"He is," Ganyang interjected. Her eyes were bright. She was finding this exciting.

Palmer continued, "I don't care if you're a Brazilian freddie. You have nothing that concerns me. This garbage you're trying to push off isn't going to fly. That pathetic piece of evidence is useless. You're wasting your time."

I glanced at Nell, and said, "Maria, open your purse wide so that Mr. Hershel can see everything in it." She snapped the bag open with the hand that was holding it, and slowly pointed it toward the bodyguard. I waited a second and looked at the guard, he nodded. Saw tiny beads of sweat on his upper lip. There's nothing better, and nothing worse, than having to deal with professionals. "Now please put the planchet on the table." She came to the table, removed the little button from the bag, and stepped back. Her eyes never left Hershel. Silently I gave her the highest compliment I knew: she was a natural. "Sit down, Nathaniel, and have a read. You'll find that I don't believe in ever wasting time."

Ganyang said, "Sir, I think we should—"

I said quickly to Palmer, "Excuse me. Have I made a mistake? I thought that you were the hombre to deal business with."

He answered too fast, "I am."

"Then why don't you have a look at my cards and decide if you want to play."

He still had his chances. He still could have walked away. He could have tried to have me killed. He pulled up a chair and sat down.

I pushed the planchet over to him. He didn't bother to be careful as he pulled from inside his jacket a platinum-plated pad the size of a debitcard. He inserted the datachip, and held the pad up before his eyes. It took a quiet minute. He was right, photos by themselves are worthless. But dates and places and a list of innocent witnesses aren't. When he put the pad down in front of him I was expecting to see damned eyes. I didn't. Something was wrong. Had Renshaw screwed up, or screwed me? No, that wasn't it. But what?

"You've been busy," Palmer said far too calmly. "Senor Meireles is the name now? Good work, but then cops are usually good at extortion. You're taught that at the training school, aren't you? It's the class between how to do frame-ups and when's the best time to use a throwdown. How much is it going to cost me to never see you again?"

I sat there silent again. Long enough for Palmer to start frowning again, long enough for Nell to cross and uncross her arms—her unintentional signal that she was getting nervous. Ganyang was a statue, matching me silence for stillness.

Let me be right. I sighed. "It's *senhor,* not senor. Know palm-sign, Nathaniel?"

"What?"

"I said, do you know palm?"

He nodded reluctantly and extended his hand across the table. I took it and talked. When I was finished he pulled his arm back as fast as he could. There was a tremor in his fingers. He looked at his bodyguard. "Timothy, leave us."

"Sir?"

Sometimes you can yell without raising your voice. "Now. And close the door."

Hershel left.

It was Palmer's turn for silence, but I wasn't about to give him any rest. "Pretty gambit, Nathaniel, elegant. Self-defense. I like it. Sorry about upsetting your timing. Does Natalie Orloff know that you're throwing a leg over her in order to set her uncle up?"

Ganyang started to speak, "Nathaniel, I think we should—"

I turned on her. "Pardon me, doña. But I don't believe I was talking to you. If you can't keep quiet then go outside and stand with the other trash."

She spat, "How dare you!"

"Easily," I replied emotionlessly. "You're not relevant."

She looked to Palmer. He was so busy trying to put pieces back together that he didn't notice her, or care.

For the smallest moment she lost it, her perfect face contorted into ugliness. Renshaw had said that she came, as he old-fashionedly put it, from class. She hadn't clawed her way out of the indescribably terrible wreckage of Jakarta. Her family had emigrated back in the last century, first to Holland, and then to North America. They were upright citizens, her mother taught comparative literature at a small brahmin school, her father, before he died, was a manager at a cloned-tissue depository. She went to Nevada State and after graduation went on a skiing vacation in Chile where she met some interesting—her term—people. That was all she had confided to Renshaw during the two years he had been with Palmer. Somewhere she had lost, or thrown away, her compass. However, she was staff, not field; she had superb control, but she hadn't learned how to stop the sudden twisting below her heart.

In her, our, world, irrelevance is a cold synonym for expendable.

I caught her golden eyes with mine. Forced her to look back. Waited until the fear subsided into hate. Then I said very softly, "You will be quiet."

I wasn't asking. She tucked her chin in and looked at her lap. I had made another enemy. It was something I was good at.

I went back to Palmer. "Now, amigo, while we both know that

I can't prove a conspiracy to murder—not in this backward country—for the Russians I have enough proof. Agreed?" He mumbled something. "Speak up, Nathaniel. My associate is trained to listen, as I'm sure lovely Doña Ganyang is. We don't want any misunderstandings later. Do we?"

"No."

I studied him for a few seconds. "Can't see any way out of it, can you?" I said kindly. "But hey, you know the old line about best laid plans." That produced a faint, rattling cough from Nell. I ignored her and went on. "Seriously, Nathaniel, relax. It's not going to be as painful as it may seem. We don't care about your situation vis-á-vis the Suratov group. Catfights between black banks outside of Brazil doesn't fall into our range of concern. And I have no special interest in ending your career, if you get my drift."

Palmer's eyes took on a glittery cast. "Then what do you care about?"

I poured myself a little more of the scotch. "Want some?" He shook his head. I glanced at Ganyang. She had most of her composure back. She was young. She was going to go far. Shame. "How about you, doña?"

"No."

I shrugged and put the bottle back down. "What do I care about? Quite a few things. Fortunately, most of them have nothing to do with you."

"What is it you *do* want?"

"A meeting with several officers of the Hsin-min. Specifically Senor Jose Gutierrez, Senor Roberto Chan, and Senor Pericles Eugenio Chan."

Ganyang opened her mouth. And abruptly closed it. In front of her was a long glimmering razor jutting into the baize just where it met the rim of the table. About eight short inches from her stomach.

Palmer and I both looked at Nell. She shrugged at us. I said to him, "This time I must apologize for my associate's behavior." I carefully pulled the razor out of the tabletop—the edge was so fine it left an almost invisible mark—and held out my hand. As Nell came over to retrieve it, Ganyang stared at her. Nell's eyes were rocks.

The young woman's face took on some of the color of the tabletop. I had scared her. Helena da Silva Carvalho had done more than that.

"Now, where were we? Oh, yes. You will contact those gentlemen and tell them that I will be in Santiago tomorrow for a discussion."

He had been working at being a professional, but the stress finally got to him. "Who the bloody hell do you think I am? I can't just call them and say that they have to see you. I don't have that kind of power and that's not how it fucking well works."

I stood up and stared coldly down at him. "You are a comprador, a position of responsibility. You facilitate the flow of dirty money. You're an intermediary between legal scum and illegal scum. You work point for a flock of whoring vultures that sell themselves enthusiastically for a piece of somebody else's dead meat. Don't you ever try and tell me what you can't do. I am going to tell how you'll do it. Pay close attention: You will tell them who I am and who my employer is. And then you will say that it involves—not the cochino Orloffs—but a French construction company and a recent personal tragedy they've experienced. You will check your board and you will tell them of the relative strength of the ecu versus the kwanazarand. And you will say personally to Pericles Chan that, like him, I also for the last twenty years have shared an enthusiasm for space research." I paused and looked at Palmer. He had no idea what I was talking about. Hadn't expected he would. "But most importantly you will tell them that it's only a *trivial* matter. Remember that; use that exact word."

He leaned back in his chair, and raised his feverish face to me. "And if they're still not interested?"

"You and Doña Ganyang are going to work very hard to see

that they are interested. And if it doesn't happen, then I would suggest you both find some place where the *vory* doesn't shine."

He rubbed his face with the palms of his hands. "I'll speak to them, but I can't—I'll speak to them."

"I'm sure you'll be successful." I stretched and yawned a little. The movement made Ganyang jump in her chair. "Take it easy," I told her genially. "The evening's just about over. As a matter of fact, why don't we all leave for our homes. Tomorrow promises to be a busy day. Agreed?" Palmer swallowed and nodded. "Excellent. Why don't the two of you accompany us to my car— without your bodyguards." I saw the expression on both Palmer and Ganyang's face. "Come, Nathaniel, it'll be safe. Why shouldn't it be?"

He was a smart man. "Fine," he said.

So we left the room. Both guards were waiting in the corridor, Hershel by the door, Springer at the far end. Palmer told them to go to the bar and wait. Hershel looked at me. I showed empty hands. Nell took my cue and spread hers out as well. The guard clenched the muscles of his jaw as he said, "Yes, sir."

We strolled Latin style the short distance to where I had parked the Lotus: the ladies about a half dozen feet in front, the gentlemen behind. My suggestion. Palmer and Ganyang were on the street side of the sidewalk. Nell linked arms familiarly with the other woman so smoothly and swiftly that Ganyang didn't have a chance to jerk away—a nice touch. Nobody talked until we got the Lotus and then I told Palmer that I would be calling him around noon. He nodded silently.

"Good throw."

"I was aiming for the middle of the table."

"Oh."

She turned to me. "What the hell exactly happened?"

I downshifted, took a curve fast and tight. "Palmer, for reasons

I don't have the vaguest about, was setting up Pyotr Orloff. He was sleeping with Orloff's niece in order to provoke Orloff into coming after him. Which would result in the abrupt end of dear uncle Pyotr."

"I got that part. But how did you figure it out?"

"He didn't have the right amount of worry. . . . Something had been bothering me about the deal. Sleeping with an attractive woman whose relative is both homicidal and a business rival may sound crazy, but who says that sanity has anything to do with sex. But then failing to make damn sure no one finds out is—men like Palmer don't get where they are by making those kinds of mistakes. Not unintentionally. And then I thought about something else Renshaw had said, that Palmer had a permit for a lethal defense installation in his office—which in itself is odd given the caliber of security the Mercantile has. It led me to the idea of self-defense, and what separates it from murder. His remark about a throwdown gun helped."

"I've never heard of that kind," she said.

"It's not a type, it's protection. A cop kills an unarmed cit, maybe deliberate, maybe not. He throws down an untraceable weapon, nowadays around here it's usually a knife. Instant self-defense. An old gag but it still works."

"Oh, yes, in Brazil they call it a *condon*."

They would. I was beyond wondering how she acquired that bit of slang. "And then I considered Pyotr Orloff. He isn't popular with his peers, and he has no relatives that would feel obliged to avenge him—the right kind of target." We came to a stop sign. I returned her intent stare with a half smile. "I guessed."

Her eyes were very wide, the amber fleck in her left iris gleaming like a tear drop. "And if you guessed wrong?"

"My credibility would have been history. At best I might have been able to bull through anyway. At worst, his other guards might have gone for us when we left."

"His other guards?"

"Renshaw didn't know everything."

She was quiet until we got close to Sunset, then she asked, "What about Renshaw? Do you think that Palmer is aware that he was spying on him?"

"I think it's possible. That's why we're going back to the hotel." The light was red. While we waited I called the Swan, keeping a wary eye on the rearview mirror. I asked for the waiter who had brought the scotch to the room. He came on quickly. I told him about the wedge under the back door, how to remove it, and that the fifty dollar bill underneath it would be matched if he would be so kind as to privately sequester the item until somebody came by to pick it up. His manners held up. He told me his name and shift hours.

Nell was shivering. I made the turn on the green and pulled to the side of the road. Her hands were balled fists on her knees; I gently wrapped my fingers around the one close to me.

I said to her in Portuguese, "You did well."

She whispered back to someone, "Did I?"

INTERLOGUE 4

WEDNESDAY, OCTOBER 27

CHLOE GROUND HER TEETH. "IT'S not working."

"Give it time." Anton replied soothingly. "I told you, it's like hacking one of those old password systems, the neurex have to try innumerable combinations until they find the one that unlocks the door."

Innumerable combinations. Chloe stared at the flat monitor. The woman was sitting cross-legged on the bed in the stateroom. She hadn't moved from that position in—Chloe glanced at the timer at the upper left corner of the screen—forty-seven minutes.

Not due to any drugs they had given her—seeing how well they hadn't worked, Chloe had stopped bothering. Thomas had said he thought that might be due to the new generation of prophylactics that supposedly the elite vipers at Groupe Touraine received early last year. Thomas knew *mierde*.

The encephalsensor she had attached to the woman's skull—after warning her that attempting to remove it would result in very unpleasant consequences—said the woman wasn't meditating. The waveforms were all wrong. But she wasn't agitated, despite her alphas—hell, who ever saw such oscillations? Not the resident expert in her Merck's Manual. It suggested that she consult with various neuropsych departments, then helpfully provided a short list of the most knowledgeable ones on rhythm analysis. The RE knew *mierde*.

"How long before . . ."

Anton shrugged. "The learning mutation rate of this particular spirochete is supposed to be very fast—I am sorry, Chloe, but this is not my field and even if it were, the sellers weren't willing to provide any kind of detailed history. It may take a few hours, or a few days. Eventually, God willing, it will work and then you will be able to introduce the correct interrogative chemistry."

How reassuring. She resumed her study of the woman. Something was going on, but what? The rest of the team—even after acknowledging the boldness of that escape attempt—refused to see her as a danger. She isn't a soldier, that stupid bastard Knut kept on saying. And even if she was, there are six of us. We have complete control of the situation. Knut wasn't even shit.

As if on cue, the cock entered the galley that they had converted into a ready room, the barrels of his shotgun bouncing noisily against the tools on his belt. He went first to the bubbling urn, poured himself a large cupful of black tea into a wide-bottomed mug, then came over to the table where they had set up the monitor. He looked over Chloe's shoulder—she jerked away deliberately. He ignored her, and asked Anton, "How's it going?"

The other man rubbed his temples. "'Who can find a virtuous woman? For her price is far above rubies.'"

"Huh?"

"You should read Proverbs, Knut. A great deal of solace can be found there."

"I'm not interested in solace, *Chaplain*. I was asking if that gorgeous bitch is ready to be peeled."

Peeled and plundered, but not just for the information that was payment for the tactical and strategic help the Furies had gotten. But Knut's crudely obvious hopes weren't going to happen, Chloe thought. They just weren't going to happen.

If Anton was annoyed, he hid it well. "What I meant was that while she is a challenging subject she will provide us with the riches of her mind. It may take some time, but in the end she will be good for us. . . ."

Knut leered at the image in the monitor. "I hope so."

Chloe wiped sweat off the back of her arms. The tracksuit she was wearing clung damply against the taut muscles of her thighs and back. The first thing they did was turn off the air-conditioning. A symbol. But as Anton was fond of saying; symbols give actions meaning.

"We will call you when she is ready," Anton said to Knut. "Where are you going now?"

"Relieving Hooker in the driver's seat." Knut clapped his beefy hand on Anton's shoulder. "Sorry about that chaplain crack—no offense?"

Anton covered Knut's hand briefly with his own and smiled warmly. "None taken."

"Good"—Knut nodded toward the monitor—"and good luck."

After he left Chloe turned to Anton. "I wish he wasn't on this mission."

Anton could have said, Really? But he had as much use for sarcasm as he had for impatience. "Knut is a good fighter, better than

Hooker perhaps. And he is the only one in the *satai* who knows Norwegian."

"We could have gotten a Translit."

"Do you know of a portable model that can successfully convey the meaningful undertones, the nuances to her words? No, Chloe, it was a wise decision to include him. Knut is strong with languages. . . . I know he is weak in other areas." He glanced at the monitor. The woman had moved her head slightly, staring now in the direction of the wide-field camera they had installed in a bulkhead. What wondrous eyes she had, he thought sadly. Anton shook his head. "Don't worry, we will do what we must with that poor twisted soul, but no more than that."

"*Oui.*" She strode away from Anton and headed for the cabin she shared with Teresa—an arrangement that suited neither of them. She would have preferred Thomas or Anton as a roommate— not Hooker; while he hardly spoke, his body shouted volumes, and she had enough anger of her own not to need the fire of his

Anton would have been her choice. Even though he sometimes looked at her the way their prisoner had that night in the Flower club. It would have been all right, he knew how to contain himself, and anyway, if he needed her she would have been willing, not for pleasure—men were nulls in that regard as far as Chloe was concerned—but for friendship, for comfort. Teresa would also have preferred Anton—if she could ever get past her hysteria. But Hooker was mission chief for this operation and he had assigned the bunks. Not from some antediluvian propriety; the cabin she and Teresa shared was located near their respective battle stations.

The still air inside the empty room was thick, cloying. She tugged open the porthole. A faint salty breeze came through. She sat on her unmade bed and looked at the small chipped mirror on the opposite wall. Even with her hair pulled back into a ponytail, the humidity dulling its luster, with no makeup, she was more beautiful than she had ever thought it was possible she could be.

The face would go when the mission was done. The body, she ran her hands over her breasts down to her hips, that she might keep—the sculpting had been subtle and she enjoyed the improvements. How her figure looked was her only vanity.

Chloe touched the reader on the stand by the bed. It was loaded with the transcript of her first interrogation of the woman—the concussion she thought the woman had received during her escape attempt had gone away very quickly, too quickly. The questioning had been a failure; Anton's spirochetes hopefully were going to be the remedy. Those bacterions—the sellers may not have provided their evolutionary history but she had taken a close look at the coiling forms under her scope before they were injected: some of their genes must have come from *Treponema pallidum*—the extinct syphilis microbe. She had felt nauseous for a moment. Until the thought came: We're doing a whore's job. Using a whore's disease fits us.

She could spend the waiting time listening again to the conversations, rerun the veracity parsers and use her own training as a psych nurse—Knut was *not* a wise decision, she hissed to herself—to try and put together a voir dire matrix that they could use to check against what the woman would tell them. But the conversations—and the words not said—were too, too disturbing.

There was the book she brought along. Araiza-Unger's seminal dissertation on Easter Island. The work that did for sociology what Darwin did for evolution. Islands, Galápagos and Easter. It reminded her of a conversation she had once with Valere, the kind of conversation that lovers had who were as easy with each other's minds as they were with their bodies. It was about whether Darwin would still have been able to give birth to his theory if the Polynesians had made it to Galápagos. Valere wasn't sure, but she thought that maybe Wallace would have been the father of evolution, not Darwin. And that might have been better for the human race. Wallace believed in the potential for nobility, for spirit. Chloe had been too young to argue. It wasn't until later that she realized that her lover was a sweet fool.

She touched the planchet. It was the popular version, of course. She didn't have the mind or the education to follow the powerful math that Araiza-Unger had developed to explain the drive to destruction. To suicide.

She read Magda Araiza-Unger the way Anton and Teresa prayed and meditated, for clarity, reinforcement.

But she would bet that Matthiessen could follow the math. She could follow anything. The old fascists fantasized about the *übermensch,* the new ones simply built theirs.

That thought spoiled her taste for reading.

From under her pillow she removed the a/v set she kept there. She put on the wraparound glasses, inserted the headphones into her ears, and curled up on her side, her knees drawn tight against her chest. Elias Lebel stood on a small bare stage, a single blue spotlight illuminating only his head and shoulders as he sang. She tried to listen to his smoky baritone, the ancient country songs that her Valere used to adore—her lover may have hated what the bastards had done to the land, but she had been true Quebecois.

What ran like an angry river through her mind wasn't the music and the memories they brought but a treatise she had been assigned to read when she was studying for her degree. It was about the Stockholm syndrome, the tendency of many hostages to bond, identify with their capturers over time. The authors hadn't discussed what the capturers might come to feel about their prisoners.

She whispered to the mattress, "It wasn't my fault. They coached me, taught me everything they knew about her, gave me every empathic tool. . . . How could I have known she was . . . Who am I betraying in my heart, Val? Tell me. Please."

CHAPTER TWENTY-SEVEN

WE WERE AT THE UCLA parking lot where Nell had left her scooter. While I was spraying Calvin Renshaw awake and then informing him on the new facts of life, she had changed back into the clothes she was wearing when we first met. Renshaw had come out more quickly than I expected from his stupor. (A residual benefit from his army mods?) Whatever anger he felt over being slipped a mickey faded when I told him the game Palmer was playing. Informing him was a calculated risk on my part; I chose to believe that he wouldn't try to use the information. Told him that his safest option was to find another life. He thought about that for a while. Never an easy decision. Then he said that his brother had been his only family. I nodded and offered him some money—Nell's brows rose a little at the amount. He looked at me as if I had urinated on him. I thought about arguing about pride, realized what I was doing, and settled for telling him about some people who could help him out with some of the technical details involved in erasure. We left each other not with a handshake. But with debts settled.

"So now what?" She was rubbing her eyes.

"You go to wherever you're staying and get some sleep."

"And tomorrow?"

"You've done enough, Nell."

"Why don't you let me decide that."

I looked at her straddling the small bike, the flywheel humming faintly, her strong legs stiff against the black pavement. I thought about risk, about loss, about giving people a chance. "Very well. Tomorrow you'll continue doing what you were about in South Bay, talking to your friends, seeing if there are any threads you can find. If any of them should happen to lead to one of the Bennies or their kin, don't pull on them. Wait until you talk to me." She nodded, but her face said she wanted to do more. All right, I offered her something else. "The labor movement in Equatorial Africa. Does the IWU have any reliable contacts?"

Part of me was hoping that would shut her off. It didn't. "What do you want to find out?"

"The African connection I told you about. It's a global called MacKenzie-Rao. One of their outfits, a rogue maybe, may have played a role in the Furies selecting Siv Matthiessen as a target. If that's true, I'd like to discover more about them."

There was a deep frown line above her nose. "And you think that the unions there may be involved?"

"There's a possibility."

"Which ones?"

I told her what Vladimir had learned about the miners who had blown up a factory. Added some possible candidates that I had gleaned from my readings . . . and some names from my past.

"I'll see what I can find out."

"Just like that?"

She didn't glare, or laugh. She simply said, "Don't push it, Robie."

Watched her drive away. Across the half-empty lot, past the double-gated exit, onto Westwood, until she was gone. A slender woman with thick dark hair.

The tune that she had been playing in my house; it wasn't Chopin, it was Jobim's *Insensatez.*

When you use occasionals you must be doubly careful. First in determining whether they are suitable, both in temperament and talent, for the mission. And secondly, you must be careful to limit your involvement with them, for your sake as well as theirs. Our work is hard enough, amigo, let's not make it unbearable. Comprende?

Sí, Enrique.

Didn't get any sleep that night. Too many things to do, to think about. Figured I could catch a siesta on the flight to Santiago. I was going, whether or not Palmer was sufficiently persuasive. Just by calling them, he was putting a foot in the door for me. If I had to, I would shove it the rest of the way open.

There were decisions to make. I went over the updates I had gotten earlier. Michael Hardesty in San Francisco had said that Rebecca Donovan, the tired Benevolence concubine, and her companion—Michael had provided a name, Lori Flores-Rueles, along with moving-cam shots edited to show both of them from front, rear, and side—had a local blade as an escort when they left the Bennington Hotel, but there weren't any guards over them within the hotel itself. That was good. Rebecca Donovan spent most of her time in the hotel, her companion was more restless. Michael thought that a delaying diversion wouldn't be difficult. Even better. Except that I didn't have the time to go there myself.

Danny. He would know how to play it—hell, he'd probably, certainly, play it better than I could. But it meant his brushing up against the edge of the Mid-City Benevolence. I went out to the back terrace, got out of the locker a man-sized foam target. I propped it up against a wall, dimmed the outside spots, and snapped ball bearings at it from various distances, angles. Elbows, knees, shoulders, groin. When the target's surface looked as deeply cratered as the moon, I stopped and called him.

He wasn't sleeping, but he wasn't happy about the interruption. A voice yelled into a pillow something that sounded like "Damn, damn, damn."

It's funny the things that can make you sorry. That can seize you up. I stumbled into the first thing that came to mind. "Your house didn't refuse my override."

"It wouldn't ever do that for you, *mate*."

Think about the worst time there is to stop making love. Add to that the prospect that it's the first time you're making love with that person. Imagine what your voice would be like. Got it? Now you know how he sounded. "I'll call back later."

"Nothing doing, Gav. I want a clear mind—and a clear conscience in case I decide to kill you."

"It's a personal situation, Danny."

"Wait a minute." The phone went blank. It was more than a minute before he got back to me. Behind him was a row of handmade surfboards. He lives in an apartment he owns above his shop. My phone told me he had all of his shields up. "Lo siento, excuses weren't easy. What gives?"

I briefed him on Rebecca Donovan. Which meant telling him about Warren Tyler; about some of the political dynamics of the Mid-City Benevolence; about the Sing On tong that Harry had mentioned; my suspicions as to the involvement of MacRao—everything he needed to know in order to do a competent interrogation. He listened impassively, closing his eyes every so often as he recorded mental notes. He didn't ask for details as to exactly how I got my information from Tyler. I was alive, Tyler seemed to be out of the picture—as far as he cared that was the end of the story.

I did tell him about encountering Nell at Lew's school, but not what went on afterward. He found the happenstance about as funny as I did. Fortunately, for his sake, he didn't ask which one of us had the bigger stones. He did say, "Cute meet."

"Tell me about her, Danny."

He nodded and settled back into his chair. "Best place is to start at the beginning I guess. Her mom was a cop in Brazil—yeah,

I know how she feels. This story is one of the whys. Her mother was part of that special division they set up so that women wouldn't be afraid to report crimes against them. They had their own stations, kept their records separate from the rest of the force. It was a helluva good idea, arrest rates for assault and rape and child abuse went up like crazy. Anyway, when Nell was three her mother was found dead in those horrible slums around Rio, fav something."

"Favelas."

"That's it. I was there once on an assignment. The guy I was working with took me on a tour. . . ." His eyes turned dreamy, not pleasantly. "Man, oh, man. You know what I think was the worst of it? They're all up on the hills—when they're not falling down— and when they look out they can see all that beauty that's still there, Sugar Loaf Mountain and the bay and the ocean. When I was a kid a stupid nun told me the story that once a year a window opens and the damned in hell get to see what heaven's like." He made a twisting gesture with his hand that ended with a straight middle finger. "The only thing that old bag said that ever caught me. It came back when I was there. . . . They never got who did Nell's mom in. But the bullet that had blown a hole in her back was an odd caliber, a nine-fifty-six millimeter."

"A caliber the Rio police used?"

"Right. Almost exclusively. Her gun was missing but the shot didn't come from her weapon. Sweet Jesus!" That same black mist came rolling in again for a moment. "Then when Nell was five her old man got killed in an industrial accident. He was manually pressurizing a storage tank when one of its seams blew. He got blamed—no matter that he was doing the job only because the servos had been behaving unreliably and he was being conscientious, and that they had him pulling seven-day double shifts for weeks. The company didn't care, it was a small town, they had a big payroll, and justice was on it." He sighed. "That must have been in Year Sixteen and things were starting to go real bad down there. She was lucky, she had an aunt—great lady, that's where most of this is coming from—that took her. Her aunt was an American pilot for one of the Brazilian airlines. Worked a steady route from Sao Paulo to here. She managed to get Nell in. So she grew up here, and then, when she got older, spent a fair amount of time down there." He paused to get a long-necked beer out of the office fridge. "Got a feeling I'm going to need some yellow courage before I go back upstairs."

If I hadn't sunk myself into the texture of his story I might have said something idiotic. He popped the cap, took a swallow and went on. "I told you how we met. That was about five years after you went away. . . ." He faltered. Danny doesn't know where I went, only that when we next saw each other it took him a long time to recognize me. "Nell and I were pretty tight until I joined the marshals. Then we didn't see much of each other. I heard that she had been doing a bit of this and that—"

"Teaching?"

He shook his head. "I don't know, maybe. She's got a degree in analytics from some university down in Brazil. Then about ten years ago she got involved with her union and that became her life. She does come into town every so often and she usually looks me up. Guess it's just been one of those ships in the night thing that you two didn't meet. Let's see, she's pretty quiet about her social life; if she's ever been serious about anybody she never told me—Nancy might know, they got close. . . . I remember she once brought someone cute to one of our beach parties, but the girlfriend was real nervous. I guess the boys in the cliqua were too high-test for her novia to handle. She didn't bring her around again." He looked away for a moment. "Hunh, that must have been a problem for her, caught between . . ." He sighed. "Wish I had noticed that then. Don't know if I could have done anything for her—"

You were her friend. "You did."

"Really?"

"You know, you are a stupid bastard yourself sometimes."

"Tell me—well, that's about it except that I think that besides being a very tough doña, she's pretty solid. I'd trust her. You got a reason not to?"

"No . . . she's got an intensity."

"That's where her thermostat's usually set."

I nodded. "Thanks."

"Sure. Now, the Hardestys—are they as good a gang as I've heard?"

"They are. I'll call Michael Hardesty and fill him in on your coming in for me. They've got a great morpher on their staff, her name's Sylvie. Let her do you."

"Can she knock six inches off the top, and give me your cow-boy looks? Take it easy. I'll get a makeover. I believe in insurance too. Uh . . . there's something else about Nell I should tell you."

"She really likes men?"

"Huh? Actually she does, but not for—what the hell does it have to do with anything? That's not your style, Gav, what made you ask?"

I looked at him straight-faced. "Stereotypes, assumptions, they're knots in the brain. I'm trying to stay limber."

He scratched at his bare chest and cocked his head at me. "You're getting better at it."

"What?"

"Pulling my leg—anyway, where the saints was I going? Yeah, it doesn't have anything to do with sex."

My line. "So what is it?"

"She knows about what happened with Dano." He saw my expression and added hurriedly, "Not me, mate. It seems that she dropped into town a couple weeks after you got back. She visited with Nancy, and Nancy, she needed someone to talk to. She doesn't know the details—nobody but you and my son know those—but she's got a pretty good idea of what you did."

It helped explain some of the oscillation in the way she looked at me. But . . . "Is there anything else?"

"No. Except what I said, she's solid, Gav."

"Okay. How's it going at your end?"

He shook his head. "The river's running dry in South Bay. If they had collaborators, they're sunk pretty deep. Oh, one thing did come up—I've got a tail."

"Did it just slip your mind?"

He laughed—imbecile—and said, "Calm down. No problema. Somebody hired one of our local sleazes. Somebody with some shrewd; outsiders stand out like—like a trout in milk. One of the advantages of living in this here colonia. But they're employing a tail who's been blown so many times he might as well have one of those skyboards over his head. I was thinking that if he gets on the magtrain with me to SF I would ask if the Hardestys could do a courtesy dump on him."

"Sounds like you've got it under control."

"Apology accepted. And speaking of which, I have a woman waiting who's looking for more than that from me—if she's not already out the door. I'll talk to you as soon as I finish the gig up north. 'Night."

Some life, Robie. Using the people you love.

Decanted a bottle of Château Haut-Brion, the millennium vintage. My birth year. My father bought two cases for me the day I came into the world—an old family tradition. While I waited for it to wake up, I got a stack of cashcards and loaded them with fifty thousand. The cards and the gloves would be waiting for Danny at my East Hollywood office. I started a fire in the living room. Asked the house to locate a station that was playing live music. Somewhere in the world it found a strong tenor singing Puccini.

The wine was still good, still alive. I tasted it slowly, listening to arias from *Turandot*. The tenor started singing *"Non piangere Liù."* I turned from San Francisco to Southern Africa.

William Mpondo's report was limited. The information he had acquired so far on the life and times of one Sebastian Broder gave me no hints. As for the notes I was sending—those had provoked a response. A "viralent" one according to Mpondo. I shook my head. Puns are what people do when they don't have a sense of humor. No danger to my African detective, the Union of Southern Africa may not have as stringent privacy laws as we do, but their national telnet isn't as sophisticated. Mpondo had taken the right precautions: posting through public phones, multiple fast routing, generic envelopes. The odds of a trace back were slim to none. The only thing revealing about Broder's reaction was that he hadn't simply instituted a pattern recognizer with a lockout. He was continuing to accept the notes. There was something about the initials SM and GT that he found engaging. I knocked the wood arm of my chair.

There was something else, a recent addendum to the file that hadn't been brought to my attention—a system glitch? I told the house to rebuild the engine of its secretarial section, and to run again the self-auditing routine I had given it earlier in the evening—accidents happen to even the most reliable software, but it didn't hurt to make damn sure it was random crap, not bad karma.

The note said that Broder, accompanied by an unidentified male companion, had left for Paris this afternoon.

Mpondo must have activated some Watchers. Most likely they would be good—I remembered those stars his firm had—I just hoped they were careful. I poured myself another glass and forcibly reminded myself that when a man is doing a good job, leave him alone.

Paris. I hadn't heard anything recently from Sophie. I suspected she had been sitting in her study, papers strewn around her feet, her long fading blond hair undone around her shoulders, sifting through whatever her niece was finding out—and nine points to the abstract—whatever some of her old sources might be providing her. I didn't think of specifically telling her not to use anybody else, and she always used to take my silences for yeses. She'd want to save me time trying to see if there was anything in the data. It was important for her to be more than useful.

A nine-hour time differential; she would be having her early lunch of *trouffade auvergnates*—pancakes made with bacon, Cantal cheese, and potatoes. Her mother used to cook that dish only for winter holidays. Sophie believes that every day is winter, and every day should be celebrated.

I ran a sweep cycle through my private line and rang the phone that belonged to her village's parish priest. When he answered, I hung up and had the house analyze the pulse. It looked clean. I put through the call to her home.

"Robie, *de tout mon coeur*, I'm glad to hear from you. I have some questions—"

"Forgive me, Sophie, but not right now. Can you give a fast brief on what you've got?"

She grumbled a bit, then said. "I see jealousy but no hate. Some friends, more lovers, all very discreet. Of her work, nothing of consequence; her Groupe is very tight. She has a modest estate of her own—according to Lila very nicely invested—but with no evidence that she has benefited from her, ah, proximity, to the president of her firm. Lila had heard of her, but they were never introduced. From the evidence of the photo Lila obtained for me, and the verbal portrait that she put together from stories in the salons, this woman, Matthiessen, is very magnetic. A woman of strong impression. That may have been one of the reasons they chose to take her."

"How so?"

"I think, and this is pure speculation, Robie, that one of the Erinyes knows her. Not necessarily closely, or professionally, but nevertheless this person has had contact with her. Why? Because within Touraine there were better targets of opportunity. For example: Lila obtained via her Desk a corporate roster, analyzed the key positions, and saw a familiar name; the chief of the civil engineering team that has primary responsibility for the first phase of the Congo Project. A brilliant man, famous for his ability at expediting problems in the field. This engineer belongs to a bicycle club that she also is a member of. He enjoys going on weekend riding excursions in the Nivernais with his daughter—and with only one guard. It would have been simple, and very damaging. Yes, I know that her relationship with Fouchet would be a strong weight in their considerations. Yet I do not believe that by itself would be enough. A bonus definitely, but by itself, insufficient. However, if someone among the kidnappers had met her—had experienced her—then I can see why she might have been moved to the top of the list for their coup de théâtre. These people, perhaps as a consequence of their cause, think a great deal not only about the past but about the future as well. I think they have the discipline to act through the present. Siv Matthiessen, if I understand my niece—and discounting the effect of the instant secondhand crush she seems to have developed—will one day be a formidable power. And as far as these Erinyes can see, one that will be arrayed against their faith. Pluck the seedling before it can put down its roots too deep. Does this sound wrong?"

Holguin has his wands, beakers, cauldrons. Sophie had a life. If I had to choose, there wouldn't be a choice. "Sounds plausible."

A faint, happy note of triumph. "That is good. I know that this would be of no immediate use to you—"

"It might. What else?"

Sophie has no fear of being in the dark, not with me. She shifted gears smoothly. "The financial data you requested, those things about the Congo bonds. I have a file that Lila assembled, but as you know, those games are beyond me. I will send you it now if it is safe. Yes? One moment, let me find it. . . ." I heard the rustling of papers. Sophie uses them not out of some atavistic nostalgia but because the sheets she uses are a special type of flash paper that burns instantly unless certain precise conditions are present, the right person handles them—given modern methods of digital resurrection, a more reliable safeguard. An unsophisticated bit of underground technology that makes the police very unhappy. She sent the file. My phone gave a startled chime and told me there was a print-only tag on it. Where should it go? I patiently told it to send it to the copier—and then double scrub the buffer. If my phone had been programmed to pretend feelings, it would have sniffed the audio equivalent of raised eyebrows. It's been a long while since anyone's sent me a paper fax.

"Have you got it, Robie?" Sophie asked a little anxiously.

"It's here."

"Good. Now, when you asked about the Africans I assumed that you saw a role for them. Ah, Robie, the rivalries, the friend-ships, all together at the same time! Lila is very cosmopolitan about such matters and even she was amazed at the incredible degrees of relationships. Let me find those notes . . . here. It seems that Groupe Touraine holds positions ranging from one to twelve percent in no less than fifty companies in Southern Africa. Some of these are in direct competition with the Groupe in a number of fields—it would seem that Touraine wishes to win even when they lose. However there are no comparable holdings by the Africans in GT Lila calls it a sweet position. There are a number of joint ventures, and, well, I could go on, but looking at all this is like trying to un-derstand the motives and relationships between the gods of India."

A good metaphor. "Do you have anything on MacKenzie-Rao?"

She let out something that sounded like a cross between a tsk and sigh. I've never been able to duplicate it. "It would have helped if you had been more specific to begin with."

"It's a recent development."

"And one that feels warm to you. Wait a moment. . . ." The tenor had turned from opera to old English folk songs. I listened to "Behind Blue Eyes" as Sophie searched for her nuggets. My eyes aren't that color but otherwise . . . "There it is. No, nothing useful. They share ownership of a node harvester company that operates a few subs in the South Pacific, but that is all. If anything, they seem to be on indifferently friendly terms with each other. Their main businesses do not overlap. No, Robie, I see nothing."

"That's okay."

"So, what is the other reason you called?"

"I don't know if you can help me with this one. There is a man who came into Paris last night. I would like to find out what he's doing there."

Silence, then, "I know a man. Older than me even. He is still employed, although mostly by suspicious husbands and wives. Last night . . . It will be a chilly trail, especially if the target has taken precautions. But I will give it to him. He does not like to fail. You know, Robie, there are advantages to the old. There are so many of us now. And we do not attract attention, we are seen as harmless. It works for him."

"You wouldn't have settled for being a Watcher."

"No? Perhaps not . . . Who is the target?"

I told her about Sebastian Broder. She asked if I had any clues as to his possible actions. I said that any guesses I had weren't reliable. She understood.

"Is there anything else?"

I shook my head, forgetting that she couldn't see me. "No. Keep fishing in the same streams, maybe something new will turn up. And give my love to Lila."

"She knows that she has it. '*Voir, mon petit loup.*'"

I stretched my legs in front of the fire and picked up the file from the phone. I liked the tone I had heard in Sophie's voice when she spoke of her niece. Maybe working together helped. Maybe there would be at least one small victory. If it lasted.

Kit, sitting on my lap, laughing at a remark I made. "You know, querido, before I met you I always thought that description, an optimistic cynic, was nothing more than a literary invention."

And before I met you, I was starting to forget what it was like to hold a woman *de tout mon coeur*—with all my heart.

A sometime cynic. There are a few things I'm faithful to.

After I read the fax, I took the claret and the glass upstairs. I had questions I wanted to ask Matthiessen's shadow. And I wanted somebody to talk to.

CHAPTER TWENTY-EIGHT

HAD A HALF HOUR BEFORE they called the executive class boarding for AirAndes's direct flight to Santiago. Palmdale's viper lounge has private booths. I entered one, the glass partition darkening automatically, and called Olivia Fouchet. The number was supposed to be a straight vertical to the top. It also had a secretarial overlay with a strong justification routine. It wasn't happy with my simply repeating Guarneri over and over. Finally it got up the nerve, or neurode, to interrupt whatever Fouchet was doing and ask her if I was okay. She came on.

"Monsieur Robie."

"Madame."

Felt queasy. There was a point during my conversation with Siv that she talked about the woman who shared her life. The curving, intersecting lines of love's why and how, an indeterminate calculus. I had listened, because clues can come from the least expected places, and because she needed me to.

"I thought you weren't supposed to call me," she said.

"Something has come up that—" I stopped and studied her face. Her dark chocolate hair was down. She was resting a sallow cheek against the bent fingertips of one hand. She looked like she'd had a sleepless night, and she showed it far more than I did. "Something has come up. What is it, Madame?"

"Your services may not be required any further."

Summary execution. It happens. A breach in security; the hostage can't be moved safely. A strategic change in plans; the hostage's value has declined, or setting an immediate example seems to be a better investment.

Siv . . . I walk with ghosts all the time, too much of the time, but they're usually dead first.

"Can you explain?"

She took her hand away from her face, glanced to the left of her, and said: "Hang up."

I broke the connection and waited for her to call me back. I doubted that Groupe Touraine used the Digital Collective; I doubted they needed to. According to Lila's notes, one of the Southern African companies they part owned manufactured black-box telcom units that were used by the security services of half a dozen countries. I rested my eyes.

It took her ten minutes to get back to me. Long enough for her to decide what she wanted to say, to find the right mask, to make sure I wouldn't continue reading her so easily.

"We believe we have located where they are holding Siv. A hostage rescue team is en route from Virginia."

In my mind's eye I saw the Marine Corps base that is situated on the heights of the Potomac. The planes climbing low over the great Chesapeake levee—the Big Stubborn—and its forest of end-lessly cranking pumps that keep the Atlantic literally at bay. The fast VTOL transport with its chameleon camouflage turning the plane's skin the colors of the sky and seas. The men and women of SEAL Team 6—this was what that unit trained for—inside the plane's belly getting nonstop updates through the eyes and ears of their helmets. The sweat slowly beginning to trickle down their backs.

"Where?"

"A polymetal extraction platform currently working off the Mouchoir Banks. That is—"

"Just east of the Turks and Caicos Islands, or what once were islands." Turkeys and storms. What Tyler said he overheard. Hadn't bothered to do a semantic search. Was I that negligent? "Don't those ships have a three-person crew?"

"Ours do."

"Yours."

"*La Sainte Maure*. We operate the platform for the Union Minere. They have a lease from both the Confederation of West Indian Exiles, and the Hispaniolan Phalanges to work that region. Apparently, the Erinyes have a deeper access to my company than we have yet found. With the information they acquired they were able to take the platform without us knowing anything was amiss." She spoke as if she were talking about a small financial setback.

"Can you tell me when the team is due to go in?"

"I was told that they should arrive at the platform's current location four hours from now."

"Are the Furies going to be given a chance to surrender?"

"Arthur Cormac says that they had the Raleigh stratego run a psychostatic analysis. The odds of a surrender, either now or after a siege, are too low against the probability that they would choose martyrdom."

And Cormac never met a bloodbath he didn't like.

I shook my head. That may be true about Cormac, but Paul Thinh and his staff would have run their own risk assessments with Groupe Touraine's expert intelligence. They must have concurred. "What do they say about a rescue operation's chance of success?"

"They said insufficient data, too many unknown variables."

They always say that. "May I call back later today?"

"If you wish. Speak to Paul."

"I understand."

It was her turn to peek behind masks. "You do, don't you. . . . I want to thank you, Robie."

I lied and said, "I did my best. *Une bonne journée, Madame.*"

"*Et vous, Monsieur Robie.*"

I took the hyper to Santiago anyway. I have friends there I haven't seen for a long time.

Woke up as we crossed the Tropic of Capricorn. About thirteen hundred kilometers from Santiago; allowing for the reduction in airspeed on the long descent, I was going to be on the ground in a little under an hour. I raised my seat and the flight attendant was there offering to take the pillow and alpaca blanket. I asked her, in the clipped, fast style that Chileans use, to please bring me a pisco and a Schweppes Bitter Lemon. She smiled brightly and went off to fetch my drink.

The ratio of the colorless, deceptively mild grape distillate to soda to shaved ice was just the way I liked it.

One of the advantages of traveling up front is that, besides seats that you can really sit in, you get free access to a far more secure netlink. And privacy. I placed a call to Brazil.

There was a delay, somewhat the same problem I had reaching Olivia Fouchet, but this time at least the secretary was human. He didn't know who I was—or rather who I was supposed to be—but he had better judgment than Fouchet's machine. The man came on after a couple of minutes. He asked me how it went. I told him I was falling toward Santiago. He offered to give me some assistance when I arrived. I said that he had done more than enough. He replied that it would be no trouble, and he would have a pleasant, personal surprise for me.

Outcomes: Siv is dead. She's alive. She's not on the *Sainte Maure* at all.

Assume the worst, plan for the best.

I suspected that he wanted to continue helping me not only for a twenty-year-old debt, but also for reciprocation. I didn't want to start working for Brazil's Ministry of Justice. I started to say *No obrigado,* then changed my mind. Theater is more than acting and a script. There's set design, lighting, music, a skilled stage crew. I was used to more intimate shows, with audiences that weren't especially discerning. I had come this far, I thought I might as well at least try to finish out the act with a dynamite performance.

And if I don't want to work for anybody, all I have to do is not work at all.

Caught a glimpse of Aconcagua as the hyperjet turned for its final approach to Santiago's Pudahuel Airport. The Queen of the Andes was the color of molten white steel. Seven thousand majestic meters.

The man who had been my first mentor in the Committee was a Chileano. When he was very young he had to flee his homeland. His crime was writing songs that were too funny, too witty. His first punishment was being forced to watch as his sister was raped by men who had sworn to protect and serve. His second was not being allowed to hold her—not even allowed to say good-bye.

He said that seeing Aconcagua from the plane that was bringing him home after a lost decade of wandering allowed him to feel what he hadn't been able to do all those years. As if the mountain, speaking for the country it oversaw, were saying to him, "We witness, we endure. And whatever is done does not diminish us. We are the Land, the Life. And so are you."

It brought him home, both inside and out.

Somewhere in Wyoming there is a valley, and a cabin. . . . Not a home. Not yet.

Customs was slow; a thousand passengers had gotten off a flight from Quito, Ecuador. Having a first-class ticket didn't save me from having to wait in a queue. Most of the crowd seemed to belong to the same engineering corporacion—not a company, it's what the locals call their associations. Chileans have always been an organized, communal people. Professional societies; craft guilds; business confederations; industrial unions; community service bodies; popular economic organizations—cooperatives, production workshops, soup kitchens, mortgage committees and such that practiced what Lionel Akawa and others called the economy of solidarity. And then there are clubs like the Cuecas, a women's group named after the national dance. But they weren't a social club; the Cuecas started during the Pinochet tyranny. Women would gather in front of government offices, prisons, military posts—all the other synonyms—and defiantly perform the dance without male partners; accompanied only by the sound of furious guitars. An inescapable reminder to all watching that their husbands, their sons, their lovers, were dead, in dungeons, or simply missing. Their ghost dance. No, not a social club.

During the Transition the government collapsed. The six clans that controlled the country's economy followed it into the maelstrom. Instead of letting their country fall into bloody chaos or yet another bootheeled dictatorship, the corporacions took over. Some people superficially call it a modern syndicracy. But it's not an oligarchy of economic interests. It encompasses with equal political measure all of the country's social, moral, and intellectual institutions. And if individuals choose to actively participate in more than one organization they have more votes, a greater voice in their country. You'd think that it would produce the chaos of fractional politics, but somehow it doesn't. An attitude of mutual respect, the only way to survive in a lifeboat. The Chilean Estructura has been touted as a role model by a few pundits who see it as the only working, and workable compromise between the two flavors of the day: brahminic technocracy or tribal fascism. The Polynomial Republic as one sage called it, a paradigm for a multiplex world.

Do I sound like I think those pundits are right? I'm not wise enough. And I don't much care about what is the best type of government. I only have a simple criterion. Akawa once said that in the end all politics comes down to the question of decency. So far the Estructura has answered the question pretty well. So far.

I finally got through Customs. There was supposed to be someone waiting for me, but there also was a mob. I waited patiently, black leather valise in my left hand, antique ebony walking stick with a silver knob in my right. After a few minutes I saw a young man dressed in the current popular fashion—a velvety blue bolero jacket, narrow pants, and short pointed high-heeled boots—gently push and apologize his way past hugging couples, friends handshaking, young children clinging to parents' legs, older children with asymmetrical haircuts practicing their cruel coolness—I've always meant to ask Kit if she thought that developmental stage might be pangenetic. The man spotted me, came up, and said awkwardly in English, "Are you the Right Honorable—"

"Haven't been either of those in a long time. Yes, I'm James Kenmar."

"My name is Christan. I have a car waiting, sir." He looked down at my valise. "Do you have any other luggage?"

"No."

"Then are you ready to go, sir?"

"Sure." He offered to take the valise. I smiled and told him I thought I could manage. Followed him through the happy throng to an uncrowded exit where private cars were waiting like patient dogs for their master's return. He led me to a forest green Bentley. On his signal the curbside door opened. I peeked inside, empty. He started to get in the front. I told him I would rather sit shotgun. The phrase threw him so I switched to Portuguese and explained that I would be more comfortable alongside him.

After we both got in and he manually maneuvered the big car skillfully into the thick bus traffic leading out of the airport. Keeping his eyes on the road, he said, "*Shotgun* . . . I will have to remember that, sir."

"A figure of speech, not tradecraft."

"Yes, sir."

"Don't."

He grinned a little. "Call you sir?"

I nodded. "Tomas would be better. Senhor Meireles if you really insist on staying formal."

"My uncle said that you were, um, casual, like a carioca."

Ipanema beach makes South Bay's coastline look like a post-card from the past. Well, spirit takes a long time to die. "Your uncle?"

He took his eyes off the road for a second and looked at me. "My full name is Christan Borrayo Aragao."

A pleasant surprise he had promised me. He didn't take after his uncle. He was taller, his face was more narrow, his hair and eyes a lighter shade of sable. "Your mother is Marina Aragao?"

His eyes came back to me, a little wide. "Yes. Do you know her?"

I watched him idly, carefully. "We met once. Years ago. At a party at your uncle's house in Petropolis. It's been a long time but I think you resemble her."

He showed no signs of connecting me with the horror in his parents' past. I was glad. He nodded and agreed politely, "Thank you. People do say that."

Marina Borrayo Aragao had been three months pregnant when she and . . . Luis—that was his father's name—were taken out of the prison where they were waiting to die. A bit of data we hadn't known, weren't prepared for . . . Christan Borrayo Aragao. I touched cautiously at the memory the way you touch a broken tooth with your tongue. There had been enough years, enough overlays—terrible and kind. I looked at his slim tan hands resting easily on the wheel of the Bentley. Another reason to be glad.

"Where are we going?" I asked.

"The Andradina. It is a small hotel that our embassy often uses for guests that wish discretion." He made a characteristic Brazilian gesture with his right hand. "A very discreet hotel."

As in no one will get at me there unless they have a court writ, and maybe an armored regiment besides. Nice. However I wanted some additional privacy for the two calls I had to make. I told him I wanted to stop at the Biblioteca Nacional. He looked at me with surprise. Only antiquarians and those few scholars still mystically in love with the smell of print and leather bother to physically visit Santiago's Central. He had to check with the limousine's directional to find the right road.

I rolled the window halfway down. A cool breeze and clear air. You could see the chestnut-colored mountains—ramparts of the Andes—that ring the city. Those mountains were the reason that Santiago occasionally still has some smog. It could be worse. Santiago used to be as bad as Mexico City.

I asked Christan, "So what do you do?"

"I am interning in our embassy's office of information."

"When did the ambassador start letting interns borrow unmarked embassy limousines?"

He swung the Bentley past a tightly packed taxi, a *collectivo,* that was doing less than ninety klicks. The limo's warning lights flashed urgently as the two cars' side panels got within a handsbreadth apart. He pulled in front of the taxi and accelerated up to a hundred and forty. All Brazilians think they're race car drivers. He grunted, *"Melhor."* Glanced at the stranger next to him and decided. "I am a detective-sergeant with the Border Patrol's Special Investigative Division."

His uncle's old outfit. "I hope I'm not taking you away from anything important."

He glanced at me again, trying to see if I was pumping him. "No, I am only here in Santiago"—he tried his English again—"to learn the local rope. Is that right?"

I kept my smile to myself. "Pretty much."

We talked a little shop. Smuggling was the local rope he was learning about and that's a subject on which I can give some advice.

The Biblioteca is located nowadays on a little rise surrounded by a wide meadow near the center of the town. The datacores and other vulnerables are under the rise. The building itself is a more or less exact reconstruction of the original stately nineteenth-century library—the first was destroyed in a quake about, oh, about thirty years ago. Santiago has had its version of Crazy Eights. More than once. I saw that the grounds were being planted with new seedlings and bulbs. It was spring down here. One of those community service groups tends the public gardens, for free, for pride. The library's few parking spaces were filled up. Told Christan Borrayo to idle around for a few minutes—then changed my mind and asked him to see if he could find a store that sold twenty-five-millimeter ball bearings. He was puzzled but complaisant. Whatever his uncle had said about me was sufficient.

I entered the beautiful marbled lobby and asked the startled, half-awake woman at the front desk—small *d*, it was a replica of a Spanish late colonial lectern—which way to the lavatory. Rolled my *r*'s for emphasis. It explained everything to her. She handed me a guide.

Followed the glowing key past the first washroom, turned left down a long empty hall—security left me alone; the guard at the entrance had seen that I was on the permanent visitor's roster, the select list—walked until I saw the sign for another washroom. The door snicked open as I came up to it.

One dark varnished wooden stall and a blue porcelain sink with polished brass handles. Didn't look like they had done any recent remodeling. I went into the stall, slipped the bar shut, and squatted by the toilet. The tile was snug. I worked it slowly loose. Behind it was the patchjack that fed directly in the upper library's telcomm system. I found the short length of fiber tucked into the little cavity behind the tile and connected my pad to the patch.

Not my handiwork. I discovered it courtesy of a man who was stealing from the Biblioteca to pay for the addiction of his young lover. It was one of those coincidences; some rare books are also works of art, but it's not an area that I'm particularly knowledgeable about. But a collector I was advising on something I did know happened to tell me that someone had approached her with an offer to sell an original volume of Diazavalos's sketches—Pedro Diazavalos was a physician, a playwright, an astrologer, and a naturalist in the late seventeenth century; not a rarity for his times, but an uncommon one for the Spanish colonies.

I didn't tell the authorities about the bypass, but then I didn't tell them who had stolen the Diazavalos folios and then gently altered them ever so slightly—I just returned what he hadn't yet sold.

It wasn't because he tried to kill himself when I found him. I'm not that sentimental.

Whether the bypass would make the system ignore my calls was questionable. But it didn't matter, the pad was inserting chaff that would keep a tracer routine confused for a little while. And I was only looking for a temporary privacy.

Priorities. I reached Paul Thinh first.

"You have no visual."

"I'm calling on an old line."

"The operation is a failure."

If Siv was dead it would have been in his voice. I closed my eyes for a second. "What happened?"

"The platform was deserted. There is a series of bombs aboard. A squad is attempting to disarm them."

Lord help them. There are explosive devices so sensitive now that a single photon detected by the trigger mechanism is enough to tell them to go off. "Any idea of what really happened?"

Thinh sounded more distant than the thousands of miles that

separated us. "We were misled. It looks like pirates took the platform."

He didn't want to discuss it. Neither did I, not then. "I would like to speak to Madame Fouchet."

"Robie, why don't you go home? Stop whatever you think you're doing. We'll destroy your file—no obligations on your part. I will explain to Madame. Just go on with your *life*."

Your pathetic life with your delusions of heroism. And stop wasting ours. "*Auriez-vous,* but I recall Olivia Fouchet telling me that the secret to Touraine's success was a willingness to try anything. Has that philosophy changed?"

That's when he called me a worthless bastard. And a number of other things. I waited him out. He finally let loose with: "All you are going to do is hurt her."

I wanted to laugh. "She's Olivia Fouchet. Her father was gunned down while on a diplomatic mission in Macedonia. She got to see it live on CNN. She lost her husband to the Potosi virus. She knows what hurt is. She knew that long before the day she decided to call me."

Cold silence. I thought I could hear the faint hiss of gamma rays dying in the ionosphere.

Olivia Fouchet came on. Just in time.

"You wanted to speak to me."

She sounded less tired than earlier. She didn't sound happier. "I need a pry bar."

A little sigh. "How much?"

"That depends on the contracts you get over the next two years in South America."

She didn't lose a beat. "Go on."

"I want a letter of intent from you stating that you will use the Hsin-min Bank of Santiago as your main financial agent on any projects you undertake during that period of time in the countries of Chile, Argentina, Bolivia, and Paraguay."

"Do you have any idea what that entails?"

"I'm not an expert on your business, but I would guess their fees should come to several million."

"More. Much more. And then there is the matter of the relationships we already have with other moneycenters in the region."

There was a long pause. I inserted into the stillness: "How much is Siv worth?"

I thought for a moment that she would lapse into Thinh's anger. There is nothing like dashed hopes, even desperate ones, to grind nerves down. But my first impression of her was true: elegance and steel.

"Why do you—no, wait."

I went back to my reading. She returned in about a minute or so. "The Hsin-min Bank ended up benefiting from an action by the Erinyes in Chile. It wasn't a coincidence? The Erinyes are working as condottieri for them?"

"It could be that the Furies have fallen into the last temptation."

"The last temptation?"

"The last temptation is the greatest treason: To do the right deed for the wrong reason."

Scorn like the sharp edge of a saber: "Very sympathetic, Monsieur."

"No more than you are when you call them an *otriad,* Madame."

"Touché . . . Now please explain to me why I should make a pact with the devil?"

"How far does my voice carry?"

"No further than my ears." It was her turn to wait. Finally she said, "Do you doubt me or my security?"

"I don't know enough to doubt."

"Your profile said that you were a difficult negotiator."

"I thought we already had a deal."

"Yes, yes, we did." She snorted. "Oh, very well. You don't make mistakes and I made my pact with you. But understand, I shall require an accounting on this matter. It concerns more than myself, it concerns Touraine. Do you understand?

"Yes."

"Very well, I will go further. This *billet* you wish will be drafted—and guaranteed—by me personally. Now tell me exactly what you want it to say."

I gave her the wording. She asked me where I could get it. Informed her where I was staying in Santiago and under what name (another favor from the minister). She said she would send the note via the law firm in Chile's capital that GT had on retainer. They would add authenticity seals. The document would be waiting at the hotel when I arrived. That ended the conversation.

I figured that Olivia Fouchet was going to order a fast-track investigation of the Hsin-min beyond the information she had accessed. I hoped that before she attempted anything serious she would reread my profile.

It went better than I deserved. I had thought about the money, and forgot business is built on relationships as much as it is on cash. The other moneycenters would be seriously annoyed and that could be a problem for Touraine. But I was right in believing that the money would be a secondary issue. Siv Matthiessen was more valuable than any fees or bruised feelings. Valuable not just because of love but because Fouchet knew intimately what her lover was, what she could be. The issue that I thought would present the most problems was what the letter meant. Giving it to me, allowing me to wield it without direction, was in effect saying that I enjoyed the power of Touraine. There haven't been plenipotentiary ambassadors for centuries—for good and selfish reasons. "You don't make mistakes." A warning, not an opinion.

I had clipped Fouchet at the optimum moment. The best thing you can say about failure is that it makes you receptive. We heard each other quite well.

My conversation with Nathaniel Palmer was brief and blessedly simple: I had my appointment.

CHAPTER TWENTY-NINE

HAD ANOTHER WAIT OUTSIDE THE library. No sign of Christan and the Bentley. Still searching for ball bearings? I hoped he didn't think I pulled the ancient gag of sending a tenderfoot off to find a left-handed skyhook. Talked for a while with the elderly guard. He was by himself and lonely.

He offered me some coffee from his large plastic thermos. I accepted. Cheap, overbrewed, but he had added a comforter to it, palm wine brandy. I let it settle angrily in my stomach and thanked him.

Asked him about the changes he had seen in Santiago over the past forty, no, forty-two years since he first came to the city with his wife. I was expecting a nostalgic reminiscing about old streets, old friends, old ways of life. Instead Hector Alonzo Garcia talked about the new architecture that had been put up since the last big quake. He pointed out some of the most noteworthy erections—from the front steps of the Biblioteca we had a good view of downtown—and commented knowledgeably about the construction methods used; how the young architects of Chile had rediscovered and readapted the ideas of Buckminster Fuller (he had trouble with that first name, it doesn't roll very well in Español) and employed the principles of *tensegrity*—he hesitantly explained that the strange Anglo term was a combination of the English words for tension and integrity—to build structures that were both very efficient and very strong.

I wanted to ask Hector Alonzo Garcia how he had learned so much about architecture, but I couldn't think of a way that wouldn't sound patronizing. Then he came to my rescue by volunteering that he had spent some years working security for one of those young lion design firms. A good job, he said, looking meaningfully around his cramped little kiosk—the people there were very simpatico. When he ventured to ask questions about what they were doing, they had answered patiently, happily—it often happens that way when people love their work, doesn't it, senor?

I agreed. He started talking about how his wife also loved the city, how each morning she would pick a neighborhood and then start walking. She would walk all the boulevards, the avenues, the streets, simply for the pleasure of it. Just then the Bentley came up the driveway. I thanked Hector Alonzo Garcia again for the coffee and the conversation—I enjoy architecture myself very much. My . . . my wife was an architect. He asked if she was with me on my trip. I told him that no, she was probably designing those interesting streets I hoped his wife was finding in heaven. He touched his chest with splayed fingers as if my remark had beat a sudden tattoo on his heart. I put my hand out. He nodded, crossed himself, and shook it.

There was a bag of large marbles on the front seat. Christan Borrayo looked as embarrassed as only the young can get. "I couldn't find any ball bearings and I did not want to be late so I thought maybe if they weren't of steel they . . ." His words trailed off while he waited to be lashed.

I got in the Bentley, and said, "Before we go to the hotel drive past the New People Bank."

"Yes—Senhor Meireles." He turned the car around and headed towards the city's center.

I looked at the bag. They were all taws, shooters. I opened it and took out a few. Solid glass. Cat's-eyes, jaspers, glassies, rainbows, even a couple of aggies. I reached in and removed those. They had the right shape, not as heavy, but they could work. I rolled them together in my hand. Somehow, the idea of using children's marbles had never occurred to me. I forgot how as kids we would often use ball bearings for our taws. I put the two into a pocket and the remainder into my valise. "They'll do. Did you ever play?"

He tried to hide his little exhale of relief. "No, not with those, but I did play Kongki Nori when I was young."

A Korean VRgame. It was played in a variable-gee sphere instead of a ring drawn in the dirt. The art was in ricocheting your taw so that it would spin into a high-grav zone that would slow it to a halt. Not hard for most modern kids, although at the advanced level it added a distance distorter that made it tricky for any age. When Kongki came out the company that produced it was on the ban list, something about soft theft. Dano had heard about it and asked if I could get it for him the next time I was out of the country. I did. I also showed him the original game, but . . .

Do I sound like I was raised in an isolated commune? Not quite, but I spent part of my childhood worshipping some older cousins who believed that games that couldn't be played outdoors weren't much fun.

Christan was aching to ask me what they really were for. I wasn't feeling in the mood to be enlightening. Wasn't much feeling in the mood to feel. Instead I asked him about certain other arrangements that his uncle and I had discussed. Even though we were in an embassy car he sensibly darkened the windows and turned on a portable scrambler—the low-pitched whine danced in my bones.

I was to meet with Senors Gutierrez, Chan, and Chan at 6:30

P.M. Not at the Hsin-min headquarters that we were driving toward but at a private home; the address, according to Christan, was in a rich colonia that nestled in the Andean foothills at the eastern end of the city.

"I will have to arrange another car for you," he commented glumly. "This one will have too great a chance of being recognized by the residents there." Watching him handle the car, how gracefully it moved despite its bulk, I understood why he felt morose. The Bentley was a masterpiece in motion. Rolls-Royce claims that over 95 percent of the cars they have crafted in the last hundred years are still around. It was easy to believe them.

I could imagine Nell saying, "Beauty and efficiency, a 'masterpiece in motion.' Are they something else the rich are only trustees of?"

Nell shaded with a bit of Kit. Now, why do I let them ask me questions that I can't answer?

Christan was saying something. Asked him to repeat it. "I think you will need another escort besides myself as well."

I hadn't planned on taking him along. "Why?"

"For the appearance. Even though this is strictly an unofficial visit—that is so?" I nodded. "With people who live in places like that, it is good to show them that you have power. That you're"— he shifted briefly into English—"not a lone wolf."

"Let me think about it." We were off the main road that ran atop an embankment down at the street level. I watched people strolling, eating their lunches at busy empanada stands, or sitting on the new grass with friends, lovers, in the small parks that separate the clusters of buildings. Some of the men were dressed in northern suits, but the majority wore the same kind of clothes that my companion had on; more than a few had brilliantly colored ponchos that swirled like the crowns of wildflowers with the wind. The women wore pastel tops tucked tightly into dark blue skirts or pants. Most had knee-length woolen sweaters as brilliant as the men's ponchos thrown over their shoulders like capes. They had large silver brooches attached to their blouses or sweaters, or at least silver earrings. A couple wore simple headpieces.

It's more than dialects, costumes.

They used to worry about the homogenization of human society, about the media puree that the global village would become. They underestimated the strength of local character, the urge to be part of a unique community, to have a history. We have an enormous capacity to resist change. Sometimes that is our tragedy, sometimes not.

They also thought once that communities wouldn't be bound by something as old-fashioned as geography, time, space. They forgot that closeness, identity, isn't simply defined by conversation, or imagination.

I decided to ask the hotel to provide me with one of those ponchos—a childhood memory of watching an old, old movie came to me. An actor that wore one constantly in a Western that didn't make any sense. My mother had all of his films in her personal library. Her odd fondness for him was due to the fact that they had worked together in the grand twilight of his career. I wasn't about to attempt an imitation—a man's gotta know his limits—but the thought was amusing.

That's right, Robie, keep working on that sense of humor. One day it might stick.

The Hsin-min headquarters wasn't entertaining. There was something about the sharp angles, even gentled by its warm terracotta coloring, that jarred me. It wasn't nerves, mostly not; perhaps it was because I'm not fond of structures that resemble a sacrificial temple, or a benevolent nuclear reactor. The art of good architectural design is as much psychological as it is material. If they were trying for an image of safety, they failed.

I told Christan to pull over and go into the bank. He was to ask if a Senor Jose Guitierrez was in today. He wasn't to tell whoever he spoke to who he was or why he was asking—his face said that the latter wouldn't be difficult. Whatever the answer, he was to say:

"Oh, never mind, it's a trivial matter." Then leave and come straight back to the limo. He shrugged and stopped in a five-minute parking zone. In his eyes was the dawning realization that I was strange.

It took him longer than five minutes. Predictably, a police scooter came by. The officer read the bar code on the back plates and grimaced. The windows were still very dark. He didn't bother to look inside. Cops aren't fond of diplomatic immunity either. He leaned hard over his handlebars as he rode away.

"He's in," Christan said when he returned. "Was that an anxiety attack?"

It took me a few seconds to realize who he was referring to. An anxiety attack. I liked it. Made certain I would remember. "Something like that."

He nodded with the happy expression of an eager student. "The minister said that I was to pay very close attention to you."

I replied dryly, "Your uncle is too kind. But I'm not exactly the world's greatest investigator."

"Begging your pardon, *senhor*—are you sure it would all right to call you Tomas?"

"That's what I said."

"So . . . Tomas, my uncle sent me some of your file—he thought it would be instructive—I feel privileged to work with you."

There isn't a file unless . . . No, it wasn't that. Tomas Meireles was invented many years ago, and had been inactive pretty much since then—by me, but not necessarily by others. It made sense, just like action groups swapping names to confuse their foes. I supposed I should have been flattered that the man had apparently farmed out that alias to some first-rate operatives. It was clear that I would have to abandon any ideas of using Meireles after this. And that I had a case of incipient hero-worship on my hands.

"Don't believe everything you read. Let's go to the hotel."

We passed through a little urban forest. Acacias and naked

alders cross-adapted, the alders fixing nitrogen for both, the acacias bending their branching protectively over the other species, providing a cooling shade in the hot summers. A graceful garden. As we left the woods and we crossed over the Mapocho River, it was swollen with runoff from the spring thaw almost up the edges of its concrete levees.

Christan Borrayo Aragao and I weren't going to be friends. For practical reasons and for his parents' sake. . . . Wrong kind of memories. I may have no choice in being forced to live with them. They shouldn't have to.

There was a lawyer waiting for me in the lobby of the Andradina. I knew he was an attorney because he told me. He was wearing red shorts and a white pullover shirt with grass stains on it. His firm had called him away from a siesta *fútbol* game. If he was unhappy he knew that counted for little when you're a junior partner and a lord wants prompt service. In one hand he held a pair of cleated running shoes, in the other a databloc that looked remarkably like a pencil—it was even yellow. He looked me over carefully—they must have given him a tight description—waited for me to formally identify myself, and then handed over the document. When I thanked him he did his best to be courteous, but his heart wasn't really in it.

He probably wouldn't ever be a senior partner. Had a hunch he really didn't care.

After I was checked in—Eduardo Mistral, another name, another packet of well-organized lies—we went up to inspect my suite. Following the concierge who had been assigned to me, we walked through an inner courtyard carpeted with early-blooming pelargoniums to a short flight of stone steps. At the top was a door and a windowed balcony that looked over the courtyard. Someone would have to fight their way through the hotel's impressive guards to get to me. Inside there was a large airy sitting room with a raised alcove in which rested a bed big enough to entertain multitudes. I mentally shook my head. My emotions were far too tangled for even a moment of innocent pleasure.

Told the concierge I needed a few things. I wanted a poncho—she politely asked me to turn around for her, then nodded; no doubt she would select a better choice than I could make. I asked for a full keyboard. They had a Kurzweil-Baldwin and a Yamaha; which would I prefer? She added helpfully, "The Kurzweil is the one that Maestro Naciamento uses when he stays with us." Decided to go with genius. I was feeling hungry—could I get some *curanto,* and—I looked at the bottle of Chilean champagne on a table—perhaps a half liter of Fuentes's Syrah? The traditional dish was no problem of course, but she wasn't sure that they had that wine in their cellar—if not, was it all right for her to pick out a substitute? I smiled my permission. Finally I asked for a sewing kit. That set her back a little. She said a bit anxiously, "We have a tailor on the premises. If it is urgent, he can undertake any repairs that you need done immediately." I smiled and told her that I preferred doing it myself, it relaxed me. She quickly got back her aplomb. "As you wish, senor. Is there anything else you require at this moment?

Yes. A truckful of good karma. I thanked her and said that should cover it. She made a little bow that was more like an extended nod and said that she would be available to assist me throughout my stay, at any time. Thanked her again and sat down in one of the comfortable chamois-covered chairs.

After she left us I asked Christan if he had those extracts from my file with him. He didn't, it was back at his office in the embassy. "It is safe there, Tomas."

"Why don't you go get it. I could use some light reading."

He hurried out. I liked the chore trick—had a feeling it might work the best. And I did want to see that history of "mine." More than curiosity. The gentlemen I had an appointment with would undoubtedly be using their own resources to find as much as they could about who I was, if not what the hell I was about. It wouldn't do for them to know more about me that I did.

The keyboard, a sewing kit, and the lunch arrived at the same time. While I ate the fish-and-meat stew along with the loaf of crusty bread that came with it and drank the excellent red that the concierge had found as a replacement for the Fuentes, I watched the houseman set up the piano. When it was ready I went over to it and ran through some scales. It sounded fine. I tipped him and offered him the champagne. He took it, but I had the feeling he shared my opinion about the quality. Before I sat down to play I looked over the document. It was pretty much what I requested— I may not be fluent in legalese, but I can follow it. There were a couple of provisos designed to protect Groupe Touraine in the case of any malfeasance, criminal or otherwise, on the part of the Hsin-min; standard contractual practice but their specific wording made it a not too subtle dig in the ribs. Cute touch, very French.

Did a few finger exercises, asked the piano to bring up a score, then played carefully through the opening movement of the *Appassionata*. An amateur's tribute to a maestro's favorite performance piece. It was a good piano. I prefer an acoustic, for visceral if not aural reasons, but the KB, like most of the better electronics, has analog circuitry designed to grow richer with age—and each unit mellows differently. This one was a bit more tart than my Bechstein, but I was happy with it.

I switched to Rachmaninoff, Rhapsody on a Theme by Paganini. Started playing the variations that Kit loved.

The Siv-that-wasn't-Siv had talked to me about her lover. I had returned the confidence. She listened and said that perhaps Katherina—she followed my example and gave it the Greek accents—a luscious name, she said—simply wasn't suited to be a whaler's widow. That threw me for a minute until I recalled that the Norwegians had hunted whales as eagerly as the old New Bedford men, and had persisted at the slaughter longer. While she talked she drew a sketch of a woman dressed in a long skirt and shawl, standing on what they used to call a widow's walk—an open rooftop veranda that looked out over the coast. The wind whipping fiercely at short dark hair, her face half turned to the churning sea. With a few short strokes Siv had limned a face filled with forlorn hope. She waited a moment while I looked at the drawing, then said, "Perhaps you are a kind man. Perhaps that is why you don't fight harder to hold her."

Perhaps.

What was more illuminating was our conversation about the Congo bonds. I handle my finances and small business operations fairly well—thanks to good intuition and the expensive expertise of my software—but macroeconomics was never my long suit. I wasn't surprised that it was one of Siv's. I managed to follow her most of the way, and when I stumbled (does anybody, human or otherwise, really understand how a delta-gamma upside-down hedge works?), she picked up and showed me the handholds on the mountain we were climbing.

She was frankly amazed by some of the sensitive data that Lila had gathered around the bare-bones facts about the Congo securities. (Mercy buckets, dear Lil. I'm sorrier than I realized that we don't see each other more often.) If Siv understood it right, she wasn't certain, some of the data was only allusional; there was a deception of sorts with the bonds. The principal on them, their face value, was supposed to be ultimately guaranteed by the EU's Treasury. They weren't, not completely. There seemed to be about a 70 percent shortfall in the contingency reserve.

"I don't see it," I said again. "They're only supposed to be guarantor of last resort. And the bonds are laddered over a long maturity period. The early ones are strips, they'll get the piled-up interest when the first profits start coming in. And even if those earnings come in slower and weaker it seems real unlikely that the reserve would be drained."

"Read the microscopic print, Gavilan. At the mutual discretion of the issuers and holders the privately placed bonds may be redeemed early."

"Okay, and refusing to redeem would torpedo confidence so that future issues would have a tough time of it. I still don't see the fraud. The Treasury can cover any shortfall."

"It isn't that simple. The EU's budget is as finely and tightly crafted as an old Swiss watch. Income and expenditures are calibrated out for ten years. I doubt that the Bundesbankers that control the Treasury are going to be willing to see that system get busted."

"But the money managers that are buying the bonds, they've got to know this. It hasn't slowed sales."

She looked at me skeptically, as if I were pretending to be obtuse. "Clearly they know. They've been assured that the Congo consortia will be able to stand by the securities."

"Touraine is the dominant partner in the syndicate."

"Touraine is dominant in whatever it does."

There was a oly question about whether she was referring to the company, or herself. I didn't bother. "Can the Groupe cover a run?"

She shrugged. "I don't know."

"Would you?"

She sat back in her chair and picked at the pleats of the cornflower blue sundress she had chosen to wear. "Did you maneuver me into talking about Livy so that it would be easier for me to make that evaluation? So that my circuits would be oversaturated with the sense of her?"

"I don't recall doing any maneuvering—I'm not that clever, Siv."

"So you say. . . . And I don't know you at all. Do I?"

"We never met."

"I hope we do."

"Yes—my question, Siv."

"Livy trusts me. More . . . she's come to rely on me."

What better business asset could Olivia Fouchet have than a Leonardo who loved her? A cynical thought. Tempered only by the knowledge that in the end hardly anyone knows or cares about the blood-soaked politics of the Renaissance, only about its great-souled geniuses.

"Is that why I was kidnapped, for what I know about finances?" The outrage that she felt on thinking that her bodyguard, her friend, might have betrayed her for money, was back in full force.

"It's not clear. There may have been other motives."

She cooled down a bit—almost literally, her colors became more subdued. "The part that puzzles me the most is the Furies. I find it hard to believe that they would . . . collaborate."

I sighed and quoted again the line from Eliot I had given to Fouchet.

"'The wrong reasons.'" She shifted toward me with troubled eyes. "I hope that isn't the case with you."

"No, more like the opposite."

I finished the rhapsody, then improvised a little tart capriccio of my own on Paganini's sugary theme. When I was done I got my jacket and started sewing a snap-release holster for the marbles in the silk lining of the left sleeve. A man of many talents. Pity all of them are terrible. Christan returned.

He watched what I doing until he thought he figured it out. "*Comprendo*. Here is your file."

I took it from him and laid it down on the chair next to me. "The other escort."

"I'll call now."

"No, get him, or her, yourself."

"But I have a secure line."

I passed along some bitter experience: "The world is full of words that pretend to be truths: infallible, secure, safe, encrypted. Go in person, Christan."

"Yes, sir . . . Tomas. Uh, I have a question."

"Ask."

"When you told me what to say at the bank. I understood you wanted me to say those words exactly. Why?"

His uncle thought that he owed me. Guess I owed him too. All right, I would teach a little more. "There are some cliques in east Asia that use a certain kind of argot. An antonymic slang. Yes for no, right for wrong, and so on."

"Trivial for important."

"Something like that."

He took a moment to look at it from different angles. "It's not just the phrasing, it's the fact that you know the slang and you know that they know. A sort of metaknowledge."

His father taught communication theory, the most useful of the practical philosophies. The things we inherit.

"Ever do any woodworking?" He shook his head. "When you want to put a screw into wood it's best to drill a small hole first. Helps make sure the screw goes in straight."

Christan laughed. "That's good."

"So was 'anxiety attack.'"

He flushed with the compliment. Careful, Robie. I switched gears, dropping my voice to an imperfect impersonal. "Go get the other guard."

When he had closed the door behind him I inserted the file in my pad and read while I stitched. It was fragmentary, enough to be instructive, nowhere near enough to be compromising. Still, Christan's uncle shouldn't have sent it to him. A personal exercise of power. A failing. A fortuitous one maybe. My human alter egos, it wasn't obvious to me how many there had been, were apparently very competent. They seemed to have undertaken operations that I might, in a different life, have gone on. They had been given mostly a free hand, trusted men. They were also willing to be grim—but there was no record of their killing anyone on those operations. Luck? Or did Christan's uncle put that limitation on those men that bore the Meireles name? It would be nice to believe that.

I memorized and cross-referenced details and then erased the file.

Finished the holster and put on the jacket. Practiced shooting the marbles into my hand. Not great. It would have to do. I told the pad to read to me the material I had brought with me from L.A. Did some exercises. Drank several large glasses of ice water. Thought about the architecture that we build inside of us.

CHAPTER THIRTY

BERNARDO DONOSO WAS THE NAME of the guard that Christan had re-cruited. He came with his car, a discreetly armored Citroën. Jet-black, at rest low to the ground, very French.

Christan's uncle hadn't told him any details of my business with the Hsin-min. Serendipity or a sign; I was willing take it ei-ther way. And I was willing to take Donoso as well. His sandy hair and complexion reminded me of the Padrino's Deacon. But his eyes, while cold, weren't dead. He worked as freelance private se-curity, mostly for foreign executives who were just passing through Santiago and traveling light. A professional soldier who chose to be his own boss and—unless I had thoroughly misread Christan—a reliable one. While I was sizing him up he was doing the same with me. I think we were both satisfied.

As Donoso drove us he talked with Christan about fútbol. Chile looked like it had a team that would qualify for the World Cup, a thing it did not often do. Christan, coming from a country that had more championships than any other, and would have had more if the Cup games hadn't been suspended during the Twenties, showed a generous spirit as they debated Chile's prospects. I rested my eyes and listened to the notes behind their words. They sounded okay. I worked on tuning myself.

When we got to the gated entrance, the sentinels, with manners as starched as their khakis, called the address that Christan gave them. While we waited, one of them asked if we would permit him to search the car's trunk. Donoso, driver's side window rolled down, hands in plain sight, told his car to release the latch.

Decency may mitigate poverty and crime; it doesn't eliminate them.

A silvery black sunwing, like a tiring giant condor, lazily trailed us as we motored along a quiet avenue lined with monkey puzzle trees, their heavy branches bending upward as if in prayer, or gratitude.

The house at the end of the winding road managed to be huge without being ostentatious. A blend of traditional Spanish country villa with the elegantly classical proportions of Palladio. The marble columns of the facing colonnade, the way they were proportioned; the subtle lines of the entablature were especially—I turned my head away for a moment. I knew whose eyes I was looking through.

Waiting at the driveway there was another set of guards, and loitering as if it were taking a relaxed break from its rounds was a microtank, its multibarreled main gun nonchalantly drooping. It's not the most cost-effective killing machine around, but it excels at creating nightmares. Christan was impressed. Donoso, maybe. I didn't think much about it at all.

The guards didn't approach. They just watched as we pulled up to the wide steps that fronted the loggia. Christan and I got out. Before we started I had given him the drill: he was to stay with the car, he could lean against its far side and chat with the guards, but if they were too tense he was to give it a couple of minutes, then get back in the vehicle. I had made it clear to both of them that this was supposed to be a low-risk gig, but if it went sour their only responsibility was for themselves. Donoso grunted at the obvious.

Christan nodded somberly. He was after all a sergeant in a tough outfit; despite his youth he hadn't gotten his stripes because of his uncle.

The broad wooden doors of the house were open, a flood of plangent light pouring into the dusk. A butler with a face defined purely by verticals stood impassively by the entrance. He handed my poncho off to an equally reserved maid, and told me in fair Portuguese that Senor Chan and the other gentlemen would join me shortly in the library. I nodded and followed him.

The octagonal room had only a single slender book. One of the thirty-nine volumes of the Ross Bible. Esther. It rested on an illuminated steel pedestal in the center of the room. I went over to it. The manuscript was opened to the blazing page where she kneels openhanded before her king, her husband. Hamman, in robes only slightly less opulent than the shah's, is still reclining on a cushion by the banquet table, staring at her. No one before or since Janielle Ross has managed to capture the tremulous, determined beauty of Esther or the concealed venomous core of Hamman. And she showed more than that. Looking at the stunningly inked figures you knew that while Esther may have won the battle, Hamman's descendants won most of the wars.

There may not have been any other books but there were five painted scrolls in unwrapped splendor on the pale amber walls. The first sign that the house was owned by a family from China. Each of the scrolls was from a different dynasty. The Sung was— before I had a chance to forget the warning that Ross was sending in that page from her masterpiece, the men came into the room.

The younger two were dressed in dark gray business suits with matching orange-and-black scarves; their elder was in a loose-fitting checkered chambray shirt over faded gray worsted slacks. He was a heavyset man, but his face was thin, cadaverous. On the middle finger of his right hand was a trap-cut ruby ring, five carats or so, pigeon's blood red.

The introductions were in English and terse: no handshakes,

just names. Roberto Chan led to the way to leather wing chairs arranged around a low circular rosewood table. I picked the point of the compass where there were no windows behind me and I could see the door.

It was Gutierrez, fingering his thick goatee, who spoke first. "You have a damned interesting way of approaching people, Mr. Meireles." His English was nonspecific; some years ago the bank had given him a sabbatical so that he could study at the London School of Economics.

"Thank you."

He coughed faintly as if prompting me to continue. When I didn't, he frowned, and said, "There is somebody else we would like to have present at this meeting."

A lawyer, or a senior officer of the Chilean carabineros? I said cautiously, "Considering what I'm here to discuss with you, I was hoping we could keep this informal. You are clear about what the agenda is?"

Roberto Chan spat out, "You believe that we have some connection to the kidnapping of Olivia Fouchet's mistress."

He was in his early thirties, the youngest member of the council within the Hsin-min that was responsible for "special situations." With his delicate, elfin face he looked a decade younger. But only the young are fooled by youth. I didn't know much about him—didn't know enough about any of them—only that his public job with the bank was as a vice president of trading in their commodities department. It's a job that calls for very fast mental reflexes, and nerve. I stared at him, and said, "Siv Matthiessen. She's a woman, a person, not a product. And yes, I am here because you do have some knowledge about her kidnapping."

Gutierrez shifted uncomfortably in his seat. He was too large for it. Despite his body language he spoke without a trace of irritation in his voice. "That is your supposition."

I kept my eyes on Roberto. He hadn't reacted at all to my first statement, and not much to the second. I said, "Oh, I see. And you agreed to this meeting in order to correct my mistake. Very kind of you."

How people of power react to sarcasm can reveal a lot. The elder Chan smiled slightly, the younger scowled. Gutierrez kept his mask. "We're here because you threatened a valuable associate," he said.

Valuable? Well, he should know. Gutierrez was Palmer's direct supervisor. On the flight down I had spent some time speculating on what the likelihood was that their L.A. comprador had authorization for his Orloff project. If he had, then perhaps that potential instability that Harry thought he saw in them so many years ago had started becoming actual. If Palmer had been acting solo then unless he had come up with some superb lies on short notice—I didn't think Gutierrez would have used that term. I turned toward him.

"I only offered him a supposition."

Roberto made a chopping motion with his hand. "Enough of this dueling crap! My question to you, *Senhor* Meireles, is— whether or not we know anything—what the devil does it have to do with your government?"

Pericles Chan had been carefully snipping the end off a Double Corona with a pair of gold clippers. He stopped and rumbled to the younger man in Chiu Chow, "Stay easy, nephew. All things will come in their right order."

The script wasn't going in any direction I thought it might. I had expected that they would work me for a while, giving out only to take. They had gone past the first act as if it didn't mean anything. Planned? The way Roberto Chan had spoken so fast. And his uncle asiding to him in a dialect that Meireles wouldn't know—or did they know that *I* did?

The first rule of negotiation is never to let the other side confuse you.

There was a large vacuum flask on the table with a set of cups and saucers, bowls of sugar and cream, silver spoons. I touched the flask's handle and asked Pericles Chan, "Tea?"

His eyes stayed on my face. "Coffee—Talamanca Borbon."

From Costa Rica. I complimented him with a slow, tilted smile, flipped open the lid, and poured myself some. Over the brim of my cup I said to Pericles Chan, "What does this problem have to do with Brazil? Specifically, it doesn't. I am a loan."

Roberto Chan jerked his head. "Alone?"

Before I could respond, Gutierrez calmly corrected him. "He means he's been lent by his department to another nation"—he directed his attention back to me—"or company?"

I nodded. "So who is this other party?"

Pericles Chan had fished a lighter from his shirt pocket and was warming his long dark cigar with its flame. He answered, "As the Americans like to say, you were beaten to the punch. Early yesterday an official of another country contacted us regarding the same unfortunate matter. We feel a joint meeting would help clarify matters."

Not only was the script going with a POV I hadn't foreseen but a new playwright had stepped in. "Who is this official?"

He paused for a second, then said, "Mei Chien. She is a member of the Censorate of Sichuan."

The Censors are the guardians of political and military morals in the Chinese Realms. An elite force. They have the power to accuse, and to condemn. They are only hampered by the sheer size of their country and by their low numbers—there aren't many who can be trusted with that amount of power. Silently I cursed my *campañero,* my minister. Odds were these men had told Mei Chien that I was coming. I didn't know yet what her stake was in this but she would have almost certainly contacted Brazil to find out what my involvement was. The relationship between the two countries was cordial. And he didn't tell me. I gave myself a mental kick. Respect the man, but always remember the politician. I stared at Pericles Chan's eyes. "It may suit you, but why should it suit me?"

With his free hand he thoughtfully brushed a thumb across a hollow cheek that had a small constellation of pinkish white keloid scars. The Potosi virus that had claimed Fouchet's husband so long ago had its terrible run through Chile as well. He looked like a man who was carefully examining his cards—after he had already deliberately dropped a few face up on the table. "We believe that the sharing of information would be mutually beneficial."

I tasted my coffee again. "What if I were to say that I am not interested in what benefits you. I can talk to Censor Chien on my own."

"Then I would say that this meeting is at an end." He moved as if to get up.

"There are benefits, and then there are profits."

Roberto Chan's eyes widened incredulously. "Are you trying to bribe us?"

As Meireles, I spoke a little Cantonese, poorly. I took a few seconds before replying. It's not easy to dumb down in a language, especially when you've worked hard for the opposite. "The young are so quick, but so full of elbows."

Pericles sat down again but he didn't speak. It was Gutierrez who asked, "What sort of profits?"

I reached into my jacket, and from the ceiling a pale violet beam focused on my left chest. I asked the air, "Should I be flattered or insulted?"

Pericles said a couple of words in a dialect that I didn't know. The targeting light vanished. I glanced first at the smooth ceiling, no trace of where it had come from, then back to him. I finished taking the letter from my inside pocket and rolled it slowly between my gloved fingers. In a way I can't explain, the beam shining down, marking my heart, had shaken things loose in me. I understood the script. They were in trouble.

There's a tactic that experienced felons sometimes use when they're hauled in called Yes/But. As in, yes, I'm involved. But I'm not the one you really want. Yes, I can help you. But you're going to have to help me. It only works effectively when the police are under pressure, aren't getting anywhere, and are barred from using torture. While I ran through the scenario I said slowly, "I once had the privilege of having a conversation with Victor Giletes. Name ring a bell?" Pericles nodded with his eyes. "Thought it might. He was a great man of business. It was, oh, a few weeks before he was executed. He said that having an excessive defense was nearly as bad as having no defense at all. It revealed too much. I thought that was an interesting insight. . . ." I stopped and glanced at Roberto Chan. "Offer a bribe? Now, that is insulting. Didn't your inquiries turn up anything useful about me?" Before he could reply I returned to his uncle. "I am prepared to offer you a deal. A very generous one. But I am going to need to know whether it's justified."

"What kind of deal?" Pericles asked.

"A marriage of convenience."

Both of the Chans got it. They bore no resemblance to each other, but they both shifted their shoulders the same way, their heads rose together almost simultaneously. As if they were smelling something unexpectedly wonderful. Gutierrez, however, didn't, although he was able to recognize that he was missing out. He said a little peevishly, "What are you talking about?"

"A profitable, legal arrangement with Groupe Touraine. And all you have to do is persuade me that you are capable of doing a good job, a good"—I used the Spanish word, it hits harder— "traición." A good betrayal.

Each in his own way looked impassively at me, then Roberto held a hand out. "Let us see what you are offering." I nodded and gave him the bloc. He took out his pad from his black silk waistcoat with mocking slowness. He started reading. Gutierrez shifted his chair so he could also see the small screen. The ease with which he moved his and the chair's bulk reminded me of a bit of confidential data my daemon had snagged. Unlike Roberto Chan, he hadn't been bred and raised to be a black banker; he had started out as a trooper for a syndicate. No name, no history, only that it had lost a war to a *vory*. Was the Orloff gig a payback? Maybe, or the Russian aspect might have merely been icing. Or it might have meant nothing to him. The most terrible men don't bother with grudges. I settled back in my chair and watched Pericles Chan. He was slowly drawing on his cigar. Studying me back, warily. I asked him, "Is the woman here?" He was too wise to make the mistake of misunderstanding. "No, the Censor is waiting to join us from the Mainland."

"I see."

"Did you really have a conversation with Giletes?"

"Are you still interested in the possibilities of space?"

"I have a son on the moon. He is a research geologist. But you probably know that."

"Not many in his field are fortunate to get that ticket. You must be proud of him."

"I am proud of all my children."

"That's good; playing favorites never works out well."

"You sound as if you have some of your own."

"Not really. I do have a number of nephews and nieces. Only one nephew actually, the other died of a *lody* overdose."

He didn't flinch. Why should he? He had been only a facilitator, no blood on his hands. The lies we tell ourselves. Or worse, the truths we don't care about.

Before we could play another hand, Gutierrez spoke up. "Pericles? We must discuss this offer."

"Take your time," I said. "I'll go for a walk in the garden."

That wasn't exactly what they had in mind. They wanted hours, if not days, to confer with their EIs, debate, analyze, ago-

nize. But I was already getting to my feet, no smile on my face—
that would have been impolite—and it was very clear that I wasn't
about to wait at their leisure.

Pericles looked up at me, and quietly said, "The center window slides open."

"Thank you." I left them and went outside.

It was a beautiful Chinese garden, which meant it was very beautiful. Between a bright moon and the light from hundreds of
glowflies that came alive as I walked on the paths I could see it
quite well. The air was perfumed with the smell of daphnes, *shui
hsiang,* the "sleeping scent"—or if you use a different ideograph
with the same sound, the "lucky scent." Staggered rows of
hait'ang, crab apples—ugly name for a lovely tree—flooded with
rose, pink, and white petals. At the end of a meandering path that
followed a stream bordered by daylilies, there was a huge peach
tree with perfect double white flowers striped with crimson lines.
I found a teak bench by a little bridge that went over the stream
and sat down.

I could have done what they were anxiously, I hoped, engaged
in doing: trying to work out the best vectors. But I had insufficient
information. I knew, sensed, that they were in trouble; what kind,
and from where, I had no idea. Only that it was something that
scared them. The Censor from Sichuan? Could be. I didn't know
how I wanted to play that. There are times to think, and there are
times to be. I sat down on the bench and admired the garden.

The minutes went by. I was starting to get chilly. I stood up.
There's a movement technique that a woman once taught me that
drives the cold away for a while. Even though I was sure somebody
was watching me, I decided to do it. I got up, started *wu chi* and
moved my arms slowly toward my chest and out and back again,
gathering the heat. It actually worked, or I thought it did—is there
a difference?

I sat back down. The memory of what Siv had said came to me: a graceful garden filled with graceful people. Was it that bad a plan? The ancient Chinese, and to an even greater extent their Japanese stepchildren, didn't think so. For them it was an ideal. A true harmony with nature. But they never dreamed how far we could take it. How thoroughly we eventually will be able to mold our, somebody's, definition of grace. Another memory walked in.

God grant me the serenity to accept the things that I cannot change. The courage to change the things I can. And the wisdom to know the difference.

A forgotten prayer she taught me. A prayer that became the remains of my life . . .

The word *nephew* must have resonated somewhere. Roberto Chan came down the path. Greeted him. "Hello. I was just about to go back. Have you come to a decision?"

"Yes."

"Excellent." I stood up and went close to him. He automatically stepped back as I came into his space. "It's quite some garden."

"My cousin, Aureliano, designed it."

"When you see him, please say how much I admired it."

He looked as if he wanted to say something sneering about how little any member of his family would care what a cop thought, but there was the minor handicap of a still-unconsummated arrangement. So instead he nodded, and said, "Shall we go back?"

"Sure, in a moment. Did you understand the Chinese I spoke to your uncle?" His moon pale face flushed. "Good." Before he could move I took his right elbow. "You know there are nerves here that if pressed in the wrong way can cause more pain than a man can stand? And the nice thing about it is that it can be done before anyone else even notices." He tried to pull away; he was stronger than he looked, but not strong enough. I said to him musingly, "No, it's not a nice thing. It's terrible, the things a cop has to learn. Almost as terrible as the lack of respect children often give us." I released him abruptly. He stumbled back. "That was a career lesson that your uncle should have taught you. Never play with people like me if you're not willing to get hurt. Have I made myself clear?"

He swore at me. Not much enthusiasm or imagination. When he ran out of words, I smiled, and said sympathetically, "I hope that makes you feel better. One should have a calm mind when dealing with money. And that's why we are really here, isn't it? A few millions' worth. We should get back to your associates. It's getting cold."

He looked very bad. The second rule of negotiations: Find the person across the table who could give you the most trouble, and break him. I started walking slowly. I wanted to let him have enough time to recover, on the outside.

"What are your preconditions?" asked Gutierrez.

I poured myself another cup of coffee before I answered him. Roberto Chan was leaning back in his chair, his composure restored, the image of a forceful financial operator planted firmly on his face. Lord, the training they're getting nowadays. His uncle had shot him a lingering glance when we returned, but nothing else. While I made myself comfortable, I wondered about how their conversation would go after I left. Would Pericles Chan be angry at what I did to a member of his *dajya*? Or would he be ashamed at the lack of control displayed by his nephew? I shrugged inside. His reaction wasn't important. I wasn't leaving until I got what I wanted, and whatever he thought afterward, he would be sensible. That is how people like him, how families like his, survive. That's why cops survive.

"Did you help arrange a partnership between the group called the Erinyes and a Southern African company?"

Gutierrez lifted his shaggy brows. "That is what you consider a precondition?"

I mirrored his surprise. "Did you think that Touraine would be so generous just for some information about who is involved?"

Pericles Chan sighed. "You wish active help."

"I would have thought that would be obvious." I looked over at Roberto. It was. They were just back to the game.

Gutierrez said, "Perhaps you could give us a general idea of what kind of involvement in your investigation you are seeking from us."

"Why don't you answer my first condition?"

Roberto Chan finally spoke. "It is necessary? You seem to already know what the answer is."

I said as gravely as Ethan Hill would, "Declarative statements are a necessary formality in my profession." I switched to a disarming smile. "But only if I thought that I might have to testify in a court of law. And I haven't done that in years, don't expect that I ever will again." That produced a faint smile on Gutierrez's face. The Chans were in varying degrees of ambivalence. "If you worried that I might have within me a recorder that your detectors haven't spotted, I am willing to accept a nod as a stipulation."

"We made the connection." Pericles said.

"Thank you. Do you know where the Erinyes are now?"

"No."

"Do the Southern Africans?"

He looked at Gutierrez. The other man cupped his hands and leaned forward. "Before we go forward on those lines I think we should discuss some details of the contract between Hsin-min and Groupe Touraine."

"The letter is straightforward. You get a customer who will provide you with some considerable profits. If you provide good service in turn there's the likelihood that Touraine will continue using you. You know their reputation. They're not petty, and they always look toward the long term. If there are technical questions about the contract, I suggest you contact their legal representatives. I'm not a lawyer."

Gutierrez looked puzzled for a second. "I thought . . . oh, I see. Never mind."

Did I overlook something in the Meireles file? Or did they know something about one of the alter operatives that wasn't mentioned? Weave a tangled web and you end up getting screwed up in it. Gutierrez seemed to have worked out some kind of explanation for himself. He continued, "The issue we are concerned about is the provision that allows the agreement to be summarily canceled by you within the next ten days."

"You think that we would renege?"

Gutierrez hunched his shoulders like a prizefighter. "What we suspect you want us to do will cause us to lose one client."

"Would MacKenzie-Rao terminate their relationship with you if you severed your connection to a unit of theirs that is engaged in activities that the board doesn't know about? I would think that they might be grateful for bringing that activity to their attention."

Either that was one of the worst bets I've ever made or they were stunned at the size of the bill I had just taken out of my wallet. I watched Pericles Chan. He studied his cigar for a while, then asked, "Why are you here, Senhor Meireles?"

"A man I know likes to say that if you know where to put a fulcrum, you can move the earth."

His face looked even more like a skull. "That is true."

"Cancel it."

"What?"

"The provision that bothers you."

Pericles Chan nodded admiringly. "Very good. I am surprised that I have never heard of you."

"We move in different circles."

His face said how poor a lie he thought that was. I said to Gutierrez, "I'll inform Touraine of the change. Will that be satisfactory?" He didn't show the respect that the vice chairman of his company thought I deserved but a smile flickered around the corners of his mouth. He nodded, and said, "Quite."

"Fine. Now, I asked whether the other party would know where the Erinyes are. Do they?"

It was Roberto Chan's turn to be useful. He started off slowly, he wasn't used to the current yet, where people can die for their mistakes; he may not have even completely realized that it was running through the room. "They assisted in the logistics of the operation. If they do not know the precise final destination, they should be able to extrapolate where it is."

I asked Gutierrez, "How certain?"

He had poured himself some coffee. He gazed at the black liquid for a moment, then said, "They are not my brief, but if I were them I would have already located where the Erinyes are. In case there was a change of plans."

Like deciding to abort, dropping a fireball on the Furies. I said to all of them, "I am going to want names, data, and a passport."

It was Pericles who asked the most important question. "How good a passport?"

I said as honestly as I could, "I'll try my best not to have any survivors hate you."

He shook his head sadly. "It has been a long relationship."

"It is about business," I replied. "And maybe about protection."

"How so?"

"Think about it. Touraine is very powerful. A tiger. One that can fight a dragon."

It was an offer that I had no authority to make. So what. The prospect of it took him quickly out of his pseudopathos. Pericles Chan looked at his companions, read what they had to say, and nodded at me. "We seem to have a deal."

"I'm glad. Isn't it customary to have a toast?"

Pericles smiled impersonally. "Of course." He said something in that strange dialect. A few seconds later a white-jacketed servant came into the library carrying a tray with the bottle of Johnnie Walker Platinum and four crystal tumblers. The servant broke

the seal on the scotch and poured a measure for all of us. He left behind the bottle and a small silver ice bucket. Gutierrez helped himself to the ice. The Chans and I kept our drinks neat. We all held
our glasses two-handed, one around the tumbler, the other underneath it. It wasn't the sort of ritual that called for a verbal salute.
We drank silently.

As we put our glasses on the table I said, "One thing before we
get started; who is it that Censor Chien is interested in?"

They all frowned. For a second a sliver of panic ran through
me. Had I taken the wrong road? Waited.

Suddenly Pericles laughed. "In for a penny . . . The Censor is
investigating the involvement of a highly placed government official in a certain financial conspiracy. The, uh, event, that you are
concerned with is part of that conspiracy."

"How did you get linked?"

He turned to his nephew. It wasn't a kind glance. Roberto
Chan flushed again. The color didn't do anything for him. He
picked up his whiskey. Pericles said to me, "The official has an account with us. He has been using trading activities to cover the
movement of funds."

One hand not quite knowing what the other is doing. I would
have been amused if that sliver hadn't returned as a knife. Not
panic, something worse. "You didn't know about his connection to
MacKenzie?"

"We thought he was on the sidelines," Pericles said.

"How far is he into the game?"

Gutierrez spoke up. "We don't know." And he hadn't known
either, not a happy man.

"Who is he?"

"The Procurator Chao Wen."

"Never heard of him."

At that moment Pericles Chan looked like he wished he could
say the same. "He is director of one of the Realms's intelligence
branches. But on this, he is operating outside of his government.

The Censorate doesn't approve of free enterprise, not when it comes to those responsible for the public welfare. "She wants his hide."

Pericles Chan had been educated at the University of Wisconsin. He had shown his familiarity with very old slang. He laughed unpleasantly. "Oh, yes. She wants him."

There was a lot more going on. But this was a level of the game that I didn't want to know about. "Will I have to deal with him?"

Roberto Chan roused himself out of his funk. "Chao Wen has nothing to do with the Matthiessen kidnapping."

I showed him my teeth. "Thank you. I'll remember that you told me that." I mixed my drink into the coffee, an insult to both. But I had overload and ache to work on at the same time. "Now, shall we get to work?"

It took a couple of hours, much of it spent by them trying to cover their asses. I was patient. Selling people out is a nerve-wracking experience. And to give them a tiny dram of credit, they weren't used to it. Their careers had been built on reliability. But I prodded them gently toward where I wanted them to go. All the time dodging having to think about Mei Chien, the scare she had put into them, the man she was after. They did try to talk to me about that problem—my hint of help from Touraine may have been as big a carrot as the letter of intent. But I fended them off with noise about discussions I would need to have with Fouchet. I thought Pericles sensed that I couldn't deliver; at the end he started becoming more withdrawn, withholding. But I got enough. When we were finished they walked me out to the main door, Gutierrez still talking about legal aspects, Roberto trying to keep his distance from me, emotionally as well as physically. Pericles didn't say anything, but he did walk beside me.

I stepped onto the loggia and turned to Pericles Chan. "How close is she to getting Chao Wen?"

A glimmer of curiosity showed behind his hooded eyes. "He bothers you?"

"I don't like crooked cops."

He thought he understood me. "I think she will take him very soon."

"That's good."

He surprised me by offering his hand. I hesitated, then thought: What the hell. I shook it.

Went to the car, got in, and told Donoso it was time to go. He smiled and started the engine. Christan asked if it went well.

"Do you play poker?" He nodded. "Ever draw four cards in a row to a royal flush?"

"I don't think so."

"You'd remember." I said dryly. From the front seat Donoso chuckled.

I leaned deep into the backseat. "It's quite a feeling."

CHAPTER THIRTY-ONE

THERE'S A COUNTRY RESTAURANT A few miles west of Santiago that I hadn't been to for five years or so. I asked Donoso to take us there. On the way we stopped at a hythanol station. While Donoso went to pay for the fuel, I got out of the Citroën and gestured for Christan to join me. We walked together out to the edge of the curving road where the station's entrance was marked by an arrow of mirror paint.

"Can you call your uncle safely?"

"I will have to patch and relay through the embassy's sat."

"How comfortable do you feel about that?"

He looked shocked. Diplomatic transmissions are secure precisely because countless millions have been spent on trying to make them otherwise. My question had addressed his opinion on the security within the embassy.

"I'm sure it is safe—I think it is."

I nodded approvingly. *Muito bem.* I want you to ask him to send the current file on a Mei Chien, Censor of Sichuan of the Chinese Realms. The most current one."

He had gone from being shocked to puzzled. "Why do you want *me* to call him?"

I said so roughly that he startled like a colt, "Because I'm not in the mood to talk to him. Go use the rest room."

"Yes, sir." He started to walk stiffly away.

Not right. Damn. "Christan." He looked over his shoulder. "Tell him . . . tell him I said, *Obrigado, meu campanero.*"

Waited until he went around the station's office. Then watched Donoso fussingly straw-boss the crew of attendants that were serving his car. Attendant was the wrong word. They were all partners in the station. It used to be part of a government chain until they sold it off, not to the ricos but to the workers.

I had Christan make his call away from the car not because I didn't trust Donoso—I didn't know him well enough to make that decision—but because when unanticipated luck runs your way, that's the time to be especially careful.

Donoso was critically wiping the corner of a windshield with his handkerchief when Christan returned. He nodded to me silently and passed along a planchet. We got back into the Citroën and went to dinner.

Bressario was once the best Italian—correction, Venetian—restaurant south of the Equator. I had heard that it had gone down slightly, making it the second or third best. Even so, Donoso passed. Said he had a heavy lunch and wanted to watch a fútbol game in his car. So it was just Christan and me. It wasn't busy that night; we were able to get seated near the large hearth—the smell of the cooking dishes was saying that you may not get to heaven, but you can get close. We shared a pot of the house soup, *zuppa di pesce*—more a fish dish than a soup, but you use a spoon anyway. Then I had the *fegato alla Veneziana*—liver and onions may not sound like much, until you had some made by a chef from Veneto. Christan ordered the closest thing to Brazilian soul food on the menu: *risi e bisi*, rice and peas. Afterward we retired to the bar where I persuaded him to try a *caffè alla Borgia*—he wasn't enchanted with the name—he took a sip of the coffee laced with apricot brandy, sprinkled with fresh ground cinnamon, and agreed there were worse ways to be poisoned.

The barman and I chatted a little bit in Italian, he was from Torcello. He looked old enough to be a refugee. We talked about the great dining rooms of Venice. He thought that Mazzotti had been the best. I didn't argue. We both sighed over the memory of Florian's, the most elegant café in the world. Then he poured for the three of us small glasses of a locally grown Bardolino that he thought might, almost, maybe—please, *signore,* what do you think?—be as good as what used to come from around the shores of Garda. It was close, very close.

And so was this room. A soft, long-fingered hand covered mine. *The serenity to accept the things I cannot change . . .*

Sometimes, given time, love can be sifted out of grief. There had been enough.

Her knuckles stroked my cheek. *Grazie, my love . . .*

She walked away.

Christan was still tasting the wine. The barman was looking at me with eyes that were ancient. Eyes that could see. I nodded at him. His hands were a little shaky as he washed a glass.

There are no ghosts, only memories that can sometimes be so tangible that even strangers can feel them. An explanation. Believe it if you want to.

Eat, drink, and be merry. For tomorrow, etc. I took the marbles out and did some tricks for Christan and the barman, Alberto. Passes; drops; the shell game—Alberto brought me another café as payment for the bet he lost; the gag I did for the Padrino's bodyguard; the fusion, that's slapping two balls together so that only one remains, the other ball appeared in the right pocket of Christan's pants—which is when I discovered that he was carrying a gun.

Alberto had to take care of a waiter's order. When he left us. Christan whispered in Portuguese, "You weren't briefed on it?" I shook my head. "Flexible ceramic. Five shot, six millimeter. Hardens when you squeeze the handle. Most arrays can't detect it."

Lovely. "It's time for us to go." I asked Alberto for a bottle of the Bardolino, settled our bill, and we left the restaurant.

The Bressario is in the center of a small hillside village with hardly any parking. We had to walk about two hundred yards to where Donoso was waiting. The cold had grown; there would be a frost tonight. I started to put my gloves back on. As we turned a corner I saw the car, Donoso leaning back in his seat looking down at the dimly glowing dash, watching his game. Nearby a ponchoed farmhand, crooning drunkenly, had his legs spread in front of a low wall that marked off a vineyard.

Too far away. I started running. He turned around. The gun coming up in two hands. Too far. I stopped so suddenly I fell forward, arm out, the marble exploding out of my hand. His head snapped back. I got to my feet and closed. He was down, the marble embedded deep in his left eye. A gurgling scream on his lips. The cat came flying over the wall. The base of my palm smashed against its skull. It twisted in midair, landed and raked my thigh. Pain so paralyzing I couldn't strike. Then the soft bark of two gunshots in one heartbeat. The cat kept moving. I rolled away. Another shot. It died, vomiting blood on my chest.

Christan was with me as I was getting up as best I could.

"Perimeter!"

He did a fast three-sixty. His gun in one hand, the throwing knife he kept in his boot in the other. "Nothing."

"Donoso."

On a crouched run he headed to the car. I went the other way.

The assassin was lying bent over on his side, one hand over his face. He wasn't screaming, just gasping, shuddering moans. I looked down at the hand I had over my thigh. It was covered in blood but there wasn't any spurting, no steady flow. Agony. Bearable. Christan called out, "He's down. Still alive."

"Medkit?"

"Got it."

I saw the weapon a few feet from the man, kicked it farther away. Some kind of sonic. The cat jerked its hind legs, an afterdeath reflex. A black jaguarcita. Three shots, two hits, both shredders. The first hit had put a hole you could put a fist through in its flank. It had taken the second between its neck and shoulder to stop it.

Christan joined me with the kit. "Move your hand away." He sprayed me with a coag bandage. "Pain shot?" I nodded. He fumbled a syringe out of the bag and hit me.

Through gritted teeth I said, "Again." He looked at me for a moment, then complied. I asked, "How bad?"

"Bernardo? Don't know. He has a pulse. Steady right now."

He was getting out his phone. I stopped him and pointed to the downed man. "Give him a full painblock." A stare. Mix of anger and postbattle fright. "Do it." He went over to the man.

I stumbled to the Citroën. Donoso had slumped to his side. Lying on the fine bed of armored glass from the shattered far-side window. Lying on what had saved his life. If it had. I checked his vitals. Christan was right. The wild, irrational thought came to me: Donoso was going to be unhappy about the mess. If he had a mind left. The sonic probably had turned his brain to mush. That he was breathing at all was a miracle.

Bernardo Donoso was a soldier, paid to take the risk. I hardly knew him.

If you think that makes it easy to file him away—go to hell.

I wrapped my hand in a handkerchief and took out his pad. There was a bright orange button on its side—an emergency auto caller. An essential add-on for someone in his job. Pressed it and dropped the pad on his lap. Somewhere in Santiago a medevac team was scrambling.

Left the car and went to where I had dropped the bottle of Bardolino. Broke the neck and used the wine to wash my hands. Returned to Christan. He pointed indifferently to the sicario. "He's pretty bad. How did you—"

"Not now." I took off my poncho and started wrapping it around my waist. "I'm going down to the PCM. I'll call as soon as I can."

"But—"

"I can't be here. I have to leave in the morning. The carabineros will want me to stay. You'll have to deal with this."

He shook his head, "I—"

I grabbed his shoulder. "Deal with it!"

"Yes, sir."

I held on to him, for emphasis, for support. "Lie like crazy but be sure that they don't get a hard link to me. There's a med team on its way. Make sure that they're both alive. Both of them. Do you understand?"

At that moment I saw his uncle. "Yes, *Comandante*."

Major. My father's bloody rank—the life he uselessly prayed I would never live—almost lost it. Instead, I left him and headed as fast I could to the village's metro station. Left him to clean up my mess.

INTERLOGUE 5

THURSDAY, OCTOBER 28

HE WAS CLEANING THE TWELVE-GAUGE. It wasn't his favorite—too old, and nowhere near as effective as the Gewehr automatic with its pulse booster that allowed its solid 20mm slugs to penetrate even the best body armor at close range. But the old gun had a special value to him. He carefully ran the brush down each of its twin barrels.

There is such a simple pleasure in working with one's hands, with tools, he thought. It was sad that whatever the others might say, they really didn't understand that. Except for Thomas. A good man, if too idealistic, a good *venn*.

Knut looked at his equipment spread across the bridge's chart table—yes, this ancient scow had one—the Gewehr; the Heckler & Koch 11mm Parabellum with the extralong clip; the Mitragliatrice sonic—he didn't care too much for that one, it didn't have enough juice to kill, but there were occasions when that wasn't an option—and what was perhaps his favorite: the Beretta Brevetto 2022, the most accurate small gun ever built. When he practiced with it he normally would set the target forty meters away. Head or groin, with it in his hand he never missed.

Hooker came onto the bridge, binoculars in hand. Knut shook his head; as if he could see something with them that the ship couldn't. Hooker went to the windows, and without raising his binoculars, stared out at the sea and the heavy clouds. He said without moving, "Teresa says that even wit' the course change there is a good chance that we will be caught in the edge of the storm."

"She should know."

Hooker turned around. "Why do you speak like that? Teresa respects you. Can't you give her the same?"

Knut swallowed a sarcastic reply and nodded reluctantly. "You're right. I should. I have no argument with her."

"Unlike Chloe."

"Did you come up here to give some counseling? I thought that was Anton's job."

"I'm the team leader on this mission," the other man replied flatly. "A team functions best when there's a minimal amount of friction."

"Now you're sounding like turbo Thomas."

"I don' care for sarcasm."

Knut stared at Hooker. A mistake, it wasn't a match he could win. He put down his grandfather's shotgun and sighed. "She gets on my nerves, and she acts as if Matthiessen is her private property."

"Which doesn't give cause for the two of you to behave like you're toms howling and scratching at each other to see who will get the bitch in heat."

"That bad?"

"Damn close."

"Then I will stop, if she will."

Hooker flashed one of his rare smiles. "I'm not expectin' you two to kiss and make up."

"Not much chance of that."

"You got a yen for *Chloe?*"

That was so absurd that Knut laughed hard. "I think maybe you should have a talk with Anton."

"Sorry. But remember, Knut, there's a reason why everybody's here. We all got our job. And Chloe's is the prisoner. She's responsible and I don' want to see her get fucked up doin' it."

He had been screwing with the little witch mostly because it was easy. And because he was uncomfortable with this part of the mission, the waiting. It made them vulnerable. He was the best tactician among them, they knew it, but they had overruled him. The fact that Chloe's job was the reason they were sailing around semi-randomly gave emphasis to his inclinations. And then there was the fact that the waiting, the interrogation, wasn't for the team's benefit. It was for the African bastards. But Hooker was right. If he kept on Chloe it might slow her down. He had never been a handicap. He wasn't about to start now. "I'll stop."

Hooker nodded. "I know." He looked back out at the ocean. "The Satfeed says that the storm will track east of us. What d'you think?"

He had been born and raised in a fishing village in Nordland, almost at the midpoint on Norway's spine. He had spent as many if not more hours on the water as Teresa. But it had been years since he bothered to focus and smell the weather. He got up and opened the door to the outside. He closed his eyes, trying to remember what his grandfather had taught him. "She's moving all right. . . . I don't know. If I were to guess I would say we were okay. Anyway, this tub should be able to ride it out as long as we don't get too close."

"Thomas thinks this is a good ship."

"Thomas thinks anything with an engine in it is goddamn poetry."

"He been quotin' that crap to you too?"

Knut laughed again, this time because it *was* funny. "Let's make a deal, the next time we see him with a book that isn't a tech manual we wrestle him to the ground and steal it."

"Sounds good by me." They slapped hands.

Hooker looked at the pile of firearms on the chart table. Distaste crossed his face. Knut had a hard time understanding that. Hooker had been in the army, although it was the blood-scared North Am—kick ass but don't get hurt—which was nothing like the Legion that he had been in—where they teach you by example that war's as much about dying as it is killing—just be the last bastard going down. Hooker may not have been in the Legion but he knew that truth. But though he loved his knives, he didn't like guns. Which didn't mean he wouldn't use one—truth was he was decent with his H&K. Maybe he had gotten infected with that stupid code that was popular in his country. That killing doesn't count unless you do it up close and personal.

"I don' want to sound like I'm raggin' on you," Hooker said, "but couldn't you do that in your room?"

Knut went over to the table, picked up the Gewehr, set it to manual, and pumped a round. He said coldly, "This is my job."

Hooker looked at the weapon and at the man. "You're right. I better get back to mine." He left the bridge.

Knut sat down on the stool behind the table. He took the shell out of the Gewehr, and returned to cleaning the other shotgun. After a while he stopped, wiped his hands on some rags, and went by the wheel. A quick look at the control panel—everything green. He raised his head and watched the sea. It was going from light blue to dark gray. Whitecaps were streaking the long angry waves. It reminded him of the waters where he grew up, the ocean he had run away from. His grandfather had told him that the ocean was always going to be there; no matter where he went or what he did, there was always going to be the ocean.

His grandfather may have been slow-witted, but he was as patient as only a fisherman can be. When they told him that he couldn't fish in certain areas, he didn't understand, but he obeyed. When they told him that there were certain fish he couldn't catch anymore, he didn't understand, but he obeyed. When they told him that he had to fish less, he didn't understand, but he obeyed. When they told him that he could no longer fish at all, he finally understood.

So he took his trawler out alone for the last time and when he got to where he had always fished, where his father and his father's father and all the men of his family had fished, he took his shotgun and blew his head off.

Knut was the one who found him. He took the shotgun and set fire to the boat, a Viking's funeral. Hell, he was only a boy.

He wasn't fifteen anymore. He didn't believe in drama, and while the team believed in the power of symbols—he had contributed his share—he didn't believe in myths.

Like the ocean, that part of him had died.

CHAPTER THIRTY-TWO

THE ONE-SHOT WAS A shoddily built little phone. The front panel was ancient Bell, the back was pure jerryrig. But the unit and its number were untraceable—as long as you did use it only once. I had carried it a long time. Now I would use it. I called Jose Gutierrez. He was awake.

"I had an accident."

"Not serious, I hope?" He actually sounded concerned.

"Grave but not fatal. I don't want to experience another."

He hissed, "You think *we* are responsible?"

I chuckled. "It doesn't make much sense, does it? But I would take it as an act of good faith if you were to personally look into it. I'll have someone send you the details."

It was a voice only. There was silence on the other end, then, "I will do that."

"Good, and don't worry, I believe in *vive y deja vivir*. There won't be any ace of spades tucked under a door."

"I am glad to hear that." He paused. "In my experience, that is a rare quality."

For criminals, and too many cops. "A matter of discipline."

Another pause. "You know, Senhor Meireles, I too am surprised that we have never heard of you."

"It's a large world. How is the passport coming?"

"We agreed that we would have it prepared for you within thirty-six hours. It will be ready."

"Excelente." I cut the line.

I didn't call Christan. I was going to wait until I was safely airborne. And he was undoubtedly very busy. He had diplomatic immunity and a powerful uncle, but murder and attempted murder weren't events that the carabineros would shrug off—especially when they had occurred during the course of an operation their commanding officers hadn't been informed about. But he would manage. Besides being a hell of a shot, he had presence of mind. But it would get tricky for him if he hadn't gotten rid of the marble before the cops arrived. There hadn't been any direct witnesses, but there was the Bressario's barman, Alberto. I made the mistake of making an impression.

Mistakes. The man who tried to murder me. His was not wearing a hat and having an expensive haircut. Mine was in almost killing him. Maybe not almost. Another reason I didn't want to talk to Christan. The discipline that is etched in me doesn't forbid killing in self-defense—the founders of the Committee were human, flesh and blood, and their goal was to try to prevent involuntary martyrs, not create them. But the definition of self-defense is very narrow. "For wide is the gate and broad is the road that leads to destruction. . . ." If I lived past Sunday, I had a long one to walk on. The judgment of my ghosts.

Why? Because I can do a number of things effortlessly. Killing is one of them.

Crossed the Equator and got Danny. His story:

"You were sure right about the Hardestys, mate. I thought I've worked with some of the best. Now I'm going to have to reconsider my standards. They had a playbook ready for me with more options than I've seen since I left Septic High. The Bennington uses a voice, keyword, *and* a print system; they had a burglary problem last year. Donovan was holed up in her room, hadn't left it for twenty-four hours. Room service only. De pas nada, Mike got me a manager's bypass—mucho impressive. Went in while they got the other conk diverted—sorry, I know you don't like that term. Anyhow, I slipslide in and there's no sign of Donovan, look in the bedroom. There she is buck naked on the bed, plugged into a VR, moaning away. I'm thinking of all the felonies I could get slapped with. So I activate a jam—praying to Jude that it's going to baffle the room's genie—and go over to her. She doesn't stir, I suck some air and touch her shoulder, ready for a brickload of hysterics. Nothing. She doesn't move. So I try again. Niente. Take off her set, her eyes have gone to heaven. There I am, the only things I've got in my bindle are the usual life-support garbage and few quickie mods, nothing that's going to get her back to realtime. I can't even curse—I'm still not sure about the jam. I stand there for a minute, feeling as stupid as I look, and then I pick her up and carry her into the bathroom and turn on the shower ice cold and carry her in. Yeah, I know, that doesn't usually work squat with the modern mierda we're doing. But hey, what did I have to lose besides trying to get out of the hotel soaking wet? Don't ever discount prayer, Gav—it actually worked. No frenzy, instead she falls to her knees and starts working on my crotch. Lucky for me it isn't one of my fantasies. I had to almost drown her under the showerhead before she got the idea—and then we had a little hand-to-hand. No education, but man, she was a witchy little thing. Finally turned her around and got her in a bear hug where she couldn't do any damage to my best parts, and I talk, and talk, and talk.

"Sometime later we're back in the living room wearing bathrobes—trying to on my part, the Bennington doesn't prestock extra, extralarge—singing about freedom. That amount of cash is an awesome thing, Gav, she was ready to fly right then and there.

And she was more than willing to pay. Here's what she had: Carlos Chou, her ex-lord and master, liked doing the same chemistry she was enjoying when I came in, only with him he would start talking about whatever was pressing on his mind right in the middle of— I made a note of that chemo, might be a fun truthdrug. It seems what was most recently uppermost in his rotten head was an operation he was handling for a Mainland associate.

"This is pretty, Gav—no, sorry, this is fucking grim—it looks like there's a two-timing game going on. This Mainlander, no luck, no name, was involved in the planning of the kidnapping. That bodyguard that got torched, she was his—oh, you know she was hooked—but get this, he also wants the Furies to be caught, alive, at least some of them. He's got some kind of built-in connection for the authorities between them and the Africans. They get into deep, deep mierda and—I'm not sure, maybe there's a bonus shot if Matthiessen doesn't make it as well—anyway, when Chou informs him that you're on the case, he tells Chou to help you, but very indirectly. Which might explain a few things, like that piece of shit Lake. And Tyler and the kid Nancarrow knowing more than they should. All very subtle, I guess they think highly of you—if I ever make that observation again you'll do what? Sweet Mary Mag, I'm sorry!

"Okay, here, for what its worth, is the best part. The Furies are in the Caribbean, south of Hispaniola—which means a boat of some kind. No precise coordinates, somewhere between sixteen and eighteen degrees. That was supposed to be the final clue dropped. Or at least that's what Carlos had the last time Donovan was servicing him. I know that's a lot of ocean, but it's better than running around the whole chinga hemisphere, isn't it? I paid her, Gav, that's all right with you? Good. If anybody needed a fresh start, she did. I'll tell you some of it, someday.

"By the bye, Emily says to tell you that she's glad you called me when you did. Seems she really appreciated how I apologized.

"Adios Gav, see you soon."

Add what Danny had to the slim info in Mei Chien's file (she had called Brazilian Justice. The minister had been tied up in a cabinet meeting. His secretary had dealt with her—he had my cover—and hadn't gotten around to telling his boss. He was in Trouble. Did I believe it? *Fa lo stesso*), to the bits and pieces that the Hsinmin gang had been trying to feed me. It made sense. For a man like the Procurator Chao Wen.

And if I succeeded in saving Siv Matthiessen, the way I had to try, what was the likelihood that I was going to help him?

When you use people, Robie, you've got to expect that you will be used in turn.

Revenge isn't good served hot or cold, it's an empty dish either way. At least it is for me. But should Mei Chien get her man . . . I think I could live with how I would feel.

Called Pericles Chan. Asked him if that passport could to be changed for Hispaniola. He grunted in surprise, and told me that as it turns out several key members of the MacRao clique were already in Santo Domingo. Ostensibly on a business cum pleasure trip.

There could be a number of reasons they were there, ranging from deadly to merely thrilling. But the passport that the Hsin-min were working on was designed to reduce the risks of those adverbs being applied to me.

Pericles Chan was nervous, and it wasn't because someone from Touraine had contacted his staff about a few niggardly details in the contract that was being drawn up between the moneycenter and the tiger. He had heard about the attempted hit. It was bothering him, a lot. I didn't offer him any comfort. Didn't repeat the promise that I had made to Gutierrez about no cards under a door—the mark in most of South America that there will be a death in that house. On my short list of potential suspects was a princeling who didn't know yet know that emotions are an unnecessary luxury in his kingdom. He was Pericles's responsibility.

As Bernado Donoso was mine. Christan told me that he had died.

When you cut at a tree, make damned sure you know how it's going to fall.

My mistake. Another one to live with.

If anything was gained, it was that the Hsin-min were going to work very hard to make me happy. Saving one life at the expense of another wasn't going to make me happy. It would have to do.

Tried to get hold of Randolph Erskine. Hernando, his butler said that he was where I was, up in the air. And when he's up he doesn't talk to anybody. Randolph—always Randolph, try Randy and run for your life—feels about flying the way Danny does about surfing, and he's about as good. He's got thirty thousand hours and five planes, ranging from an ultralight to a custom Mach 2 jet. When he was young he started his pile by running guns and medicine into various wars—got out when shoulder-mounted missiles became both cheap and accurate—parlayed his money with an unbelievable run at a baccarat table, and then invested it all in a new species of diatoms. He retired before he was forty. He's now sixty-four. Randolph claims we're kin; he's one-sixteenth Cheyenne. That he is Southern and I'm Northern is a minor detail. That's how we know each other. We met at a Joint Council Meeting. (How he persuaded the chiefs to accept him into the tribe is a mystery; a quarter has been the firm minimum for a long time). The Tsistsistas had a serious problem that together we could solve. We did. He has his quirks—like telling Katherina that if I don't marry her he'd be more than pleased to make up for my stupidity. His other principal eccentricity—sorry, Kit—is buying into the whole daredevil/brave warrior myth. He's old enough to know better.

Maybe that's how he got in. We've always had a soft spot for fools.

He also has a great laugh; a face that shows all the storms he's flown through; a sharp appreciation for what is possible and what isn't; a tremendous talent for beating the odds—and he's willing to go to hell with me. Likes my style, he says.

The people you know.

Told Hernando that it was very important that his boss gets back to me. Crossed my fingers and gave him my private number—Randolph's past may be buried, mine isn't. Not anymore.

Went through everything I remembered about Hispaniola and the waters around it. Called for weather reports, hazard warnings, traffic flows. Burned through some of my fractional lives and made some calls. The last one was to a cemetery system, ordering the irrevocable destruction of those alternate identities.

A couple of them had real friends. They would mourn.

Never delude yourself with the idea that you're a kind man, Robie.

Went over the fight in my head. The only alternative scenario I could come up with would almost certainly have resulted in Christan being killed. I didn't have any choice. Just an incredible amount of luck. Thought about a drink, but I knew what any doctor would say, considering the condition of my leg. I try to listen to my doctors.

CHAPTER THIRTY-THREE

GOT HOME FROM PALMDALE VIA a chartered limo. The house said that I had messages in my mailbox. While I changed clothes and dressings it read to me.

From Ethan: Calvin Renshaw was the older brother of Robert. That was followed by a short bio on Calvin. Nothing relevant, just the stark bones of a man's life.

From Vladimir Holguin: There was an unusual amount of short interest being generated on the Johannesburg exchange against some of the publicly traded companies owned by MacKenzie-Rao. "Interesting, *n'est-ce pas?*" And there was a rumor that he just heard about a certain NGO and a small convoy of theirs that had picked up some people from an airstrip and moved to a location somewhere in the Massif des Bongo—that was in the Ubangi-Shari Republic. Did I think it was related to my problem?"

If it did, then Siv was dead.

From Sophie: Sebastian Broder only used Paris as a brief layover. Spent a few hours in an apartment—she gave me the address, it was a few blocks from the French legation of the Chinese Realms—he then left on an Air France flight to Havana. The man he is traveling with is Dhan Rao (not Chenna's husband, or son . . .

Sometimes you do get a wish). There was no way to determine if Cuba was their final destination. *"Chéri,* I got up early, my hip was aching. the sun was very red this morning. Like it was in Africa. If you go ahead . . . remember, you promised to wait for me."

Her left hip got shattered while she was dragging a fourteen-year-old boy out of a minefield. I said she was shrewd, that she had great hands—they are the utterly unimportant things about her.

Wait . . . Neither of us believe in any kind of heaven. But if it's a promise that can be kept—

From Randolph Erskine, in very bad Cheyenne: "Are we going coup hunting? I have to spend a few hours today with some pales that think they can make me richer, then the Eagle is free. Call me anytime, cousin."

From Nell: "I have some information. Can I see you tonight?"

I rubbed my hands on my knees. Left an answer for her: "I'll fix dinner."

Went over to the fireplace. Opened the vault and took inventory There were things I would have to buy. Had to change again; the neighborhoods where the merchandise was for sale weren't the safest for linen slacks and a silk shirt. It was pouring when I got in the Land Cruiser. Took it on manual anyway. I didn't have the time to have Jonah do another sweep. Nothing hard—the house hadn't reported any visitors—just paranoid.

Finished shopping. Half the people I dealt with had connections to various Bennys. So what. Almost threw out of a second-story window one of them who had tried to palm off garbage. Stopped before I got too stupid. The sin is in the thought as well as the deed. The chinga irony is that my reputation wasn't going to suffer.

Went to the County Museum. Spent a half hour with their Turner. One of the live guards who knew me came by and sat alongside, her somber black face carefully not watching me. When I was done I thanked her; it's good to have a Sitter. Left a thousand-dollar cashcard in the donation box.

Drove down to South Bay. Met with Danny. Told him everything, and then I told him some things about me, some memories I wanted to share. The ones I was thankful for. He listened the way you are supposed to.

Afterward, he got up and depolarized his window, sunlight flooded. He looked at the sea. "Let me go with you."

"We've had this conversation before."

"But this time I won't be strung out."

"That was only one reason, I don't want to have to repeat the others."

Once, only once, I had to tell him about his inadequacies. A very hard conversation. He's a better man than I am.

Without turning he told his genie to play again the last album he had been listening to before I arrived. He asked me, "How are you going to get on the ship?"

I said that it depended on a lot of variables. Talked about a couple of options. He didn't comment—except on one. "A windboard?"

"If they're under way. It's fast and I'll go for twilight. I shouldn't show any profile for the ship."

"What if one of them's on visual?"

"You know how hard it is to spot someone."

"Risky."

"I know."

"Take my board."

He'd built it himself. As strong as he was. "Okay."

We talked a little while longer, then I had to leave. But before I did, he put a hand on my shoulder, and said, "Listen." A harmonica started blowing thinly, and then a very old rock and roll ballad poured into the room.

A song about summer promises, about being strong because you're not alone, about leaving but not being gone.

When it was over I took his hand away, and silently went through the door. To my back he repeated softly the words the singer used to introduce the song. "Here's one for friendship."

He's not corny, or maudlin, or sentimental. He is what he is. What some can become. If you grow up. If you can keep the courage to feel.

Returned home. Called Randolph. Gave him the outline of what I was going to do.

That daredevil mask got a little wobbly. He poured himself a tall glass of thirty-year-old Beam. Would have been nice to join him. After he finished half of it, all he said was, "I'll see what kind of seaplane I can get."

Randolph is slowly dying of a disease they can't yet cure. The only reason he was coming.

Put a time lock on certain files, accounts. If I didn't return a large part of my electronic life would disappear.

Checked my will. It's complicated, like the life I led. Worked on simplifying it. Danny gets *Shiloh* and enough money to have the all-time greatest beach party in history; Nancy and their son get whatever they need; Leah gets the cabin in Wyoming—I entered a note on the flowers for the graves on the ridge. Ethan was my executor, he would give the note to her when she was ready. There were letters to other friends, answers to questions they were brave enough not to ask; Rafaella and Josifia, her baby sister, are already taken care of. The house in L.A. is to be sold, the proceeds go to the Kenmar Trust, ditto for some other properties I own, except for the small parcel in Brittany that overlooks the sea—that was for Sophie. She knows the history of the ruined house where my Breton *grand-mère* hid two families of Jews, and a very badly burned Scottish RAF pilot—her future husband. . . .

I took another sip of coffee. There are libraries filled with books on the effects of growing up in a dysfunctional family. I never found one that seriously discussed what it does to a child to have the complete opposite.

I returned to the will. Jonah gets the Lotus; he wouldn't keep it, it's not part of his Path, but he would appreciate the gesture; Len would find a home for the Bechstein; Jessie goes back to the

Tartinis—I didn't lie to Olivia Fouchet when I said she was a loan, for whoever has her she will be only that—and Aldo will make her happy; Katherina . . . There was nothing I could give to her, except the things I should have.

I folded the papers and put them in a drawer. If it was necessary, Ethan would know where to find them.

"Hello, Gavilan."

"Hello, Siv."

She was wearing jeans and an oversized dark green sweatshirt. "Do you prefer speaking in English?" she asked with a smile.

"Italian makes me feel uncomfortable."

"Does it?"

For the first time I realized that deep inside it always had. Are you still there, *cara*? No answer, just a warmth that was always there. That I had always missed.

"I'm not fluent in Norwegian, but I can try it if you would like."

"How many languages do you speak?"

I counted. It took a while. "Seriously, fifteen. I can follow fairly well a good deal more if they're in the same family—like Romanian and Catalan in the Romance group. And I know useful bits in a bunch of dialects."

She leaned forward and stared. "Are you like me?"

And what are you, Siv Matthiessen? What will you be? Another Leonardo, touching us almost unintentionally with transcendent greatness? Or will you be as he was for too much of his life, a creator of bright entertainments, clever toys, fabulous machines, for a cold calculating audience of princes and princesses? And at the end of that long life will you become like him, a self-imposed exile in both body and mind?

Questions that can't be answered. No one can see their future.

"No. I'm a bit before your time. . . . Before the Lorca and all the other major psychobiologicals were developed. I even have all but a couple of my original genes. I am good at some things, bad at others. Those things that I needed to learn, or that I love, I work very hard at." I shrugged. "If I have anything that is extraordinary it's a memory—that sometimes seems to have a mind of its own. . . ." A very long pause, "I also had an extraordinary family."

"Could you tell me about them?" She sounded so wistful. She wasn't real and she had no life pulse. Would that be the greatest hurt, if one day we were able to sustain an entirety permanently? That while there might be others like them, none would be truly kin? Family isn't necessarily of the flesh, but . . . I told her about my mother and father, my grandparents, my cousins, the people who made me what I am, my essentials, my shadows, my universe.

"Were they that good?"

I laughed gently. "Nobody is that good. But yes, they were great people. I was very lucky."

She rested her chin on her hands and looked off into a space that was imaginary, that I couldn't imagine. "You've come to say good-bye."

"Yes."

She bent her head down, her neck a long, lovely curve. "Could you talk to me a little longer?"

So I told her a story, the one my grandmother told me the last time I saw her. It was about a maid who got lost in the forest, the one the white men called Yellowstone, and how she met a gray wolf, who was also lost. How they got past their fear of each other and became friends and together searched for their homes, their tribes. How, despite the cold, the hard blowing snow, they did find their families. And then, even though they had grown so fond of each other, they had to go their separate ways, for a maid's life is not a wolf's.

A romantic lie of a story. Except that my grandmother did tell it to me. Her bony hands with their faded strength gripping mine. And she died so many years ago.

Siv said, "It's time to send us away, Gavilan."

I nodded. And said good-bye.

Nell arrived at seven, the time I had picked. The house let her in and told her that I was in the kitchen. She was wearing a severe burgundy tunic over dark gray slacks. Her hair was tied back in a bun. She looked very serious. I bowed, and said, "You have a choice, Madame. *Filet de sole Marguery*—only in this case it's Colorado River sturgeon—or *domates yemistes me rizi*—that's baked tomatoes packed with rice and stuff. A lot tastier than it sounds."

"I talked to Daniel."

"For dessert I thought we would have white peaches and macadamia ice cream—one of my neighbors hand-makes it; she sent me some. I'll let you pick the wine, I have a couple of hundred bottles in the locker. You should—"

"Gavilan."

"Yes?"

"You want to tell me what's going on?"

"Never distract a chef. It could prove fatal. Pick a wine."

She looked at me for a long time. Then went over to the locker. Smart woman.

"A Montrachet. Guess you want the fish. I'll decant it. Why don't you go into the dining room. It all should be ready in another five minutes."

She left wordlessly.

It was closer to nine minutes. Cooking is not an exact science. I brought the dishes and wine in. Lit the candles and sat down opposite her. "There we are. *Bueno gusto.*"

She pushed her plate away. "I'm not going to eat until you talk to me."

"It's a lot better hot than cold. . . ." I put my silverware down and leaned my elbows on the arms of my chair. "It's simple. I think I found her. And tomorrow I am going to see if I can get her."

"Alone."

"I'm never alone." I smiled. "I'll have help, Nell. And I've done it before."

"I know you have."

I shook my head. "No, you don't." Lord, how do you tell the truth without sounding boastful, or like a fool. Something else to practice. "I'm good at this. Once upon a time I was very close"—Siv would understand, the place you can reach, when the body-mind is one, when you can do anything, when there are no limits—"to being as good as you can get. I'm a ways down the slope from that, but not too far down."

She saw that I wasn't lying. That at least I thought it was the truth. "Then why does Daniel believe that you think you're going to die?"

I said slowly, "This time it feels like the best way to prepare. A way I learned from some of my ancestors. Before a fight they would make their farewells, to their families, their friends, their world. So they could set their fear behind them. It works for me."

"What about their family's, their friend's fears?"

"It's hardest for those who stay behind. I know, Nell, I know." There aren't any easy answers, ever. "You can't bury fear in the moment."

It was her turn to shake her head. "You are . . ."

"Why don't we finish this conversation after dinner? I'm hungry. And I do like my own cooking."

She nodded. We ate in silence.

After I cleared the table, and poured her a generous dram of my best eau de vie—I avoided making a joke about the water of life—and asked her to wait for me in the conservatory. She took her drink with her, and the bottle.

I went into the living room, got Jessie out, and joined her. She was sitting on the bench under the mimosa, the silk tree, my favorite spot.

"I'd like to play a little. Hope you don't mind."

"Another farewell?"

"Something like that."

She made room for me on the bench. I rested my hands on Jessie for a moment, then started with *"La fille aux cheveux de lin."* We were delicate, as light as a girl dancing in a summer's moonlight. Then Ishi's "Valse." Long sustained lines of blue. Finally the last movement of the Kodaly. I thought I might have gotten it at last. Jessie thought so. I stood up, wiped her carefully, loosened the bow, and put her back to sleep in her bed of whiskered titanium.

I looked down at Nell. She was rubbing the thumb of one hand against a palm. She glanced up at me. "What time are you leaving?"

"Early, about four."

"I noticed you didn't drink anything."

"Doctor's orders."

"Your lover?"

I wasn't the only one who asked questions. "No, I'm afraid not."

She poured herself some more of the brandy. "Do you think she'll come back?"

"I don't know."

"Do you really think you'll come back?"

"I have to."

She stood up and emptied her glass. "When you do, I won't be here." I said nothing. She put her glass down on the bench and looked out at the windows. It was beginning to rain harder, the panes hissed and rattled as the drops hit them. "Can I stay until you go?"

"Nell . . ."

She said without facing me, "It's not about sex, you know."

"I know."

She turned around. "Do you? Do you know who we are?"

"Sometimes." I took her hand.

CHAPTER THIRTY-FOUR

FLYING THROUGH RAIN. IT SEEMED I had been doing nothing but that forever. Flying through storms. From the moment that Randolph and I took off from L.A. in his Stiletto, moving across the country, turning southwest over the rad, truncated Mississippi, out over the waters of the Caribbean, the quick refuel in Santa Clara, Cuba—the speed we were doing ate hydro like nobody's business.

Randolph played Rock through the jet's speakers as we raced toward the dawn. He was born at the end of an era, I had been born at the cusp of another. We both loved the old simple music. We both knew about loss.

Nell lying snug in my arms, a smaller woman than I had become so used to . . . If you think that intimacy requires sex, then either you're very young, or a very sad soul. She asked softly, "Why?"

I had given her one answer. Not something I often offer to strangers, or to friends. "Sometimes I think I have one of those metanormal sets. No, not music. If I have anything that way—and most days I doubt it—it's a small inheritance from a grandmother who was going to be a concert pianist . . . and a composer."

"Why did you stop, Grand-mère?"

She looks at wrinkled hands resting quiet on the keyboard. "I am afraid my arthritis is acting bad again." I am very young, but I know it's a lie. She says in English with the faintest trace of her husband's Scottish burr, to enjoy the alliteration, to distract me: "Chopin was a show-off, but he is not that hard." She points to the score. "Try again from here; think of it like, like a poem, concentrate on the rhythms." She looks at me, wondering if I will understand.

I don't—I am only a child—but I try.

Always try.

I said, "She was going to study with Nadia Boulanger. . . . Sorry, that once meant a lot, but it doesn't answer your question."

She murmered something about way points and head winds. "Why didn't your grandmother become a composer?"

A story told at a graveside by my father's father. Wanting his only surviving grandchild to know exactly why he was crying. A man who could have been terrible, unwilling to live that way. "A hundred years ago—Lord, that long—she was a girl who didn't care anything about politics, only cared about music. She was an orphan; her parents had left her a four-hundred-year-old house, a small pear orchard, and a strong sense of morality. . . . For the latter she was supposed to be put against a wall and shot. A German officer decided that he ought to have her body before he took her life. She managed to . . . to please him." His certain surprise. Her desperation? In the end, when we think we are at the end, our motives become as mysterious as death. "While he slept she broke a mirror and cut his throat. She didn't expect to live. Then somebody kindly dropped some bombs from the sky on the chateau that was the local SS headquarters. She crawled out of the rubble."

Nell was the third woman who had heard that story. And, like them, she didn't need to hear more, she had made the leap.

A diminishing series of perfect chords.

An eighteen-year-old girl before a Steinway in a small, bare rehearsal room. A girl who should have been scared out of her mind, whose mind was only on sound, poetry. A short, very handsome man sitting on a plain wooden chair, his hands on his knees, his eyes in the music. When she was done, he was silent for a while, then nodded once, and said with his famous charm, with truth: "Mademoiselle, you play Chopin as if you are a Pole. Thank you." Arthur Rubinstein.

Je ne regrette rien. I regret nothing. That's a hard measure to follow, Grand-mère. I think I can try to do that now.

Nell brushed away the hair from my face and held her hand against my cheek. I said, "I don't know about the nature, but I know about the nurture."

"You never had a choice?"

"It wasn't intended, but it was never a matter of choice."

Randolph helping me stow my gear in the belly of the jet. A small leather bag falls loose. A plastic coin and a ribboned piece of iron roll out. He stoops down and picks them up. He looks at them in his hand. Inscribed on one side of the coin: Ten Years. On the other: One Day at a Time. He doesn't say anything. My mother's triumph over alcohol. Long before I was born. Like all the ones that really matter—private. He stares hard at the other token. He whistles softly. "I know this, it's the VC."

"Put it in the bag."

"Your father's?"

"No. My grandfather."

He rubs the old, very old gunmetal. "The goddamn Victoria Cross . . ." He looks at me. "It's heavy."

Deliberately misunderstand. "It was made from melted-down cannons."

Because he's my friend, he asks: "I'll bet this didn't mean that much to him."

Because he's my friend I answer: "Not to him, not to my father."

He shakes his head, so sorry for me, and picks up the pouch. He carefully folds the ribbon over the Cross and puts it into the spirit bag.

We went across the lifeless desert that was Haiti. Once, before the Europeans, there were around seven million natives on the island the Spaniards named for themselves. The land was that good. It took about fifty years to go from seven million to extinction. Holocausts blur into the past; time is an indifferent, ruthless eraser. But you could argue that at least that one left a curse, a toxic sorrow that sank permanently into the ground. A plague on everybody's houses, black, white, brown. A country where the worst consequences, intentional, unintentional, always seems to prevail.

Santiago de los Caballeros, the biggest city and current capital of the Confederated Democracy of Hispaniola—a bad joke of a name. Haiti doesn't exist anymore, and democracy never really did—traffic control put us on a restricted approach to Santo Domingo. The privilege of arriving on a two-hundred-thousand-dollar toy. We landed between lightning strokes.

Randolph had arranged a place for us to stay—a staging area actually; I wasn't planning on being in Santo Domingo for very long. It was a penthouse that belonged to a rich friend of a richer friend of his. Since said friend also owned the building, the penthouse's external security was very tight and the internal security was under our command. With any luck, there would be no residual history left behind. We both had local shopping to do and so after working out a series of meeting places and timings— Randolph had been in and out of Santo Domingo since before the remains of the city got moved ten kilometers upland—we went our separate ways.

Simone Mendoza was a woman who had never met Jacques Condé. He was way too low for her, but with Calderon she had done business. Purely professionally, purely for money. That is how she deals with the world, with her life. About thirty years ago she came here from somewhere in the Northeast. Fleeing some botched crime, not quite killing a pimp, so the rumor said with all the reliability that rumors have. Even though she had been born in Hispaniola, she was still considered after thirty years to be a gringa dominicana. But that hadn't stopped her from trying to do an Evita—climbing on her back to the top. Having, apparently, naturally golden-brown hair and fair skin was an asset. She made it as far as the heavy favorite to be the next generalissimo. Then one night, when she returned to the garden of her little hillside villa with her lover's favorite aperitif—champagne dusted with cocaine—she found him floating facedown in the hot tub. She didn't bother turning him over, which was good seeing as how he didn't have a face anymore. She checked on the bodyguards; they had vanished, forever. Simone wrapped a sarong around her naked hips, sat down on a bench in her pretty little garden, sipped some of the champagne, and reflected on the fact that someone had allowed her to live. She decided it was time to change occupations. That isn't hearsay; it's a true legend of the calles.

The door of her store identified me and opened. A couple of wall-mounted pulse guns swung smartly in my direction. She doesn't bother to be subtle, and she has no use for human bodyguards. From the air came: "Oiga, Rafael. I'll be with you in a moment."

Patience is a virtue the universe is determined to make me master. I took a look at the display cases. Simone Mendoza sells gold. Necklaces, rings, bracelets, all just pure gold. Nothing else. The workmanship ranges from very good to occasionally breathtaking. She owns the small factory where they are made according to designs she . . . borrows . . . from the very best masters. The craftswomen—she doesn't ever hire men—are paid well enough so that stealing isn't a worthwhile option. And if they are still tempted, there's the prospect of ending facedown in a river. Her version of the carat and the stick.

There's always been gold and silver in eastern Hispaniola, less than what the Spanish hoped for, tortured for. There were some alluvial deposits of *doré*—solid nuggets. That was all they got. Providence's sense of satire, it was a hundred and fifty years after they left that the biggest open-air gold mine in the hemisphere was developed and started producing annually almost two million ounces. And then, when the oxide ores began diminishing, a way to cheaply process sulfides was discovered. The gold flows and flows.

It's not justice, it's not funny, but it sure as hell is ironic.

It was mining that had brought the MacRao party ostensibly to Santo Domingo. Besides gold, the island nowadays produces a significant amount of some critical industrial minerals. The local mining industry is supposed to be controlled by the parastaals—hybrid state and private corporations—but it was the great mining combines that put the Phalanges that really control things into power. A really nice piece of design work on their part: a decentralized dictatorship. It was a good fit for a historically quasi-feudal culture: strong enough to be efficient, not so strong as to be able to effectively challenge the real bosses. And while having to work through a bunch of caudillos might be at times wearisome, it was better than having to deal with the possible capriciousness of one. Latinos are so unreliable. Sometimes they start believing in their myths.

MacKenzie-Rao wasn't part of the incestuous group of mining combines. But they had their interests and alliances. They had put some money in—"Capital is extremely tight." Lord, I was quoting Holguin—and their research labs had come up with some new wrinkles on ultrapurification. The people that I was going to have a conversation with were here to get a firsthand update on how their firm's investments were doing. And to enjoy one of the hemisphere's five-star free-fire zones for vice. And, if it was warranted, to take possession of the broken husk of a young woman.

The dataflow that my own new allies were giving me was close to being up to Vlad's level. Maybe better. Was I worried that their cooperation was more than generous? No, I was operating way past worry.

Simone Mendoza and a man came from the back office. He was carrying a small package covered in plain brown wrapping paper—a trademark of her famously expensive shop. The man lifted her free hand—the other was holding a flute of champagne, another trademark—and kissed it. He said something softly in her ear that caused her to smile—if it wasn't false then I'm not my mother's son—bowed to her, glanced indifferently at me, and left.

When the door closed behind the customer—a slight whisking sound as bars rolled into place—Simone said in English, "So, Rafael, you aren't dead yet."

"Was I supposed to be?"

"Oh, yes." She emptied her glass. "Come kiss me."

So I did. She kisses very well. Another one of her old assets. Very professional. No affection; it didn't need any. The sensuousness and morality of a cat. As for me, well, I've learned to have a lot of sympathy for whores. But the kiss was likely to be my very last. I made the most of it.

We spent a longer minute than she intended. Her mouth tasted soft, swollen like an almost too-ripe papaya. . . . She broke away from me, and said, "You took me seriously."

"You didn't want me to kiss you?"

She gave me a disgusted look. "I need a refill. Want some?"

"Cliquot?"

"Of course."

"Sure." I'll always take some of the Widow's best.

We went into her office. She got a half-empty bottle from the ice bucket, showed me the label as if she were a sardonic wine steward, and poured for us. She sat down in her chair; no desk, only a small back-lit table, undid the top button of her black knee-length tunic—the color she always wears to accent the paleness of her skin—and stretched her legs on an ottoman. "What do you want to buy?"

"I liked that necklace with the three braids of different colors; white, pink, yellow."

"How much do you want to pay?"

"This year's gross domestic product."

She laughed. Only two things matter to her, money, and very long, very sweaty afternoons. But if she has any redeeming quality, it's that she manages to have a sense of humor about her passions. When I didn't say anything else, she sobered, and thought. Rafael Garcia Calderon doesn't have the resources to buy anything, everything. But her best asset is this: She has a frightening talent about knowing men. I don't want to think about what kind of opera could have been written about her.

"I didn't make a mistake, did I?"

Calderon was going away, a man better than I thought he would turn out to be. "You didn't."

She nodded, seeing how it was. "So, what do you really want to buy?"

For most people, her shop would be more than enough. Not for Simone Mendoza, who almost became queen of Hispaniola. She had gone into the same line of work as Palmer, but she was a comprador who worked only for herself. And in her sphere she could do a lot more. Anything you wanted in Hispaniola, she could arrange. Anything.

"There is going to be an invasion. I want absolutely clear skies."

She looked at a window that showed the rain stripping away the flowers from a bird of paradise, drowning the plumage. "Absolutely?"

"Flesh, blood, and machines."

"How soon?"

"Very soon."

She looked at me with eyes that said: I embraced men who died. You're another. "Payment in advance?"

Didn't trust her. Didn't care. You do it, or you don't. No regrets. "Yes."

"Tell me what I need to do."

The hotel. The party, the conveniences, the inconveniences I wanted for them. Ingress, egress. Timetables. Everything I needed to go to hell.

She didn't take notes, she didn't have to. When I finished, she named a sum that wasn't the gross domestic product, not quite.

"Fine"

I think I expected to see a flicker of disappointment. That she hadn't asked for more. I was wrong. Maybe she was content with her greed. Maybe I had underestimated little, unimportant Rafael Garcia Calderon. Who knows? I am not that good at reading souls.

She said, "I don't think there should be any difficulty."

"No, there shouldn't be."

I wasn't trying to scare her, that's impossible. Just clarifying.

She silently held up her glass for Champagne. I obliged. "Gracias. A one-man army, eh?"

I shrugged. "They don't deserve more."

Simone Mendoza looked at the bubbles rising to the top of the flute. Counting the ephemeral. Finally, her eyes came back to me. She slowly ran a pink nail from throat to waist. "Later, would you be interested?"

Men are at their best after they've done something dangerous. Something she said to me once. A personal truth that stung.

It might be the last time, Robie. And it would be very good.

No, the last was with Kit, and while it wasn't the best—how could it have been, through tears? It was the last I wanted to remember.

"A rain check?"

The heat in her eyes faded, leaving amusement as an afterglow. Then even that winked out. She said, "Go away. I have money to earn."

I didn't take her hand, or bow. I'm not a gentlemen, she's not a lady. She's a pure binomial; as for me, all my fractions were coming together in one frightening integer.

Jeder Engel ist schrecklich.
Every angel is terrible.

My face was different. The work was aminochemical and plastic—
it would last a few hours. Should be enough. Didn't do anything
about my height—bone takes too long, and shoe lifts might throw
off the bodymind. My clothes had lines that made my proportions
vague. If I resembled anybody it was the Padrino's henchman, the
Spanish Deacon. I didn't need a mirror to practice the look of his
eyes. The voice wasn't his; it belonged to someone worse. The
bridge of my nose itched from one of the injections. Ignored it,
didn't want to leave any hint of discoloration. Clenched and un-
clenched my hands, getting used to the thin, steel-ridged gloves. I
was in a café. Alone. There was a sign on the door saying Closed for
Health Inspection. A key had been under a garbage can. I was
waiting for a taxi to take me up a hill.

Thought for the last time about who I was going to. Four men
and two women—a typical ratio. One was a doctor who had done
his residency in a police hospital somewhere on the Indian subcontinent. Didn't know the man, but somewhere along the road I
heard about the hospital's basement. "When I was young I never
thought . . ." Neither did I, Madame Fouchet, neither did I, none
of us did. Another man was a geological engineer, who just happened to hold a few other degrees, those involving digging for
pain. At first that bothered me. Then I thought about the others,
what kind of lives they had, about impact. It was going to be fine.
Just as long as there weren't any dead heroes, on either side. One
of the women was a whiz with numbers, a maven of risk analysis.
That was good, if she had the capacity to keep her presence of
mind. The other woman had a variety of skills: a pilot, she had
flown the hyper that party came in on; a communicator (silver wire
running from skull to fingertips—did her body resonate to this
land's weeping veins?); an expert on speculative forms of propul-

478 MARC MATZ

sion systems, in that capacity a backup for Broder; a superb fuck—a gratuitous byte that actually had meaning; a director among other things of a tiny, almost imperceptible, division of MacKenzie-Rao that went by the sweet, silly, poetic name of Butterfly Works. Named that because it was supposed to deal with unintended consequences.

Pericles Chan had thought that was an enchanting touch. Sure.

Dhan Rao was the head of that division. And a senior director in a number of other, public, ones. But not a member of the board. He was old enough; his branch of the family had a lot of shares, and incompetency wasn't a privilege for a Rao. There were many reasons why he was passed over. Mostly unknowable. Went deep in my memory of Chenna, what she said about that family, what she omitted. Balanced their admiration for success against their caution. Took the last guess: he was off the leash. Running for a score that would put him over the top.

Sebastian Broder could be the linchpin. I made him to be as much observer of the game as a participant. Especially if I was right about it not being a board-sanctioned gig. He was more than run-of-the-mill smart, he was a wise one—hard, annotated data from William Mpondo.

Lord, am I burning up my luck as fast as Randolph's jet burns hydrogen?

"If you let it, your life makes your luck. I think you better." The hand that is gently kneading the ruff of his main dog rises and left to right makes Christ's sign. He is an atheist. My Basque grandfather speaking to a ten-year-old boy. Not a poet, not a prophet. Just the first to see himself in me.

Broder would play to win from any outcome. Unlike me.

Saw the cab pull into the alley behind the café. Went out the front and walked around. The driver was very black, Haitian, one of the underclass. We didn't speak, he knew where to take me. Afterward, the car would be recycled, and he would be on a plane to French Guiana.

A short ride. Nuevo Santo Domingo is an island on an island. A moral wilderness surrounded by a wasteland. I won't describe it. I don't want to.

Strolled into the Grande Posada as if I were invisible. I was. No one would see me, nothing would remember me. The people I wanted were collected in the finest hospitality suite in the finest hotel, waiting they thought for a commandante who was higher up the *tutumpote*—the local hierarchy of clans—than his rank indicated, and his wife who had an even more significant ancestry, skyboard legs, and a monumental taste for decadence. They were all going to discuss some unimportant matters and then head for Santo Domingo's most exclusive hell club.

The couple wouldn't show up—and it isn't obvious who Simone bought. She plays from an almost endless deck. The alcohol served to them while they waited had been very slightly, undetectably, altered—it would have an effect just a little quicker. If any of them had blockers in their bloodstream, well, I take whatever edges I can. Since they were traveling semi-incognito, they had brought with them a minimum of muscle. And those individuals would be, oh, distracted. The party had been maneuvered and the feedback was that they were unaware. Most of the arrangements probably weren't that difficult for Simone. This was a town that was quite used to *handling* tourists. Being rich and powerful by itself doesn't always help. Ask Simone about a body floating in a garden.

It wasn't a bad setup. Once I would have planned it better. Once I was responsible for lives.

What about Siv? She's dead, and probably will be.

Like my grandfathers, both of them, I don't have any faith in heaven. But like them I believe in the certainty of hell. We all knew about the quickest way you can get there, about the worst sin— becoming what you hate. I can't ask the living for forgiveness, but I can ask the dead. . . . Squeezed away the haze from my eyes.

*   *   *

Double doors covered with gold leaf, closed and locked. All but one of them were standing by the huge expanse of bulletproof, shatterproof glass, watching the drama of the storm—lightning bolts steeplechasing each other across the twilight sky. The suite's bafflers were turned on a notch to make the thunder bearable. The world is Theater.

The engineer was sitting in an overstuffed chair, a drink in one hand, a canapé in the other. He was quick: he threw his glass at me as I came on him. I caught it without slowing down. My trick trumped his, he hesitated for the smallest part of a second, and I smashed it into his face.

Hammered twice, destroying his strength. Slapped a narco-patch on him—he would stay awake, just. Wanted him for a back-drop. My leg almost gave out as I pivoted toward the frozen tableau. Didn't let them see that. I said, *"Bôa noite."*

What shocked them the most? The suddenness of my calling card, or that the room's defenses hadn't blown me away? Gave them a moment for their senses to revive.

The risk maven glanced at a purse on a nearby satinwood table—she hadn't any training—and the top of her gown went from solid to transparent. I quickly held up a hand covered with shards of crystal and dripping blood. She worked out the equation: distractions would have a very negative impact. Gown and face went equally opaque.

The doctor was slack-jawed, a stain running down his leg. "As ye sow . . ." The torturer's nightmare.

Dhan Rao's principal associate in the Butterfly Works was rock still, trying with her body to get through on any band. Discovering what emptiness really felt like.

Sebastian Broder—Siv had drawn him so well—had his hands in his pockets; he took them out slowly, showing empty palms.

Rao stepped forward—no cowards in that family. His voice was only a little shaky. "What the fuck is this about?"

"Siv Matthiessen."

"Who?"

I walked over and put a welt on his cheek. He stumbled back—a little too obviously clumsy, he had some training—and went for something on his belt buckle. Stopped when he felt the razor against his throat. I said, "This can be either a slaughter-house or a salon. Your choice."

The risk maven miscalculated. Silky blond hair flying, she went for her purse. A man can't be in two places at one time. I can. The fist that held the razor snapped into Rao's jaw. Got to her be-fore she touched the purse and swung her down by the back of her gown. Didn't take the purse—it might have been biokeyed, booby-trapped—instead I put her back on her feet, necessarily tearing more of her gown, and marched her to where Dhan Rao was recov-ering. "Hold his hand and stroke his brow. Do it, Juliet." At hear-ing her name she flinched as if I had struck her again. I cut the belt from Rao and threw it behind me.

The razor went away somewhere in my clothes. A parting gift from someone who had an idea of who I am. I said to Dhan Rao, *"Wer zeigt ein Kind, so wie es steht?"*

"Who shall show a child just as it stands?" The woman who was trying to reach salvation. "Rilke?"

Nodded at her. "Yes." Gestured toward the storm, "That is real, and so is this room. This now. The *unexpected* effect of the pain you give. I hope I am done with this part of the lesson." I took them all in. They were silent, except for the engineer who was crying. The doc-tor was trembling; the woman who knew Rilke was slowly shaking her head; Juliet who thought she was brave was dealing with the fact that it didn't matter; Dhan Rao was touching his cheek and jaw with the incredulous fingers of a thirty-year-old boy; Sebastian Broder was watching, afraid, but still trying to determine the vectors.

If they had all gone for me, they might have had a chance. Maybe.

I said to him, "Did you know that the Chinese were going to double-cross you?"

A simultaneous "What?" from Broder and Rao. I smiled. "Oh, yes. Apparently a war between you and Touraine is in their better interests." Whatever the hell they were. "I can't imagine it being much of a fight—not just because Touraine is a company that literally moves mountains—but because I can't imagine your board not handing you over with a million apologies." Snapped my fingers. "Maybe that's what the Chinese really want. It would be funny, wouldn't it, if you all are the people they really want to get rid of."

Data, meager, but there, was pulling Juliet back into the gestalt. This was what she was trained for. Broder and Rao were having a harder time chewing on the stone. She absently played with the remains of her dress, and said, "Can I ask who you represent?"

Said very cleanly, clearly, so that they would have no doubt how far I was prepared to go, how far they could end up, "I represent Siv Matthiessen."

"And her ghost?" That was from the other woman—give her a name, Iola. An amalgam of lifetimes kept me from breaking. "If it comes to that." I sighed heavily, deliberately. Which brings us to the crux. The Chinese are your problem—and if you are really nice I might mention a few other snarls—getting the woman back is mine. You are going to help me, aren't you?"

Sebastian Broder was sixty years old, old enough. He looked briefly at Dhan Rao and said, "Yes."

We didn't move to a table, we didn't sit down. We stayed like actors on chalk marks where we were. I asked some extraneous questions—curiosity will be the death of me, I know, I know—like: "Was there a particular reason for having Matthiessen's bodyguard killed?"

"She discovered who had procured the terrorists. We didn't want that information available." Dhan Rao. Not lying. Telling his version of an inexplicable truth.

"Did the group know?"

"No. One of them was told that it had to be done immediately. There would have been too limited opportunities later—Touraine is too thorough." Juliet of the long blond hair, and a mind dedicated to risks.

"What was the hook?"

"The what? Oh, I understand. A relative of hers was infected with a singular virus. We are the only ones with the cleansing therapy." He paused and added, "She is Cuban." He didn't have to say: Despite everything, her family is very important for her. The doctor. I won't give him a name.

"So, Sebastian, was Matthiessen really that scary?"

A jerk of the head. He stared. I pushed a little more. "Is she going to make you obsolete?"

He shrugged, holding on to secrets that aren't is a waste of time. Looked at me, but not really. He was remembering another fear, one mixed with awe. "It is not her field . . . she is an amateur in nothing—she might."

My lady da Vinci, you may give us a flying machine after all. Will you give us another Virgin of the Rocks as well? I hope so.

Didn't ask about the Congo. I've had enough tragedy.

Details came mostly from Iola. It figured that she would be the de facto operations officer. If I had been certain of that earlier, I would have targeted her only—a female made defenseless, hopeless, sitting in a dark room; generations of my women screamed inside—No, I wouldn't, couldn't. And anyway, I was also trying to start a process that would help protect Matthiessen later. Did try my best to leave Iola with the impression that I was going to wait and hit the rendezvous point—just in case their fear lifted too soon. Only once was there a brief interlude when I had to remind one of them again what a storm feels like.

So they talked. Except perhaps for the doctor, spilling your guts or having someone cut it out of you wasn't an option they had ever encountered in their reality. Money, knowledge, violence. Each alone has power, together—

They gave me the Furies.

CHAPTER THIRTY-FIVE

THE SEAPLANE BUCKED AND DANCED as it crossed down through a thermal, Randolph almost unnoticeably moving muscles in his arms, his hands resting easy on the interface. The left wing dipped, then steadied. He was a damn good pilot. The plane was good too. He had bought it from a Cuban smuggler for cash— "Shut up, Gav, I'm richer than you. And what the hell am I going to do with my money?"—it was as stealthy as the best movers of contraband could make it. But nothing can be made invisible to the eye. He was going to drop me off a few miles from the ship. Hopefully, dusk and weather, and a final approach five feet above the waves, would keep us safe.

The ship. I went over the 3-D layout. Its last official owner but one had been the Sisters of Grace. They had sold it to a company that was owned by another, by another near infinitum—and then back again, shells swallowing themselves like the serpent with its tail. The *Savanna-La Mar* (the name it was christened; sailors are superstitious about changing that) had originally been a Jamaican coastal, one hundred and eighty feet long, thirty wide, six hundred tons. The Sisters had converted its marine diesel, created an infirmary and emergency operating theater in what was once the cargo hold, and modernized some of its cyberelectronics. The new owners hadn't done much to it except to restore its carrying capacity. That meant that Siv was almost certainly being held in the central superstructure. My fingers traced corridors, staterooms, platforms, searching for the places I would put people. I had been on similar vessels before. That helped. That the *Savanna-La Mar* hadn't yet been fitted with a cannon—the Sisters of Grace didn't fight, didn't discriminate, didn't ask questions, had grateful friends; pirates usually let them be—that was also helpful. Also the fact that I had, to use the truth that the pales think is so quaint, walked in moccasins very similar to theirs.

I looked out. We were moving away from a force twelve, the far trailing edge of a very minor hurricane—the weather report clocked it at only a hundred and forty miles per hour—down to a seven: Winds from thirty-two to thirty-eight, breaking, foaming waves. Lord, I thought to no one, could I do it?

"ETA is four minutes."

I nodded at Randolph and wiggled back into the plane's small hold. Everything looked right. He started to slow the plane down, pontoons skimming dangerously close to the swells. Then with a shuddering bounce we were down. I rolled open the door. This was going to be tricky. Stepped onto one of the pontoons and brought the board down. The low, wide wishbone spar didn't want to come up. Damn. Wrenched at it. It popped into place. Sat on the board, and started paddling away from the plane. When I got sufficiently clear, I headed into the wind, stood up, and pulled the sail from its slot in the mast. And fell down. Dove under the board, came up on its other side and righted it. Tried again. Two tries. Then the sail was out and I was streaking like a comet.

Put everything Danny tried to teach me into my body. The *Savanna-La Mar* was only doing ten knots. In a few minutes she would be doing far less. I could catch her. If they didn't catch me.

The ship, a gray silhouette against the dark sea and sky. She was slowed to a speed barely above idle. Her "owners" had installed a remote throttle, part of their contingency plans—the Furies hadn't found it. I leaned back, pulling the sailboard into an arcing intercept. Counted, fixed vectors, then went into the water.

Five minutes under, the orange timer in the corner of the airmask marking off how long I had before it ran out of oxygen. The feel of water moving. I was at the ship. Came up and shot the grapple. Its magnoplastic hooks caught a rail. I went up. Halfway the ship picked up speed—someone had found the secret governor—started swaying, forced myself to move faster.

On the aft deck. A man coming. Reached for a stunner, no time. He slashed at me with a knife, saw it had no effect and something popped into his left hand. I twisted, threw him down, pulling his arm out of his shoulder. For the briefest second in the twist, unendurable pain ripped through me. I went down with him. Which saved my life.

A burst of shells slammed into the coaming above me, and went through the quarter-inch steel as if it were aluminum foil. The man beside me was still trying to move. I put a hand over the fist that held the s/m, thumb placed right—broke his wrist. He finally screamed.

More shots. Whoever it was didn't care that he could as easily hit his companion as me. Rolled away. Threw a grenade. Sound-and-light show. Unrealized courtesy of my father's old outfit. My ears were plugged, a hundred and twenty decibels still came through. Like standing next to a jet engine firing up.

Went through an open hatch, and back out again as a volley shrieked along the passageway. Reached for the second grenade—not there.

Started climbing. Second level. An open space in the middle of the superstructure. The bridge was above. No one coming down the ladder. Looked below. The man was rolling on the deck. With his useless arms and a moving surface he couldn't get up. Then I saw the nozzle of a gun sticking out from the hatch. Jumped. Something tore in my thigh. She swung the gun toward me, not firing until she had me centered. Training. I threw stars at her face and took away her gun.

Then we fought. It didn't take thirty seconds, but it was *capoeira*.

My left arm was dead. She was at my feet, her plain, strong face flooded with blood. I limped inside.

Got out the tracker. Matthiessen had an implant. Touraine's newest, supposed to be impossible to find, still a secret—if I'd had a free hand I would have crossed my fingers. It's only active on receiving a short-range signal. Got a response, closed my eyes for a second, visualizing. Moved.

Another man coming up from below, fumbling with a submachine gun. I closed with him, my hand ready. Then stopped. He looked at me, saw my eyes. He knew. Then he whispered something. I grabbed the cloth of his sweater around his chest, lifted him off his feet, and slammed him into a bulkhead. He didn't get up. Took his weapon.

Went into a galley. A monitor and some other equipment on the table. The tracker chirped once loudly, then died. Heard a shout, not Matthiessen. Too easy to fall for. I swore, then headed in that direction.

Open stateroom door. Ejected the clip, threw the gun down the corridor. Nothing.

Thirty years. Too many ancestors. My body decided before I did.

Rogen was standing beside Matthiessen. An automatic in a two-handed grip. Tears flooding her face, and under the tears, almost unbearable resolve. And under the resolve . . . Matthiessen was sitting on the edge of a bunk, eyes glazed, a dark bloody spot on her chin where the butt of a gun had hit it. The targeting light blinded my right eye.

Then Matthiessen moved. I am fast. I know those who are

faster. None of us are her. One fist punched Rogen in her ribs. A weak hit, bad angle, but enough. I put Rogen down.

Got Matthiessen to her feet. She leaned against me for a second. My leg almost collapsed. Her eyes were clear. Absurdly I made a note to ask her someday how to do that—her voice was even clearer as she asked, "Where are the others?"

Wasn't sure who she was referring to. "Four down, I don't know how many are left."

"I only saw five. Your team, where are they?"

"Just me."

"Tell me what to do."

Nobody has that presence of mind. I don't. Knelt by Rogen and checked for weapons. Just the gun, a Taurus .45. Life is nothing but bloody coincidence. I took it.

Matthiessen said, not cool, not angry, first something in Norwegian, then, "She was supposed to kill me."

"She couldn't."

"She couldn't decide.

You never decide whether to kill someone you love. I didn't know if that was the truth. It didn't matter. "I got two women, three men."

"Then there's at least one more man. That was the total that came with me to this ship. I think the man uses a shotgun."

The shells that had almost killed me. No shit. He was still on the bridge. It had the best vantage point. The Furies were certainly comlinked. He would know the status of those he couldn't see. And that, so far, there was only one invader spotted. If there were any other Furies, they would be positioning themselves at points where they had the best lines of fire and cover.

Or would they? One invader, that might be confusing the hell out of them. No organization sends in a solo—there couldn't have been a smile on my face, I was in too much pain—James Bond and all of his imitators were pure myth. That was one of the reasons I'm crazy enough to try it—if they can't suspend their disbelief . . .

I remembered what the boy had whispered.

"We are going to have to leave. Right away."

"How?"

Damned if I knew. Even if there was only one left, his spot was too good. There would be deck cameras covering fore and aft. Matthiessen might be fast enough. I wouldn't be. Not a good bet. If we split up? No, he would take out Matthiessen first. I would have to go after him. Distract him long enough.

I took out a sealed pouch. "There's a transponder and pills. We're going to the hatch that opens to the front. You'll wait until you hear a scream, or any very loud noise. Then you go over. It's an easy dive"—Lord, the stupid things we say—"swim as far and as long as you can. The red pills are metabolics; they'll keep you going." The blue ones were exotic versions of Sobert, she wouldn't need them. "All you have to do is squeeze the 'ponder. A plane will get you. Do you understand?"

She took the pouch, tucked it deep into her pants, and nodded. "What about you?"

I said in Cheyenne the worst cliché, the worst truth.

"What?"

I muttered, "It's a fucking good day to die. Let's go."

Had to assume there was only one active; otherwise, kiss it good-bye. The only way up was the stairs. That was death. Climb? With one arm and one leg? Sure, why not. I was unstoppable, wasn't I? Come on. Think. Okay, cameras, fore and aft. Port and starboard? The compartment ran across the entire beam of the ship. Maybe not. There were few handholds; it was wet. But there was an opening on the port side that I could crawl through and up. It would take time. Needed a diversion. I stopped Matthiessen with one hand. "Wait."

She looked very pale under the dim passageway light. She was beginning to sweat. Sweat . . . the environmentals were off. There weren't any extinguishers in the stairwell—"We have to start a fire."

She looked at me blankly for a second, then said, "The mattresses are cotton."

We hauled them to the stairwell. All the time I was looking in every direction, waiting, scared.

They were piled, and we didn't have a light. Then Matthiessen said, "The galley." She was off before I could move. The young and the careless.

How long is a minute? A lifetime.

She came back with a box of matches. They were old. Took three. Waited until the smoke started pouring up. Then I went with her to the foreward hatch. "You know what to do."

"Yes."

"*Ciao, cara.*"

She looked at me oddly. I went to the other hatch. The woman was still lying there. The man was gone. Damn. I found the port opening, unlocked it, and started.

Halfway up I heard a hum, fans kicking in. Well, it was good while it lasted. I kept climbing.

There was a small platform sticking out. It looked like an insurmountable overhang. Okay, nothing's impossible, they just seem that way. I needed another diversion, and all the bloody strength of my totem. Rogen's gun. I couldn't use it, not simply wouldn't, couldn't—biokeyed, remember? If I could swing around and throw it on one of the decks. Terrible. Even if he went to that side, it would only give me a second.

So, what did I have to lose?

Remember to scream, Robie.

Gunfire. Smoke. Pain blasting through my shoulder. A blond man with a frozen face. A strike to that face. Another shot, into the air. Hit him in the groin. He spasms. Grab hair, ram him into a console.

I can't do anything more. . . . Matthiessen must be in the water. . . . Thousands of laps . . . I go out. Sky, water, equilibrium . . . I fall into the sea.

Hooker makes his way to the bridge. Knut is lying facedown. Hooker goes to the captain's chair. He can't activate it. He can't feel his arms, just agony as he moves, a bird with broken wings.

Someone comes up to him. Chloe. She looks good. He tries to tell her that, but the words don't seem to come the way he says them. He can't hear.

She looks at him. Waiting. He points with his head to the chair.

She's crying. Chloe never cries, Teresa never cries, Anton never cries—where was Anton? Oh, yes, he had left yesterday, to get more drugs. What they had wasn't working. Wasn't working. He points again.

She goes to it. Opens the channel to the explosives. Says something. He can't hear. As she presses down on the send switch, he says: "Abbie."

Matthiessen found me. Impossible. Everything was impossible. I shouldn't have been conscious. I was. I shouldn't have seen the *Savanna-La Mar* blow up. I did. I knew it would. Too many legacies. The stupid, stupid words in Greek the boy said. "Go tell the Spartans."

Randolph came down. Like the angel he should have been. They got me aboard. They went home.

EPILOGUE

I MAKE MY WAY DOWN the ridge, slowly, very slowly. I had put a fresh set of hothouse irises on the graves. My mother's favorite flower, and my wife's. They never met. I could walk with them all together, but it wouldn't be the same thing. I do know the difference between the living and the dead.

Olivia Fouchet says that Siv Matthiessen wants to see me. I think not.

Irony—my life is that word. I live with ghosts, but whatever, wherever they are now, they once were real. Perhaps too real. I never had an imaginary friend. And while I love magic—that I've had it is a true blessing of my life—I have always been aware of the truth behind illusions. Even those about myself. So, how is it that I find myself caring so hard about someone who never existed? I haven't tried yet to see if she is waiting with the others in the shadows. . . . I do not regret. I learned how to do that. But someone should mourn a little.

"When lilacs last in the dooryard bloomed . . ."

Whitman wrote that for Lincoln. When he heard.

I have no flowers for her, no poems.

Fouchet also says that my fee was paid, in full. That I've become another ghost.

Maybe.

She sent me a Turner watercolor. One of the late ones where line becomes color, color becomes mystery, wonder. A favorite of hers, she said. A forever loan. I haven't decided what to do with it. It is lovely.

There is still so much unanswered. Who was doing what to whom, and why? I don't want to know. I'm tired of knowing. Of knowing that I know.

I make my way across the long meadow toward the cabin. Jessie has been coyly hinting that she might be interested in Bach. And later, a young cousin would like it very much if I would go with her and help pick out a yearling. A paint.

A woman is walking toward me across the snowy field. She's tall and slender. Her cape is emerald green.

I stop and wait. My footing isn't terribly good.

When she gets five yards away she stops as well.

"Hello, Gav."

"Hello, Kit."

"Danny told me you were here."

I listen to the wind, the sound of the land.

"He said it was crazy."

A word she never uses, unless she believes it is true. "It was hard."

Her eyes run over my body. A professional look. Not completely.

"Gav . . ." She looks at my face. A heartbreaking woman. She doesn't know what to say. What can you say to a man who wakes up most mornings not quite sane? "I'm starving. Could you fix me breakfast?"

"I'm hungry too."

She bites at her lower lip. "Can Jessie say hello to me?"

"I think she would like to."

A smile that melts the snow. That wets her eyes. "Oh, Gav, querido, what am I going to do with you?"

"Talk."

The gifts we give, when we finally learn. At first she is afraid, she is very smart. Then she looks at me the way she did the day we first saw each other. The ache, the promise. Her voice drops low, husky. "But can we listen?"

"There's always a chancc." I hold out my hand. "Always."